ELEVATION
OF
MANA

ELEVATION OF MANA

OF

MANA

✦ ✦ ✦

WANDERING AGENT

Podium

Published in 2024 by Podium Publishing
www.podiumaudio.com

ELEVATION
OF
MANA

CHAPTER 1

JUSTIN

Justin," a voice called out to me. I waved it away, wanting nothing more than to catch a few more minutes of sleep.

"Justin!" it repeated insistently.

"What?" I yelled as I sat up, looking around for the source of my irritation.

Beside me was Professor Keeburn, a brunette bombshell in her late twenties, and my advisor. I hardly had time to process what was going on.

"You fell asleep again," she said, pointing to my desk.

Again. It was happening more and more recently. As I tried to work on some of the more interesting bits of this program, I found myself waking up here a lot. I was the low man on the totem pole in my department, but that would soon change. No one else was capable of building the kind of machine that I was. Not with the problems they were running into.

Did I really care about their proprietary little computer, designed to keep others out of the base processes? No, not really; but I did care about getting access to the lab for my own work, and so I needed to play the game for now. That meant listening to Professor Keeburn. I knew I was her first advisee and would have to fight tooth and nail to pass in the end, but that was fine. She was the only one who could get me here to work on what I wanted.

Crystal structures that could hold a program, forming it with their very design; that was my dream. Was it particularly useful? Well, not in its current iteration. But it was beautiful, almost organic, and had so much potential for growth. The math was hard, but that was fine, I liked the challenge.

"Sorry, must have lost track of time . . . When is it anyway?" I looked down at my phone and paled. It wasn't evening at all, but rather morning . . . on Saturday.

"Yeah, as you can see, your weekend has already begun. Now, go home and rest. You've still got classes on Monday and need to be fresh before we continue here."

"Yes ma'am," I said, hopping up.

She waved me out of the lab after I'd had a chance to pick up my things. With my bag over my shoulder I made my way home. The campus was huge and well spread out. Sadly, that meant that it would take me a while to get across. But I had the whole day off, and the walk would at least be nice.

I stopped by Sub-Mart—a little off-brand shop—to pick up some snacks.

"Hey! Look who's here," the man at the counter said, looking up.

"How's it going, Jose?" I said.

Jose began making my order before I even said anything. He laughed when I asked him to double up, and grabbed a bottle of water.

"You doin' good? Look like you're about to fall over," he said jovially as he packed my stuff for me.

"Fell asleep at the lab again."

"Man, you gotta learn to relax some, and not work yourself to death."

We shared a laugh as I nodded to him in agreement. Jose and I had something of an understanding. I was always polite, not just here, but to everyone who handled my food, and he was friendly. We got along particularly well because I'd told some woman screaming at him about the lack of peppers on her sandwich that she needed to shut up and pay for her damn food, or leave. Jose wasn't the owner or manager or anything, so he couldn't really do that himself, but having a good relationship with people often paid for itself.

In this particular case it paid for itself in spades. When Jose was alone in the shop, he'd often refuse to take money from me. The only cost for lunch on a really slow day would be what I tossed in the tip jar, which was always at least a couple bucks. Today was one of those days. He gave a discrete nod as I put some cash in the jar and headed out the door.

A few minutes later I turned off the sidewalk, heading into a little back path. If you spent enough time around any institution you'd find little sections like this—trails and the like that had been made over the years. I was pretty sure that this one was used mostly by joggers, and those who, like me, didn't feel like walking an hour around this wooded lot.

I'd walked this path a hundred times—in the mornings, afternoons, and evenings—though never at night. So it was a surprise when I tripped, rolling down a small slope and into one of the many gullies that were all around here. The little hill above me was perhaps twenty feet, and steep.

"Ow, shit," I said as landed.

It was no big deal in the end. While climbing back up there would be a pain, I could follow the creek down for a few minutes until the slope was a lot closer. *At least nobody had seen me*, I thought as I walked along the shore, finally coming to a large stone pipe.

It was one of those pipes they put in to channel water—seven feet tall and set deep into the ground, maybe ten feet long. Sure, it was spooky, but I could see the other side no problem, and walking through would be no issue at all. Didn't even look like there were spiders or anything in it. Waving my hand a bit in case there were any webs, I began to trudge through.

In the brief darkness of the pipe, the world began to shake, violently tossing me against one of the sides. That was weird. This area of the deep south wasn't exactly known for earthquakes, but I had little time to think about it. As soon as the shaking stopped, I stood and bolted for the far end of the pipe, unsure if there would be any aftershocks or if something major had happened.

As I came out, I looked up for the path, only to find it obscured by trees. That was fine though. With a turn I headed into a patch of denser brush, aiming to cut my time down. I pushed and pushed, finding it thicker than I'd have wanted, with thorns and vines wrapping tight around me. It was also a bit darker; not night, but twilight. As I passed through the underbrush, I found myself in a deeply shaded grove, perhaps thirty feet across.

"What the hell . . ." I looked around. Above me, the trees wove into an impermeable canopy. On all sides was an unbelievably dense thicket. In the center was a pool with crystal blue water and vines spreading out over patterned stone.

That wasn't here before. I carefully walked forward, still trying to head for where the path should have been.

If nothing else, this place was beautiful and might make a good place to show friends or whomever when I had the time. The vines were glowing, enough so that I was hesitant to touch them.

As I made my way toward the thicket, I noticed a problem. As soon as I reached the edge of this surreal oasis, I felt my hand begin to shake. I could push through, out of this grove and back into the normal world, but the thought of doing so filled me with terror deep in my soul. One step forward, and I shook like a leaf. Another, before the pool could even be out of sight, and I fell to my knees.

This wasn't good. I ran back the way I came, determined to head through the hole I'd pushed on the far side, only to find the same thing happening. No matter how I tried, how I worked, I couldn't leave sight of the pool; my body simply wouldn't move that way. I fell to my knees and tried to crawl, only for the terror to sink deeper and deeper, like death pouring into me. Within seconds I found myself turning back to the pool and running toward the comfort of the soft blue light it gave off.

I began to panic in earnest and pulled out my phone. I'd call for help. Something was clearly wrong, and the authorities . . .

No signal.

That was impossible. I was near enough to a major college campus that there should be signal for days. At worst, there was always at least one bar. As I looked at the ground, I began to consider that I might be in real trouble.

Observe. That was what I needed to do first. I needed to understand my situation and then come up with possible explanations that I could test. Science had taught me at least that much. To that end, I poked and prodded at the fear barrier, trying to find a hole in the terror it inspired, only to no avail. I tried closing my eyes, only to find my feet would refuse after a few steps. I turned to the pool and tried walk away backwards. Same result. I took out my phone and snapped photos of everything I could see around me, looking for patterns.

The pool was in a divot on a solid stone foundation, and that foundation was surely important. There were carvings too, decidedly some kind of graphed-out mathematics that tickled at the bits of non-euclidean geometry. It was more complex than anything I'd seen before but somehow strangely similar to how I might try to graph something in two dimensions.

Carefully, I began to document with my phone. I moved the vines here and there gently, taking picture after picture of the patterns until I was sure I'd gotten the whole thing. This took several hours, and as noon approached, I broke into my food, taking a bite out of the sandwich Jose had been so generous to make me.

"My friend, when I tell you about this, you're gonna call me a damn liar," I said, thinking about the friendly worker. He'd certainly get a kick out of this place.

Luckily, my laptop was in my bag and undamaged, so once I was ready, I imported the photos to my computer and began linking them up, trying to get a picture of the full pattern. That took a while—resizing and editing, pulling bits together. I knew computers, but photo editing wasn't really my forte. When I finished, I could see that there was indeed some kind of pattern, repeating out from the center like a fractal and painfully complex.

All the while I checked my phone, only to find the same message repeated whenever I looked. No signal. Whatever was going on, it certainly didn't want me to communicate with anyone else. I went on like this for a few hours, trying to compare what I saw to anything I had saved on my computer. With access to the internet I might have made more progress, but sadly, I was lacking such, and try as I might, I had no luck.

I saw the power button lighting up, telling me that my laptop would soon be dead. I rushed to pull everything I could onto my phone—a rather weak prospect, but it was all I had. Not much longer after that, the battery gave out, pushing forward a dark screen.

As I looked up, I saw that the vines looked almost brighter. I hadn't noticed until now, but for some reason they'd started glowing ever so slightly more. I checking in my bag for ideas, coming up with a few notepads and pens. The bag had one of those little solar chargers on it, and from that I might be able to drip charge my phone and laptop, if the light of these vines proved enough.

After two days, I had finished up my rations of sandwich and was faced with doing something I was not particularly proud of . . . I drank my own urine. It was gross, but it would buy me time. Time was what I needed— time to think, time to reason. The one drink from my lunch wouldn't last forever, and the rule of threes said I had only days before that was a potentially fatal issue.

Further attempts to leave the grove met with the same result, but repeating experiments was no folly. It merely confirmed what I had previously suspected.

Above the little spot where I'd holed up, a flower had bloomed, brilliant and beautiful. Some other part of whatever nightmare I was stuck in. I considered destroying it but didn't want to risk any blowback. Whatever was keeping me here had already demonstrated that it could.

I made calls and yells for help, to no avail. I hadn't really been expecting it to work, so I wasn't too down, but it didn't hurt to try every now and then. While doing so, I noticed that I heard no birds or insects; nor did I see any. That alone was worth noting, as bugs were everywhere.

I worked off and on for another two days, and the vines were certainly getting brighter. I knew the time because the light was enough to charge up my phone a bit, if slowly, and even get a few minutes of laptop time.

There was no way this was natural, and I began considering supernatural options for how I'd ended up here. I was leaning toward fairies. I wasn't an expert on them or anything, but this kind of story was their deal, right? Either that or I'd hit my head quite hard and was no longer all here.

This was reinforced by the fact that the little flower had bloomed into the most delicious looking periwinkle fruit, tempting me with succulent looking flesh. I was determined to resist it though. That screamed trap.

I knew I could last weeks without food if I had to. No, my main problem was water. Even with my attempts at . . . extending my water supply, I was out, and the tap was dry. My mouth was bone dry and painful, and there was no source other than the pool, which I was similarly afraid of.

I was too weak. Two-and-a-half days with nothing substantial to drink, and I was in agony. I wept as I tried to pull myself over to the pool, having just woken up from passing out. I'd said I wouldn't drink, wouldn't fall for the trap, but my body was betraying me, and if I didn't, I would die here. I didn't want to die.

The water was cool and perfect, so I drank and drank, sating my thirst before sitting up once again. When I finished, I screamed in rage at whoever had brought me here, cursing them to a thousand deaths. This water, though, would give me more time to think, more time to figure out how to escape this place.

After two weeks, hunger had become a real issue. I tried eating the vines, only to find that the terror hit me whenever I tried to damage them. Same with the seemingly normal vegetation around the edge. The only thing that looked appealing was that fruit, still hanging there, teasing me. My notebooks filled up days ago, and my pens ran dry. For the last few days, I'd been eating bits of the paper here and there, trying to sate my appetite. That worked well enough.

Nobody was coming. Wherever I was, I was isolated from the world at large, apart, alone.

*　*　*

"Regardless of what I try, I can find nothing. I'm starving and tired. Won't you just let me go?" This is the last message I left on my phone, hoping that someone would find it.

I rose to take the fruit, pulling it down with a gentle plop. My brain screamed that all I had to do was bite, but another instinct came on strong. I turned and threw the offending plant into the pool.

"Fuck you!" I screamed at the world before collapsing to the ground and weeping.

Minutes passed and I looked up, only to see the thing bobbing there, and I lost my nerve.

I waded into the water, nearly knee deep, and picked it up. Tears fell as I bit down, letting the juices run down my throat in heavenly bliss. As I finished, I wept salty tears, relief washing over me.

When I wiped my eyes, I saw the world brilliant blue. The vines around me pulsed in time, brighter and brighter, to a fever pitch. I was afraid. I'd done what I knew I mustn't, what every story told me not to do. I'd taken the offering, and now . . .

My stomach exploded in pain, driving me down to my knees in the pool.

"Why!? Why!? Why are you doing this!? Why won't you answer me!?" I bellowed as the pain spread through my body, lines tracing up and along my skin.

I screamed and screamed as my skin began to flake away, trying and failing to exit the water, only to sink in, only for the bright light to overtake me.

CHAPTER 2

NEW WORLD

I'd been in this new world about a week. A new world it could only possibly be.

There was some evidence of this. First, I noticed that everyone's ears were elongated into points. That alone was enough for me; there weren't elves where I was from. As I looked around at the many, many elven women in the circle around me, I couldn't help but think about how many people would love a chance like this.

Not everything was ideal, of course. For one thing, I was a baby. I had turned into a literal infant. And it appeared I was stuck this way for now—severely hoping that wouldn't be the case for decades as I grew up. I knew the stories from back home said that elves lived like, forever, but they grew up normally, right? Being a baby was no fun; none at all. I could barely move, and speech was limited to various forms of crying. The diet . . . while some could see it as a bonus, it was uncomfortable for me, and very, very plain. Milk morning, noon, and night, and all times in between. I couldn't even use the restroom on my own.

It was hard to tell, but I was pretty sure that I was also somewhere in the stone age. I'd seen no sparkle of metal at all so far to indicate anything greater. Tools were mostly shaped rocks and wood, with a bit of bone here and there for variety. There were no pots, nor pans, nor knives that weren't stone. Baskets were popular with the women, and I could see them all around me weaving in the evenings.

An anthropologist would probably give his right arm to be where I was right now, but sadly that wasn't me. I had concerns, big concerns. There was no tech here, no computers, no, well . . . anything. This was a tribe, a small one—perhaps a couple hundred. It was kind of hard for me to tell. Other than some clearly sewn clothes and items like bone or wooden flutes, the greatest objects seemed to be coming from the man who looked to be my father.

Father, as I would now be calling him, spent his evenings with a piece of leather draped over his leg knapping flint. He sang as he moved the bit of stone around in his hand, tapping place after place and sending little flakes down to the ground around him. He knew his business and could turn out things like arrowheads or spearheads faster than I would have thought physically possible. Each was a perfect little shape, the points seeming almost artistically done.

He would sing, and I could see a bluish sort of mist flow around him whenever he did. It ebbed and eddied, coming off him in small waves. I suspected this was some form of magic but couldn't be a hundred percent sure. My thoughts kept going to how sometimes it looked like the stone would meld in his hands, changing in just the way he wanted or smoothing just a bit too perfectly.

He wasn't the only one to display such phenomena. There were two or three others who had something similar going on. Particularly of note was a woman who had a growing white streak in her black hair. I couldn't yet understand the words everyone was using, but it was clear as day that she was a person of respect in this tribe. Though several women were near her, she'd always been the one offered something by the men when they came back from hunting trips.

Along with the white-streaked woman was a man who seemed to lead the hunters. He and Father often sat near each other, and while my dad was a bit scrawnier than most, this guy was ripped. I'd seen him and Dad trading the arrowheads for meat, and while they were different, they acted like the oldest of pals. Dad's friend moved like water flowing between stones, and it was clear that a number of the women in the group rather fancied him. I hadn't seen him too interested in most of them yet, but maybe he was biding his time.

Then there was my mother. Frankly, she kind of scared me, not because she did anything violent, but because of the way people reacted to her. If the white-streaked woman had been respected, Mom was downright feared. She spoke softly most of the time, not bossy or anything, but when she spoke, people listened. When words left Mom's mouth, those from others stopped, and if there was a disagreement and she spoke, it ended. She and the white-streaked woman were clearly the powerhouses in the camp.

Finally, there was me. All around my skin, tiny green bubbles played, floating and hovering just at the edge of my view. I could tune them out most of the time if I wanted, but whenever I looked, they were there. Others around me had seemed giddy in my first few days of life, always coming by to play with the bubbles. This phenomenon was important somehow, but I wasn't yet sure how. It did clue me in on the fact that they could see my bubbles, though, as much as I could see the various things going on around them.

As for the other members of the tribe, sometimes I would get little flashes of light from them, but nothing sustained. This normally accompanied some kind of odd behavior in the world, lending credence to my theory of magic. Perhaps a fire would light suddenly, or a rock would be thrown perfectly at a bird. One guy had even demonstrated the ability to perfectly straighten a piece of wood using only his hands. That was a neat trick—limited usefulness, but very neat.

Our accommodations, such as they were, consisted of a woven, dirt floor . . . hut? It was not a perfect descriptor, as it seemed to be made of living interwoven branches and vines, but hut was probably the best descriptor. It was maybe twenty feet in diameter and shared by several other couples and one other child. There was no fire pit or anything; those were all in a little communal area in the center of the settlement. Everyone just slept here on piles of leaves, branches, and a few furs. I was placed in a little basket for the night, but it, too, was just lined with moss and soft plant life.

Morning broke and my new mother came to get me. She was dressed much as she always was—in a leather outfit that when done up covered her and provided at least some level of support. My father wore something similar, as did most of the other members of our little tribe. It wasn't much but looked functional and easy to deal with. The sewing was prim and exact, clean lines that had been put together one by one into the simple shapes of the garments. There was no cloth, though. Everything was leather.

As I looked at the various patterns on the clothing, I began to think about all the other decorations. While food seemed hardly an issue here, there was a great quantity of what could only be considered art. Stone tools had intricately carved wooden handles with geometric patterns or clear animal motifs. The baskets that were made for various things all seemed carefully shaped, with color gradients to them and even some simple patterns here and there. Then there were the beads.

Pretty much everyone in the tribe was wearing some amount of beads. The men had fewer, normally only woven into a couple of strands of their hair, but for the women . . . It was like a strange contest. Though I lacked the ability to understand much of what was being said, it was clear that these were some kind of marking of status. Brighter colored, or more intricate beads were more valuable, as were those with odd properties or materials.

Like most things, Mother seemed to be winning. While many of the women in the tribe were wearing wooden or bone beads simply carved and rather plain, hers were different. Most of Mother's strands had carved stone beads of bright colors. She also had a few carved from what could only be shell, the slight luster of pearl shining bright. The only person in our tribe to beat her, and soundly so, was the white-streaked woman, who was decked out three ways from Sunday.

In fact, most of the women from our little cohort were decked out in comparison to their peers. Even the men outshone some of the less decorated women. It sufficed to say that by whatever standard stone-age elves held, we were rich, really rich. The products in our little group were nicer than most, and though it was hard to tell, I thought we were even getting more meat, the only foodstuff that seemed to have much in the way of value.

Dad decidedly had something to do with this. His stone blades and points were sought after, and I suspected that he probably carved a lot of those trinkets Mom was wearing, which made sense. A good stone-knapper in this society would be a cornerstone of any group.

As Mom put on her basket/backpack, I was handed off to who I assumed was one of my aunts. She looked almost exactly like my mother, and they spent much of their day together. My assumed aunt had no children of her own, at least not that I saw, but that only meant she doted on me like any relative would a cute baby, playing peek-a-boo and making faces as she held me. It was kind of adorable, and I wondered what we'd be doing today, as I saw the many women gathering their things up. While whatever it was might not be my chosen activity, I was sure to learn something, and perhaps even pick up a few words.

CHAPTER 3

ELIAN

In the morning we headed out to a field. It wasn't farming as such, but rather an open space near the village where the women, collectively as a group, were going to gather. Everyone trudged along a small path, chatting the whole way. I began to get a feel for the area around me.

The village was nestled in a valley, and either by geography or design, the area around it was fairly clear. It was hard to tell which it was, at least for now, but it meant that a small stream meandered down past us and provided water to our little home. The sides of the valley afforded great sight lines in every direction, and while there weren't any walls, the huts seemed to be arranged so tightly that it didn't much matter; there wasn't any way in without going through the main opening.

The huts themselves were the only trees for hundreds of feet in any direction, and were clearly abnormal. Either by magic or by hard work and arrangement, the branches and leaves had been shaped and formed into huts, woven tightly into a form of walls. Even above the main area of the huts, there were makeshift paths between the larger trees, bridges formed by the interwoven wood.

Each hut was dug a couple of feet down into the ground and placed in what looked to be circles around several large communal fire pits in the very center of the village. This too seemed to indicate things, since our home neatly opened into the central square, while those who I thought looked poorer seemed to live farther out on the edges.

Regardless of the clear indications of status, there wasn't much in the way of wealth disparity. At least not so much as I could see. The huts near the edge looked much the same as those near us, and while there were demarcations in things like decoration, it wasn't as if there were skyscrapers and slums. The hierarchy seemed mainly focused on maintaining some form of organization.

Following the stream out of the village, one could go either upstream or down. I wasn't sure where down led yet, as we seemed to prefer going upward, like we were today. In this direction, the small stream met up with a larger one after perhaps a half-hour of walking, with a wide and well-worn path snaking alongside it.

Once we got to our gathering spot, the various cliques spread out, each going after a different area and product. It was hard to get a look at all of them, but it was clear that each group had a certain thing they were after in particular. There was some overlap, and I could see people taking the easy-to-get stuff in the area that they chose, but they also mostly stuck to whatever they were doing.

By and far the most common ones were the diggers—groups of girls who used little stone-tipped spiky tools to carefully remove the dirt around roots of a common fern-looking plant. They were pulling out something that looked like a small potato, about three inches in diameter.

Then there were the nut gatherers. The first thing they did was take one of the few children with us, a boy who looked about ten, and send him up a tree to shake it. Then the group would work its way around, systematically searching for everything that had fallen and could be used. I had to say that the boy in question was energetic about his task and looked to be having a blast.

White-streaked woman had only a couple of women with her, and I got to see why she was so important. There were a number of trees that had large fruit, but it was clearly too early in the season, and they had yet to fall. She reached up and I could see her aura flare. Suddenly, one of the fruits popped off of its stem and floated down to her. Her pair of companions could do the same, but it seemed that it was far more draining, leaving them looking tired and waiting minutes before trying again.

Mom and our group seemed to be going after berries. This was wild to me, as I could see when we approached that there were none, but that didn't matter. With a wave of her hand, Mother caused the little patch of bushes to burst into flower and fruit. Nobody but me was surprised, and I made a little cheer from the little holder I was in on her back.

Could I do that? I wondered as I watched her.

Perhaps magic here was inherited like that, the skills being passed generation to generation. She hadn't used any kind of incantation or markings, but rather just a flex of power. I'd have to figure it out later.

Mom had heard my cheering and brought me down from her back, holding me since I was awake. While the others picked the berries she'd made, she spoke.

"Oha . . . Nida . . . Elian?" I could barely keep up with her words, but a few were repeated often.

The last was one she said a lot to me, but not much to others, unless it was something to do with me. At least that was my working theory. I couldn't do much to confirm other than make cute faces and try to get her to talk more, but if I could work out a few words, I could start to learn for real.

After a bit, Mom went back to picking fruit, an all-morning exercise. None of the people here seemed in even the slightest rush, each woman keeping deep in conversation as she picked, dug, or gathered. They had enough, and without a good way to store things long term, there really wouldn't be much of a reason to pick more than needed. So they didn't. They enjoyed their time together as the day's work got done.

When we finally returned to the village that afternoon, almost all the men were gone. This didn't seem to surprise anyone, and the evening's cooking commenced. Roots were buried in the fire pit while everyone gathered round. The gathered nuts were brought out and were cracked open on large stones. It was informal, and while everyone had gathered different things, almost all of the goods were shared equally.

While Mom and the woman I'd taken to considering my auntie had taken care of me for most of the day so far, now there was a line. It seemed a lot of the younger girls wanted a chance to hold me, and they gathered up, each clearly offering in turn to take care of the baby.

Perhaps they wanted to practice for when they had kids? I couldn't help but notice that I was the only infant. Even the number of children was low, with perhaps a dozen total in the village. I tried to parse that with the lack of birth control and the current state of society, but couldn't; there just weren't enough children around for a society like this to continue to exist.

There also weren't any old people, at least not that I'd seen. Twenties seemed to be the cutoff, with white-streaked woman looking like she was perhaps thirty, max. That was odd too. Perhaps elves aged differently? I knew a little about fantasy, and it seemed to indicate that they lived for a long time, but the complete lack of elders was weird, and I didn't know enough about anthropology to take much of a guess.

Being passed around was helpful, though, as several of the girls who reached for me kept saying "Elian," and that was about as much confirmation as I needed for my new name. I wasn't sure how I felt about having a new name. I'd always been Justin, and rather preferred that to Elian, but I could tackle that later.

Now I had to deal with the constant moving around as the girls tried to get some time playing with me. They'd reach for me, and depending on how I reacted, I might be passed over or left where I was. I'll admit that I got frustrated by this after a while, as some of them downright sucked at holding babies.

I couldn't even properly hold my head up on my own quite yet; instead it lolled around, too big to be supported by me. So, after a while of discomfort, I tried crying. This led to a number of responses, and eventually my mother came to retrieve me. From that point on through the evening, the curious girls were rebuffed, either by Mom or Auntie. Eventually, I fell asleep, something I did off and on, and spent a good chunk of the night in that state.

When I woke up in the night, I thought about my situation.

Being a baby sucked in a multitude of ways. I was helpless, truly helpless—unable to walk, or eat, or, well, pretty much anything except cry. I could look around whenever I wasn't falling asleep, but that seemed to happen a lot too, and much of my day was a blur as every hour or two I'd simply doze off. I couldn't even use the bathroom on my own, which was painfully embarrassing for someone who'd been an adult.

All I could really do for now was learn. Learn what was what here, and try to grow; that was my goal. I really, really hoped that the stories were at least not wholly true, and I wouldn't spend the next century or whatever as a baby. The chances of me making it out of that sane would have to be almost zero.

While I was thinking, I heard a small humming tune, so I made my wakefulness known with a light cry. This ended with Dad coming over and sitting beside my basket. Normally I'd be unable to see, but in his hand he had a small light, pale yellow like the sun but barely visible. He smiled down at me and continued to sing in a low voice.

As he did, he spread out his hands, and small stars of light bloomed, swirling gently around my crib. I wasn't sure how he was doing it, but it was clearly part of whatever magic he had. Even though it seemed draining to use magic, he chose to use his to try and keep me happy and calm.

I hadn't been in this world long, but there were a few things I knew. I knew that my parents cared for me—the sheer love and kindness they displayed and their peaceful smiles showed that too much for anyone to debate. Because of this I couldn't think of them as anything except Mom and Dad. While they didn't know where I'd come from, or the secrets locked away in my little head, they knew that they loved me and showed it every time they looked down at me. That kind of feeling was irresistible, and I found myself responding in kind. It was like it was hardwired in, like the only option for their care was reciprocation, and honestly, I didn't mind. It made me happy, and I could tell that my smiles and laughs brought them the same joy.

CHAPTER 4

SEASONS CHANGE

As I realized what my parents were doing when they utilized their magic, I began my own experimentation. It was slow going, painfully slow going. First, I had absolutely no clue what I was doing. If I'd spoken more of the language, I could have asked, but I was grasping blind here. Then there were the twin problems of never being left alone and the difficulty bringing it to the fore. I suspected that the latter had to do with my age; the former certainly did.

My first attempts were mimicking my mother and trying to push out my magic and make a few blades of grass grow one day while Mom was gathering. No matter how hard I tried, I couldn't quite reach the ground from her back, and my repeated hard pushing just left me with a messy diaper. This body was hampering me severely.

During one of the breaks that the women took throughout the day, I was set down on a leather blanket, and from there tried my hand again. Finally reaching my goal, I managed to touch the little green blade. I tried and tried to make it grow, but it just refused, eventually twisting a bit and turning brown as I stared at it. This was going to be harder than I thought.

Several failed attempts ensued over the next couple of weeks. After repeated failures, either resulting in the death of the plant, or an outright refusal of the little jerks to do anything at all, I moved on to Dad's form of magic. He always sang, so I took to watching him as he worked, something that made him very happy and ended with me being brought over and shown his work. He could clearly tell that I was looking at it, and got my auntie to hold me nearby so I could watch. I wasn't allowed to touch of course. His tools were sharp, and I was still a baby.

So I learned a few of the songs he used, and as soon as I was able to get hold of a rock I tried them out. The results were underwhelming. I managed to easily force my magic to interact with and feel the stone, and it almost felt easier pushing magic into it than it did into the grass. That was about where it ended though. No matter how hard I tried, it didn't want to flow like it did for him. The singing didn't seem to matter as I hummed his tune while I did so; my rendition was poor, but I sensed no change regardless.

I was getting really frustrated, and quickly. There was something I was missing, some trick or skill that I didn't have to make this work. I needed to observe more, learn more. I also needed to work out the language more than I had so far, so I could ask questions. Even if the answers weren't perfect, or even scientifically or magically correct, they worked for everyone here, and that would be a start.

It took months of work, but I made great progress. I could now properly understand most of what was being said around me—at least the simpler things. I also noticed that everyone who used magic in a major way seemed to focus. Mom only ever used her magic on things like plants, whereas the white-streaked woman never made anything grow. Dad I was still trying to work out. He seemed to have a wide range of abilities, but he did always sing when he used them, so that was some information. My own attempts at magic were put to the side though, until I could ask how to use it.

At this point, I was around six months of age and happy to see that I was growing like a normal human baby, at least as far as I could tell. I couldn't talk yet, though, at least not anything even near properly. No matter where my mind was, my body just couldn't keep up. Even as I gained some physical ability, I was still limited by my size and weird musculature. Huge head and tiny limbs, I struggled with the simplest of things.

"Elian, no," Mom chided as I approached a small tanning hide that was hung in our little hut.

"Guu," I responded as I kept heading toward the stretched-out skin.

"No," she repeated, finally coming over to pick me up.

My mother had learned that I understood at least a few words like *yes, no, good,* and *bad.* Not managing to fool her for longer had probably been my biggest mistake, because now she knew I was ignoring her and was cross with me.

"I know you understand 'no' Elian." She let me see her frowning face to know how cross she was, but other than that and a shaken finger, she didn't give any real punishment beyond carrying me to the other side of the hut.

"He's moving a lot more now. I'll admit I was worried for a bit there," my auntie Atie said.

"Me too; he's always been so quiet." Mom looked down at me as she said that.

"Coo," I responded, lacking any real complex verbalizations.

They were right; I didn't cry much. Unlike most babies who were still trying to figure things out, I had a pretty good handle on what I wanted. Therefore, I just needed to come up with a few different cries for the things they were likely to give me, and one for general displeasure, and I was done. I didn't need much, and didn't see much point in making a racket.

"Well, at least he isn't trying to put everything he finds in his mouth. Though I would appreciate it if he would stop getting into everything he sees." Mom gave me another scowl. She wasn't wrong though. I was trying to get into everything and figure out what people were doing.

"Weird. You had to have a weird baby, didn't you sister?" Auntie asked.

"Indeed I did, and I'm not looking forward to when he discovers how to use his light." That was how they referred to the aura around me, and some others, at least as far as I could tell.

"I remember how happy Mother was when you first found yours. I also remember how much she screamed when you started playing with it for real." My auntie had a grin as she spoke. There were stories there. "Is it still growing?"

"It is. I asked Elaya, and she's only ever seen a few children born with a light proper. She said they normally turn out strong, if very troublesome when young."

Elaya was the name of the white-streaked woman. I'd learned a few things about her. One was that this village was named after her—Elayatol or "Elaya's village" in the local tongue. The other was that people spoke as if she was way, way older than she looked. It was possible that like in the stories I'd heard as a human, elves aged differently, and she was undoubtedly the elder of this village, having founded it "many summers ago" as said in one of the stories told around the evening fire.

There were other villages, though I knew only names. I got the feeling from what I heard about them that none were particularly near, or talked about much. All seemed to report to a larger settlement named Atal, though, which was somehow connected to the village elders.

"What are we after today?" Auntie Atie asked.

"More berries," Mom responded. "The dark ones are still in season."

"Boo, they're too small, and you can make anything grow if you want." This was a conversation Mother and my auntie had all the time.

"You know it's hard on the plants to grow things out of season, and bad for them."

My aunt pouted but adjusted her buckskin dress and beads and got ready to go. While she prepped, Mom put me in my holder and I cooed more. I'd yet to see any cloth still, which seemed kind of weird, but everyone looked to be still in the stone age, so it wasn't that odd. Perhaps I could look into that later, though I knew only the most basic theory on how to make cloth from even something like wool.

There was a reason the dark berries were unpopular with many of the women. They were too small, and while they tasted good, were a right pain to bring home. There were a number of different techniques, but the little things just slipped through baskets like water, dropping everywhere and constantly getting lost.

We were by the creek today, as that was the easiest place to go after our particular fruity prey. Many of the women took the time to add the largest leaves they could to the bottom of their baskets—not that it seemed to help too terribly much—and got to work. After several hours, and seeing too much of her work spill and get trodden underfoot, Auntie lost it.

"All right, I'm done. This is stupid, and I hate these things," she declared, marching down to the water's edge.

"Atie, what are you doing?" Mom inquired as her sister picked up a handful of goopy clay from the bank, only after having dumped her current haul in a pile.

"Stopping my food from getting lost," she angrily responded, and began lining the inside of her basket with a thick layer of the clay.

"But . . . they'll get dirty . . ." one of the girls in our group pointed out. She quickly shut up as my aunt shot her a glare that could peel paint.

"Then we will wash them. We've several that can make water to do so," Atie's tone was venom as she kept on lining the basket, until a thick layer of clay now lined it.

I laughed as the beginnings of an idea started to tickle in my head. If I could only figure out a way to do it.

"See, even Elian thinks it's a good idea," my auntie said at the little sound I made.

"Or he thinks his silly aunt is acting dumb," Mom tried, shaking her head.

CHAPTER 5

FIRST SPELLS

I had been waiting, watching. I hadn't had a particular need to engage in magic before, so I'd let my experiments fall on the back-burner while I figured out language and tried to milk those around me for information. Though the actions of my aunt and her little clay-filled basket now gave me a goal.

My back-burnering of magic hadn't been some whim; what I felt was a logical conclusion. I didn't know the dangers or how to control it yet. I didn't know what would happen if I ever did. Most of all, I wasn't in a hurry. I now had a second chance at life and really wanted to get this one right. Ending it with some magical mishap while playing seemed stupid.

This was a goal, though, and one I would wager I'd need magic for. I planned to pull this stone age society as far forward as I reasonably could, and that mission could start now. Who knew if my auntie would ever repeat her little basket trick, or how long I might have to wait for her to try again. No, now was my chance, and I could make it look like someone else was making the new tech too; a sincere bonus.

There were several days of berry gathering where my aunt used her clay lined basket. I just couldn't get a good chance to practice quietly. I had to wait it out, as there was no way around the fact that I, as a baby, was almost always being observed. I needed to do my work here quietly if I was to remain unnoticed. That was the goal, as it would achieve my aim, while giving my auntie a big boost.

So, as I was sat down in the grass during the afternoon break, I began my attempts yet again. I'd been watching everyone around me and divided them up into a number of groups—broad categories. Mom could affect living, and only living things; Dad, on the other hand, had a wider power gap, but always sang; and white-streaked Elaya did neither, and couldn't make things grow; and then there was Dad's friend, who did something physical.

I'd also been looking at the minor powers the villagers displayed and tried to put those into categories too. I was happy to find that a number of them seemed to fall well into the groups I'd already made. Some had to sing, some could work on living things, and some never could work on living things. There were also a few who could do small superhuman feats, just not too drastic or very often.

During my brief attempts at learning magic myself, I'd found that noise did nothing for me. I was also fairly sure that I wasn't some kind of super-baby, so that left me with two options. Either I was like Mom, and doing something very wrong, or I was like Elaya and was still figuring things out.

There was a rock nearby and I began to work. I was working on the assumption and hope that I was like Elaya; and so began to move my magic, my light as the locals called it, around the bit of stone. First, I tried to soak it in magic, which worked well enough but didn't seem to do anything. Frowning, I tried some other things, starting with a spectral hand. I tried to imagine a hand grabbing the rock and picking it up. This made the rock shift and move a bit, but felt . . . unnatural.

I sat there looking, thinking about my issue. There had to be something I was missing here, some fact . . . Okay, what could make things move? Forces, right? There was kinetic force and gravitational force. Those seemed the most likely candidates, but how to make the magic do it? That was the issue I faced.

On a whim, I tried to focus instead on the idea that the rock was in an area where all the gravity equaled zero. Trying to move the forces around it instead of *it*. At first nothing seemed to happen, and I sighed, letting the magic keep running as I started to think again. Moments later, I saw the strangest thing—the rock began to slowly float. Bit by bit, it lifted off until I released the spell.

I worked for several more minutes, trying to work out the best way to move a rock like that. Imparting direction seemed to be easy enough, though I worked very carefully, so as not to alert any of the adults who were always nearby. It was clunky, though, and I had to constantly try to work out the forces in my head, imparting either a gravitational or kinetic vector with care.

Several times as I was working, one or more of the women came by to check on me and make sure I was all right. Surely Mother was nearby watching as well, but right now I was being a quiet baby, running my fingers over the little leather blanket I was on and looking off into the distance silently. Since I wasn't up to anything visible, they seemed to not want to disturb me. Let sleeping dragons, or potentially screaming children, lie, or something like that.

All things must come to an end, though, and soon enough Auntie Atie came to sit down beside me. I was getting rather tired quickly anyway, so it wasn't an issue.

"Hi, little Elian. What are you doing?" she asked in an almost baby voice.

"Uuh!" I tried while stretching my arms up at her. Forming words with my current mouth was still proving near impossible, and my attempt at "up" didn't really work as planned.

"Well, come here then," she said, picking me up and setting me on her lap.

I wanted the higher viewpoint, particularly as she'd sat her basket down beside me. It was drying nicely. At the same time I was fading fast, tiredness taking me even as I fought against it. My aunt hummed some tune as she rocked me gently on her knee, and I soon found that I was drifting off into a deep sleep.

Adia

My sister, Atie, had the smuggest look as my child got her to pick him up and rock him to sleep. He seldom sought things like that—just another way the boy was a bit odd. I'd been standing back with Elaya, watching closely for the oncoming disaster.

I'd seen it first—the small movements in his light that indicated he was using it somehow—and immediately had one of the girls grab Elaya. There was no way to be sure what he was doing, not without some great skill and lots of potential for harm.

The elder quickly came when the situation was explained and made her way over to where I was, sitting back watching.

"He's doing something?" she asked, looking at the little bubbles moving around him, much as I was. It was both a question and confirmation.

"Yes, but I can't tell what. Any thoughts?"

Her eyes scanned him and the ground around him. "Nothing obvious, not to my eye. Normally those like me start with throwing things around—fire or light. Something that should be really visible. Children don't have the control for small movements."

"Nor mine. Nothing growing, nothing dying. We still don't know how he'll manifest, but he isn't singing, so I doubt he's like his father."

Elaya tapped her chin. "Children are often like their parents, but not always. Can you check on things in the area, make sure he's not affecting them? If he's like you . . . we'll need to be careful; a baby with that power could do some terrible things by accident."

I pushed my own light out to cover the area, looking for the influence of another on the plants and people around us. There was nothing obvious, nothing like the mess I'd made when I was little. Elaya still told tales sometimes. I'd been a right little disaster for a bit, having to go off with her until I learned control and good morals. I spread my light over little Elian, and his power was pushing back, but not enough at his age to stop my own.

"Nothing, and it doesn't even look like he's enhancing himself. That can be hard to detect at smaller levels though . . ." I furrowed my brow, still worried.

"We'll keep an eye out for now. Don't worry too much, dear. Children learn fast, and if anything happens, you'll be able to fix him up, no problem." Elaya patted my shoulder comfortingly. We were all family here, by marriage or birth, and my great-great-grandmother had plenty of experience.

As my child's eyes slipped closed on his aunt's lap and he drifted off to sleep, I wondered about him. He was strange, a good boy, but deeply strange. What would he do? Where would he end up? Perhaps he would stay in the village like so many, or perhaps he would take to traveling. I'd dreamed of that once, before I'd found that I had all I needed here.

Elian slept most of the rest of the day, stirring only a few times as he was passed around. Whatever magic he'd been working had worn him out quite thoroughly. That was concerning, as it could mean he'd be awake, keeping us all awake, all night. A good boy he might be, but he also had a habit of constantly getting into things, and leaving him alone for hours would be foolish.

We made our way home and began processing all that we'd gathered for the day. In this case, that meant crushing the berries in a large rock hollow my dear Eduan had made for us. It'd taken him a long time to make it right, but the huge bowl was good for pounding things like the dark berries. The juice would pool at the bottom and could be soaked into roots or anything for sweetness, while the berries ended up as a nice paste that could be dried in the sun and kept for a long time.

Atie's little mud trick was sort of dumb, and her berries did need washing, but it worked. She ended up with significantly more of the annoying little fruits than anyone else. If it was dumb but worked, was it really dumb?

"Mind if I take a look at that?" one of the cousins asked, pointing to it.

"Go ahead; it worked perfectly," my sister responded.

The other girl poked at the dry river mud for a few moments. Then she nodded and passed it back. "Interesting, but heavy" was her conclusion.

Elian

I woke up as the sun set, still feeling groggy. Everyone had returned to the village and was sitting around the fire for stories and dinner. People sat with their cliques and were only interrupted when something big was announced.

Mom fed me some of the fruit paste she and the others had made at some point. It was delicious, something like blueberry. I wasn't given much of this, but the variation in diet was as welcome as anything, and I voraciously munched the dark colored goop.

"You like berries huh, Elian?" Mom asked, taking a bit more from a basket where it had been lain after being formed into patties.

"Guu!" I said in response, about as positively as I could, reaching for more.

There were laughs from her and several others in our little sub-group. Everyone shared about what they'd done, be it hunting, gathering, or whatever. Then the little bits of gossip and chatter about other goings-on happened. Someone from outside our village had come by while the women were gathering and traded with some of those who'd remained behind. He'd had dried fish that came from far away and had a better flavor than what we got here, and had left with a number of beads and dried fruit.

Dad had gotten some of this fish in trade and shared it around. Sadly, no matter how hard I reached up and made angry noises I was denied fish by the adults. They worried that it would be too much for my little stomach and were probably right, but I still wanted the taste of meat again.

As we all turned in for the night, I had one last thing to do. Once I was sure all eyes were turned, I looked up and over Mother's shoulder and began working. As quickly and silently as I could, I turned Auntie Atie's basket over into the low fire, then pushed sticks from the nearby pile atop it. Leaving a fire was wasteful, but there was nothing near the fire pits that would burn, so it wasn't exactly that frowned upon either. As I was taken inside, I saw the flames creeping up the side of the clay-lined basket. I sincerely hoped this worked, because if it didn't, I'd have wasted all the effort my aunt put into her project, and I'd feel really bad about that.

I nearly passed out from the effort, though, and the headache creeping up on me told me I'd pushed a little too hard. As soon as I was put into the basket that served as my bed, I passed out.

The next morning, I was awoken by Auntie Atie's enraged yell.

CHAPTER 6

POTTERY

I expected my auntie to be mad, but she was not mad. No, no, she was furious; she screamed and raged so loudly that my mother even looked up.

"Who?" I heard her exclaim before a series of words I didn't know.

"What in the world is she screaming about?" Father asked, moving to the front of the hut.

I had a feeling I knew, and knew well. I'd really thought that she would be mad, but this was on another level. Perhaps I'd underestimated how much she liked that particular basket, but even if I was sure that she valued it, this seemed extreme. Really I should be worried that she might ever find the culprit, because if she did, I might have earned my first beating.

There were a few more sounds of incoherent rage and the gathering of a crowd before Mother picked me up and headed outside.

"Atie, what are you screaming about. You'll wake up the whole village," Mom said as she stepped outside.

My aunt turned, her face in a horrid expression of anger. Seeing who she was talking to and the baby in her arms, my aunt calmed considerably, lowering her voice to a hiss.

"Someone burned my favorite basket!" She pointed to the ashen remains of the fire.

I looked to the ashes and was glad to see that my first secretive attempt at a pot had survived. There was a real chance that it would burst, or chip too badly to be useful, but it seemed to have come through relatively unscathed.

"Are you sure you didn't just leave it too close to the fire last night?" Mom was trying to be a voice of reason, even if she was wrong.

"Even if it was near the fire, look at it, Adia. It's turned over and buried. You can even see where someone piled sticks on top of it." I could see her jaw strain in anger as she spoke. She was right. There were a few bare remains of twigs that I'd pushed on there.

Mom looked with a deepening frown at the fire pit, clearly thinking about the repercussions of this. This was a very, very small community, and someone going out of their way to destroy other people's things may well be a rarity. Before it could continue, though, another person showed up.

"What is all the noise about?" Elaya asked as she approached.

I noticed that most of the men had stayed back a little. There were, for the most part, two separate groupings in our village. The men spent most of their time away, while most of the women were on their own as well. I suspected that the men viewed this as something to stay out of, at least unless violence broke out.

"Someone burned my basket," my aunt explained.

Elaya listened before turning to the small crowd of elves. "Don't you lot have things to do?" When she raised her voice, people quickly found things to do. With the elder around, you might well be assigned something if you couldn't find something yourself. She turned back to my aunt. "Who?"

"I don't know," Atie hissed, still quite mad.

Elaya's hand snapped out like a viper, grabbing my aunt's ear and twisting. I wasn't sure, but the little "Eep," sound she made indicated that it was probably quite painful.

"Don't take a tone with me child; you're not too old for me to twist your ears." After a second or two she let go, leaving the younger woman rubbing her ear.

Mom looked irritated but said nothing. There must be some organization to how things were done when it came to . . . crimes, I supposed.

"Sorry," Atie pouted, "Nobody should have. Not like I've had any real fights with anyone in years."

"Well, if you didn't see anything, I'll ask around. Don't expect me to find the truth, though; not unless someone else saw something. If I do find who did it, you'll get a pair of new baskets, but that **will** be the end of it." Her voice was hard, and she stared daggers at my aunt, looking for confirmation.

"It was my favorite . . ." Atie continued to pout, but was still cowed by the older woman.

"They'll be nice. If I can find whoever did it."

Finally, my auntie nodded, confirming she understood. That gesture was the same here. Though, there were only so many simple gestures like that. As she turned to start talking to people, Atie continued to rub her ear.

"You know better than to mouth off to her like that, sister, particularly when she's trying to help." Mom was still trying to be the voice of reason.

"She didn't twerk your ear," her sister complained.

"I didn't do anything to deserve it. She also knows better than to do anything that would put a child at risk." Mom bounced me up and down ever so slightly to indicate my presence. "At any rate, looks like the mud at least survived."

My aunt turned toward her new bowl with a scowl, marching over and picking it up from the fully cooled ash of the pit. I worried for a minute that she might throw or break it in anger, but it seemed she'd calmed down. When she felt it, she made an odd face, like it was something strange. Then we all headed back to our hut.

With the village elder asking questions, we'd be a little late getting out this morning. As that was going on, Atie sat there with the pottery, examining it deeply as she ran her hands over it, tapping it in places, making a nice ringing sound.

I could see the gears turning in her head as she looked at it with a critical eye. Many people from my previous world thought that so-called "cavemen" were stupid. To an extent, that was a misnomer though. Sure, humans of the past hadn't had the tech that we did in my age, but they still knew things. More than that, they knew how to look at things and how to solve problems just like any modern person would have.

This was happening in real time with Auntie Atie. She seemed to know she had . . . something, in her hands, but not quite what to do with it yet. I saw her looking for cracks, or imperfections. To be true, the edge of the pot was really rough, but that was mostly because it hadn't been designed as a pot, but rather as a simple basket coating.

"Eduan, will you take a look at this?" she finally asked.

My father had been working on some tool or other, shaping stone with a critical eye and a few hard thwacks. At her request, he rose from his spot and moved over to look at the little clay bowl. He didn't seem all that interested, but she'd asked nicely, so he held out a hand.

"Just dried mud, right?" he asked, confused as to what she'd want him for.

"Doesn't look quite like dirt, or feel like dirt, and it makes noise if you tap it."

Dad brought it up close to his face, turning it around a few times and running a fingernail along the surface. "Hard, not good stone hard, but hard."

"You could make something like that from stone right?" she asked.

"Yes, but it would need to be thicker or it would be very brittle. It would also be a pain to do." We didn't have any stone cups or bowls in our hut, so my guess was that he just didn't ever feel like making such a thing was worth his time.

"Do you think I could still use it to gather berries?" My aunt asked hopefully. "It's a lot lighter now."

"Sure, it might break though, so I'd be careful. I could clean up the edge if you want; it's still rather bad." He pointed to the parts that were starting to chip away, and at my aunt's nod went back to his corner.

Dad was careful in his work and filed the edges with one of the stones he used for shaping, before singing for a few moments and frowning. He was trying to shape it like it was stone was my guess, only to find that it wasn't quite the same. A few more rounds and he finally got it to move a bit like he wanted it to, making a nice, smooth rim.

My aunt seemed quite pleased with her new item, giving it many, many looks. I hoped that she'd take up pottery, and based on the smile that was forming on her face as she held the pot, I guessed it was fairly likely to happen.

Elaya showed up after a while with a frankly terrified looking girl, one who I'd seen a number of times, by the name of Aria.

"Couple people said they saw Aria here with your basket yesterday afternoon," the elder declared.

'I-I was just looking at it. I even asked, and I gave it right back. I just wanted to know how to make one myself for the berries . . ." The poor girl looked pale; understandable after Atie's rage not so long ago.

"She's telling the truth. She borrowed it to look it over for a bit and returned it. Whoever burned it did so last night, far later." She could have let the poor girl be a scapegoat, but Atie didn't, quickly explaining the truth to the older woman. She might have a temper, but at least she didn't go after those she knew were innocent.

I sighed internally in relief. If they had punished that girl for something I'd done, I'd have felt obligated to do something. It would be easy enough to float a few of the things around the room into a pile, baskets particularly. That would have been enough for them to know the true culprit, but I didn't want my aunt mad at me. I had only been trying to improve things, after all.

"Well, I got no other reports, dear. We'll keep an eye out for any other mischief, but without anything, there's not much to do."

Auntie Atie frowned, but there really was nothing to do without a culprit. In the end, she took up her new pot, which she seemed quite taken with, and we went out to gather, like we did on most days.

CHAPTER 7

FIRST WORDS

D ing!
[Achievement: Pottery]

Well, at least that's what I'd been hoping for. Sadly, this was not some game world. No, in this world there was no *ding*, and there were no achievements that magically made you understand what to do. Unfortunately, you had to just go ahead and do it.

I spent six months watching my aunt trying to work out the basics of pottery. Something which seemed so obvious to me was still a mystery to her, so she had to work it out the hard way.

Her first attempts were doomed to failure. She'd taken regular mud from near the village and packed it into baskets, which she then put in the fire. With no clay and no chance to dry, there was no success. Her frown as she looked at her first experiments was a bit disheartening, but she was a trooper and moved on.

Part of the problem was that she had no context for what was right and what wasn't. She didn't know what part of the process was important, and therefore didn't know where she was making mistakes.

She seemed to think for a long time that the berries were the secret. Something about them, or their juice, had made it so that she could form these new pots. That was untrue but an interesting guess. Mother was very, very irritated after a while by Atie's constant pestering to make the dark berry bushes fruitful; again, a change from her previous stance of hating them.

After those didn't seem to work, though, she looked into the basket she used to form her pots. Did the weave pattern matter? What about the plants it was made of? Maybe they burned differently, or they did something to the mud.

After each failed trial, she would sift through the mess she'd made, trying to work out the point of failure. Time and again, she had pots that broke because they were just mud or exploded in the fire. After a while, she realized that they needed to sit for a time to dry first. I think that was accidental, as she'd been aiming to have the plants impart their essence or whatever into the mud she was using.

Did the time of day the mud was gathered matter? What about the shape? Perhaps it was an issue with the fire? After repeated failures, she laid back in the grass one day. Mother had been getting rather tired of her spending so much time on this, but she was away tending to some emergency with one of the hunters for the moment. I hadn't heard what the problem was, but she'd run off quickly.

"What do you think, Elian? Where am I messing up?" She asked in a singsong voice as she held me and looked at the mess.

I wanted to yell and scream at her that she needed to use proper clay instead of regular mud, but I was still a baby, and I didn't know the word for clay, if it existed in this language at all. I'd been quietly practicing a few small words recently, mostly the equivalents of "mama" and "papa," something my parents were repeating to me all the time.

"Coo," was the only response of note I had to her question, but she nodded along sagely.

"Hmm, you think so? I don't know."

"Another failure, Atie?" Dad asked as he came over to join us. "Look, I don't mind, but your sister is getting tired of how much effort you're putting into this."

"I know, she thinks it was just some one-off mistake or something, but I'm close. I can feel it." My aunt was persistent. Most people I knew would have given up in much less time than she'd put in.

Each basket was a chore to make, and while she was now using simpler ones and had gotten much faster, it was still time. It wasn't a problem for the group as such, since there was plenty to go around, but she was using a lot of time and effort on this that could go into other things that Mom wanted done. I feared that if she didn't get it right soon, she might face some real repercussions to her place in the village.

"Hmm, perhaps there's something you're missing? I've run into issues like that working stone, and it's often something that seems silly later down the line, like, learning how the stone cracks along certain lines." Dad shrugged. He too knew nothing about making pottery.

"Any thoughts on what I'm missing?" she asked hopefully.

"No, but you might try working the exact same way you did with the first one, see if something stands out. That's what my father taught me when I first started knapping stones, and what his father taught him."

"Hmm, have to try that then. Now, that day we were . . ." She began musing to herself, drifting off as Dad took me from her arms and sang to me.

As my aunt began making yet another basket, Dad held me. He seemed content, happy with life and the way things were. This world was different, but here he was, happy to have his child in hand and the world around him safe.

Mom eventually returned, looking tired. She sat down near us and took me from my father. "Say, 'mama,' Elian," she encouraged once more, looking at me as she tried to elicit words.

"Were down by the river . . . maybe . . ." Atie was still mumbling to herself in the background.

"Oh give it up, sister. That bowl you got was nice, but whatever it was, isn't going to happen again. See, you're even bothering Elian. Even he knows you're silly, and he's a baby. Isn't that right, Elian?" She looked at me, and for once I was irritated.

Mother sometimes spoke as if I had an opinion that was the same as hers, but I didn't, and frankly, it was rather annoying. This was particularly the case here, where I not only disagreed, but I disagreed heartily.

"Papa!" I said, reaching my arms out to my father where he sat nearby.

Mom looked like she'd been slapped. She was the one trying to teach me to talk, and her favorite word to get me to try and say had been "mama." I'd also done it at the perfect time to indicate that I wholly rejected her opinion. At least it seemed that way to me.

Dad, on the other hand, looked elated and quickly reached out for me. It took a few seconds of grumping and a few more shouts of "papa, papa," but eventually I was handed over to him. I could have called for my aunt, but that would have just been mean.

"Hmm, perhaps he doesn't agree with you, dear," my father teased.

Auntie Atie had smartly said nothing and was instead trying to hide her laugh at my clear rejection.

"Betrayed by my own son," Mom said with mock darkness. "Fine then, do what you want."

She pouted, sitting there working on cracking some nuts she'd gathered up. As the night went on, though, I took pity. It wasn't a big thing; she just needed to know that she was wrong sometimes, just like everyone else.

Dad finally put me on the ground as the sun went down, something that was being done more and more as I grew. I was always watched, partially because there was a fire nearby and nobody wanted me to get into it. I'd made a few inroads to walking as of recently too. There were mostly halting steps and a few paces of running, which I put to use now.

I ran quickly over to my mother, crashing into her since slow speeds and stops were still giving me a good few problems. "Mama," I declared as I grabbed on, eliciting a smile from her as well. It would seem all was forgiven.

"Two words in one day, that's great!" she declared. "He even knows what they mean!"

Mom was happy, I was happy. I was also happy that I'd managed to get a little bit going for me. Being a baby was tiring, and now that I was approaching a year, I was finally getting past the worst of the helplessness. Soon, oh so soon, if I continued to grow normally, I would be able to talk freely, and walk, and run, and all the good things that I'd missed out on doing for the past year.

There were a few things I had noted over the past year. The first was the seasons, or lack of real ones. There were a couple of months where it definitely rained more, but nothing like the deluge that one might get in some places back on Earth. Other than that, it was just cycles of plants, rather than a major change in temperature and weather.

Another important note was that my memory was . . . different. I found that everything seemed to come back to me easier, so much easier. I could remember formulae and the like that I'd learned once upon a time, like it was ingrained into my memory. Heck, on a whim one night I'd started going over the periodic table, each and every element crystal clear in my mind, and I didn't even really study that, other than a few chem classes. Perhaps this was something about being an elf. My working theory was that since we lived longer, our memories were just different somehow, stronger. How or to what extent, I didn't know, but it was really cool to be a walking encyclopedia.

That wasn't to say there weren't gaps in what I knew. If I hadn't looked at anything with a hard eye, or studied it, it was still not there. I could recall things like algebra and geometry well enough, but the single semester of piano I'd taken didn't mean I could think of anything more than the basic pieces, and I wouldn't be playing any masterpieces anytime soon. The things I liked were also definitely clearer in my head than those I hadn't cared much for, or not tried to learn.

The next day my aunt took her basket and did as Dad had suggested, following the one she'd made previously as perfectly as she could remember. It was as she got down to the creek bed and began taking the clay out that she began laughing maniacally.

"Adia! I've got it! It's the mud; the mud here is different! It's all weird and strong and stuff!" She cheered as she got to work on her new pot, and I laughed with her.

"You seem sure," Mom said doubtfully.

"I am sure. Just you wait and see!" She struck a pose like something out of a TV show, proud and upright, and I nearly fell out of my carrier, I laughed so hard.

A week later, her first pot—the first she'd made intentionally and without my direct influence—came out of the fire pit, and she began a little dance. The difference was clear to her, and to everyone else. She'd managed to make something new, something truly new, and that was special.

"What do you think Elian?" She asked after passing the new pot around to everyone else.

I looked at her and clapped my hands, "Atie, Atie," I was proud as I could be of her success, and happy she'd managed it with only a hint from me.

This world had its first potter, a major step forward into a bright future I hoped to make. If I had centuries like I thought and a memory as good as I hoped, I might actually manage to bring us somewhere; only time would tell. That one of my favorite people in my new life had been the first to make inroads toward the brighter world I imagined only made me more elated.

CHAPTER 8

DIAMOND IN THE ROUGH

I took a few more weeks to sit back and get back to the main task at hand: language. As my mouth developed and things came into their proper place, I found that I was having an easier and easier time talking. I was struggling, though, because while I wanted to start going for full sentences and questions that I desperately sought the answers to, I was still a baby.

People didn't expect babies to be able to have full conversations, and while I would definitely stick out a little, standing out too much might be bad. I didn't know the traditions or superstitions of the people here yet, and so I was more than a little afraid that I might run afoul of some of them. Ancient cultures, back where I was from at least, had been really brutal to those they didn't like, and I could absolutely not survive on my own yet.

So I slowly started adding things to my publicly known vocabulary. A few words were there for communication, but others got added shortly thereafter. *Yes* and *no* were my first additions. Those two were needed for communicating what I did and didn't want, which solved a number of problems. Then we got to the really fun ones, *why* and *how*. Like most children, my favorite new word was definitely *why*.

"Let's go Elian. It's time to go for the crackle-nuts," Mom declared as she picked me up to put me in my carrier.

"Why?" I asked.

"Because they're coming into season now."

"Why?"

"This is the time of year they always do, Elian," she answered with immense patience.

"Why?" I wanted to know what the people thought as far as seasons. It might give me some insight.

"Well, a long time ago, when the world was made, it was made with seasons. These seasons come and go in a cycle, one to the other, before returning. As for why or how they do that, I don't know, son. Maybe one day you'll find out." Mom spoke as if this was something that had been told to her again and again, over many years.

There was a lot to unpack there. She said the world was made, but not by who or how, so perhaps they didn't know, or had no story to that effect. That was strange, but elves weren't human, so I couldn't argue. Then she did something really amazing. My mother admitted that she didn't understand everything, to a baby, and then told him that one day he might figure it out.

Most—the vast majority even—of humans wouldn't do that. The good ones, the really good ones, might admit that they didn't know, but for her this didn't seem to be some philosophical musing, just common wisdom. These people seemed to know that there was a lot they didn't know, and were interested that someone might find out.

It explained why they'd let my aunt play around with her new pot for ages, working and working with almost no progress. They knew that there was a lot they didn't know and encouraged others to look. Perhaps there might be a limit, or other philosophies on it, but my mother at least, I felt I could depend on to let me put forth new technologies.

Crackle-nuts, I decided, were one of my new favorite things. They looked to be some form of paper-thin shelled pecan variant. I knew that pecans were more of a temperate fruit, but these looked—and from the few that I was given, tasted—almost exactly the same. The name, I soon came to learn, was derived from the fact that the shells were so thin that they would crackle and break away when squeezed even lightly.

The little field we were gathering in had a creek bed, currently dry, running down its middle. The worst of the rains had passed not too long ago, and with them, a few of these had dried up once again. They made for an easy path through the woods and were used as such.

"Oh, pretty!" I heard a high voice declare from nearby, a call that got more than just my head turning.

Aria, a younger girl who'd once come close to drawing the ire of my aunt, was bent over in the dry creek bed, reaching down for something she'd seen. A few of the other curious women tried to get a look at what she'd found. One of the boys, on the cusp of adolescence, was looking too, but I could see that his eyes were somewhere slightly different.

When she rose, a small stone was in her hand—quartz or something, if I had to guess. It was clear and shining brightly in the sun. It got the attention of all the women. Eyes were shooting around, looking at the ground near her, and at the other parts of the creek bed.

I learned a few things in quick succession. The first was that I'd seriously underestimated how much the women here liked pretty rocks and the like. As soon as a few of the onlookers got a good look at what she'd found, all gathering for the day stopped.

To my eyes, it was just a little crystal, maybe the size of a man's thumb. To those around here, though, it seemed much, much more important. One of these seemed to be worth the rest of the day's work, and the whole group started searching for more; well, almost the whole group.

I was strapped to Mother's back, so I got a good view of the bidding war, and that's how I learned another important fact. Mom, along with several other representatives from other huts, all gathered around little Aria, who looked quite intimidated. She may have folded, but the elder Elaya came to her rescue with a glare that made everyone back off.

A bidding war ensued, and I learned the purpose of all the beads everyone had. That was the second, and perhaps most interesting, thing I learned this day; they weren't just decoration, they served as a form of currency.

The first bid came from a woman who didn't have many of the little trinkets, and she took off her nicest string. These were mostly wooden and, while prettily carved, were certainly nothing special.

"All of these for it," she offered. While little Aria considered, several other women in the group scoffed.

"Wood is worth almost nothing. Most of those aren't even colored," one opined. "Here, these are much nicer, no?" She took off one of her own, a smaller string, but the beads were carved stones of various colors; there was even a little one that looked like it was some kind of shiny shell.

This went back and forth for a while, and I couldn't help but notice that while Mother and Elaya both seemed very interested, neither made a bid. They were both by far the most bedecked of the women in our village, and I suspected their magic was the cornerstone of that. I wanted to know why they weren't bidding, but the words were still too much for a baby to ask, so I just watched.

"What do you think?" Elaya finally asked, after a number of offers and counter-offers had been made.

"Hmm . . ." the girl thought for a few moments. "My brother has been talking for a while about us, and a few others, perhaps getting our own hut, but none of us has been able to get enough together."

Those words were enough, and with them, and a few grumbles, most of the women fell back. Why, I wasn't sure, but for some reason that was enough for them. Only Mother and Elaya stayed forward near the girl, each sizing the other up.

"I could make you an offer to raise it, but then I'd need Eduan to carve it for me," the elder said, looking at my mother. "We both know what the fair offer on that would be."

"We do," Mom agreed. "And it would be a lot. Do you really want this one? Perhaps someone will find another."

Here the true bids began. They'd both abstained, it would seem, because neither wanted conflict with the other. Now that they were the only two in the running, though, it was a game.

"An arrangement? If I don't oppose you on this one, will you oppose me should I want the next?" The woman with her little white streak of hair appraised Mother and her answer.

Mom tapped her lip and thought. It was a risk for both. If Mom didn't agree, they could bid each other poor. If she did, she might get a good deal here, only for her opponent to get a free bite at a possibly juicier morsel.

"If another is found before the moon goes through its cycle again, I will not bid against you on the first."

That one took me a while to puzzle out. I had noticed that the moon did change phases here, and even that those phases were of a similar length to those back home, but nobody seemed to care about how long something took most of the time. This was also the first time I'd heard anyone try to use it as a measure of time.

"Agreed," Elaya said without a moment's hesitation. Then she too backed up.

Now it came down to Mother and Aria making a deal. Mom could have strong-armed her, but instead pondered for a bit, before removing a few beads from one of her own strings. They were nice, all very detailed carved stone.

"These, and a hut, for that one," she offered, and I could see the girl's eyebrows raise.

My mother had almost all the power here, but I could tell from the murmurs of those who had already bowed out that this was a pretty good offer. Even the elder nodded along.

"Could . . ." the lucky girl tried. "Could you get Atie to make me one of her pots too?"

Mom looked put off but called my auntie over. They had a very hushed conversation, whispering in each other's ears so low that not even I could hear it.

"Of her offer, I will take the bead you like least," Auntie Atie eventually made her gambit. "And of the five pots I have, you may choose that which you like best."

"Agreed," Aria said.

Their trade quickly concluded, with Atie being given her prize, and Mother hers. They then discussed briefly where the new hut would be, and several people congratulated the girl.

I could have watched this all day. Trying to work out what was best for trading, and how they determined it. Color was important, clearly, as well as size, and artistic skill. There was also a bit of opinion going on—some of these little pieces of currency clearly had more value to some of the women than others. It wasn't a simple monetary breakdown with clear denominations like I was used to, but it definitely worked.

As we headed back to the village late that afternoon, I couldn't help but look upon the parade of rather disappointed looking elves. Nobody else had managed to find something even close to that first stone, and they'd even missed out on an afternoon of work.

I was excited, at least, to see a new hut being made, and to find out why Mother would be the one to do it.

CHAPTER 9

BIG FISH

Getting time to practice magic was a real problem. Sure, I'd figured out one small thing, but I was still bad at it and had no time to try it out, because I was always being watched. Regardless of how the days and weeks passed, I was just never left alone. That was pretty good policy for a baby in this level of civilization, but it still irked me that I was unable to get much done.

It wasn't like many others were often alone though. People traveled in groups, large ones. The men who went out to hunt did so in large parties; the women to gather, much the same. Everything was done with others, it seemed; the idea of privacy nearly nonexistent. That brought up some questions in my mind about how . . . new generations were made, but I'd never seen anyone going at it, so it must be somehow hidden.

I did make a few inroads, small movements and the like, and even one attempt at making a fire, in one of the fire pits for safety of course. Every time I tried, though, it seemed one of my parents, or Elaya, came running shortly thereafter. I didn't know how they were seeing what I was doing, but there must be some way. The fire attempt had led to an almost panicked look on Elaya's face, and me being even more tightly watched.

A new watcher even joined. My father's best friend was a man by the name of Larus. He was without a doubt the most well-toned man in the village—not large like a bodybuilder, but hard and chiseled like a lightweight prize fighter. He also had an aura which seemed to indicate magic, but I'd never seen him do anything.

The downside to Larus being around was the number of girls he brought with him. He was clearly single, and just as clearly, several of our female residents would be happy to change that for him. Learning as I had, it was clear why—magic was power, and he clearly had it, as well as good looks. I didn't know what his thoughts were on magic, though, since he never commented much on it.

He would sit and tell stories while my parents attended to their own tasks. All of the children gathered round for these, and he told us of the hunters and the beasts that they went after. He described deer the size of huts and birds that could eat a man whole, and how as a group they'd go and take them down. He always downplayed his own role, instead regaling us with stories of how this man or that had landed a critical blow on the creature's side, or of the trap they'd set.

Eventually, time came for bed, though, and I was carted off. His stories were good, and while I'd personally prefer games or a good book, entertainment was thin here. I very briefly considered trying to convert some of the stories from my old world, but the truth was that I didn't have the skill for that, and so I let that thought fade.

Days came, and days went, and I grew bit by bit. I could walk now, and talk a bit, though I did little of the latter. There was so much to see, and I was even given time to play with some of the other children. Honestly, there wasn't much for me to do with them, as they all seemed to be ten or so, but that was fine.

I thought this might be something at least a little distracting, where I may even get a bit of time alone to practice magic; but alas, it was not so simple. The first time I was brought over, I was swarmed by about four girls who really, really wanted to play their variant of "house" with me, obviously still as the baby. Sadly, none of them were as skilled at handling me as my family was, and all were far too eager.

Perhaps all would have been lost, but then a hero appeared. Well, not a hero exactly, but someone who'd surely save me this time. A boy came to us a few days into my torture and stepped up to the girl who seemed to be running this little clique.

"Hey, Elian should be playing with us," he declared. "We need to teach him boy games." He stood with his head held high and a weird, three-pronged spear on his back.

"He's playing with us," the girl, by the name of Ayla replied. I'd learned her name as she ran this group harshly. "Elian doesn't want to go with you, right Elian."

"I do want to go with them," I said, which was probably the longest sentence that I'd spoken in this world.

"He-he doesn't know what he's talking about; he's just a baby!" she objected, and several of the other girls agreed with her.

It launched into an argument between the cadre of girls and two of the boys. The latter stood there taking all of their anger and letting them be drawn closer and closer. I noticed that I was now not being watched by my previous jailers and began to slip backwards.

The adults were watching on but seemed content to just let it play out. I was sure they even saw me trying to slip away. As long as the children were safe and not hurting each other, it seemed they'd let small things go.

As I tried to get around a small bush and out of sight of the two groups, I met a boy creeping around like I was. He was small and lithe, probably the youngest of the boys, with his face and body painted to blend in with the surroundings. Or at least that seemed to be the goal, but his camouflage was less than perfect.

We looked at each other for a full second, and he smiled. "Good going, little brother; we're here to rescue you."

"Thanks," I responded, and began following.

He nodded and began leading me back, near the edge of the clearing that we were in today. I thought he might take me out of the edge, but he didn't, getting just close enough that we had periodic cover, but never outside of the gathering women's area. Several nodded to him conspiratorially as we passed, not trying to hide from them, but from the group of girls. My aunt had to cover her mouth to keep from laughing as we crept along near her.

I didn't see when the girls noticed my departure, but I certainly heard it. By that time, I was well and away, and enough of our guardians had seen us that they began laughing openly. Even calling out that we were fine, just hiding.

We were near the creek again and I was led far upstream by the painted boy. We were soon joined by the rest of the boys, who'd slipped away shortly after. There were five in all.

"It worked?" The spear-holding boy asked, smiling as he approached.

"Yeah, he was escaping right as I was coming in."

"Great! You're Elian, right? I'm Ninden, and you've already met Olond, I see," the same boy said. "Want to come with us? There's lots to do."

"Sure, what stuff?" I asked.

"Fishing today, but there are rules." At my nod he continued. "Never ever go outside of the clearing we're in. We're safe here, but there are monsters that will eat you." I suppose I looked like I understood because he continued. "And don't go anywhere alone until you're a bit bigger. The women don't mind if you're playing with us, but while you're so small, they'll get mad if you're alone."

"Okay," I agreed, and we headed off up the stream.

We arrived at a pool, just near the edge of our allotted area, one swarming with little fish. Each of the boys had a spear there, and they were quickly taken up, each except me. There was a little branch though, one just about right for how tall I was. I was as big as a larger two-year-old at this point, and this was the first bit we had to do. While some of the other boys went off to begin, it was the oldest Ninden who came over to me.

"All right, you need a spear, so I'll show you, huh?" He took out a small stone knife and cut prongs into the end of the little branch, so it made a little three-parted spear tip, well almost. "You cut these like this, and then you get a stone, about the size of your thumb. Can you find one?"

I looked on the ground and found one that matched close, a small round one, and presented it to him. "Here, like this?"

"Yeah, then take some vine and tie it here, like this." He showed me where and how and then took the time to let me try and get it myself.

It was simple enough. The stone parted the points by sitting between them and was held in place with several wraps and clove hitches, nothing complex. I got it on my first try, and he patted me on the shoulder.

"Good job. Now, you should ask Olond to teach you to spear fish; he's the best at it."

Olond did indeed teach me how to use the spear. The trick, it was explained to me, was to aim low and thrust fast, the fish were lower in the water than they looked, and very quick. Other than that, I needed to stay still. He set me up in a good little area with a rise I could stand on, and the boys let me have at it.

I was not really good at spear fishing, but they were. While I tried, I was still very small, and couldn't quite manage it for most of the day. The older boys didn't seem concerned. Every now and then, they called out to give me encouragement or to repeat the instructions.

Near the end of the day, I was tired but still determined. I was also having some thoughts on how to do this. There was a fish right in front of me, one of the largest I'd seen today, right in my sights, and I had a plan.

I extended my will, my magic, into my spear, and as I went to thrust I pushed it with me.

The spear, with my magic in it, went fast as a bolt and lodged into my target. Things went sort of wrong then, as I'd underestimated the size of my prey. I had the spear, and it was lodged in well, but the huge fish struggled, pulling me off my feet.

I wasn't alone though. The elves of this world, even the young ones, highly valued each other. Within a second, the other boys were with me, helping me up, and with the spear. I got a bit of help hauling my catch out of the water, and Ninden smiled.

"You got one, and a good one too!" he enthused.

"Yeah," I agreed with a smile.

It was the only fish I caught all day, and my mother had doubts when they explained it was mine. It did make a good dinner though; it was added to our family's food for the evening. Dad asked me to tell him the story of how I got it, and while I hesitated, I eventually gave it a shot. He wasn't the only one to listen either. Most of the hunters in the area leaned in. It was polite, after all, to let someone tell you how they got a good bit of prey.

CHAPTER 10

FLIGHT OF THE BUMBLEBEE

Every day with the boys was different, or at least interesting. There were a number of games and the like to do, all of which were led by Ninden. He was the oldest, and while he wasn't the most skilled of all of them, it seemed part of his position as the eldest boy was to make sure that all the other boys were taught what they needed to know.

Of course, every game we played or task we took up was related to hunting or finding food. Men in our tribe primarily went out to search for high-value and high-risk targets, like beasts and meat, while the women went for the safer and easier-to-attain foods. Everyone wanted both, but there were many days when the men of the group came back with almost nothing to show for their labors, particularly if some prey had led them along all day. Nobody was terribly bothered, though, because sometimes they came back with a bounty of food for their efforts.

One evening I even got to see several of the men, one clearly Ninden's father, giving him lessons on what to teach the other boys with the changing seasons. He nodded along, paying close attention, for while it was clear he knew these already, it was his job to make sure all of us did. I didn't know how much longer he'd be with the children, though, as he was one of the oldest of us, and would, in at most a few years, be pulled away to join the men in their daily endeavors.

I was somewhere around the age of three now and had finally been getting a decent amount of magic training in. While the adults still watched me like a hawk, the boys not as much, and it was easy for me to push a bit of magic into spear throwing, or fire lighting, things that we did often. I could feel my skills improving almost daily as I worked more and more of it, seeming to grow like a muscle.

I also confirmed that I needed proper visualization. Just making the idea of what I wanted wouldn't work; I also needed to visualize how it worked. Fire, for example, didn't need just the thought of the bright flame, but, for it to go well, I also needed the understanding of flames being plasma and the idea of oxidation reactions, even the three pillars of fire— heat, fuel, and air. While I was careful about it when I was unwatched, I could throw small balls of the stuff with very minimal effort when visualizing all of these.

Today though, we were after bees. Honey was a rare treat, and while it was much beloved by everyone, it wasn't something people went after much. The women didn't like messing with the bees, and the men seemed to be more inclined toward larger game that could feed more. We boys, though, had the time and inclination to seek this target with viciousness.

The fine, cool day, that was as much spring as there was here, glowed with early morning light. For the last few days we'd been planning, readying for our hunt. There were small baskets, replaced now with a few little pots, to ready, and one of the men to recruit. The boys weren't allowed out alone, no matter the reason, so a chaperone was needed. We'd established that there was a beehive somewhere north of the clearing used for this time of year, but not its exact location.

The man we managed to snag was Ninden's father, Niyen. He didn't talk much, staying back a bit as we caught a bee and held it under a small pot.

"All right, everyone, you know the plan. When we let him out, we follow close back to his hive. If we're lucky, we won't need to catch another, but if we do, be ready," Ninden said, looking at all of us.

Ninden and Olond had spears for this trip, as both were more experienced than the rest of us. Niyen, who looked at us before we could let loose our quarry, also had a spear.

"Boys, we shouldn't run into any beasts, but if we do, you're to run back here. Myself and the older lads will throw spears to slow down anything, but we're not hunting animals today. If you see one, you run, understood?" Niyen said, and there were nods all around.

With the warning given, the boys looked at me. "Well Elian, you're the youngest, so what say you to starting the chase?" Olond asked, always happy to give me something that I could do to help.

"Let's go!" I enthused, lifting the pot and releasing the bee.

A cheer went up from our small group as we set off after the insect. It flitted left and right, and we kept eyes on it the whole way. I'd never been out into the woods proper before and struggled a bit to keep up, but with a good push, I managed. The bee led us through several patches of trees and bushes before finally coming to a rocky hill.

"We can't be far; bees don't go much farther than this from their hives. Keep an eye on the trees as we go up," Ninden declared.

While most of the boys flew up the first few rocks, they were a real issue for me. Niyen stood back watching as I tried to pull my way up the first, and at a small cough from him, our leader turned, jumping back down to help me up.

"Thanks!" I said, as he offered a hand, the both us quickly ascending the stony hill.

Before we'd made it to the top, I could already see the problem. The bee, fast as it was, didn't need to slow to climb up the hill, whereas we did. I looked around for a few moments before finally looking at Niyen.

"Er," I began.

He shook his head. "It's your hunt, boy, not mine. I'm just here to make sure you're safe."

Olond, who had by far the best senses of all of us, pointed after a few moments. "There!"

Easily fifteen feet up in one of the trees was a hole, in and out of which dozens of insects flew every moment. It was the hive, and in a very inopportune place. We'd prepared for that though. While Ninden had skins tied over him to keep the stings away, the rest of us got to work. I prepared the fire, with lots of green leaves in a little pot to smoke the bees out while the other boys set to readying baskets and the like.

While it wasn't fun pissing off a hive of bees, the whole operation went as by the book as possible. Half a dozen elves, mostly young boys, passed the readied smoke as our brave leader took a stick and broke open the hollow full of golden sweetness. He chucked down the pieces of hive into our waiting baskets and pots as we all cheered, retreating as each one filled.

As soon as we had our prize, we retreated. The angry bees wouldn't follow us too far, even if we had raided their home, so getting away was our first priority. Everyone took a few stings, myself included, but that was the price to pay for what we got.

And oh, did we ever get. We had filled up to the brim on honey, and as we laughed through our retreat, we couldn't help but smile. Everyone had a bite of honeycomb when we reached the bottom of the hill, a prize for a successful hunt. Ninden got his first, as he'd been the one to climb, but soon each of us had a small bit of comb to chew on, spitting the wax into the smoke pot when done.

I pulled off a piece, the same size as the ones we boys had, and offered it to our escort.

"It was your hunt, not mine," he said, smiling.

So I shrugged, breaking it in half and offered again. "Maybe, but you helped too."

"Yeah," one of the boys replied.

"You did," Olond agreed with me.

"Take some, Father," his son finally said, leading the man to smile.

"Very well. What will you do with the rest?" he asked as he finally took the small piece.

"Share most of it with everyone else, of course," I answered.

That was apparently the right answer, as a cheer went up. This group of elves, tribe, was not like the humans of my old world. We were all too close for anyone to be stingy with their work. Sure, some things weren't shared, and many weren't shared equally, but most of it was, particularly food. All of us boys would go home with a private stash of honey to do with as we and our family pleased, but a fair bit would be shared with everyone. Even those who didn't have sons on this excursion would get a small bit of the honey.

The way home was filled with chatter and a quiet song of victory. Each and every one of us was thrilled at the day's successes. It didn't matter that we'd all taken a few hits from pointed butts; we couldn't help but be happy.

As I thought back, I found that there were few, very few, times in my previous life that I'd felt like this. I was proud of a job well done, satisfied and happy that I'd done my part, as we all had. I was also thrilled with my friends, each who recognized the success of the other. It was refreshing in ways I hadn't anticipated, and brought a true smile to my face.

As we were approaching the clearing, something odd happened. From just in front of us, behind the cover of the trees, a purple star shot upward. It climbed and climbed, making an ear-splitting, high-pitched noise as it reached toward the heavens, where it exploded with light, a brilliant marker for all to see.

I'd never seen that before, but I was clearly the only one, as the whole group froze briefly in terror.

"Boys, back to the village, now!" our chaperone yelled, pulling us from our stupor.

We had to follow him a bit forward, as the path to the village intersected the clearing, and that would be the fastest way. All of us ran, with Ninden reaching down to pick me up from the ground. My short legs would not do for the run we needed to make.

The scene when we got there chilled my blood. The star had to have been some kind of warning, as a bear of incomparable size stood in the middle of the clearing. It was covered in spiky growths and roared in anger at all around it. Many of the women had scattered, fleeing back to the village path, while a few stood firm, covering their retreat.

From here and there, a few bolts of energy flew at the beast from the fleeing elves. None had more than Elaya though. From each of her hands came a barrage of flames and water balls, homing in and slamming into the beast, who seemed to care little. Based on the colors, my guess was that Elaya must have been the one to send up the call for help.

Mother was there too, sending ripples of energy out toward the beast, while others aimed at the ground around its feet. The bear seemed to quickly find the source of the vines and roots trying to keep it in place, and with a shake, ripped them before charging at Mother in rage.

Niyen was running forward, but too slow. With a flash of magic around him, he blurred and threw his spear like a missile, the point lodging into the beast's side. His son let me down for the briefest of moments, sending his own smaller projectile into the fray with an identical movement. It seemed he'd inherited the trick that his father had.

Now on the ground, I readied myself. I'd never used my magic to fight, but I'd thought of one or two things. There was a small trill of fear until I saw Mother turn, trying to flee or dodge the charging beast. The look of terror on her face as the monster tried to take her steeled me like nothing before, and I let my hands raise. That was my family, as true as any I'd ever had, and this thing was not going to take anyone from me.

CHAPTER 11

BATTLE AGAINST THE BEAR

Elaya was using fire, which was good, but I was thinking of something a bit more . . . energetic. In my hand, I visualized a spell, pulling my thoughts together cohesively faster than I'd ever thought possible. Force pooled in my hand. It was odd, so very odd, to feel pure kinetic energy warp and mold in ways that really shouldn't be possible, but within an instant a spear of pure force hovered there, waiting for direction.

With a minute flick of my small hand, I sent the spear flying. The air hummed as the force was imparted with direction. I saw grass and bushes shred as the missile of directed force rocketed, silently screaming through the air.

Before it landed, before it could even make it half way toward the creature, I was spinning up more of them, one in each hand. I even began my own slow plodding toward the monster, aiming to save Mother from the oncoming abomination of fur and spikes.

As the first of my projectiles struck, there was a thunderous boom and the beast faltered. Several of the large bone-like growths protruding from its body cracked, but the effect was far, far less than I'd hoped for. Something about the creature seemed to push back against the magic, resisting the force that sent a plume of grass and dirt back from the point of contact.

The next two flew similarly, but to little avail. One missed, striking a nearby tree and making its base explode; whereas the other landed true but merely pushed the creature back again. Either this monster was unbelievably resilient, or it was somehow negating my magic.

The next problem with this fight made itself known instantly and with its own potency. As I tried to step forward, my body faltered, like all the energy had been wrung right out of me. I'd never cast like this before, and it was clear that it would be a problem.

Ninden was nearby, and as the passing energy made itself known, he looked back at me, eyes wide. I could see him trying to process, trying to understand how I could do what I'd done. He could ask questions later; for now, we still had an enemy present.

"More spears," I wheezed to Ninden, sure he could hear me.

"I can only throw once!" he protested in panic.

"More spears," I repeated, trying to work my way through the fog.

He turned to run. The other boys may have had one or two spears between them; they weren't great, but would be better than nothing. If nothing else, we could brace them, because I wasn't leaving until my family was safe.

Our assault of wood and spell had an effect though. The bear's charge had been stopped dead, looking from my mother to us. It must have spotted our group because it turned from my fleeing parent right at us, roaring with rage and defiance.

Niyen met it halfway, his own speed gaining as he sprinted, a small stone knife from somewhere making its way to his fist. The man might not have too much magic, but the scream of rage showed he also had no fear. He was determined to do all he could, as much as any of us would.

He also had skill. I barely saw the monster pull back, but it attacked with a blurred claw at the man, which he ducked somehow, either through insane reactions or practice the likes of which I could barely fathom. The furred appendage left his hair rippling in the passing wind, and his hand slashed up, scoring a hit. Sadly, the backstroke of the monstrous bear caught the hunter, sending him flying a good twenty feet back, spitting blood.

Mother turned her head mid-run, and her eyes widened as she saw where the creature was now heading.

"Elian!" she shrieked in panic, seeing me in the path of the abomination of fur, bone, and flesh.

"Mother," I said quietly in return, knowing she couldn't hear me.

"Nooo!" came the roar a second later.

I didn't know if this creature was male or female, but I did know that I had a mother bear of my own. Mom stopped running as she yelled, hands blazing brighter than I'd ever seen before with power. Her right hand became a green fist, causing innumerable vines and roots to spring forth to capture the beast.

Her left hand was more terrifying. A black torrent, raging forth like an angry thundercloud in fast forward, and where the cloud touched there was only death—grass turning black and almost liquefying at its passage. It slipped close, but didn't touch the fallen elven man and slammed into the bear.

The struggling beast hadn't fully stopped before the cloud hit it, but it mattered little. It screamed in agony as wave after wave of my mother's rage washed over it, pulling and yanking as it came to a complete stop.

That power couldn't last forever, though, and after only a few scant moments, the cloud faltered and soon died. A quick look confirmed that Mother had collapsed, presumably from the same exhaustion that I could feel eating at my own strength, pulling me down into a sleep that might well never end if I succumbed to it now.

Ninden returned with two spears, and I grabbed one. I didn't know much about how to use a spear, but even I could brace it on my foot against a charging beast. That was good, since after Mother fell, the creature ripped with impossible strength, pulling the vines until they broke and tore with a sickening snap. It looked at her, but seeing her no longer standing, returned to charging us, slower than last time.

It forgot, though, much as I had, that even with her gone, there was still another to contend with. The tree I'd felled flew at it at an angle, the broken wood now a spear. The old elf had spent the moments we'd bought her, weaving her magic around the spar of wood, and now she threw it at the rampaging beast.

I could see her hard face, experience from many years telling her to hold her attack until the right moment. While her features were young, now they hardened like an ancient general, planning her attack. The wood slammed into the bear, and then it turned to pull away from all its combatants; the creature's back was now facing the woods.

Our enemy wasn't crushed, though, as I might have hoped. Bears could climb, and this one was quick, turning and bounding up a tree like a squirrel. The giant wooden spear crashed loudly into the forest, but the creature bounded, landing winded, but facing us all.

"Stupid beast; they're not alone," Elaya smiled. For a second, she seemed to sense something and her smile grew. "None of us are."

The monster was breathing heavily but still looked at her as if it understood she'd said something, but the meaning was lost on this beast. A second later, it screamed in renewed pain, turning and revealing another spear lodged through the bony spines and into its back.

More wooden projectiles flew, along with more of the minor spells some of our kind could manage interspersed, as the woods disgorged a screaming horde of angry elves. The hunters, who must have seen the same screaming ball of purple that had drawn us to the fight, had finally arrived.

At their head was my father's friend Larus, the largest and most built man in our village, roaring a war cry as he separated from the group and sped forward like a freight train. The only thing that beat him on his course was Dad's own scream of burning anger. That yell took an almost physical form in a wave of magic that slammed the beast, making it flinch and the air blow around it.

The furious men swarmed the bear like bees, or perhaps wild dogs, surrounding it in a flash. Though I was still struggling to keep going, they formed a circle around it, small strikes landing in practiced cooperation, making small hits while the lead warrior struggled to hold the animal's attention.

I wasn't one to flinch from this fight, though, not if it would leave any of my new people vulnerable. Seconds passed agonizingly slow as I wove magic around the spear in my hand, like a net. I no longer had enough for another of the pure force balls, but I might manage something else.

As the monster finally pulled back onto its hind legs in frustration, I loosed my spear straight at its now exposed chest, the point just below where I thought the sternum would lie. Earlier in the fight, it probably would have been able to bat the wooden spear from the air like nothing, or used whatever inhuman resistance it had to survive. Now however, the beast was spent, and my spear slammed home digging deep, joined by dozens of others shortly thereafter, none willing to risk the monster getting back up.

As the men descended upon the dying beast, I saw blackness creeping in on the edges of my vision. I laughed as the exertion caught up with my small body, sending me falling face-first into the soft grass.

When I woke, it felt like someone had crushed my skull with a hammer. My eyes snapped open to the cool darkness of evening and the pain screaming in my head. My wakefulness did not go unnoticed by the villagers.

"Elian is awake!" Father declared. "Now the stories can begin. You ready to tell everyone your part, Elian?" he said smiling.

I'd been laying against Mother's side and now hurriedly rose, moving toward the fire. Everyone looked on expectantly as I pitched over and emptied my stomach into the fire pit, along with a fair quantity of bile. The general uproar it caused seemed to indicate that was not the answer everyone had been hoping for.

"Not now," I answered after the spasm of my stomach stopped and I'd managed to spit a few times. "Head hurts."

Mother looked briefly alarmed, but from behind Elaya spoke. "He's fine, just pulled out too much of his light. Let the boy rest for a bit." At her words, the whole crowd settled down.

My mom scooped me up into her lap, as I was still very small, and held me. I could feel her very subtly pushing a bit of her own magic into me to heal anything that might be wrong.

"Rest, shh," she cooed.

I saw a hand near her ear from the older woman, who grabbed and twisted, if very lightly. "You already pushed too much of yours out, too, girl. The child needs only rest, not for you to pass out again."

For a brief moment, Mom looked angry, until she saw the soft eyes of the elder. Elaya might not look it, but she was something of a grandmother to us all. The other woman patted Mother's hair after her censure and took a seat beside us.

Meat was being passed around to all of us. There was almost literally a ton of it, and while some could be dried and stored, it was better fresh. There were smiling faces, as each and every member of the tribe could eat to their fill on nothing but the tasty protein, a very rare treat.

Stories began, with or without me. There were a lot of perspectives, and since the women were there first, they got to start, telling where they were and what happened. There was rapt attention, and I quickly learned that while there'd been injuries, quick action had prevented any deaths.

Our group went next. I learned part of why they were waiting for me. My spear at the end had apparently dealt massive damage to the monster, going through both its lungs, so it had been decided that the kill was mine. I'd been aiming for the heart, but lungs were not a bad place to hit. I was urged to tell what I'd seen first from our group.

I tried to weave a tale for them, struggling with some of the words, but managing well enough. All eyes were on me as I did so, everyone happy to hear about my magic, though some eyebrows went up when I spoke of it. My mother and Elaya were among them. I did stick to tradition, though, and try to make everyone else look like the hero, which got me smiles and nods.

Niyen went next, though his story was short, being that he'd been dropped quickly. Everyone was quite impressed at his bravery, though, and when he told of how he'd dodged a straight-on strike, there were gasps. The woman, who could only be Ninden's mother, clung to him like a vine, making it clear that he was very much hers.

Ninden went next, telling us all about it from his perspective. I noticed one of the girls who'd held me captive not so long ago inching closer with rapt attention. I also noticed that the boy didn't seem to mind, but instead passed her a little of our hard-won honey after he'd finished his story. He was nearing the age when girls stopped being icky and started being very, very interesting after all.

The hunters went last, telling their stories with gusto. How they'd finally surrounded the beast, and of the single spear that flew like a lightning bolt into the creature's open chest. They indicated that it was the work of those before that had made the kill so easy.

When it was all over, I sat there, full to the brim with tasty food and my hair being played with by Mom's gentle fingers.

"I want to learn to fight," I said.

"You're still too young," Mother said without hesitation.

"He'll need training, particularly since he is so young," Elaya interjected, still near us.

Mother nearly growled at the older woman. "He's still little." I was— only about as big as a three-year-old.

"More the reason, and we both know it. From what I've seen, he's like me, so I will teach him. That power he let loose is dangerous, and we both know it."

"You are not taking my child off into the woods for months," Mother declared through gritted teeth.

"Only until I think he's safe. Those strikes against the beast would destroy a hut, and we can't have that, and we can't have him hurting or killing any of us. You know I'm right, and you know it must be done."

Mother seemed ready to spit fire, but a hand landed on her shoulder, calming her almost instantly.

"What do you want, Elian?" Father asked, looking down at me.

"I want to learn," I said.

Mother looked irritated, but with the nod my father gave, she could see that she was outnumbered. "You will bring him back every few days for me to see him, or I will come and find you."

"Very well," Elaya said. "Rest child, for tomorrow we'll go to teach you what you must know."

Excitement or worry might have kept me up most nights, but I was tired, and with a belly full of meat, I soon found myself drifting off before I could make it to my bed.

CHAPTER 12

AWAY FROM HOME

I didn't have much in the way of clothing or possessions, but Mother still fussed something awful when morning came. She wrapped food up for me and checked it again and again before sitting down and giving me words of wisdom.

"Elian, if you want to come home, I want you to let me know when Elaya brings you to visit. I don't care what she says; you're still young, and you should be with your family."

"I'll be fine, Mom," I replied.

"I know. I know you want to learn, but it won't be fun; it'll be hard, and if it's too hard, you don't have to try right now."

"I know; I'll be okay."

"Elian, promise me that you'll take care of yourself, and if Elaya tries to push you too hard, you tell me. Tell her she has to deal with me if she tries." She didn't seem to consider that I might actually think I'd be fine.

"I will. If she goes too far, I'll tell her no." It was getting a bit ridiculous. Sure, the town elder wasn't the nicest of people, but she wasn't that bad.

Before long, the woman in question showed up. She had a pack much like the one Mom was making for me, but significantly larger. It was made from rolled-up hides, and my guess was that there were things in them that would help us for whatever training we would be doing.

She and Mother looked at each other for a long moment, before my mother spoke once again. "If my son comes back anything other than healthy and whole, I will be inconsolably angry." Her stare was hard.

"Good grief, child. This isn't my first time training a youngling," Elaya replied. "I'll keep him safe."

"Like you did Jolin?" Mother asked, a biting tone in her voice.

Elaya didn't have the face or body of someone aged, but in that moment she looked ancient. Her eyes darkened as she looked at my mother with sadness and regret. For a moment it looked like all the years fell down on her like a hammer.

"I will take care of the boy. You have my word." This time Mother nodded.

Mother put my little pack on me and gave me a kiss on the head before I left. It was sort of like the first day of school or something, and before long I was walking off with the village elder. There was a small, slightly disused path that worked its way through the forest to the north.

"Elian," she finally said. "There are a few things to say. The first, no matter what it seems like, you're not in any trouble. What you did the other day was very good, very good, and this isn't a punishment."

"I know," I said, nodding.

"I know that you've been told, but no matter what, I want you to remember that nobody is mad at you. In fact, most of us are pretty happy that you can use your light." I nodded, and she continued, speaking kindly like a caring teacher. "But, what you did is very dangerous, and we need to make sure that everyone is safe. That's why we're going to go out into the woods for a while and learn some, so we can keep you from hurting yourself or anyone else."

While isolation seemed like a good idea, I really wondered why Mom wasn't coming along. From what I'd seen, she could heal even really bad wounds pretty quickly, so if someone did get hurt, she'd be the person to go to.

"Why isn't Mom coming? If someone gets hurt she can help them, right?" I asked, since it was so often easier to ask than to guess.

"She could, but she also cares about you a lot and would always be fussing, which would make things harder. Your mother does like to fuss."

I laughed at that. "Okay, where are we going?"

"A cave to the north. We'll stay there for a while, and I'll teach you how to use your light and how to handle it. We'll also talk about what you need to do for the village." I raised my eyebrow at that last bit. "All of us who are strong have to help a little more, like I do when I pull down the high fruits; things like that."

"Okay, who is Jolin?" I saw her wince at my question, but I still wanted to know.

She sighed. "Jolin was a very smart little boy, like you, and he had a very bright light, like you. He was your mother's little brother, and was very cute. It . . . sometimes things happen that aren't good, and no matter how hard we try, they don't go well."

I could tell that whatever it was, something terrible had happened. I may not be very good with names, but that was a name I'd never heard before. My guess was that whatever had happened had ended either with the death or disappearance of the child, and for some reason Mom blamed Elaya. I could also see that the elder had taken it very hard, so I let the subject drop for the time being.

The path wound through the woods like a snake, going for a long time. Elaya was careful to go slow, and we took frequent breaks throughout our trek. Always making sure I drank a bit and wasn't hungry or anything.

"So, why are we going to the cave?" I finally asked.

"To teach you to control your light."

"No, why can't we do that at home, in the village?" I clarified.

"Oh, because it can be a little dangerous. We wouldn't want someone to get hurt by accident."

"What is the light? Where does it come from?"

She thought on that for a while. "I don't know for sure. Everyone has a little light, Elian, normally enough for them to do one thing a time or two before taking a break. Some of us, though, have a lot more, and nobody really knows why. Families normally have about the same amount. In some people like you, it's bright from the time they're little, but in others it grows as they age—a lot if something big happens."

"But what is it?" I pressed.

"Nobody knows, Some people call it their power, or their fire, or mana, or magic, but it's all the same. It lets us do things that we normally couldn't. Like how I can move things and make fire, or your mother can heal."

"Or how Dad can shape rock? What about Larus?" I asked.

"Yes, wait, you can see Larus' light? Can you see them already?" she asked.

"I always have," I said, nodding.

"Normally that doesn't come until you're older . . . But yes, Larus' light lets him be strong and fast, far stronger and faster than he should be."

We walked in relative silence for a long time. I was enjoying the forest, somewhere I didn't often get to go. Everyone in the village knew that it was dangerous to go alone, and the children were watched, particularly the younger ones, like hawks. That wasn't to say nobody went off alone, just that at my age I'd have been descended upon by adults had I tried.

Teenagers did seem to scamper off from time to time, as teens were wont to do; though that was generally in pairs.

As for us, with one of the more powerful magic users in town, I was about as safe as I could reasonably be, even if I didn't have my own magic to protect myself. I'd played with one or two more ideas for spells—plasma, electricity, and flight were all desirable—but I hadn't worked them out quite yet.

It took a lot of time, but eventually I realized that we were traveling down. The effect was subtle, but in the few places the trees cleared a bit, I could see it. I knew we lived in a valley, but the walls were getting ever so slightly higher.

At last we came to the place. There was a bare rock and a small divot, a small pool, no larger than an Olympic swimming pool from Earth, and looking of similar depth was fed by a trickle of water from the opposite direction. Behind it, from our orientation, was an unnatural looking hillock of rock, pushed like something had tried to come up from the ground. A large boulder blocked what looked to be an entrance, sealing it.

"Been a while since I've been here, but it's a lovely spot, isn't it?" my caretaker asked.

"Pretty. Are there a lot of caves? Why don't we use those like huts?"

"Just the one, and when I first came here, we did. It's deep, that cave. Let's go see." Elaya began trotting toward the rock, and I hustled along behind her.

We stopped before the rock and waited.

"How do you move it?" I asked.

"With your light." she responded. "Can you?"

I reached out, wrapping my magic around the big stone. It was huge, and heavy, and no matter how I pushed and pulled, it didn't seem to want to move with the amount of magic I could feed into the spell. Elaya waited off to the side, watching. She didn't offer to help, apparently seeing this as some form of test.

If it was a test, there had to be rules, rules and a result she wanted. Was I supposed to figure out how to move it? Or perhaps I should ask for aid, since it was clearly beyond what a small child should be able to do. How would she respond if I just broke it? The last thought seemed like a bad idea; her stated goal was to make sure I was safe, and she was probably looking for that kind of reaction.

I put down my pack and looked at it intensely, thinking about the options. Pure force would require more energy than I could manage at the moment, at least applied directly. I began to look around for what I had, and what information I had.

The rock was roundish, seeming to have been fit into the opening near perfectly. That said, it was only a portion that was serving as the barrier; most of it was outside. There were some other large rocks, and a few fallen trees nearby, along with the water.

I looked back at Elaya, who'd taken a seat on a rock to watch me.

"We need to put the rock back when we leave," I said, a statement, not a question.

"Yes," she answered.

"Okay, I have an idea."

The elven woman, with the face of a twenty-five year old and the eyes of an elderly grandmother, watched as I moved another rock over. This one was large, but not nearly as big, and was placed to the side of the entrance. I had to take several breaks during this process, as well as a few while positioning the tree. My magic was amazingly strong. I was able to pull things around what I'd associate with a horse or draft animal, but it was also tiring.

"Do not put anything heavy on that. I think I see what you're doing, but you need to be careful," she finally said, looking at the giant lever I'd pulled into place.

"No, nothing heavy, just a push." I moved well back before using my magic to slowly put a force on the far end of the ad hoc see-saw.

The boulder began to move, slowly at first, and then lifted. It went bit by bit until it was about halfway through the motion to push it out of the way; that was when the log broke. The crunching sound was horrible, and I was fit to curse.

"That was the best idea I had," I said after a moment, dejected. "Will you help?"

"I will." With a flick of her hand, magic poured out, wrapping around and pulling away the stone.

"Was I supposed to do it alone or ask for help?" I finally asked.

"There isn't a wrong answer, just an answer that teaches us. Some try to move it themselves, and fail, and get mad, or try to break it, and that's not really good. Breaking things should only happen when we need to. Others don't even try before asking for help. Why didn't you after your first try?"

"I thought you wanted me to do it on my own," I answered. "So I tried what I thought best. Then it was time to ask for help. Has anyone ever moved it on their own?"

"I've only trained about ten, but none have," she said with a shrug.

"How many times have you had to replace the rock?"

That got me a laugh. "More than once, but that's okay too. It just meant that I needed to teach them to be calmer about using their light."

"Well, at least we have wood for a fire," I said, pointing to the bits of broken wood. I could see now that it was dry as a bone, and perhaps rotting just a bit. I even lit a little flame over my finger just to show her I could.

"We do, and now's a good time to talk about it. We *do not* play with magic, particularly fire magic, understand?" She frowned until I put the little flame away.

"Yes," I answered.

I was totally going to play with magic though. It was too cool for me not to do some experimentation on my own, and games were a good way to do just that. I just needed to be careful and not make a mess.

She led me through scouring the cave with water to clean it, but did most of it herself. I could, if I tried, make some water, but it was slow and failing. On the other hand, she could produce something like a pressure washer, which made short work of the cleaning. So, after a bit I was put to practice, while she finished up.

By the time that was done and we'd pulled in a few ferns for a make-shift bed, I was tired. We sat for a while, her telling a few stories while I looked into the fire.

She did eventually get up to step outside, for reasons I could easily guess. While she was doing that, I idly picked up a stick and moved it around and poked the fire, something I did regularly back home.

There was a sudden flash of pain from my right ear as something latched on and twisted. I nearly lashed out with my magic as I turned to find the clearly angry face of Elaya, her hand just out of my view.

"Let go!" I protested loudly.

"What did I tell you about playing with magic, Elian?" she asked, the hand not moving an inch.

"No playing with magic?"

"And what were you doing?"

"Playing with magic," I answered.

"Do you understand why I have your ear now, little man?" she asked.

"Yes, please let go." It hurt more than I'd have ever expected, like there were extra nerves there for just this purpose.

She did finally, and pointed at the makeshift bed. "Time to go to sleep."

I went and laid down while rubbing my sore ear, now having received the first equivalent of an elven spanking. She, on the other hand, stayed up longer, eating some sweeter berries that she had brought along in her pack, and occasionally gave me a light glare that made it clear I was being denied dessert for not listening to her.

Eventually, I was joined by my still cross teacher. Most elves seemed to sleep kind of closely in our village. It was still really awkward to me, though, since I didn't even really know her, several times great-grand-mother or not.

CHAPTER 13

TRAINING MONTAGE

I had several days of what could only be described as frustrating training. Elaya kept an eye on me and made sure that I wasn't doing anything stupid, and she was pretty bad at answering questions. She didn't
know where magic came from, or how it worked, or why, or any of the
stuff that I really needed to know. At the very least, she didn't pretend to
know things she didn't, which was refreshing, having had a public-school
education.

"So, you need to observe the fire and how it moves. See how it goes
up, always seeing higher places. See how it needs fuel and air to grow. By
learning all we can about it, our magic using fire will get stronger. You
must focus on how fire works when you use it in your magic."

"Why?" I asked.

"Why what? Why does fire do these things? I'm not sure," Elaya said.

"No, why is it that we need to think about how fire is for us to use it
better?" I clarified.

"Oh, I don't know. There are a few people who've tried to figure that
out, but as far as I know, none have come up with a good reason. It isn't
like that for everyone though. People like your mother and father use a
very different method."

"What do you mean?"

"Well, your mother needs to do what she thinks is right, but she can
only change things that are alive," Elaya told me. "And your father needs
to . . . feel it, understand it more through feeling and sensation than
thought."

"But why?" I continued.

She shrugged. "I don't know. Your mother is a believer, and your father a performer, and that's just how they are. We, on the other hand, are thinkers; at least that's how I name things. In other places, they're called other things."

"I want to know how it all works, though, and why us," I said in a complaining tone.

"Then try to find out later. I'd like to know too, so if you figure it out, come and tell me. Back to fire now though," she continued.

There wasn't a lot for her to teach me about things like fire. I understood it very well—the chemical reactions, why it moved up, and what it was. All this was basic science, and she was quite frankly just ignorant about some things, particularly the whys.

"And you know the most important thing about fire?" she asked after her explanation was done.

"To not play with it unless there's an adult around?" I asked, remembering my ear twisting from last night and her lecture.

"I was going to say that it's dangerous and you should never play with it, but that works."

"So what's next?" I asked.

"We need to get some lunch. I'll show you how to gather a few things."

"Not hunt something, or get fish from the creek?" I asked.

"No, not with two of us, little man. Learning where to get easy food may seem like a girl thing to you, but you still need to know." She turned and led the way into the woods.

Gathering was mostly what the women in our village did, and there was a sharp division in labor. Never did the men join for their sessions; nor did the women seem to go hunting. Sometimes the boys would help the women by climbing trees to shake them or something, but that was about it. Even the games were more gender-divided. I didn't mind though. Knowing what berries were ripe and easy picking might well prove useful one day.

"Why don't you or Mom ever go hunting? With how strong you are, you'd be pretty useful, right?" I asked when she'd shown me what plants had the roots we'd be digging to munch on for lunch.

"You've already seen the answer to that question, no?" At my look she sighed. "If your mother and I had not been at the village, how many of the women would that monster have killed? What about other monsters? Anyway, the two of us are really helpful for gathering, too, as I know you've seen."

She wasn't wrong. I supposed that was a decent enough reason, and perhaps the women in our village just didn't want to. I honestly didn't know.

"Do you want to though? Go hunting?" I asked, trying to get her opinion on the tradition.

Elaya thought for a few moments. "No, I don't personally like wandering through the woods, and with my abilities, I bring more food back than any of the men can, even if they try." I had to snort at her answer. She wasn't wrong, and since food was often enough used as a form of value, she was doing very well for herself.

"Does doing this bother you?" I indicated our place right now.

"Not at all. You'll be very useful once you're trained, and I'm sure you'll remember who taught you, won't you, Elian?" She grinned evilly.

I looked at her and squinted. "What do you get out of this?" I asked.

She just laughed in response, sounding more like a cackle than anything else.

After lunch, we covered air in the use of magic. She knew that air was a thing. That was surprising, since I got the feeling from most of my history classes on Earth that a lot of people in the past didn't quite get that. Then again, she had magic to test against.

"So, you can see the stuff that makes air floats, and it will move above water and earth when it can," she said as she pointed out the bubbles.

We had several days of this, spending most of our time going over various bits of her knowledge. She didn't even let me cast any magic during that time, and always kept a keen eye on me.

"When will I be allowed to actually do magic?" I finally asked on the fourth day.

Elaya laughed. "Do you think you're prepared? That you can control it?"

"Yes."

"All right then, show me; fire first."

I moved beside our fire pit and reached my hand toward it before looking up. She nodded, and I let a small fire pour out to fill the pit. I was careful not to put too much out at once, slowly feeding the flames with magic as I kept them steady.

"Make it higher, and to look like a tree," she instructed.

I was given shapes, lines, balls, instructions like "flows like water," and even more esoteric commands. I spent nearly an hour working the flame in different ways before I finally stopped.

"I'm tired," I declared.

"One more. Can you change the color?" she asked, looking on.

"I could, but I'm tired." I wasn't going to budge.

"Do you not want to push yourself? Try new things?"

"When I am not tired, I do. Now it would just make me pass out. I don't want to. Mom said to tell you you'd have to deal with her if you pushed too hard." I was done for now unless there was some emergency.

Elaya laughed. "You must have been born older than I am, little man. You're right; don't let anyone push you if you don't want to do something."

"Sometimes you're a really good teacher, but sometimes you're really irritating," I finally declared.

"Perhaps, but if you can't figure these things out on your own, I will eventually tell you," was her response. "I want you to learn by doing first, if you can."

Over the next few days, I got to try out one spell after another, mostly creating and manipulating things like air or water. I could create water, but not stone or dirt, which was weird, but quite normal, I was informed. Elaya liked to go from one subject to another, trying to get me to learn a little bit of everything. That meant that I never got really good with anything, but rather a small smattering of abilities.

On the tenth day of training, we made our way back to the village. It was slow and a general waste of time, but Mother had declared that if we didn't come back enough, she'd be coming to us, and I had no desire for that.

"No magic in the village, at all," Elaya said. Do you hear me?"

"Yes, I understand."

We were descended upon by the other children when we arrived. It was later in the evening than either of us would have liked, but that was the thing about traveling through woodlands; it took time to go not all that far. The boys and girls nearest me in age all wanted stories about what was going on, the rumors flying. Mother just looked on, letting Elaya come to her so they could talk.

Elaya

The boy's mother wasn't happy when I motioned her to join me, but she could see he was fine. She'd surely be asking him about things later, but for now we could talk.

"Your son was born old," I declared.

"What?"

"He doesn't get mad or lash out at all, even when I push him. At worst he just tells me to stop."

Adia stared. We both knew that training, mine in particular, was . . . not fun for any child involved, and normally left them rather disliking me. That was fine; I needed to know what they could do, and if they were dangerous. I needed to know if they'd lash out if someone pushed them too hard, and I was the best equipped in the village to stop them if they did.

"Nothing? I know what you're like when you want to irritate, Elaya, and at his age . . . He never has been prone to tantrums though . . ." She seemed surprised. "But that's good, it means he can come back."

"I've still got a few basic things to run him through, dear, just so he knows how to use his light. I also want to see how he responds to danger. We'll ask Larus to help with keeping an eye on it; no accidents, but I want to pull something small to test him."

Adia gave me a cold look. "If my son comes to harm . . ."

"He won't; calm down. That's why I want Larus to help, dear, or Eduan, just in case."

"Why not me?" she intoned, clearly irritated.

"Because you dote on the child too much. His father will want to see his training, as will Larus. You'd just stop anything from happening at all, and that would ruin the whole surprise." I knew she meant well, but she really was too protective.

"I'll get both to go." At my look she continued. "They will if I ask; when do you want them?"

"Three more days, then send them. We'll talk when they get there."

Elian

I got to spend the night with my family again, which was great. Auntie Atie was still churning out pots and was steadily improving her skills. About half of them still broke when she baked them, but it was an improvement, and she showed me her newest work.

Everyone wanted stories, but I didn't really have any good ones. Our training had been mostly boring. At that explanation, a few more asked to see my magic but relented when I told them I wasn't allowed to do it in the village.

*   *   *

A few days later and we were back at the cave. It was nice enough, I guessed, and decidedly cooler than the huts normally were. Elaya had stepped out to use the lavatory, and I knew better than to follow the sometimes-irritating teacher.

So I decided to give a quick look around the cave. We only ever used the front part, and the back was blocked off by another boulder. With a look behind me to check that my ear wasn't going to be twisted again, I made another light to check it out.

The rock at the back was tight, but not nearly as tight as the one at the front, and while no adult could have possibly fit through the little hole there to the left side, I was quite a bit smaller. Surely it'd be fine if I just saw what was back there, right?

CHAPTER 14

DEEP CAVES AND WILDCATS

The small cave widened behind the rock, but not by much. I could now comfortably stand and walk, but it wasn't anything that could be described as roomy. It went back, and with a small light produced from my hand, I could see a good ways.

I wouldn't stay long, only a few minutes, only long enough to see just how far things went. Yeah, that was a good plan. I began to walk, making my way forward with great care. This place had been blocked off for some reason, and caves in my world were famous for being a good way to get yourself killed.

Within only a few moments I began to find some odd things. First was the moss; some kind of luminous lichen or something was covering the walls, subtle at first, but soon I didn't need my light to see by. I didn't know what could have made this, as there weren't any signs of monsters or anything else, just bare rock.

Further and further I went, making my way across the stone, deeper and deeper into the earth. Soon enough I came to a ledge, a small one to be sure, but one that was clearly too steep. The land went down quickly, and light or not, I couldn't see the bottom because of the slight twist in the stone.

I could probably have floated down, but I didn't know how deep this would go, nor did I honestly have much time left on my little tour. So I slowly backed away.

Something floated up from below as I moved to leave, a bubble. I'd seen enough auras at this point to know the look of one, and this clearly was. An aura of what though? It was small and faint, like it was far from its home.

It looked like mine, just like mine, how curious. I reached out to poke the little bubble, but as my finger closed in it popped. I gasped as a wave of mana washed over me, the little plants covering the cave brightening into an instant light show.

Then I turned and bolted. Something was down there, and I wasn't ready. I'd come back when I was strong and prepared, with gear and flight and combat magic. For now, though, I needed to retreat. If something was alive in that hole it would eat me for breakfast.

Luckily, it hadn't been too long. As I exited the back of the cave, I saw that my teacher hadn't returned. I'd suggest more fiber in her diet, but half the stuff we ate was raw fruit and veg already, so there really wasn't any point. Perhaps she'd gotten into something that just disagreed with her.

I kept waiting, and kept waiting. Eventually I got to the point that I was getting worried. I could probably make it back to the village on my own if something terrible happened, but where was she? Elaya had never been gone for anywhere near this long before; it was just odd.

I prepped a little bit of magic in case I needed to protect myself, readying one of my water spells as best I could, and moved toward the entrance. When I got there, I found everything quiet and no sign of the village elder.

Then out of the corner of my eye I saw a face in the bushes. It was hard to see without alerting the watcher, but after a few moments I managed to sneak a good glance. This led to all kinds of other questions.

Why was my father here? More importantly, why was he hiding from me? Should I call out to him or let him think he was still hiding from me? I didn't think most children would normally see something like this, so I decided to let him be for the moment, assuming he was just checking up on me.

While I was pretending to look around and contemplating these things, a small cat wandered out of the nearby woods with a lot of loud thunking and the like. It didn't look like it wanted to be here, and quite frankly looked like it was on its last legs.

The animal was just a bit bigger than a bobcat, something around that size. It was also visibly ancient, with grey hairs all over and a slight wheeze. That said, the thing was still pretty sizable in comparison, and even I could tell that it was very unhappy.

Another glance out of the corner of my eye showed Dad smiling from his hiding place. I sighed internally. This was clearly some kind of test, but to what end, I didn't know. I could easily kill this animal. Was this the stone age version of that Japanese TV show where they sent toddlers on errands or something? We could call it *My First Kill*. Except it wasn't, I'd already fought a magical beast way worse than this poor thing.

The animal spat angrily as it bared its teeth and extended the claws all along its feet, which were significantly longer than I thought they'd be.

Oh right, I should pay attention.

With an almost easy gesture, I sent a ball of water straight at the animal's face, hard enough to hurt it, but not enough to injure. The sphere traveled straight and clear, right past the now dodging cat.

"Go," I said to it.

The animal didn't speak my language, or probably any language, and instead of heeding me, bent down to leap. I caught it midair with a much harsher attack, which threw it back several feet. This didn't seem to improve its mood, though, as it quickly rose to face me again, now soaked and hissing like water on a hot stove.

I frowned. Was I supposed to kill this thing? Would we even want to eat it? I mean, there was plenty of food already, and fish or literally anything else would taste better than old, stringy wildcat. I didn't have any issue with hunting, but I'd never really done it. This just seemed like a weird test though.

My opponent, however, had other thoughts and charged. Another blast, this time of pure force, sent it back again. With a thought, I sent up a much smaller and lower version of the emergency signal, perhaps they wanted to make sure that I'd call for help if I needed it?

Nobody moved, and I knew where Dad was. Surely Elaya was still here somewhere, ostensibly also watching. Fine then, if they wanted me to deal with it, I would.

As the creature rose again and turned to charge me once more, I lifted my hand. This time I didn't bother holding back and sent a bolt of force straight into its head. This wasn't like the much lighter attacks, but rather very harsh and very fast. Poor thing didn't even have time to realize how screwed it was before its head jerked and it fell spasming.

I might have needed to kill the creature, but letting it suffer was not an option. Another spell snapped the spine, and it went still instantly. While standing back to observe what I'd been encouraged to do, I heard a noise.

Elaya "suddenly" came out of the brush, acting like she was running.

"What happened? Why did you send up an emergency signal?" she asked.

I needed a good excuse and had one on hand since I'd never seen any old folk in this world. "Big animal, and it looks sick."

"You killed it," she observed.

"Tried to get it to go away. Can we eat it?"

Elaya looked like she was thinking. "Yes, this animal isn't sick Elian, it's old."

I cocked my head at her explanation. "But you're old too and you don't look sick." There was always time for a dig at someone who was testing you.

She frowned at my observation. "I am pretty old, but animals get all sickly and like this when they get old, people don't, that's how you can tell the difference. When we get older, we only grow in strength, whereas they get weak and eventually die from the weakness."

"Okay," I said while I began to unpack that.

I'd never seen any humans in this world, but if I did, how would we even interact? It sounded like Elaya at least didn't consider anything that got old as a person. How did others feel about that kind of thing?

"Do you know how to clean an animal?" she asked, moving forward.

"No," I shook my head.

"Time to learn then."

She went back to her things and pulled out a flint knapped blade and began to lead me through the process. The stone blade was put into my hands and each cut was described, with her picking up the skin where I was supposed to and pulling it, pointing to each spot and telling me, and in a few cases even holding my hands in the right places.

It was a mess. There was blood everywhere, and the smell was a butcher shop without any fans. Luckily I didn't poke a gut or anything, since even I knew that would be bad, but the whole experience was less than enjoyable.

"So only animals get old?" I asked as I was pulling organs away.

"Yes, only animals. Well, plants too I guess, but they do it differently. Look, you can see how it's grey and all loose skinned—that's a good sign. They also get less muscular." She pointed out the traits on the animal.

"What if a person got old though?" I asked.

"They don't." Her voice made it clear that this was law as far as she was concerned.

After the work was done and the last of the skin scraped clean, we washed ourselves in the nearby pool.

"How would you feel about going back to the village tomorrow, Elian?" Elaya inquired.

"Aren't we out here to train?"

"We're out here to make sure you're safe. If you can have the forethought to call for help when you see something you think is dangerous, and the care to kill an animal like that, you should be safe. I still have a lot to teach you, but we can do that somewhere your mother won't be mad at me."

I laughed at that one. Soon we pulled the meat back to our little cave. We'd eat well tonight with only the two of us. Then I'd get to go home and back to normal.

CHAPTER 15

COMING HOME

Coming back home was . . . refreshing. It even came with a few benefits. Since I'd been "solely responsible" for the death of an animal, that particular animal's skin was mine to do with as I pleased. Elaya had claimed a few things as payment for helping me, but little other than meat, and nothing I really cared about.

"Why did you want the teeth?" I asked, as we walked back.

"Surely, you know the answer to that?"

"Beads?" I guessed.

"Yes, one of the lads in my hut likes to carve them and isn't too bad at it. Though bone beads are almost worthless, barely better than wood most of the time. Well, unless they're really good."

"How is that all decided, Elaya? Is there some reason one is better than the other?" I understood how money from my world worked, but not here.

"You've seen them traded, and understand some of that, no?" At my nod, she continued. "Well, it comes down to the fact that girls like pretty things, and being able to have pretty things shows that you're able to get what you want. Food is similar, as both you and I eat more meat than most of the village. We like it, and can demand it for services, so we have it. Meat isn't something you can show off though."

"So it's about showing you're better?"

"Yes and no," she said. "It shows power, that you're one to be listened to. Like my hair: not many get old enough for a silver lock like mine."

"I'm still unclear on how you know what's good or bad."

"Rarity is important, as is color, and how good it looks." She considered for a few moments. "With your light, you could probably make a few beads from either wood or stone to trade with the trader." At this point she pointedly tapped my ear, not grasping it, but letting me know she could. "Get your father to watch you."

"I didn't know there was a trader." There was a lot, to be fair, that I didn't know.

"He doesn't come often, since our village doesn't make anything particularly special. Well, if your aunt shows some of her pots, that might change."

For the rest of the walk I considered my options. Crystals, like the little piece of quartz that Aria had found, seemed to be some of the most valuable types. I was no gemologist, or chemist, but I could probably make fake diamonds if I really, really tried. That would attract all kinds of attention, and all of the wrong kind right now, so I thought I'd hold off on that for the time being. As for wood and stone, I'd have to try some and see what I could come up with; something good, I hoped.

I'd like to say that I came back to a cheering family. Sadly, everyone was still out gathering when we returned, so all I got was several more hours of sitting with Elaya as she made her rounds—cleaning up the camp and insisting that I help her. Chores were not my idea of a good time, but any chance to work on my magic helped, I supposed, so I didn't complain too loudly.

When Mother was on her way back down one of the many paths out of the village, she saw that we'd returned and hurried, beating all the other women back to us. As soon as she had somewhere to put down her daily haul, I was scooped up and held tightly, like she'd never let go.

"Hi Mom," I croaked.

She began to ask questions in rapid fire. "Are you hurt? Are you hungry? Did she do anything mean to you?"

"I'm fine, Mom." It was clear by the daggers she was staring at Elaya that she didn't trust the other woman with her child, regardless of how well I'd been taken care of.

I was carried off, my own opinion apparently unimportant on that point, and doted on until Father came back. Unlike Mom, who'd had a worried expression, Dad looked to be in a great mood.

"Elian! How was your time with Elaya?"

"It was fun," I answered.

"Do anything new? Any hunting?" I could see the slight smile on his face. He knew well that I'd done at least a bit to kill that cat and wanted me to tell the story.

So I obliged. I told him of how the beast had made its way to the cave when I came out looking for Elaya, and how I'd killed it after failing to drive it off. Then I spent a lot of time telling about how she taught me to clean it, and how it wasn't sick or anything. I did leave out the part where I saw my watchers, though, as that might get me drug back into the woods for more 'safety training.'"

Later, I even showed him the skin. He looked over it happily, giving all the encouragement he could. He showed me a few places where my knife had slipped and told me about the angle that I needed to hold it.

"You did a good job, and you'll do better with practice. One day you'll be as good as any of us." He ruffled my hair a little bit, and I was glad I'd gotten a good dad.

I looked around and saw Mom had walked off, so I decided to ask him another question. "Dad, will you help me carve some beads? I want to learn about it."

In a slight panic he looked around, locating his wife with ease. "You've done well to come to me with this, Son." He locked eyes with mine, a faux serious look on his face. "I'll help you, but if your mother finds out you want to carve beads, she'll have you doing it until you hate it. She likes them, but too many isn't good for anyone in the village, so you can't do that."

I put on the kind of serious face that could only be pulled off believably by a child and nodded gravely. "I understand."

"Good, then find some stones or something you like, and bring them when she's not looking one day. Do you know what you want? Or do you want me to show you good ones?" I could learn more from him, but for my first try, I wanted something simple.

"I just want practice, not anything fancy, so I'll pick some." He smiled at my decision, patting me on the head.

The next few days I got to go back to playing with the other boys. There was a little bit of a change in their attitude; that was clear. Someone must have spoken to them because they were no longer surprised by some of the things I could do, seemingly without effort. I was also having to be way more careful about my magic, because I knew I was being watched.

"Elian," Ninden asked four days later.

"Yeah?"

"Did . . . Some of the fires you made, and fish you caught . . . Were you using your light?"

I chuckled in response.

He laughed. "You scamp. So, gonna show us what all you can do then?"

None of them had asked to see my magic as of yet, at least not in so many words. The boys all looked up from the various spots they occupied today. We were looking for clams in the stream, a hard but fun job, and one that would leave you with cuts if you weren't careful.

I looked around, making sure nobody was paying too much attention. "Yeah, but gotta be quick about it."

Everyone popped up to give a quick lookout, then settled in. Olond and Ninden were the closest to me, but there were others. Alun and Ulun were cousins, but could have been brothers, and were eager to see what I could do. The last of the boys was Rindal, who seemed, at best, uninterested in me.

I started with small and easy-to-conceal things. My spear-throwing spell sent a small stick into the water at a high speed and got a good laugh. Then I moved a bit of water, not too much, but enough to show how I could manipulate it. One more quick look around and I started on the fun stuff. The first was a light, small but a pretty color.

I barely got a few sparks out for a fire before there was a quick movement from behind us, and someone seized me by my ear. I'd made a horrid mistake in my haste to show off. I'd failed to see an enemy until they were upon me. The boys had been so engrossed in their interest that they'd failed too.

"Hello, Elian," the light feminine voice said from behind me. It was sickly sweet, a sure sign of impending doom.

"Auntie Atie," I choked.

"I'm certain I didn't see you playing with your light, did I?" she asked.

"Er . . ." I was unclear here: lying might get me in more trouble, but telling the truth certainly wouldn't be helpful either.

"Interesting." She'd clearly come to her own conclusions. "And it certainly wasn't fire, was it?"

Run, I mouthed to the other boys, who were all going pale at this point. She must have noticed the movement because the twisting started.

"Ow, ow, I'm sorry!" Now, it seemed, was the time to admit, and perhaps mitigate, my punishment.

"Hmm, since you want to play with magic, you'll need to be watched, no? Why don't you come and sit with me today? The girls are nearby, and I'm sure they'll be happy to play with you." Her voice never rose from that sweetness.

"Mercy!" I begged. Playing with the girls was one of the worst punishments I could think of.

"Hmm? Well, I could take you to your mother so you could explain to her what you were doing."

"No, no, I can just play with the girls . . ." I may not be able to think of something worse, but I had no doubt she could.

"Good, come along then."

The boys watched on, as if I was being led to my death. Atie didn't even look down, just pulled me lightly along by the ear. I was marched up the stream to another area, where she had settled in with some friends and the girls. Mother was thankfully nowhere to be seen, perhaps off to help someone else.

"Bit of advice, Elian. If you want to do something secretly, don't look around like you're the guiltiest little boy that ever was." Atie released me as we closed in, but I was clearly expected to follow.

"I'll remember . . ."

"Good." We went over to where the girls were playing, making cord of some kind with a plant as they chatted. I couldn't keep up with all of it, but clearly there was a game of house being played, each pretending she was a certain person.

"Girls," Atie said as we approached, "Elian here wants to practice, but needs supervision to do so. Would you be good enough to let him in on your game?"

"Of course!" Ayla said, looking excited.

Ayla was the leader of this little cadre, and the only one of them I knew by name. She was . . . excitable and young, and very eager to play with 'babies,' which she still considered me. If I had to guess, she wasn't much older, if any amount at all, than Ninden, but it was hard to tell. Other than myself, all the kids seemed to be about ten; it was weird. The other three girls looked equally eager.

I settled in. This was sure to be a long, long afternoon.

CHAPTER 16

PLAYING

Ayla moved as if she was going to try picking me up, but I avoided her grasping hands like they were snakes.

"No, don't pick me up," I said with the harshest voice I could manage, and a glare.

"We're playing village," she said. "You're clearly a little one."

"No, I am practicing. No picking up."

Some of the nearby women began to laugh, and the girl tried to step forward and pick me up again; but I thought up a secret technique. She reached under my arms, and as she did I placed a small force there, just along my skin, pushing down to keep me in place. She tried to lift me up, only to find that I might as well have been a boulder. This went on and on, and I eventually heard a lot of laughing.

"I said no picking up," I declared to the exasperated looking girl.

" . . . what?" She just looked confused as she found herself unable to lift a small child.

"He's using his light. Which he will not be doing to harm anyone, will you, Elian?" my aunt finally said, emphasizing the last part.

"I'm not hurting anyone; I'm just not letting her pick me up," I retorted. I wasn't some maniac who'd hurt a kid for acting like a kid. At the same time, I didn't want some random girls thinking they could just carry me around whenever and wherever they pleased.

"Be careful," Auntie Atie said with only a slight frown.

I nodded and began to walk over to where the girls were, looking around for something to do. I watched the girls for a while and began to realize that their game was deeper than I'd thought. They were discussing who would make what, what for, and how much as they worked. There were a few who had different skills, or different preferences, and their magic played into this slightly.

Most of the girls here were now able to use the one magical ability that each of them seemed to manifest at some point, and while they weren't big things, they did affect their lives. For example, one girl could make plants grow slightly, and so her position was to either get the other girls' favorite fruits or to make the stems just right to harvest materials for little crafts like they were doing now.

Ayla could make a small force that would throw things away from her. I, of course, knew well that she was pushy, but the joke didn't seem to fit the language quite right. This ability enabled her to get fruits to fall that grew really high, and to scare away small animals. She was odd in that she seemed to have far more uses for it than average—not like me, but also not like the others, somewhere in-between.

"What are you playing?" I finally asked.

"Village," one of the girls answered. "We make things and then trade them. Right now we're doing cord since the plants are good for it."

"But you're all making the same thing?" I asked, not seeing how they could trade when they all ended up with the same stuff.

"No, look," she replied. "My cord is really small, while Ayla's is really thick. They're for different stuff. You could use mine for decorations and things, while Ayla is making cord for hanging things or making soft baskets."

"And you trade?" I asked.

"Yeah, we use the cheap beads when we can get them, or just trade for each other's stuff. I'm Isha, by the way," she explained.

"Nice to meet you, Isha," I said as I watched their hands move. It was true that each was using a different amount of fiber, even if they were all using basically the same quick twisting motion.

"Your dad does pretty stone carving," Ayla said, interrupting us. "Maybe you can too?"

"Not like he does. His light and mine are different," I explained without even looking over.

I could see the group all pouting at that. They knew I wanted to practice my magic, and I knew if I started carving stones, most of them would be begging me to make them some. Even if what I made was of poor quality, the beads would do for their games. I had an idea that was not the worst; it would ingratiate me, and it was something new to try.

"I have another thing I could do though; one moment."

Nobody cared too much if I wandered a bit, so long as I stayed fairly close. To that end, I made my way to some of the trees and began looking upward. There were all kinds of branches—some green branches, some old—that were nice and thick, and some that were stuck in the trees that had fallen long ago, but none of those were quite what I was looking for. What I was looking for right now was dead hanging wood, nice and dry, but hopefully not rotten.

Soon enough I found some dry, hanging wood that looked right, up in one of the trees used for nuts. With a wave of my hand, I sent a little bolt of force up, and the dead wood fell to the ground. I got a lot of looks, and some of them rather disapproving, but whatever; nobody really cared so long as nobody got hurt.

Upon inspection of the branches, I realized that I'd erred slightly. The branches were a lot bigger than I'd expected them to be, and far more than I needed for my plan. Searching through them, I found a length that was a couple feet long and around an inch in width. Through a mixture of magical bolts and pulling, I liberated it from the rest of the wood and headed back over to the girls.

They all watched on with curiosity as I held the branch in front of me and set it to spinning. Faster and faster it went, wobbling slightly since it wasn't perfectly balanced. That would be the first thing I fixed though, no problem. Force was probably my favorite magic to use, if only because it was really easy to understand, and therefore, easy for me to do, and the outcome was always cool.

Slowly, carefully, I made a little blade of force, shaping the angle and making it really sharp. Then, I began to lathe the wood down. I only needed it to be around a quarter of an inch, so that was the first thing. It was hard at first but got easier to shape as I went along, the branch shrinking over the course of a few passes.

I nodded at my work and made a quick and dirty drill bit, shoving it through the piece at the center of rotation. This was easy to find as I was the one doing it, and I had to say, far easier than using any drill. Slow and steady was the name of the game when it came to drilling, so I took my sweet time, looking up to count the girls while I did so.

By the time the hole was made, I was feeling it. My energy was burning to nothing, so I needed to hurry this up before I was completely tapped out. The last part was easy enough; just cutting the little bit of wood into roughly appropriately sized beads, five for each girl, ten for myself.

Each and every one was basically worthless. They had no color, no designs, and all looked the same. That said, the girls were over the moon when I gave them each the equivalent of a handful of change to play with. My aunt quickly came over to inspect what I was passing out. She'd been watching, and this apparently was something she had great interest in.

"Very plain, and rough," she observed, picking one up.

"They're toys. The girls can make them pretty if they want." I was done and moved back over by Isha.

That was my concession to good sense. I didn't want to ruin the local economy, just provide the girls with something to play with and learn. Playing was important for all kinds of social development and whatever, and I liked to see people smile.

"Fine, but don't go doing this a lot. You'll make people mad," Atie said before returning to her seat and shaking her head.

I pulled one of my beads out and asked Isha, "Trade for some cord?" If I was going to be stuck over here, I could at least do that much, and I wanted some string.

"Three," she said, smiling.

"Um . . . two?" I didn't even have to tell her how dumb she was being; she got it herself.

"I could make my own cord, and I don't need much."

Timidly, she took the bead and handed me a small roll of her work. It was way more than I really wanted, but whatever. I could use string every now and then. After our trade, I did the logical thing and strung my own bits, content to leave it at that and crash in the grass while I recharged.

The girls were going on and on, and eventually I looked back up to see Isha trying to figure out how she wanted to store her day's takings. The other girls didn't seem to have anything she wanted at the moment, and she was trying to use a strand of hair to hang them. It was not going well.

"Here, I'll help," I offered. "Can you make another really short bit of cord?"

"Um, sure," she said.

I braided her spoils into her hair. It was easy enough to do. When I'd been a kid in my first life, one of my first friends had been a girl in elementary school. I was awkward and she was sickly, so we both sort of kept away from other people. While she didn't do much in the way of social things, she'd been all about arts and crafts and had shown me hair braids, bracelets, and all the standard young girl things that had run through the school. All of those were easy as pie too.

I froze. I hadn't thought of her in years, literal years. There was no way I should remember things like that. I did though; all of it. Everything she'd shown me, every technique I'd learned was burned into my mind. Before my rebirth, I probably wouldn't have recognized a picture of her if you'd shoved it in my face. Now, though, I felt like I could draw her from memory and it would be perfect.

"Everything okay?" Isha asked.

"Yeah, sorry, fine." Quickly I finished, taking the bit of cord and tying her hair in place. It wasn't the nicest in the world, but it was good enough, and I had things to process.

As I laid back down, I thought. Everything I practiced came to memory with ease. All the techniques, all the hard studied things that had once slipped my mind now seemed to stick there like glue. It wasn't totally perfect, but it was getting clearer, way clearer, and the memories I was making now? They had a crystal quality that seemed unlikely to ever shatter. What could I become in a decade? In a century? More?

CHAPTER 17

THE CALL

I was forced to spend the next few days playing with the girls. While I knew Mother had been told of the reason, she pretended not to notice since I was taking my aunt's punishment in stride. It was at least fun to be able to freely play with my magic.

There were of course some downsides. The girls constantly pestered me to make them things using magic, and I knew that if I began, it would never end. Therefore, I outright refused to make anything else for them. They also wanted me to teach them how to braid like I'd done Isha's hair. That one I agreed to, since I had a lot of downtime waiting for my magic to recharge after playing with it myself, and I only had to make sure they got it once with how good everyone's memory was.

There were, to be clear, a number of braided hairstyles that the girls and women would sometimes wear. However, since these were different, and the only real use for money in the town was decoration, they consumed such ideas like they were starving for them. Any form of art, particularly one you could wear, would be infinitely popular among the females of our tribe. Even some of the older women came to sit and see what I was showing them.

"These are fancy; where did you learn them?" Isha asked one day after I'd finished braiding her hair. She could see the other girls repeating my movements, to various levels of success, and looked at me with questioning eyes.

"Hmm? They're not that hard to think of once you understand the idea," I lied. It would be best if I didn't share that I'd been reborn in this world. Who knew how they'd take it?

"Fine, don't tell me," she answered.

One of the things I liked about her was that she wasn't nearly as pushy as the others. If I said no, or indicated that I wouldn't agree, she mostly let it sit at that. She'd still ask, and sometimes make faces, but she didn't prod without end. Two days into my forced playtime with the girls, one had brought some bones from somewhere, and they'd decided to make some small needles. Most of them griped and fussed when I'd told them I wouldn't be helping, but Isha had let it drop after only pouting for a few moments.

"Shame I can't see my own," she mumbled, while touching her hair.

I thought for a few seconds, then nodded. "I might be able to do something about that."

The only real source of reflection around here was water, and everyone was familiar with it. Sadly trying to get water that was calm enough for a proper mirror was really hard, so getting a good look at yourself was rather rare. I could make water though, and I could make it still.

There wasn't a lot of water in the meadow we occupied today, but there was ample shade from a few large trees. I found one, cleared out a small divot in the soil, and filled it up with water. From there, a plane of force to keep it still was easy.

"Oh thanks!" She said as she looked in the makeshift mirror.

"That's pretty clever, Elian," Mother said, appearing behind me.

"It's just a pool," I answered.

"True, but it's still clever, and nice of you to do. Shouldn't you be playing with the other boys though?" She gave me a little head nod in their direction. "And not using your magic when alone with them."

It took a beat to register, but as soon as it did I quickly responded. "Okay Mom, bye!" Then I ran before anyone else could keep me stuck any longer. I didn't hate the girls anymore, but fishing and trapping and making fires was just more fun to me than sitting around talking and making little hand crafts.

Finding the other boys was easy. They were off to one side of our clearing, away from the adults and practicing making small traps. They welcomed me back with open arms and cheers, as well as some light teasing for being punished. I knew for a fact that some of them had gotten fussed at too—getting the youngest kid to do things he wasn't supposed to was a bad mark in most parents' books.

Around a week later something very new happened. When we came back from our daily gathering, those left behind were in deep discussion with an elf I didn't recognize. He was long and lanky with a small patch of salt in his otherwise black hair and had a pair of friends with him. All three were armed but didn't seem in the slightest bit hostile to us.

"Ah, lad, there you are. It's been what, ten seasons since last I saw you? Come here, come here," Elaya said, embracing the black-haired elf.

He and his companions were led to the main fire pit, and the rest of the group came happily along. Several of the single women were checking him and the others out. The dating pool was painfully small in our little village, as almost everyone was closely related. Even these stone-age elves knew that mixing too much blood was bad.

"How are you, Auntie? I see the village is doing well." He motioned to the huts with a smile.

"Good, very good. We've been lucky these past few years. And yourself?"

"Wonderfully! My wife gave birth just last year to a healthy son." The elder smiled, and then a worried look came over his features.

"You didn't come out here just for a social visit, did you?" Elaya asked.

"Sadly no. Atal is calling all the elders of the villages to meet." His statement hushed the crowd immediately.

"War?" she asked worriedly.

"I don't think so," he continued. "I've heard reports from the southern villages, the ones up in the mountains, but no confirmation yet."

"Confirmation . . . a cold season?"

"Maybe. I think you'll be told everything when it's time to meet," he answered with a shrug.

"What's a cold season?" I asked my mother from where she sat beside me. From what I could tell, it was only a rumor right now.

"The wind gets very cold and the skies turn grey. When the rain falls, it's slow like leaves and is hard, kind of like sand. During very bad cold seasons, the streams and ponds become hard like rock," she answered.

So . . . winter? I'd never really had a proper winter here; it seemed like a tropical climate. There were cooler times and warmer times, and times when it rained and rained, but never snow, not even close.

"Is it bad?" I asked. Our village didn't keep much in the way of stores.

"It isn't either good or bad, Elian. It is the season, and it just is that way." I assumed she could see my frown in response to her answer because she sighed before she continued. "If we know and can prepare, we will be fine, my son, but we will need to prepare. Many of the plants will lose their leaves and die. There will be a few new plants, though, and the animals tend to be very good hunting during a cold season."

"How long will it last?" I asked. This sounded like a rare and odd occurrence.

"Five moons, perhaps six. We only get one every thirty or more years though."

The time in this world was measured by the natural phenomena. A year being a full cycle of the seasons, then by the season, then the passage of the moon, finally days and their parts, of course. It seemed . . . natural, and with the slow pace of life here, there was little concern for the exact time for most things. Though, the moons were about a month, and that would make this a very, very long season.

"What do we do?" I asked.

"For now we sit quiet and let the adults talk," she answered.

I gave her an angry frown, but apparently that just came off as cute because she shushed me again and patted me on the head. The rest of the night I listened to their conversation. Nothing much came of it. The messenger didn't have any real news other than the call for Elaya to come with him to the meeting. They did prattle on for hours about friends and distant family. I learned that in her youth, Elaya had been from the central city of Atal.

Interestingly, they also spoke of the city as if it were both a person and a place.

CHAPTER 18

WHILE THE ELDER'S AWAY . . .

As Elaya prepped to leave, most of the village met. She didn't travel much—nobody really did—so it was a huge occasion. Well wishes were given, and the departing party's gear was checked and refreshed by everyone. There were also a few cheeky requests to bring things back from the big city.

Larus and Mother were called forward, and I didn't know why.

"You two are in charge until I return; keep the people safe," Elaya declared almost ceremoniously.

"I shall see to it that the hunters are protected," Dad's friend said.

"No harm shall come to the women or children," Mother answered.

"Huh?" I said, confused.

Father was staying back for the moment with me. "It is tradition for an elder to leave their village in the care of two of those with light when they must leave. Elaya has chosen your mother and Larus, which she almost always does."

I only knew Larus a little. He and Dad were always together, and while I spent more time with Mother and Auntie Atie, even I noticed.

"Why not you?" I asked Dad.

"Not a good idea to have both from the same home. If they agree on something others don't like, there would be arguments of favoritism. Your mother's the only real option for the women, and there are only three men in town with enough light for it to fall on them. Since I'm far too close to her, it must be him."

"Not me either," I said.

Dad laughed. "No, you're too close, too, but even if you weren't, you're also too young, Son. You would only be picked to look after the village if there were no other options, and that would be a desperate time indeed to have one so young put in charge."

"What if there wasn't someone?" I asked.

"Hmm, that would be bad. Few villages are that small, though, and even in the worst case would only have one to look after them while their elder is away. There must always be someone who can use their light."

I could keep asking, probing why the others weren't considered, even though they could utilize magic, but I didn't need to. This world was dangerous, and the best thing to fight against that danger was the power we wielded. There were no guns or weapons that could fight against something like that bear we'd all gone against. Not that I was that sure that a gun would have been enough on its own.

It was clear within a day or two that the men were staying near the gathering spots, regardless of the hunting there. There was a charge in the air—not panic, but caution. Our elder was gone, and everyone was feeling it keenly. The hunters didn't want to stray far, and many found excuses to work on their crafts near the women and children instead.

While this meant that the amount of meat available shrank significantly, it also meant that we boys got to spend more time with our fathers during the day, something everyone seemed happy about. It gave me a chance to ask questions I'd never gotten answers to and to practice magic at the same time. I wasn't being forced to go sit around with the girls, and Dad knew quite a bit about making things with magic, even if his was very different from mine.

"Have you ever been to Atal?" I asked.

"Yes, though not in a long time. I even met Atal once," he said.

"Isn't it a place?" I said, seeking clarification.

"Atal is the elder of Atal, which is the biggest settlement around here."

"How big?"

"Well Son, Atal is big enough that if each villager of our village were a village like ours, we'd be around the same size," he said after thinking a bit.

"And the elder?" I asked.

"Is very old. He was very old even when Elaya was born. There are others like him, far away in their own villages, but they seldom meet, and are all very powerful. When you get old like that, you get strong, even if your light wasn't when you were little." At my confusion he continued. "Most villagers don't live as long as Elaya has, but those who do always develop a light, even if it's a small one, that they can use, like you or me. Of course those with a bright light already are more likely to survive that long, and we do grow, slowly, over time."

"So if you grow for many, many years, like being old when Elaya was little, you'll be strong?"

"Yes," he said.

"Are the other old elders nice?" I asked.

"They fight sometimes, but not often. None have fought during my lifetime, or even Elaya's."

"Okay." I waited a few minutes before asking another question, but I had it ready. "Why did you go to Atal?"

"I was a traveling merchant," he said. "I went from place to place and traded things. Some things I made; some I got other places. When I met your mother, though, I wanted to stay."

"Oh, I see. So you're not from our village?" I asked.

"No, Larus and I were both from another, about two days away. He was my friend there, and when I'd heard he'd moved here I decided to come out this way. Not many traders care to come this far."

"Are we far from Atal?" I asked.

"Depends on how fast you are." My father was technically correct. Larus would surely be faster than I would.

There were no maps or even good directions, for the most part. People knew general directions, and landmarks, and where villages and the like were, but we just weren't there technologically. That was something I might be able to work on later, but for now, there was little I could do.

I couldn't, no matter how hard I tried, meld stone like my dad could. That said, he couldn't make a lathe like I could, and he seemed to really like the idea when I showed it to him. I knew some of the many things that could be made with such a tool, even if I wasn't any kind of woodworker in my previous life, and I could see the gears ticking behind his eyes.

"I have a few ideas, Elian. Would you mind helping me with them?" He chuckled under his breath as he looked at a small decorated stick I'd made.

He liked the idea of spears a lot, and between us, we could make a really good one. My shafts were to exacting standards that would take him far, and he made the best flint heads. I'd really like to make a bow, as that would be a big step forward in the way of things, but I honestly didn't know how. I knew enough to know that making a bow would be very difficult, and failure could result in injury, and that stopped me, for now.

Elaya was gone for a few weeks, and she was certainly missed. I got to spend time with Dad, so I didn't miss much. He and I made spears, with him walking me through each and every step. He also looked on as I used my magic to fish. Everyone was happy about the latter, because when I really let loose with it, I could bring in lots and lots of fish every day.

Larus also came by one day while all the boys were playing to talk to us.

"Hi, boys. How are things?" he asked, looking us over.

"Pretty good, sir. Something happening?" The tone Ninden used indicated his respect.

"Nothing much, but I know you boys heard the rumors about a cold season." There were nods all around; it was the talk of the village. "We had one when I was young, you know, and do you believe that the boys were a huge help?" He smiled at us all, leaning down to tell his story.

We were regaled with tales of how the young lads of the town had spent day after day putting up traps. Many of the big animals either hibernated or died, and some became very hard to catch, but the little ones, the little ones could still be gotten. This wasn't something vital as I understood it, but rather him trying to prep us for what might come.

"Show me the traps you boys know, and where you'd put them," he said.

So we did. We displayed all our tips and tricks shown to us by the various men in town, and at each one, he smiled. He knew that, for us, this had been mostly play and practice, but we'd done well regardless.

"Good, good, but look here, boys. Look at the grass." He pointed to a spot we'd all missed, where something had moved through the little field. It was subtle, but it was there. "As for traps . . . the ones you've got will work well, but make sure to practice making them; the trigger is the most important part, so make sure it's right."

He showed us the triggers again and then pointed out where each would have issues. We drank it in. This wasn't him being mean, but rather making sure we had what we needed to do what we must. The whole time he laughed and smiled, and I couldn't help but watch all eyes on him from around the field. How he was single to this day I couldn't figure out.

When Elaya finally returned, she looked exhausted. She, and two other elves who'd agreed to travel with her, arrived late in the evening. All were frowning, all unhappy at what they'd learned.

"Gather everyone," Elaya said. "We have much to discuss."

CHAPTER 19

PLANNING FOR . . .

As the whole village sat down and looked at our elder, I couldn't help but sigh. It was clear that her news was bad from her expression alone. The only thing we were to find out was how bad.

"A cold season is coming, and we must begin preparations for it," she opened. "In more than three, but less than ten years, it will arrive, and with it will bring hunger and the chill. If we begin now, and set up our food and blankets for when the time comes, all will be well, but these things will take time to do."

Food preservation was hard in this world, as there were no freezers or the like, though I could probably build one. They also lacked things like fermentation, and salt was not nearly as prevalent, though I'd seen a bit. Meat was basically eaten right away, and while some fruits and the like were dried, it was honestly poorly done. I was still too young and still too untrusted to introduce many new conventions, but I might manage to get something easy in if I tried. Smoking perhaps? If I could do that, it would save us much effort.

It was also wild to me how far in advance we knew this disaster was coming. While the time frame was huge, the ability to tell that something was on its way would save lives. I wasn't sure, but if this new season appeared without warning, the straits would be dire indeed. Mother could only grow plants so fast, and there might well be starvation from it.

"There is no need for worry though; only action. I will request the men to quickly begin gathering honey where it can be found, and to make as many stone holders as we can for it," she said.

That was actually a brilliant idea, honey never went bad, and apparently even the people here knew it. If we could gather a bunch of it in the years between now and the six-month winter, there'd be a great source of calories just waiting for us. I did have one or two ideas though.

"What about Auntie's pots?" I asked, knowing that clay would hold honey perfectly, and be a lot faster and easier to make.

Eyes swiveled in my direction, and more than a few of them looked irritated that I'd interrupted Elaya's speech. Mother put her hand over my mouth and made a shushing sound. Elaya, on the other hand, looked at me and quirked her eyebrow.

"Hmm, we'll try that, but ask questions later child. For now, though, we need to look into gathering seeds for the plants that we can have grown during the cold season. While it will be a chore, we also need to start saving the skins we can where we can for warmer clothing. That will be enough for now."

A lot of questions were being taken to Elaya now, and people were crowding forward. We held back, waiting while others sought answers. Atie slowly moved over toward Mother and me, and sidled in close.

"Do you think one of my pots can hold honey for a long time?" she asked Mother.

"I don't know," was her answer. "Regardless, it is rude to interrupt the elder when she's speaking like that." I was fixed with a light glare now, not that I cared too much, so long as they listened.

"They hold water, right?" I asked, looking up.

"True, will you make a small one to try, Atie?" Mother asked her.

My aunt nodded as the rest of the members of our hut's little group started gathering around. Mom was distributing jobs to everyone and being very clear about the preparations that she wanted for us in particular. The whole village would be making changes, but for what each of the sub-groups in particular would do, that was up to them. We were one of the strongest, and it wouldn't do to lose any amount of prestige, much less have our people suffer, because they weren't prepared.

Off to the side, Father had moved over so that the representatives from the other huts could come and speak to him about getting stone pots made for storage. He was the best in our town at it, and offers were being put to him quickly. There were also discussions about different tools and hunting implements, as the game would change with the season. Those were less vital, but people still wanted to get their requests in now.

The next day, I finally got a chance to speak with Elaya. There were a few things I wanted clarification on, particularly about how we could store food.

"So, I heard the water will get all hard in the cold season," I said from where I'd set up near her. "What's that like?"

"A pain to deal with. You can't drink hardened water, you have to heat it up first, but cold water tastes nice. Some of the villages up in the mountains to the south have a name for it, it's 'icha' at least to them," I mentally added that for ice.

"Can you make it? Like you can water?" I asked. She'd long ago shown me she could summon water without much effort. I suspected that I could make ice if I really wanted, but didn't want to demonstrate something I'd never been shown.

"Hmm? I don't know . . . never tried to." Absentmindedly, she began to hold her hand out and concentrated for a few moments, a small ball of ice appearing there. "You can," she finally answered.

I took it from her hand. "Cold!"

After that, I began making a bit of my own. I was careful to make it smaller than the piece she'd formed, but it came easy. I could picture ice on all kinds of levels without any real effort. I knew how it felt, tasted, and everything else, even the chemistry of it, how it formed, and what the crystals looked like. Heck, I could remember almost all of those classes in school where the teachers showed us that kind of stuff, like I'd been there just this morning. And, it all came flooding back to make a beautiful little crystal in my hand.

"Oh, you got that quick. Good job, Elian."

"Do other things get hard when it's cold too?" I asked as innocently as I could.

"Plants do, and they get a little covering of ice, sometimes they break and come apart," she said.

"What about animals? Will they get all hard and break apart? What about us?"

"No, animals don't. Well, I guess dead ones do, the meat stays good a little longer like that, too, which is one of the reasons trapping and hunting will be so important." She was now giving me a look that seemed to indicate I should get back to my own lessons for the moment, but I had one or two more things I really wanted to push forward.

"Can we do that even when it's not a cold season?" I asked. "We can already make the ice; can't we use it to do the same thing?"

"As soon as it warmed up it would go back to normal, and I don't have that much light to constantly cool it," she said shaking her head.

"Okay, but what if we just put the ice somewhere it was already cold, like in a hole, or in a cave? That cave was cold before we started the fire in it."

"Well, you're welcome to try if you want, Elian. I don't think it will work though," she answered, now actually waving me off to leave.

"Okay, I'll do it!" I said before turning and sprinting away. I didn't want her thinking too hard about what she'd just given me explicit permission to do.

I now had to go find Ninden and the rest of the boys. Even with my magic, I'd still need help for this. I briefly considered trying to get my mother to help with the building, since she could probably make what I needed in an hour or two, but I doubted she'd approve of my plan. On my way to the boys, I started coming up with my arguments, arranging each and every one, not that I thought that the first would fail.

The boys were fishing, hoping to get a little extra meat since a lot of the men were already going after honey to fill what stone vessels we did have. We knew that this meant the village would be a little light on meat for a while, and they wanted to change that.

"Hey!" I said excitedly as I approached them. "I've got something I need help with back in the village if anyone wants to help. Elaya told me to try it if I wanted, and if it works, it'll be great." Sadly, the word *cool* with my intended meaning didn't exist, so I couldn't make the pun.

"Why should we?" Rindal asked. None of us really hated each other, but he certainly liked me a lot less than the others did.

"It'll be good for everyone if it works, and if it doesn't, we'll have a place to play at the village away from the adults or the girls," I said.

There were some things that transcended time, culture, and dimensions. The love boys had for digging and secret bases was one of these things, and all eyes were on me very quickly. Details were demanded, and eyes set to sparkling. Heck, the only thing I might have suggested that could have gone down better was if it were a secret tunnel, and I wasn't ruling out making one of those later.

"Okay, let's plan all this out. We'll need to start quickly, or they'll try to stop us . . ."

CHAPTER 20

SURREPTITIOUS CONSTRUCTION

Adia

As soon as we were home, the boys ran off, and all I could do was sigh. They were all hard working on their trapping, though, so we could let them skimp on the evening chores. Even my Elian was trying to help, though he often came up with the strangest of ideas. But he wasn't the only one.

Atie was still more interested in her pots and things than anything else. She'd kept up with her gathering, though, and I had to admit, having something to store water in around the hut was nice. I wondered if any of the merchants that passed through would be interested in them.

All that could wait for later. For now I had things that needed doing. Our group headed over to the best section of rocks and began the arduous process of cracking all the shells from today's nuts.

Boom.

"I've been saying for months that we need to put back more skins for clothes, but Mother won't listen at all," a younger woman complained.

Slam.

"Well, she wants bedding, right? You need both, and getting someone to part with a larger skin isn't a small thing," one of her friends added with a shaking finger.

Crack.

"I hear they use tree branches up in the mountains for that. Why can't we?"

Thunk.

"Dear, they have different trees up there. Oh, that one's no good," an older woman said, tossing a rotten nut.

I smiled. None of this was really intense; just letting our hands work as we chatted. Someone was always thinking about what came tomorrow, even if it was all small stuff. The seasons came, and they went, and year after year we grew, families getting bigger, members of our village getting stronger. We were still small, and still weak by comparison to most other villages in this region, but we'd only been founded a couple of hundred years ago, so that was to be expected.

Shina, who I'd known since childhood, looked over, eyes gazing off as she ran a hand over her belly. She knew, as did I, her condition. She'd come to see me a few days ago, wanting to be checked after she began suspecting herself, but it was too early to make any kind of announcement. Children were blessings, and even though we got one every few years, there was no reason not to celebrate. They were also so very fragile as they came into the world, no matter how much I tried to help.

Thinking of my own, I looked around. "Where's Elian?" I asked.

"The boys ran off to play," answered Isha, one of the younger girls who often joined in our evening chores.

"All of them?" I asked.

"Mmm."

"Has anyone seen or heard any of the boys?" I asked, rather loudly.

Several women looked around, increasingly bothered. Nothing would ever bode well when the entire group of them couldn't be found.

Elian

All of us knew we had to hurry. We all knew the stakes. Once we'd found the proper spot, we started with haste. I'd used my magic to do the initial digging while the others had gathered tools and the like, and now they were getting the few logs we'd managed to secure in place.

Our little project was very makeshift, mostly just a hole with a bunch of wood serving as the roof and covered in dirt. It would work as an ice-house, and once it was done I was sure that I'd convince the village that it would work for ice, and to let me make another for us to play in. I sort of felt bad about tricking everyone into helping me, but I believed myself right, and if I wasn't . . . we'd still have our secret base.

Many hours of labor had already gone into this project, be it planning or prepping the wood. Most of that had been distributed here and there, us putting things where they needed to go slowly so that when the time came, we could get construction going, but some things couldn't be easily hidden, and the building process was one of them.

The cousins, Alun and Ulun, were the fastest by far, and I could see the little bits of magic as they worked together, pushing the roof into place. Ninden and I were pulling more materials over, along with Rindal, who'd never liked me but loved this idea. Finally Olond, our best at stealth, was keeping an eye out.

Most of my magic had gone into the digging, so I couldn't well finish it all myself, and teamwork was fun. Once we had the rafters in place, we took our borrowed tools and began covering the whole thing with dirt, leaving only the small entrance. It was as we were piling the soil high that the first calls came from the direction of the village proper.

"Olond, where are you?" came the first shout, the voice feminine.

"Alun!" followed soon after.

Olond soon appeared, looking at us with large eyes. "They realized we were gone; they're coming."

All of us took a moment to freeze; we all knew it was coming, only hoping that we'd get enough time to finish before it did. It was still too early, still too soon for the disaster that would soon be upon us.

Steeling himself, Olond looked out upon us. "I'll go, I'll keep them distracted for as long as I can," he said solemnly.

I placed my hand on his arm, and in the most serious tone I could muster, I said, "Your sacrifice will be remembered."

He soon turned and fled into the lingering twilight, a hero to us all. If he could just keep them until the men returned, we might have a chance, a slim hope that they'd see the greatness of our work and protect us from the retribution that was sure to come.

As soon as he was gone, I got back to the project. Most of my magic was spent, having gone into the initial push. That was part of why I'd used so much in the beginning, though, just in case we needed a hard push at the end. I reached out, grabbing as much of the dirt as I could and piling it on top of our makeshift base. It would insulate, and we needed it done before we were found.

My world briefly spun as I overtaxed my magical muscles, leaving me spent as all the power left me. It didn't change things, though, and soon I'd returned to the pile, helping spread and pat down the mound of dirt. A few minutes later, we were as done as we could be and looked upon our new building.

It wasn't much, honestly. All in all, it was just a hole dug into a hillside, with sticks and dirt piled to make an impromptu roof. The entrance was small—small enough that most of our fathers would struggle to enter—and long, about five feet. The main room inside was around ten feet wide, and nearly just as long, with a low ceiling and a few larger logs to serve as supports. I'd need to get rock in there later to replace those, but it would serve for now.

No sooner had we gathered for the final inspection than the call came from behind us.

"Found them!" came a familiar voice, and I turned to see Auntie Atie yelling back toward the main part of the village.

Soon mothers, older sisters, aunts, and the like all descended upon us, all looking quite cross. I saw Olond, the bravest among us, being hauled forward by the ear. He gave a smile when he saw us, resigned, but pleased his mission was successful.

My own mother soon made her way to the front of the gathering group, several of whom looked upon our creation with clear anger.

"What exactly do you boys think you're doing?" she asked as she looked at us.

"Elaya gave us permission," I blurted out, hoping . . .

"I most certainly did not!" came the hollered reply. I should have known she'd be nearby. The clearly displeased elder stepped into the dying light of the late evening, scowling.

"You said I could put ice in a cave or a hole or something. So we made a cave, or a hole, or something . . ."

That excuse flew with all the grace and beauty of a chunk of sandstone, and it was clear from the looks alone that nobody was buying it. Several were already advancing on their sons. There was only one option left.

"Run, scatter!" I yelled at my compatriots, turning to the nearby woods. We didn't need to get far, just into the shelter there to wait out the worst of the storm.

I made it not even three steps before I felt the magic wrap around me, lifting me from the ground. I pulsed my mana, trying to undo a spell that could only have originated from Elaya, but to no avail. Tired as I was, there was little I could do as I was pulled back. The other boys didn't make it far either, each in turn being levitated or wrapped in vines by Mother as they tried to dive into the bushes. None escaped.

When the hunters finally returned a couple of hours later, they all had a good laugh at our expense. Both for the severity and number of punishments being thrown about. Our whole group had been sentenced to hard labor in the form of all the evening chores, overseen by merciless wardens who assured us that we'd be taking care of them for the foreseeable future. I myself was tied around my waist with vines to Mother, who seemed determined that I shouldn't leave her sight for even an instant.

Elaya took time, now that her work was being handled, to fill our little icehouse up, calmly informing us that since that was what it was for, there should be no complaints. I just hoped it worked, and that they let us keep it.

CHAPTER 21

THE REWARD FOR GOOD WORK

Weeks after what was now being referred to as the "ice cave incident," a number of the men gathered us boys up. At this point most of the anger had fallen away and punishments had ended. I was sometimes even allowed outside of sight of a "responsible adult." Big progress. They looked us over with smirks.

"Now, since you boys like building so much, we've decided to take the day to teach you a bit about it," Larus declared. Whenever the men did something as a group, he tended to lead them. "Now, you should always try to have access to someone like Adia, who can just grow a hut, but sometimes that doesn't happen, new villages, or those where some of those with the light have left, or long hunting trips. So knowing how to do this will help you."

"Can we not just make one like we did before?" Ninden asked looking confused.

"Nobody will be using their light for this one," his father clarified. "Also, do you think it's a good idea to remind any of the girls about that little game of yours again? The one where you deceived all of your mothers?"

"I mean, it worked," I said. "We were right."

I got a lot of looks from every adult who'd come to this little outing. Then they looked at each other until finally my father spoke.

"Perhaps you should bring that up with your mother then," Dad suggested. "Or maybe you'd like me to tell her that's your opinion?"

The boys had nothing to say to that.

"I didn't think so."

The first thing we had to do was gather up materials. That was straightforward enough, as nothing we wanted would be too large. All of us were shown what to use, the right and the wrong pieces, what would rot or break too easy or burn. Some of it we knew, some we didn't. Then came things like the outer structure and lashings, and finally the roofing. It took all day, but by the end of that day we had a pretty good little lean-to type shelter on the edge of the village.

It wasn't big, but it was more than large enough for our group of boys to collapse inside at the end. While we rubbed sore spots and took a break, our teachers gathered around it humming and hawing.

"Not bad, not bad at all," Dad said, shaking one of the spars lightly.

"No, this should do quite well," Ninden's father agreed.

"I'd say it'll stand for at least a year if it's taken care of," Olond's father added.

"Sure will," and "Without a doubt," agreed the fathers of Alun and Ulun, brothers who, much like their sons, were peas in a pod.

"Ah, but that will be a chore, won't it? Have to have someone take care of it 'til it needs to come down," Rindal's father pointed out.

"You know, while their mothers have punished them for digging up part of the village, I don't think we have," Larus declared finally. "Boys, listen up." All of us sat up from where we'd taken to resting and looked at him. "You lot are in charge of this for the time being, got it?"

All of us nodded, and they left, chuckling lightly. I understood immediately, but it took everyone else a bit to realize what had just happened. Once we all had, we burst out laughing. Sure, we'd made a mess and had irritated a bunch of our elders; and sure, some were still peeved that we'd not properly asked permission, But we'd done a good job and provided something for the village as a whole. And the men had seen that, and seen fit to provide us . . .

"We got our own place for us," Olond whispered, as if it were a secret. It sent us all into a fit of laughter.

Unfortunately, our gains caused a whole new slew of problems for us. Well, more like one big problem. The girls saw we'd gained something they didn't have and were more than just a little bit jealous. It had started with suggestions over dinner, and increasingly nagging remarks here and there.

"It's not fair, they did something bad and got rewarded for it," their chosen representative announced, having cornered us after the day's gathering.

They'd picked their time to strike carefully. All the hunters were away; therefore, our strongest supporters were absent. Somehow they'd even managed to pull our village elder into the area for their ambush. Elaya was supposed to arbitrate any disagreements that weren't too serious on her own, and she looked at us with raised eyebrows. It was clear that they'd gathered allies for this battle.

"She has a point," the elder declared, turning to us.

"No, we all got punished, a lot, and you sat there laughing at us while it happened," Ninden said, not backing down.

Elaya now turned back to the girls. It was clear she wanted some response from the girls.

"And then the hunters built you a hut like you wanted."

"No, they showed us how, and we built it. If you want one, build it yourselves."

This argument had played out to this point several times already. There were some problems though. We'd been shown how to do it, and they hadn't; and then there was the whole division of labor thing. In our village it was uncommon for the women to do things with stone tools or larger items; it was almost always the men who used those. There were, of course, exceptions, particularly when it came to using magic rather than muscle to make stuff, but they didn't have access to much of that. It was unspoken, but clear to everyone that it wouldn't really be socially acceptable for them to just up and make something like we had.

That was why Elaya's eyes hadn't left us yet. The elder understood all of this, and it was being made clear to us that not only should we also already know, but that it wouldn't serve. Ninden faltered, not sure where to go and understanding that we'd lose if there wasn't a better retort.

"You could ask my mother to make you one," I offered. "She might."

"We already did. Adia said that it shouldn't be done often, or it will hurt the ground near the village. She won't make us a place like you have." It was Isha who spoke this time.

I blinked at the change in speaker, and then understood. While on the whole we didn't have the best rapport with the girls, all of us got along with some better than others. Their chosen speaker hadn't been picked because she was the oldest, but rather because she got along best with Ninden. They didn't think we'd be as harsh with them that way. It was also why they'd picked Isha to counter me, as between our groups, they knew she and I got along best. It wouldn't work, and might backfire, but I could appreciate the effort.

Ninden and the others looked at me. We didn't have a ready answer for that one. After a few moments, I looked at Elaya.

"We need to talk about this," I said.

The elder seemed to get a kick out of that and smiled. While she'd arbitrate, I got the feeling that she liked it better when we sorted our own problems out. It made sense. If we lived for centuries, there was a good reason to avoid fights. Who knew when someone would be important later on. If we came up with our own solution without being dictated to, there shouldn't be any hard feelings, toward her at least.

"Thoughts?" Ulun asked, looking at all of us. "We need something or they're going to make us build them a hut too."

"We could do it," I said.

"Pfft, for you that might be easy," Rindal said angrily, "but for the rest of us it'll be hard work. We're doing a lot of extra work because of your ideas." Every time the subject of using magic came up, he became bitter.

"Not for free," I said, ignoring him. "If they want one, we make them give us something in return."

"What do we want?" asked Ninden.

There were a few blank looks, and I just shrugged. There wasn't anything they had that I really wanted, but I did want to stop being nagged.

We broke our huddle, and Ninden looked at the girls. "We're considering; do you have anything you'd trade us to build you one?"

Now it was the girls' turn to huddle up. The women of our village did a lot more trading than the men. These girls were knowledgeable of what they had and what they could get, and what they might trade for it. While the men spent most of their time out hunting or making tools, it was often the women who handled the households and carried most of the beads—money. The results of the hunts were shared between all participants, with only those who did a very good job getting extra, and even then, sometimes they would only take their normal share.

Negotiations went back and forth for a while. They didn't have anything we really needed but agreed to make various amenities for our clubhouse—baskets and some woven mats and the like. At the end, I realized we were kind of being screwed over on the deal, but at the same time, we were buying peace, and peace was pretty expensive.

"Why does it feel like we always end up with more to do when you start speaking?" Rindal asked.

"Oh Rindal, it's not because I'm speaking, but because we're doing a good job at stuff."

"That makes no sense," he complained.

"The reward for good work is more work," I answered. Elaya was close enough to hear and nearly fell over laughing. The rest of the kids didn't seem to understand, but at some point they would.

CHAPTER 22

WINTER ONCOMING

The next few years were much of the same. I slowly tried to figure out what to add to our tribe, while also trying not to draw too much attention to myself. Magic slowly but surely grew in skill and strength as well, but the best thing for that seemed to just be using it.

And before I knew it, I was eight. I was perhaps a bit smaller than I'd have thought I should be, but between my diet and being an elf, I assumed that was probably normal. My friends looked almost the same as they had the past few years, all seemingly lacking as I caught up. This was normal, it seemed, with our aging slowing significantly right as we neared puberty.

Today when I'd awoken it was unseasonably cool outside. I frowned as I looked up at the sky, which had turned slightly grey. Rain in and of itself wasn't terribly uncommon, but those clouds normally came in rolling storms, not like this. I frowned, as this was something we'd been waiting on for quite some time.

"Yes, it is here," Elaya said as she came over to where I was.

"Took longer than I thought it would," I said.

"Don't hurry it along boy; it's going to be brutal."

"It will, but can we be any more prepared?" I asked.

"Not by much. Come then, I need to make the announcement."

I stood by my parents as everyone was gathered. It wasn't like anyone could change the weather. At least I didn't think any of us could, but it might be something to explore later. Mother looked grim, as did most of the village; all thoughts and worries written clearly on their faces. The children, even us, who hadn't seen such an event before, mirrored our parents.

"As we all know, the beasts of the woods will shortly be in a frenzy for the last of the food, and that is why we need the hunters to keep near the gathering party and aid where they can. Meat will still be available for a while yet, but once this growth of nuts and berries is gone, we will likely get few more until the season is done," Elaya said, finally ending her speech.

It was odd for the men to spend too much time with the gathering parties. Normally some were nearby, and our territory wasn't that big, so they could always come running. Now we'd have them on hand more. The idea of losing out on some meat wasn't too big a deal for the moment. Our little icehouse had as much dried and frozen meat as Elaya and I could manage to store, so it wasn't like we'd have none, but we'd certainly have less than we were used to.

We boys made our way to the local stream. If nothing else we could get fish aplenty there. We settled in, and I used my magic to help us all along sometimes. I could see the others doing similar things. Ninden in particular had been practicing his throwing trick quite a lot and could now do it several times before he failed.

"You've gotten stronger," I commented as I watched him once more.

"You're one to talk, Elian," he returned with a smile.

It was true. Over the years I'd gotten quite decent at magic. I'd focused mostly on pure force, since it was the easiest to work around others without causing undue concern. Ice was coming along well too. If nothing else, I was filling up the icehouse periodically. Fire was still frowned on by all though; and while the restrictions on some of my abilities had loosened considerably, if I were seen tossing out fire someone would quickly drag me off by the ear, generally my aunt.

"So, you going to join the hunters soon?" I asked my friend.

"Hmm, after the cold season; at least that's what Father said. I am old enough now, but it seems they want me to hold off until that's over. Not like you boys need anyone to look out for you all." He gave us all a proud smile. We were all his friends, and he'd taught us well.

"Guess I'll be oldest after that," Rindal commented. He was indeed a couple of years younger than our leader.

I didn't comment. Rindal's general irritation at me and my magic had evolved into a full-blown issue. He didn't like me, and at this point, the feeling was quite mutual. I'd have been happy to let it drop, but he was just too jealous of magic, and of the fact that I was given a lot more leeway because of it. He wasn't wrong though. The adults of the village did generally listen to me a lot more than they did the other children.

Not that there were many of us. In the time I'd been with the boys, not a single male child had joined our little tribe. Two girls had been born, but no boys. Elven birth rates were truly dismal though. With how long we lived, that might be a good thing. A species that were biologically immortal could easily overrun their lands if they also reproduced quickly.

"Anything going on?" one of the other boys asked.

I popped my head up to look at the adults. A few of the men were climbing trees to get down some fruits, and also getting a good look around. My own father was sitting near our creek knapping flint. There were also some scouts coming in and out of the field.

"No, not as such," I responded. "Though it looks like Auntie is getting yelled at again for making too many pots." There was a round of laughter at that.

"Yeah, she likes those, huh?" Alun commented.

We kept up with our fishing and trapping and all the like for the next several days. Though eventually we did end up in a clearing where there wasn't enough water for the former, and we had more than enough of the latter going on. I decided to try my hand at pottery, and see if I couldn't add to Auntie's own efforts.

I'd been thinking about things for a long time, particularly tools and the like that were achievable in our current state. Honestly, there was still a lot that I couldn't do right now, if only because it would require space I didn't have or explanations I couldn't give. I'd put most of that on the docket for later, but there were some options, even with things like pottery.

Two of the easiest were a basic magic-powered pottery wheel; that would enable me to make some really nice little cups and stuff. The other was glaze. We weren't using any glazes at this point. Now, I wasn't a potter of any renown in my old world, but I had taken an art class in middle school, and with my new memory, I could remember it almost verbatim. One of the things I remembered was an offhand comment from the teacher about how some glazes had been made with nothing more than slip—watered down clay—and ashes. Both of those things were easily available to me, so I decided to give it a go.

I wasn't glazing my little cups, of course. That would be impossible to hide from anyone. A few tiny beads in the shape of decorative animal heads I'd made and fired at home though? No problem getting those in and out at all. So I sat around watching the little pit my aunt and I were using today while she was gathering. The most interesting thing happened. Of course, the fire was hot and required almost no wood at all . . . I got looks but admitted to nothing.

At the end of my day spent doing, well honestly, very little, I broke open the makeshift kiln. Several pieces had broken; though, that was expected. Bits of pottery were always breaking, so no problem there, and I'd be introducing the idea of using them in new pots eventually. Some of my little cups had come out well, so that was good. In the very bottom, though, was something that alarmed me.

My little trials had almost all succeeded, and something about the mixture of the slip and whatever was in the ashes had made rather unexpected results. They were all brilliant shades of violet, bright, very visible violet. I knew nobody had anything violet in the whole village, save for a few flowers every now and then. As soon as I knew they were cool enough for me to grab them up, I did, looking for a place to dispose of these before anyone else saw.

"Oh they're done, how did things . . ." Auntie Atie was walking over, but stopped, narrowing her eyes. "What did you do, Elian?"

"What . . . nothing," I attempted, looking for an escape.

"Your face says otherwise. You always have the guiltiest face, boy." She was already advancing, and we were attracting too much attention.

"Lies and slander! I've done nothing wrong!" I said backing away.

I had no choice; I had to run for it. Without any further worries, I turned and bolted, aiming for an area away from some of the others. My auntie had far longer legs than me, but I had something she didn't, magic. I used force judiciously to push myself along faster, aiming to escape.

That came to an end quickly as Mother saw me. With a wave of her hand, a massive section of the ground sprouted into a soft blockade of grass. I landed in it like a pillow, stopped dead in my tracks. I heard Dad off to the side laughing as the stern disciplinarian of our family descended upon my location, looking unamused, her plants wrapping around me to keep me from flight.

"Elian, what in the world has got you so worried that you feel you need to use your light to run from Atie?" How could her voice be so sweet and so angry all at once?

"Nothing, she's accusing me of doing something wrong!" I said, pushing my hand and its contents into the grass, hoping that dropping them there would work.

"He had something; that's for sure," my aunt said as she joined us.

Mother went for my ears, why was it always the ears? All the while, my aunt looked at the ground, eventually finding what I'd dropped, at least some of them. I knew I'd failed when she breathed in loudly and her eyes widened. She at least had the good sense not to show off her prize as she drew in close, nose almost against mine.

"Elian, where did you get these?" she asked.

I was trying to come up with a lie, but something interrupted us. A loud series of booms and a light filtered over our field. It was the signal to gather—not extreme emergency, but immediately.

Elaya stood near the center of the gathering area, the rest of our people filtering in quickly in small groups. Her face was hard and set.

"Check for everyone in your hut. We need a head count right now," she said. "One of our scouting parties has gone missing."

CHAPTER 23

BEASTS OF DARKNESS

Distracted Mother may have been by the crisis, but forgotten I was not. While her sister, the traitor, quickly wrapped my creations in a small leather pouch, I was led back to the group.

Elaya was counting. Each and every group was also making sure that all of their members were there. During the counting, she sent up several of her little light and sound shows, trying to attract the attention of whoever had gone missing. After the main gathering, though, nobody joined us.

"One of our scouting groups didn't come back. We know their path, and several of the hunters will need to go and check. Larus has agreed to lead that group while the rest of us stay here," she said.

The leader of the hunters did not look pleased as he picked out several of the men to join him, Father included. I now knew almost everyone in the village, and his choices were clear. He was taking all the strongest fighters. I didn't know what he was expecting, but it seemed it may end in a fight.

As the group of elites disappeared into the brush, everyone else took up defensive positions. The smallest children were kept near the middle, along with those who didn't have much in the way of defensive abilities. On the outside were the remaining men, backed by Mother and Elaya, eyes scanning in every direction.

Time crawled for us in the field, unable to help our friends and family. We waited and waited for what seemed like hours, hoping for some indication, some sighting. Sentries eventually switched, and the sun soon began to fall.

Before twilight could take us, the group reappeared. They had two large skeletons with them, as well as two injured elves. One of them was Larus, head lolling side to side as he was carried from the brush. The largest man of our tribe had seemed invincible, but now he couldn't even walk. Dad was there helping haul him along, a panicked look on his face as he sang, wisps of mana flowing over his injured friend.

Mother hurried toward the injured, and Elaya just froze, looking at the bones. The men were in a panic as they put down the two large piles of bones.

"Put up lights, now!" she yelled at us.

Without hesitation, a dozen or more balls of light shot up all around. Most were dim, but mine crested high up, bathing the area in radiance. I thought the elder would move to Mother's side and haul her up from the way she looked over toward her, instead she began yelling at everyone nearby to get ready for battle.

"What's going on?" I asked loudly, slowly feeding magic to the ball above us.

"Why did you fools bring the bodies back?" she asked several of the men.

"Larus told us we needed them," one said, looking worried.

"Of course he did. Didn't think he'd get hurt, did he?" She nearly screamed.

"What's going on?" I repeated louder.

"Well, I can tell you what killed our scouts. There shouldn't be more than three, but there will be at least one, and it will be coming for us."

"What?" Mother asked, looking worried as the injured men's bodies knit themselves back together under her care.

As if to answer her question, there was a deep, pained-sounding howling. The keening noise echoed again and again, spreading throughout our little valley. It seemed to come from everywhere.

"Twilight beasts, pack hunters, and about the most dangerous animals in the region," she answered. "Get ready, everyone. They're smart, fast, strong, resistant to our light, and they know we killed two of theirs. They'll come soon, tonight if I were to guess. Everyone stay within the bright area; they're able to shrug off injuries in the darkness."

"The bodies?" someone asked.

"Have to draw them in to kill them," Larus wheezed, finally stirring from his sleep. Mother tried to push him to the ground, but he struggled his way up, her magic giving him just enough strength to sit up. "Only way is to kill some; they'll want vengeance."

"Yes you daft boy, but you brought them back *to where the children are!*" answered our elder. "How did you even manage to kill two of them?"

"They were eating, one of ours," he said. The pain in his voice was clear; everyone here was close, either by blood or friendship.

"There!" said one of the hunters.

I followed his pointed spear and saw a huge form trudge out of the darkness. It was a wolf, only it was nearly the size of a horse and seemed to flicker like a shadow in the light. The most striking feature was the eyes, filled with hatred and rage as it made its way into the clearing.

"Another!" came a call from the other side of our group. I couldn't see, but I was guessing that a second beast had appeared.

"Elian," Elaya said. "Whatever you do, keep the area bright."

I watched as the two beasts circled us. They took their time, treading carefully, looking at all the members of our group. Not once did they leave the shadowed edge of the forest; not once did they charge and try to rip us apart.

We waited, and eventually they fled back into the darkness. I didn't understand it. If what Elaya had told us was true, they should be coming, and quickly, but they didn't. They didn't attack, and I got the sense that they wouldn't just . . . leave, not like that. I wasn't sure why, or what was going on, but there was nothing else, no scratching, nor another howl, just . . . nothing.

"Did they leave?" someone asked.

"How smart are they?" I said.

"Smart," Larus and Elaya both answered. He was still in and out but tried to speak. "I don't know why . . . normally they just come in and attack . . ."

"There's a lot of us, and only two of them. They know the light is bad, and we can't flee right now." I surmised. "Do we have anything else that can hurt them?"

"In the light everything hurts them," she answered, still looking around.

Night deepened, and they didn't come. The moon and stars rose, and they didn't come. We stood there, stuck in the circle for hours, and they still didn't come.

As the stars and moon made their trek across the sky, I felt myself begin to weaken. Keeping the light above us wasn't too hard, but it was effort, and physically I was still a child. My eyes began to droop, and two or three times I nearly fell asleep, only to be jolted back awake by fear.

As all things must, though, night ended. Darkness gave way to the morning light, the growing brightness in the eastern skies, until finally the sun crested the edge of the little valley and bathed us all in its golden rays. I nearly passed out, finally letting my own illumination fall after holding it in place for so long.

Slowly our group moved back to the village proper. If nothing else, we could fortify it and wait them out. With our stored food for the oncoming winter we had a couple of weeks to wait, something Elaya didn't seem to think our enemies would do.

When we all finally stumbled our way home, what we found was devastating. Huts were torn from their foundations, ripped like paper in the hands of an angry child. The few watchers who'd stayed behind yesterday littered the ground, eyes staring lifelessly into the sky. Tools and goods were strewn about, torn apart. The monsters were smart enough to track us, smart enough to know where we'd come from. Even our cold room was dug up, the meat inside now out in the morning air and attracting flies.

It was devastating. All we'd struggled to prepare for the last several years was now wrecked by a pair of vengeful monsters. I could see several people on the verge of weeping; others were just happy to still be alive.

"Where do we go?" Mother asked to no one, looking at our hut, now little more than a dying bush.

"Cave," I said tiredly.

"What?" my aunt asked.

"The cave Elaya took me to train. There's only one way in, but we'll need to move the rock at the back."

I could see the elder's eyes widen as she looked at me. "Smart boy! Everyone, grab whatever you can carry that's still good. We don't have much time; we need to go before the sun is fully overhead!"

I heard a few people start running toward their ruined homes as sleep finally overcame me and my eyes shut.

CHAPTER 24

REGROUPING

I awoke to find myself laid down on the cold stone. While it took me several moments to realize where I was after the initial shock of waking up somewhere new, my brain caught up. I'd suggested this place; there should be no surprise that I was now here.

As I rubbed the sleep from my eyes, I weakly sat up and looked around. Here and there were the people of my village, all looking exhausted and resting where they could. Their faces, those that were awake at least, were hard. Much of my own family was curled up around me in a pile, which at least was our normal way of sleeping. Those that were awake, though, looked rough.

Niyen was near the entrance of the cave, as was Larus, both keeping an eye out.

"Want help?" I asked the two hunters.

Both looked back at me with a slight smile. "Sure Elian, but keep back in case those beasts show up," Larus said. "If they do, though, use your light like you did against that bear if you can."

My father was still out cold behind us, so I took some time to sit with them, keeping about ten feet back from the opening.

"Did you two rest at all?" I asked.

"Not yet. Some of the others will wake soon, and when they do, we will. Until then, we're just keeping an eye out," Larus said.

Soon enough, others came to relieve Niyen, but Larus stayed up. They wanted at least one magic user on the door at all times. As the current guards were replaced, the others went into the giant pile of elves that was the current sleeping arrangement. This cave wasn't big. With all of our stuff and the people we had, it was packed.

Luckily the sun hadn't gone down yet, so there was still light spilling in from outside, but judging from the color that was coming in, it wouldn't last too much longer. People awoke one by one, taking up what little space they could and looking positively nervous. The fact that our elder had finally woken up and was calmly eating breakfast before addressing the village was also off-putting to some.

"Everyone not guarding the door, gather round so we can talk," she finally said.

There wasn't a whole lot of moving around, as we were basically sardines right now, but that got everyone's attention. She took a few moments to look around and meet people's eyes. Even I came a bit nearer to see what she had to say.

"Things are grim, everyone. It is sad, but the truth. Those monsters left, but went after our loved ones, and we will be paying them back for that; but for now, we need a few moments to mourn our dead." Everyone sat silent, waiting for her.

"Good. The hunters will soon venture out to kill the remaining two beasts, but they must rest and recover first, so we will be spending a few days here. Once they've finished them, we'll return to the village, and we'll repair what we can. It will be hard, particularly with the cold season on its way, but we will survive."

A few more platitudes were given before she motioned me to her side. We retreated to the very back of the cave, near the big boulder that blocked off the tunnels behind it. When I'd first come here I could easily squeeze past, but I'd grown a good bit since then, and now it might be more difficult.

"Mind helping me shrink this down, Elian? We need more room for everyone." She motioned to it and we set to work.

"Why is it here anyway?" I asked.

"Surely you can sense the power coming up from below?" she retorted.

"Yes . . . what is it?'

"I don't know."

"What do you mean you don't know? You just blocked it off for no reason?" I was flabbergasted at her response to that question, but she seemed amused by my questioning.

"I don't know because the cave is very deep, and there's never been a good reason to go all the way down. As for why it's blocked off, that's simple. The energy leaking up from whatever is down there has attracted magical beasts in the past, and I've no desire to let them get into whatever it is. Most wouldn't, but we use this cave sometimes, and I don't want to have to clean it out every time I come out here."

We cut away little bits of the blocking stone until it could be pushed farther into the cave. With a few quick motions, Elaya managed to make it roundish and just let it roll back. I watched as we went deeper, stopping before we'd gone too far.

"Should we keep going?" I asked.

"No, we'll need to use our light so that everyone can see. It is too deep and we'll have issues. We'll all just be cramped I suppose."

When we returned to the front area of the cave, we could see the sun had fully set. Mother seemed to have taken the initiative and grown what looked like a wall of thorn bushes in the entrance. It seemed nobody was going in or out for now, at the very least. She and our elder shared a look before the older woman took up a spot near the opening.

"I'll help the men on watch for a bit, if you and yours would like to take a place. It might be useful for you to settle near the back of the cave so that Elian or Eduan can keep a light on for people . . ." Elaya said.

My father, along with Mother and my aunt, appeared and led us to the back. There were a few others who shared the hut with us that moved with us, keeping close, but at a slight distance. My direct family got the spot at the very end by the boulder, and I threw up a light for everyone, as I was still very fresh and that particular spell was quite easy.

"Let's talk, privately," Mother said pointedly.

Father hummed a few lines of a song, and the low mumbling of our neighbors fell to a barely audible buzz. Mother looked at us all.

"Can the hunters take those monsters?" she asked Father, not holding back.

"Yes, but it will be a hard fight, and I'll have to go with them." His answer didn't seem to please her at all. "We also need to worry about them coming after the people who stay behind. You saw what they did to the village."

I cringed. We'd lost people, nobody close to me personally, but those were the first deaths our village had seen that I'd witnessed. Elves were ageless, and with healers like Mom around, most things could be stopped from killing us, so long as we caught it quickly enough.

"Can I help?" I asked, and Mother gave me a hard glare.

"You'll stay here, Son, but that doesn't mean you won't. You're stronger than a lot of the village, and we'll need you to keep everyone safe while we're away. That's an important job." Father bent down to my level as he spoke, placing a hand on my shoulder and smiling.

"The monsters though . . ."

"They won't go far. Remember that they'll want to come for us. We killed some of theirs, and even with our village wrecked, they won't stop. So we'll fight them, and we'll win." Father sounded sure, and his eyes blazed.

"For now, dear, you rest. I'm sure Larus will want to gather the strongest of our men as soon as dawn arrives, and you already said he'll need you," Mother chided.

Dad took to checking his weapons, as well as those of the others in the cave. It seemed he wanted everything in proper shape. While he did so, the women of our little tribe tried to prepare some food, struggling due to the lack of fire. Eventually I offered to help with the food, which was more than welcome. A good meal was just the thing to raise spirits.

CHAPTER 25

VICTORY AND MOURNING

The men had left us some hours ago, heading out to try and destroy the last of the monsters hunting our tribe. I stood near the back of the cave, watching, keeping an eye on everyone. Ninden was watching us boys, but the girls were nearby, too, and I was doing what I could to keep an eye on them as well. There shouldn't be any danger, but if something did happen, it was likely I would be the last line of defense.

There was something throwing me off, though, and it was Isha. Even though we were in the same age group, we hardly interacted, so I'd never noticed it before, but there were little bursts of magic around her. Nothing like Mother, Elaya, or I had, but also much stronger than that of Ninden and the other boys, or even other adults.

I could see a sort of . . . aura or something, some indication of magic. In those of us who were really capable, it was a near constant flow, but in everyone else, it was just the briefest little puff every now and then. Almost everyone had this going on continually, and a few questions I'd asked had indicated that most people who couldn't use magic couldn't actually see them at all.

For example, the other boys had no answers when I asked them about it. As far as magic went, they were basically blind to it. My auntie had come through, though, and explained that while she couldn't see it like I could, it was common for people like me to be able to. Those whose magic left them and went out into the world gained the ability, while those whose magic remained bound to their own bodies oddly lacked it. My working guess was that it was somehow relevant to the casting of magic, but that was only a guess.

"You've noticed, huh?" Mother said as she came to settle near me.

"What is it?" I asked, continuing to look at Isha.

"She's going to be like us, able to use her light soon. Well, maybe soon, maybe a long time. It's wonderful news for her, though perhaps at a bad time."

"But why? Why is it like that?" I asked.

"Nobody really understands it, Elian. Even the oldest of us are sometimes surprised."

"Very well. What kind of power will she gain then? Like me, or you, or Dad?" I asked.

"That is sometimes easier to tell. For those like her, they tend to gain more of whatever they had before. Your friend Ninden, for example; if he were to change the same way, he'd likely become like Larus. I don't know what ability she has, or if she's manifested it yet, but if you did, you might be able to know."

Mother and I sat in silence for a long time after that. There wasn't a lot of room here, and I was sure that someone had overheard us, but we'd not said anything bad, or even indicated who we were talking about, so it was fine. I got the feeling Mom just wanted to be close to me while Father was out fighting, so I sat down near her.

"I'm worried about Father," I finally said.

"Your father and the rest of the hunters know what they're doing. These are bad beasts they're after, but by no means the worst, and our hunters are strong, stronger than most villages. Let us instead worry about the things we can change now."

"Like what?" I asked.

"Like the fact that the village is wrecked," Mother replied, "and we need a plan for what we'll do when we get back. We need to rebuild, and quickly before it gets too cold. We also need to think about how to fix our food issue, or we'll be in real trouble."

"I can't do much about food, but I can think of a few quick ways to build. With my light getting stronger, I think I can re-dig the cold room, but I'm not sure if that's something we should do right now or not." At her questioning look, I continued. "We don't have the meat to fill it, and with little time wasting, the effort to put more ice in it is probably a bad idea. I think new huts should go up first, and I can help with building those much faster."

A scream came from the front of the cave, and both of us leaped up in alarm. Mother tried to run ahead, and I was right on her heels, but something was odd. The scream wasn't afraid, or hurt, no . . . it was cheerful.

We charged into a blooming celebration, as the whole village began pouring out of the cave to meet the hunters. The men were roughed up, covered in cuts and bruises—one even had an arm tied in a makeshift sling—but they were all smiles. At their sides were two new skulls, large and full of teeth. They'd succeeded in killing the monsters. We were safe and could go home.

The party turned into a parade with little prompting. The hunters were quickly patched up, and the skulls of the beasts were tied to sticks. Our supplies had been gathered quickly and hardly unpacked. Since everyone wanted to get home, there was no reason to stay where we were. It was chilly, sure, but not cold enough to keep us from sleeping outside at the clearing we'd called home for generations.

Father and Larus took turns leading the group. Each wove the story of where they'd fit into the hunt, and where the others had played their part. Tracking the beasts had been long and hard, but one of the men I didn't know, a tall, chocolate-maned man, Onai, had shown skill in following their tracks, leading the group to the den. He had some form of super-smell or sight or something, not incredibly potent, but enough to give a potent edge to any decent tracker. Father had woven spells for the wind to silence their approach, the dirt to hide their smell, and at the moment of attack, the light to brighten their way. Larus, of course, had been the point of the spear, and if things were to be believed, had grabbed one of the beasts, snapping its spine with his hands.

Once the story was told, Father led several songs. The march was in no hurry, and a number of us took to dancing as we walked. I . . . tried to join in on that, but it was a skill I sorely lacked, and other than a few laughs from my friends and family, little came of it. My eyes fell to Isha as she danced, if only because of the sparks of magic she was emitting; I worried for a moment that something might happen, but it never did.

As we entered the village, the mood sobered. I'd not noticed, but all of us came together to the center of the village, where there were several small piles of dirt. It was almost silent as one person for each approached.

"What's going on?" I asked, slinking up beside my aunt, Mother nowhere to be seen.

"Oh . . . that's right, you passed out. We didn't have time to bury them properly, so Elaya just sank the bodies into the dirt. It's time for the dead to be taken care of. At least we have the bodies."

One by one, Elaya went to each of the mourners and raised their loved one from the ground.

"This was his favorite fire-making stick, would you let him burn with it?" The woman asked, laying the tool upon the dead man, his body, sadly, already in a state of decomposition.

Elaya moved forward, and with her hands, fire extended forward, consuming the body in moments, along with the tool.

The next body was requested to simply be buried deep in the earth, which she did. The third relative requested his lost love's song. Father stepped forward and sang, using some sort of magic I didn't know to break the body into something like dust. The final rite of passage was odd as well—a boy requesting his mother be turned into the tree that bore her favorite fruit. He had a piece of the fruit in his hand, and Mother took it and dropped it onto the body. Roots quickly spilled out from the point of impact to consume the corpse and left a small tree in its place.

It was an odd funeral, but very personal. There was little crying from those outside of the direct families, and even they seemed restrained. You'd think that the death of an elf would be jarring, but there was something I'd forgotten. We started to become like Elaya after only a couple of hundred years, and while biologically immortal, we were still very killable. The lives of most of us, therefore, had to be . . . cut short; violence killed my kind and little else, and there was no good chance for most of us to properly mourn.

I wanted to be sad, sure. I knew the dead only in the briefest sense, but with everyone else so reserved, it didn't seem appropriate, so I let it pass. When the ceremonies were over, we spread back out. It was evening, and things needed to be taken care of before we could rest.

By some universal decision, it was decided that the huts of those who'd gone after the monsters would be the first made. Mother was regrowing our hut, while my father helped one of the other hunters construct a shelter. Larus needed no help at all, able to fell trees and stack them with ease. Elaya had moved off to another who needed aid, which left me. I approached the tracker, Onai. His hut was located on the edge of the village.

"Want some help?" I offered.

"Of course, come. I think enough of the branches of our home survived that we can make a temporary shelter with it, but help would be nice," he said with a smile.

He was right. With what was left of his home, a temporary place should be easy enough to build. I began moving the larger bits into place and holding them tight with magic while he and others tied branches and the like together. I noticed that Isha was with us. This wasn't her home, but she lived near it, and I supposed she'd likely be staying with Onai and his group until her place was rebuilt.

"So you can track beasts, I hear?" I asked Onai conversationally as the sun finally fell below the tree line.

"Ha! Yes, it's not much, and on twilight beasts, it's hard, as they have little scent, but one breath in . . ." he said as he sucked in air through his nose, and I saw a little spark of magic. I expected him to say something funny, but instead he froze like a statue for the briefest second, and then his head snapped to the tree line. "Light!" he yelled.

I didn't hesitate, tossing up a bright ball of illumination just in time to see it. They'd missed one, and the horse-sized wolf now tore out of the field, using the setting sun and long shadows to hide its approach until I disturbed it. The creature charged, and before I could cast another spell, was leaping in the air, mouth open and teeth shining as drool dripped from them.

CHAPTER 26

BURN

The rest of the village was still moments away as the monster slammed its jaws down on the hunter. If it was smart, it might have well understood the danger this man posed to it. He definitely appeared more dangerous than the rest of us.

Most animals would only hunt for food, but as Onai's corpse was abandoned, it was clear that wasn't the case here. The twilight beast looked up from his kill for its next target. The rest of the village's strongest people were moments away, moments we didn't have. This beast seemed determined to cause as much damage as it could.

Before it could charge at us, I blasted out with force, trying to push the creature away. At first my spell seemed to work, the form coming together well. The monster had some resistance, though, some power to fight against my magic. Moving it was like trying to keep hold of water, constantly shifting around the spell to escape. In the end, the creature flew back thirty or so feet but landed upright and turned toward me.

I wasn't alone, though, and as the lupine tried to leap, another joined us. Isha screamed, and my ears exploded in pain. She wasn't even facing me; rather looking at the monster with small fists clenched at her sides. Pushing back the pain, I managed to get a look at her, seeing that the monster had fallen, yelping from the pain of the girl's voice. Her aura, which before had been pushing out small explosions of power, was now rippling and golden like the surface of the sun with arcs escaping it.

While she kept it distracted, I rose. We'd had enough; we'd lost enough—our homes, our tribe mates, friends, and family. I was done, and while most of our members had spent the day on lookout or casting magic, I'd come into this fight fresh. It was time to see just how far I'd come in the last few years.

"Burn," I commanded, thrusting my hands out.

Fire magic was frowned upon by my tribe. We lived in a jungle, and in a jungle fire was a terrible danger. That said, I'd managed to push through some training in the fires that we kept, feeding them with magic. I'd even practiced when firing pots with my auntie, insulating and strengthening the flames slightly so that I wouldn't need to get more wood.

A virtual bonfire appeared atop my enemy, sending out a wave of warmth. It was enough to even spook Isha out of her screaming, a less than ideal situation. There was no time for that though. The beast needed to die, to be done.

Even as I saw the hairs on the wolf's fur start to burn and drift away, it tried to rise, tried to get out of my spell; I was having none of that.

"Hotter," I said under my breath, pouring more mana into the flames until they grew in both size and strength.

"Hotter," I repeated, pushing, using walls of force and wind to feed the conflagration. It seemed to be growing blue as its temperature skyrocketed. Now my foe screamed, struggling as bits of its flesh melted.

"Enough, enough, just burn!" I screamed, pouring everything I had into my magic. Ideas of how oxidation worked flowed through my mind—the chemical bonds, the movement of electrons that let loose the heat, and I fed them into the spell.

It hurt my eyes to look forward at the end of the creature as the heat grew from uncomfortable to something akin to a furnace. The ground seemed to melt under the onslaught, shining like liquid glass. I could smell the slight singeing of my own hairs as I finally ran out of juice. As for the beast that had menaced us, there was nothing before me now but a molten circle, angry and red in the twilight.

I fell to my knees, spent, and began to look around for my friend. Isha's eyes met mine moments later as I found her, from where she'd fallen back in the grass. They were dinner plates, huge and afraid.

"You okay?" I wheezed out, snapping her back to reality.

"Yes, I've . . . never seen anyone use their light like that before," she said with stumbling words.

"Fire is dangerous, don't you know?" I laughed as I began to fall to the dirt, all the strength leaving my body as my mana was fully spent.

Isha let out a slight giggle in response, which helped my mood a bit. I liked Isha; well, as much as I liked anyone, and it would be a real shame for her to be scared of me now. Personally, I'd rather be the one to protect and nurture this tribe into the modern era rather than some destructive maniac. As I'd thought about it, that was a viable option too. Provided I could live long enough, I could absolutely pull people forward in technology, and magic could fill some of the gaps that my knowledge couldn't.

Before we could say much else, the adults were upon us. Between our yells, the ball of light I'd sent up, and the blazing ball of fire, we'd attracted quite a lot of attention. Larus, of course, was the first, skidding to a halt near us, but followed quickly by several of the others.

"What happened?" the hunter said, looking down at the body of his fallen comrade.

"There was another one. Elian . . ." Isha began, looking nervous.

"Where is it?" he asked, still looking between us and the circle of dirt that was slowly losing its glow.

"I got it," I replied, trying to motion to where the beast once stood, but finding my hand mostly lolled in the general direction.

" . . . good, good job."

Elaya and my parents arrived in short order. The former's eyes bulged as she recognized just how hot that fire had burned, while the latter ran to me in a panic. The elder let her gaze roam over us before it settled on Isha with a mixture of sadness and happiness.

"Elian!" Father yelled in a voice that pained me, clearly thinking I was hurt or dead.

"I'm okay," I replied as he scooped me up, still feeling as if my muscles had been replaced with balls of yarn. "Just very, very tired."

It occurred to me that it was probably very bad to be passing out as much as I had been recently, as the darkness finally overtook me.

When I woke up I received several things. The first was a rather irritated elder berating me on the danger of fire magic. I tried to look repentant, even if I didn't feel it, and she knew that I'd done right. The primary source of her irritation was that she had to tell me off for breaking rules in a way that probably saved lives. She seemed to want to congratulate me, but the fact that I'd stomped on the village rules prevented that from happening.

"Enough, you've made your point. Now let him rest," my father soon asserted. Normally he wasn't at all protective, but it seemed thinking I'd died had increased his instincts.

"Thanks," I said.

"Elian, it's not said around the women, but we hunters do what we must to feed and protect the village. This is twice you've saved others, twice that you stepped forward when needed. I assure you that all of us are proud of you, no matter what the elder says." I let out a chuckle before he continued. "That said, please try not to get into any more fights for a while."

I also discovered in short order that I hadn't managed to make glass yet. The flame I'd made had been hot, and perhaps even hot enough, but far too short for that process, and nowhere near the right material. What I'd thought was a sheet of glass had really just been an illusion from the temperature and my own eyes fooling me.

However, it had gotten hot enough to wreck that section of ground, and even make it glow slightly for a short period. Some of the shards of dirt and sand had even coalesced into small, brittle orbs. The heat was enough to vaporize the water, but not to fully change particles into something else.

When I went to look over the site, I was met by Isha.

"There's nothing left of it," she said, looking at the ground.

"The bodies mostly turn to skeletons anyway; the heat just destroyed the bones," I said.

"Maybe, but that was pretty cool. Think I'll be able to do that?" she asked.

"Depends on what your light manifests like. I'm still learning myself."

"It's odd, seeing the light around me and others, but pretty," I said, laughing as my friend held up her hand, waving it to look at how her own power moved.

"You'll learn to ignore it. At least Elaya hasn't dragged you off for training yet," I said.

"Eh, she's busy. Who knows, maybe she'll forget."

Fat chance of that Isha. Fat chance.

CHAPTER 27

A PLAN

I had dreams of shining cities of steel and glass, beautiful in form and in function. Sadly, I was very limited by the materials available to me. Currently, I was looking at a mostly destroyed village barely into the stone age, and trying to think about what kinds of improvements we might make. For now was the time for progress. It was sad, the people we'd lost, and the houses; and with winter approaching, too much work would be bad, but if we were going to make something better, it should be now.

"You're up to something again," Auntie Atie said, frowning. "I can see it in your eyes."

"I am, but I need help," I replied.

"Oh? Well, you know your mother and I have something we want from you. Perhaps if you were to share your secrets, we'd be willing to help out," she said.

We spoke as we worked on our newly regrown hut. Mother had whipped it together in an afternoon and was currently working on others. Normally, people would have to pay for their new huts, but being an emergency and all, she was willing to replace those lost, albeit with slightly lesser versions.

"We need a wall," I finally said.

My aunt looked at me blankly for a few moments before she began to laugh.

"We don't have anywhere near enough people for us to get a wall, and where would we get the stone anyway? It would be nice, sure, but walls are hard to make, and we don't have the people."

"Do you know much about them?" I asked.

"Only from the stories of travelers. They say Atal has walls like cliffs, sheer stone all around the whole place. Then again, it might not be a good idea to make one, since I also hear that all places with walls tend to stink."

That told me two things that I needed to get around. One, everyone pictured walls as stone, or something similar; while I wanted wood, it might be a bad idea for some reason. Two, sanitation was something that would need to be sorted out before building; though, on that front I had some more ideas as well.

"We don't need stone; wood will do just fine," I said.

"It will rot," my aunt argued.

"Eventually, but it will give us safety and time while it does."

"I don't think most people would like the village to stink either," she countered.

"That can be fixed I'm sure. We just need to make it so the things that stink can wash away."

"You're not giving up on this are you?" Auntie Atie asked.

"No, no I'm not," I replied.

Mother and my aunt had not forgotten that I knew how to make shiny purple beads. It was currently a sticking point between us; but after a rather heated, if private, argument, they'd stepped back for the moment. My suspicion was that they'd find something I wanted to trade for the knowledge.

Father had eventually heard and stepped in to stop them from trying to force my secrets out of me. I'd never seen him angry before, but he'd made it very clear that if I didn't want to tell them, and refused to give it to them in trade, that was tough. Even my mom had been stymied by how hard he'd put his foot down, something he almost never did.

I'd never paid too much attention to Dad, but now I started to look more. He didn't get loud often, didn't take sides in much. Larus led the hunters, often declaring when and where things would happen, but he also listened when my father spoke; everyone did. The thing was, Dad may not have been as front and center as Mom or Larus, or anyone else, but that didn't mean he didn't do things. He was always there, putting forth a gentle influence and making connections.

People came to Dad with their problems, and with things only he could provide. Oftentimes, he helped them, at least with advice on how to get what they wanted. Those he turned away were told why, and generally it was because what they wanted was dumb or too much of a pain, but sometimes because they just irritated him. He seldom chose to use the soft power he had, but that didn't mean never.

Reflecting on this, as soon as I finished my work for the afternoon, I went to see him. He was currently near the center of the village, repairing some of our many lost tools and helping Isha figure out the very basics of her casting. She was like him, someone who needed to perform in order to do magic, and frankly, their magic was a bit weird to me. They could both make things from nothing, with some restrictions, and mold things in ways that I just couldn't and without a lot of effort. It also seemed more feeling based than knowledge based.

"Hi, Dad," I said as I approached his little knapping area.

"Elian, care to help? I need some more handles," he replied pointing to a pile. Each was sized and laid out near what he would be attaching to it.

"Sure, but I've got something I want to do, or something I think we should do, maybe? Kind of like the cold room," I said, sitting down.

Many people would think that a good handle would be circular, or close to it. Those people needed to spend more time around hammers. A good handle was a rounded rectangle, with a slight bulge for the center of the hand. There was an art to it, one I was only passably good at. That said, magic at least made me fast. I could carve the general shape with planes of force in seconds, and then get down to much more delicate work.

"What's that?" he asked.

"I think we should build a wall."

"Not thinking small are you, Son? I don't think that's possible right now." His reply was instant.

"I know stone is too hard to acquire, but what about wood? Even if it doesn't last forever, it should help, and I don't want more monsters wandering into the village," I insisted.

"A good thing to want, but where would you get the wood? Too much to take out of the forest without almost everyone involved, and your mother can't grow that much at once; it would destroy the ground. She won't do that, and the trees would die before making it to full size. Even the huts we use are pushing what's possible."

We bounced ideas back and forth for a while as I used reeds to sand my work into the exact shape I wanted. It was meditative, and I understood why Dad didn't just use magic for all his work. It wasn't something I'd be doing full time, but something I could do for the moment. It allowed me to go back through my memories for something, anything.

I remembered an old TV show, in which a group had spent time in Africa. They'd stayed in a place surrounded by thorns to sleep, though the exact construction had been a bit unclear. There were a few thorned plants around here, some nastier than others, and one that nearly reminded me of the brambles that were a constant hazard in the childhood of my first life, minus the berries.

"What about a net of spiky bushes around the village, enough to keep larger animals out? Is that possible?" I asked.

"Hmm, maybe. It won't keep anything really big or really determined away, but it should at least slow them down. You know what your mother will want in exchange for helping with this though?"

"Let's find out if it's possible first, and then see what others think. If all that goes well, Auntie is the one working with clay anyway. I don't really care that much beyond wanting to be left alone." That got me a chuckle.

"Good answer," he said.

CHAPTER 28

WINTER PART ONE

The day had been long and I was tired, but there were things that deserved my attention.

I stood back and watched as Mother wove the last of her magic—vines flowing and grasping as thorns sprung up along their length. The inner net was thicker, with larger spars about an inch in width. From the central bit, more sprang out here and there along their length; those were far less controlled. The whole thing was woven around a series of wooden poles in the ground. They had been sunk deep and burned on their outer layers. Eventually those would fail, but by that time the whole thing should be pretty solid anyway.

We'd gone back and forth on the price and settled on the arrangement thus. I made a full batch of the little trinkets my mother wanted—fifty in all—shaped by my aunt, since she was better at it, but didn't know how to glaze, and then finished by me. Five, I kept; five went to Elaya—as a bribe, since she helped us with getting the poles made and put in place—ten went to my auntie for making them; and Mother got the rest of them.

Mother then went on a spending spree, not because anyone had anything she wanted, but because she was smart. Hoarding that much money to herself in a village this small would only cause problems. For that reason she made sure that at least some of her currency made it to each of the huts for their leaders. Several more were spread around with those she considered friends, and were now something of a status symbol.

Mom and Auntie were very tight-lipped about where they'd come from too. People thought that I had been paid off for some special service, like an impossibly hot fire that might be needed for the process, something which I encouraged. Getting something like a proper furnace or kiln at some point would allow me to really accelerate the technology of this world without too much messing around. Someone might even figure out how to make metal without my help!

Everyone needed a mission, and mine was to bring about modernity, at least parts of it. There were some ideologies that we'd be skipping, and I would personally be stomping on as an adult if they ever popped up around me—too dangerous—but many parts of modern life could be brought to this world. Father mostly wanted us to be happy, as far as I could tell. Mother seemed to be making a run at some kind of stone-aged mercantile empire or something. Auntie Atie, on the other hand, had found a technology she liked and was now putting her all into its perfection.

Things needed to go slow for now though. It grated on me, but my first job was to make it to adulthood. That clearly would be a struggle all its own since our food stores were basically nonexistent. The only reason Mother had agreed to my project at a time like this was that she honestly didn't have anything else to do; there were no plants in season right now. The hunters were on double duty trying to get what they could, but I could tell that they were struggling with the workload.

That was where we boys came into play. We weren't hunters, and couldn't go after the kind of game they could, but we could trap all around the areas near the village and close to a few of the nearest water sources. It'd been weeks since the twilight beasts had attacked, and the woods were declared . . . not safe, but safe enough that we could go out.

Back on Earth that would have seemed like madness, but here, well, not as much. We didn't go out very far at all, and between Ninden being nearly an adult and my magic, there wasn't much in the local area that would threaten us. The hunters, of course, were always out and about in groups and had thoroughly scoured the area near the village at this point. I was also pretty sure that one was always assigned near the area we were in, too, just in case. Even if they didn't bring back much in the way of meat, letting us experience things on our own was important.

As our group walked up to the central fire pit, I blew a stray hair from my face. It was pretty long now, and I often missed a few strands when tying it back. We'd refined our clothing from the nearly nonexistent leather loincloths to something slightly more modest—tying sewn-together pelts on ourselves. It was still pretty cold, though, no getting around that.

There were makeshift shelters all around us now—whatever improvised scraps could be put together for comfort. Elaya and I were switching out in the evenings, each tossing up a weak barrier around the area to keep the wind out and to keep us all warm as best we could. Dad could do something similar with some effort, but he didn't get involved. He reserved his magic for the hunts and for making more tools.

The women were all grouped together as they worked on dinner to decrease the size of the needed protection as much as possible. They also had the fire going to produce as much heat as possible. Shield or no shield, it was still cold.

"Got something for us, boys?" one of the women asked. I think she was one of Olond's aunts.

We just smiled and held up our hauls. In all, we'd caught only five kennits. These were a type of rodent, or something that looked like a capybara, though only about the size of a rabbit. Nobody really liked the way they tasted, but it was better than an empty belly, and their fur was warm enough that they were still around.

"See you lot found something too," I said.

They were all busy preparing tubers. They were mashed into a paste and then cooked on rocks. These were not particularly flavorful; more like a potato pancake without butter or enough salt. Again, though, it was better than being hungry, and on a lucky day, someone might find a few berries that would sweeten them well; either that or a bit of honey.

I settled down after we passed our haul of meat over near the fire to warm up. While it was possible for me to warm my body with magic, it took a lot of concentration to not overheat. Most of the time it was just easier to be a little cold.

"Want one?" Isha said from the side. She was cooking several of the little cakes, looking sour.

"Sure," I replied, taking the offered food. "Bad day?"

"I just feel useless. I get my own light, and it's not good for anything. Nobody really needs healing, and I can't keep us all warm for more than a few moments yet, and I'm bad at shaping stone like your dad. There's nothing for me to do," she vented.

"Do you want me to listen, or to propose solutions?" I asked.

"You're not like me. How would you even know what to do?" she asked with more than a little heat in her voice.

"I don't, not really, but I also don't really know what you can do. Just offering to look from a different perspective." I held my ground, looking at her calmly.

"Sorry, it's just irritating," she said.

"Be angry all you like. I did offer to just listen, didn't I?"

That got me a laugh, a small one. "Well, your dad doesn't know how to do much other than heal and mold stone. Some little tricks like making water, light, heat, or that sticky sap he uses for holding things together, so I don't really know either. He said those like us are weird, because we can supposedly do a lot of things, just not well. If I could grow plants like your mother that would be great, since there's lots of demand for that, but it's so slow when I try, it almost hurts. We don't need anything else either, other than food, and I can't make tubers or animals; I tried."

"What about salt? We lost most of ours, and I know I can't do it. Even a little would make the food better, and it's easier than trying to go get it right now." I'd tried, too, but salt, along with metals and anything mineral, just drained me. I could get a few grains, but no more.

"No, I thought of that one. Just trying gave me a headache. Your father said liquids and stuff are doable, but not solid stuff." She seemed dejected.

"Isn't the stuff you're making these with kind of liquid?" I asked, waving around the little cake. "For that matter, honey is too. Have you tried that? Or did you try to make living plants and animals?"

"Living ones . . . hold on." She sang a few bars of one of the songs Dad hummed while he worked, and a little dollop of paste appeared in her hand, which she quickly deposited on the hot rock. "It worked . . . maybe."

While it was cooking she tried honey, which did work, if the way she froze and let her eyes widen were any indication. She didn't say anything, but the look told me that she'd found something sweet.

"You okay?" I asked.

"Shh, don't tell anyone," she said. Greedily hoarding valuable secrets was a running pastime with this crowd.

"You should be the one to do it. We really could use the extra food. How about the cake?"

She flipped it, letting it cook until golden before splitting the little thing in half and making us more honey to go over the top. We bit down at the same time, and I couldn't suppress my smile. It was a bit off flavor-wise, but still pretty good, and very sweet; something I seldom got nowadays. At that point, our winter, which had pretty much sucked up until now, got significantly better.

CHAPTER 29

CONTRACT

Isha had pulled me to the side; we had a rare moment of privacy so we could talk.

"I kept practicing last night," she said, bouncing on the balls of her feet.

"Cool, what did you learn?" I asked.

"I can make them already cooked, which is good. I think they taste better like that, too, but I was hoping for your opinion." She held out one of the little faux tuber cakes for me, and without hesitation I bit down on it. She was right; it was better.

"So, you tell anyone else?" I asked.

She frowned, looking divided on how to proceed. "No, did you tell anyone?"

"It is your power, for you to use and share as you like. If people were starving, I might have felt divided, but they're not. It's your secret to share when you want to. Though I do think you should," I explained.

"Not sure if that's what I want. Mom and Dad will be happy, and our hut will do better, but they might push me for more and more. People are like that. Look at some of the things they ask you to do."

She wasn't wrong. My parents would step in if people got pushy, asking me for things, but it didn't mean that I didn't get requests all the time. Lots of it was stuff they could do with a little effort, or stuff I didn't know how to do. Mostly it was my wood lathe trick that people wanted. Elaya couldn't get the visualization on it quite right, and there were plenty of things that could be made easily with one, but some things just weren't possible for me. I was still keeping the idea of quick and easy wooden cups and bowls for later, people might have known carving them was possible, but they'd not made the connection yet.

"Maybe talk to my dad? If he could learn the same thing, it would make even more food for everyone, and having someone teach him would help. He might even make an agreement to pay you for making food to help the village. If someone strong made a deal with you that restricted what you could do, that would be that."

There were agreements, not contracts as such, but close enough. Quick things where people traded might be worked out alone, but for larger things, the terms would be presented to the influential people of our village publicly, so that everyone knew.

"What about you? You already know, so if we can't figure it out, at least nobody else would." She gave me a questioning look.

"I'm still a kid," I said.

"Yeah, but a scary one. Your mom and dad would take your side if someone tried to push things, too, and if we had an agreement, I could hide behind that." That was fair enough. After killing a full-sized monster with a massive blaze of heat, I was pretty well respected by most of the men in the village.

"All right, how many of those little cakes are you willing to make for everyone?" I asked.

There was a sort of noblesse oblige, or since it was based on magic, magus oblige. Something like that. The more you had, particularly power-wise, the more you were expected to make available to help others. It wasn't everything, of course, but something. Mother and Father both worked for pay most of the time, but if there was a need, they quickly stepped up to fill it. Again, this also helped keep the peace with our neighbors. I hadn't been pushed too much into this yet because of my age, but I could do something for others here, particularly my friend.

We went back and forth for a good while. Eventually, we decided that our contract would last through the winter. It would be long enough for her power to grow, and for others to acclimate to her abilities. I managed to push through two major points. The first was that she would teach my father her magic, if he agreed to learn. The second was that she had to provide a set amount of her little cakes to the village. There was a third point, and it was from Isha. She wouldn't be allowed to work for any-one else for the duration of the winter and was expected to push excess amounts of her light—I hated that term—into making me honey. I didn't expect her to make much, but I did want some of the stuff, and it would be a perfect excuse. There were some exceptions. She could do things for herself and her family, but there was a minimum amount of honey I'd be getting every ten days regardless.

From me she'd be getting two of my purple beads; I didn't care about them and could make more if I really needed to. The first bead was for the teaching, the second for her work for an unspecified amount of time. I also had to pay her a pittance in either small woodworking projects, like tool handles or equally agreed upon items every ten days. Things that I could do in minutes, but something to show that our agreement was ongoing. It was important to have something that could be easily pointed at, and my little payments to her would be it.

Once everything was hashed out, we went back to our tasks until dinner. That would be when we told everyone and when she got her first payment. Things were easier that way, as everyone was together to witness it.

As we prepped for the evening meal—getting things together and finishing up the last of our tasks for the day—my aunt stared at me. Auntie Atie always had the most annoying ability to tell when I was up to something. I'd asked her about it a few times, and she simply told me that I had the guiltiest face ever. That said, she also knew when to step in, generally right before things went off. She and several other of the women in our hut were now loudly discussing what I was up to this time, and suspecting it had to do with Isha, since we'd been seen together.

I didn't think too much about most of the others who lived with us all that often, but they were there. There were two couples and two single women other than my parents and me, and all were closer to my parents than I was. This was a normal enough thing, as most of the huts in the village were a sort of communal affair. It mattered because of the potential futures.

Both of my parents were strong, quite strong, both magically and socially, and there was the possibility that if one or both of my parents started to gain a white lock of hair like Elaya, our village would probably split. Not immediately, but there would be a push to gain enough members, and it would occur. The reason was simple enough—an elder was too respected, and too many cooks in one kitchen would cause problems. In larger settlements, there would be a hierarchy, like Atal being ruled by Atal, but Elaya wasn't that far along yet and wouldn't be able to just force things through like she could now; this would cause strife.

I thought about this and looked at my parents and aunt as we made our way to the main fire pit. It was cold, painfully so, but my actions attracted Father's attention eventually.

"Something wrong, Son?" he asked.

"Just wondering if you have any white hairs," I responded.

"Ha! No, not yet; nor does your mother. She gets me to check her over every now and then." He gave a wry smile. They were private about their affections, but I was a direct result, so I knew what was going on. I wasn't sure where or when, though, as while people were clearly having sex, everyone seemed to hide it pretty well.

"What about Auntie? Maybe she'll beat you both to it," I teased.

"Not likely. Her light hasn't fully manifested yet. She's getting stronger, but slowly. If and when it does, it would be at least another twenty years or so before she started to become an elder. At least that's the most likely thing. Rarely do people gain white hairs without a fully manifested light, but that is very, very rare." I wanted to ask more questions on the subject, but we'd arrived to dinner, and Isha was sitting there nearly bouncing as she waited. "On another subject, why does your friend look so anxious to see you?"

"You'll see," I answered with a chuckle. I thought several of the people in our hut might object to our deal, but Dad probably wouldn't be one of them.

As soon as we arrived, Isha and I went to Elaya and sat with her social group. She raised an eyebrow in curiosity, while Mother glared at Isha. Isha's mother was also looking at me with a mix of curiosity and unhappiness. It seemed she hadn't told anyone about our deal yet either.

"We've come to an arrangement," I told the elder, who stopped what she was doing to look at us. A number of representatives from the village, as well as those who were curious, came over to listen.

As we worked our way through the arrangement, the reactions were mixed. Dad's reaction was laughter.

"This is a major thing," Elaya said. "Are you sure?"

"Isha, we should talk," her mother said. "This is months of work he's getting from you. It's a good price . . . but you still should have talked to us first." Isha's mother was clearly interested in what exactly her daughter could now do.

Mom looked less than pleased. "She's getting a lot from you, and she's using you to protect herself. You get little from this, Elian."

"I'm aware," I answered my mother. "The thing is, she's not getting anything that I care much about. However, a good source of sweet foods is something I want."

My father howled at that one, as did several of the other men of the village. None of them cared about money or trading so long as they had what they needed, and everyone liked good food. They understood my side instantly. The women of the village, on the other hand, cared about pretty things because they wanted the status. Men got theirs through their hunting skills or by making things; but for the girls, if you didn't have magic, it was much more about how much decoration you could accumulate. Social connections were important for everyone, but for them, who spent so much of their time in large groups working together, hierarchy was important.

Dad eventually stopped laughing when Mother fixed her eyes on him , so he explained, "Both of them are getting what they want, and we'll gain too. She's teaching me her trick as part of this, so don't worry so much, love."

Mom moved her eyes back to Isha; they were not kind. "I do not like my son being used."

"He's using her too," Dads said, waving it off. "Better, he's doing it to help the village, not just for selfish reasons."

Our parents could, in theory, stop us from this; they didn't though. Mother didn't like it but would admit that my things were my own, whereas Father really did approve. Isha's parents were a little trickier, as they didn't like that their daughter was making such big decisions on her own.

"If you do not allow it, I'll refuse to help anyone other than myself," she said finally in a threatening tone. "My power is mine to use how I want, and I won't let you tell me I can't. Perhaps I'll just make a deal with Elian's mother or Elaya to let me get my own hut too. I'm pretty sure I could manage it if I wanted."

Those were some real threats, and while I thought she'd get an earful later, it was enough to quiet them for now. It also quieted everyone else, because a magic user putting their foot down so harshly often did. There were only a few in the village who could oppose her on this, and they either didn't care too much, or thought our deal was a good idea.

After a few more objections, Elaya read our terms to us once again, putting it a bit more formally, but keeping everything the same. "These are the terms you accept?" she asked when she'd finished.

"Yes," I said.

"Yes," Isha answered as well.

"Your initial payments?" she said, motioning to us.

I produced the beads Isha wanted, while she began summoning the food as required, looking winded by the end of it. When it was all done, the elder nodded. All of us had basically perfect recall, so there wasn't really a need to write these things down. Most of the village had been present for the verbal contract, and everyone that had witnessed it could recite it verbatim if asked to.

CHAPTER 30

WINTER PART TWO: THE HUNT

Ninden and I stood over our empty trap. There were enough in the area that we were splitting into smaller groups. Everyone was nearby, but for the moment, we were alone.

Winter was in full swing, and I was frankly thrilled that it only came to call once every several decades if this was what we were getting. There'd been colder winters in the north back on Earth, but this was supposed to be a tropical jungle, not a temperate forest. The normally green trees were now replaced by dead-looking spires. The world was grey and brown, with a bright white covering the ground where snow had fallen over the past few days.

"Another empty," my friend declared, shaking his head. "Not even getting the small game now. If we're lucky, maybe we'll have enough for a sliver of meat each."

I shook my head. There was really nothing to do about it. The game was in hiding or dead; none were out and about right now. Even the birds, normally so vibrant, had disappeared. I suspected they were all in some torpor somewhere very hidden, probably high up or buried, but we had no confirmation of that.

"Well, at least we won't starve," I pointed out. It had been a real worry that not everyone would make it after our village had been wrecked.

"Fair, but I'd still like some different foods," the older boy responded.

All day, we'd only caught two of the little rodents known as kennits. They were small, thick furred, and the taste was not great at the best of times. We were all quite ready for something slightly better. Our group met up as we began moving to the next site, slowly working our way through the brush.

"Anything from you guys?" I asked, only to be met with shaking heads. "Dang."

As we rounded a bend, which overlooked one of the little creeks that crisscrossed our lands, we saw it, down by the stream.

There was a small waterfall-like area, the water forming a pond above on a few large rocks before spilling over and continuing its journey. At the bottom was a small pool formed by the erosion of ages, and one of the few places liquid water was still widely available. Most of the creeks and rivers had at least partially frozen, but this one was just deep enough that the water continued to flow beneath the ice, leading to a small cascade.

At the pool was one of the small deer that were endemic to the region. Its coat had taken on a flecked white and brown coloration, making it hard to see in the new conditions. The animal's head was down, drinking deeply of the water, the same water source in which we probably would have stopped to refill our own water-skins.

All of us froze and slowly hunkered down. We'd gotten lucky, approaching from downwind, our sound masked by the noise of the water on the rocks. It hadn't seen us or noticed a thing, at least not yet. Though it was still a good hundred or so yards from where we'd fallen back.

"Far shot, not sure I could hit it," Ninden whispered to me. "Can you?" His personal ability was a boost to his muscles that allowed him to toss a spear like a missile.

"Mmm, not sure," I responded. It was indeed a far shot, further than I'd tried using my magic yet.

"Okay, plan," he said, and we all grouped up.

Olond was still, by far, the sneakiest among us. I suspected that there was some form of magic going on there. Whatever his ability was, for the life of me, I couldn't pin down exactly what he was doing. There was definitely some sound muffling going on, as when he began to move around, keeping downwind, I couldn't hear him. He probably had some sort of reactive camouflage illusion, too, but I lost track of him before I could get a good look.

The general plan was for him to get around to the other side of the deer and spook it toward us. If we could get close enough, either Ninden or I would make the shot to take it, but there was a good chance we'd miss, so we were going to be extra careful. The other boys, Alun, Ulun, and Rindal, joined us, trying to form as tight a net as possible.

We had plenty of time to get into position before a small spear flew forth from the vegetation on the far side of the river, followed by our scout. I don't think he believed he could actually hit it, but he'd come pretty close. The flint point had struck the air over the deer, only inches from the animal's spine.

Without hesitation, it turned and ran, right toward me. I was silent as I popped my hand forward, unleashing a small bolt of force. This was my fastest spell, invisible and easy to aim. The animal's leaping and bounding threw me off just enough for the bolt to go wide. Rindal was near me, his shot going wide too.

It turned and headed downstream, down toward Ninden and the others. Ninden threw first, scoring a grazing hit on the deer's flank, a bright red joining the white of the snow. The others missed, but the animal still turned. We as one began to run after it, joining up as we did.

A wave of my hand retrieved spears mid-stride as I joined the others, the stationary objects easy to target once I'd gotten within a hundred feet or so. The others smiled as I brought them back to our troupe.

"Now?" Rindal asked as he plucked his from the air.

"Chase," Ninden declared, pointing to the trail of red in the snow. His spear hadn't bit too deep, but it had given us a good way to track the creature.

We spread into a loose formation, with Alun taking point. His sight and tracking were marginally better than the rest of ours, and with us keeping an eye out for any crisscrossing trails, we should be able to follow easy enough. The wounded beast headed along the creek, nearly parallel to our village—a small bonus for us, since we weren't really supposed to get much further away than we were now.

All of us knew the hunting tactics our fathers used, and now we employed them. This wasn't a sprint; the deer was far, far faster than any of us at this kind of distance. No, this was a marathon. We settled into the jog that a lot of us used when going out to help the older men, plodding along at an easy pace. Elves, much like the humans of Earth, were built as persistence hunters.

We were in a good position; the trail was easy to follow, bright on the pure white ground. The blood also showed that the animal was injured; how much remained to be seen, but any injury was enough. We could keep this pace for at least a couple of hours, harrying the beast bit by bit as it lost fluids and energy, never letting it rest, always keeping the wound open and moving, never letting it close. Every ounce of its life-blood spilled onto the snow was one step closer to us filling our bellies tonight.

We drew in as the trail seemed to slow; most animals didn't run too terribly far before trying to rest. We found it hiding in a small thicket, trying to catch its breath. There would be none of that on our watch though. This was food we needed, that our village needed.

Ninden and I were the ones throwing out shots as we came upon it, both of us better at hitting over the sort of distance we were looking at. This time it was he who missed, his spear's tip shattering loudly as it struck a tree and broke. It was of no consequence, a destroyed spear nothing compared to the potential gain. I got three force bolts off, the quick movements of the deer not quite as fast, though it only helped one of them land.

My shot scored on a back leg, one more injury onto the pile, as the harried beast flew off again. I'd have preferred a clean kill on the first try—every hunter would—but I was taking anything I could get at this point. Ambush kills were always ideal, but in a world like ours, ideals were not often what one got.

Alun passed his spear off to Ninden, busy with tracking and not as good a thrower as the other boy. Normally, we kept our tools our own, but right now the goal was to eat, so we were all in. I realized that Ninden could now use his ability at least twice, maybe even three times in a day if he was getting another spear. That was great, and it meant he'd been practicing a lot.

I didn't know how long the chase went on, but a few hours at least. Our wounds had hurt the creature, but it was resilient and wanted to live. It ran, and ran, and ran. All things must end, though, and the deer was not made to run for so long, particularly not while losing fluids, heat, and energy like it was.

Our group was ragged as we approached where the deer now lay exhausted. We, too, were tired and covered in sweat, some of our fur clothing even loosened to let the air cool us down better. I was lower on magic than I'd have liked, and Ninden had finally used all of his small reserves on a few more close shots. Even those who hadn't been using minor or major magics were wiped, having run for longer than any of us were used to.

"Anyone want the last shot?" Ninden asked as we closed in. The deer tried to rise but couldn't, instead struggling on the ground.

"I'll take it," Rindal said, looking at me challengingly, as if I wanted to use even more of my reserves than I already had.

"All yours then," our leader declared, waving forward.

I didn't like him, but I had to give him this. Rindal was professional. He closed in as much as was safe on a wounded animal and did what he could to make the strike clean. The deer, tired, in pain, and on its last leg, died quickly after that, finally bleeding out onto the snow with only a few more halfhearted kicks.

After a basic cleaning we began to head back to the village, only now realizing just how far we'd gone. It was getting late, the sun much lower than we normally let it get before heading home, and well before we got there, a light went up into the sky.

Elaya had a system of flare signals she used with my father before I was even born. Most of these were fairly simple light colors. The one sent up now was the one for non-emergency gathering. The same Elaya had used when our scouts had disappeared. In this context though, it was a question. "Where are you? Hurt? Come here."

I responded with the color signal for "Safe," or rather, "We're fine, coming."

The other boys looked at me as I sent the flare up. "We'd better hurry back; they're looking for us," I told them.

When we finally got home, the sun was setting. We were briefly met with unhappy gazes from parents, angry that we'd not come home on time. At least until they saw what we were carrying.

CHAPTER 31

FARMING, FIRST ATTEMPT

Months after the cold had begun, it slowly began to lessen. It ended much like it started, with a warm wind blowing through the village. Sure, there was still snow, and it was still cold, but that blessed kiss of warmth told us that things were changing, that soon, very soon, things would be back to normal, and we could go back to our old lives.

I, of course, had some other ideas. Our old lives were good, but couldn't they be so much better? Well, there were potential pitfalls, some issues here and there that I'd need to navigate, but I had trust in my own abilities and a perfect memory of my history classes. There were a few places we could start, but some glaring advancements that would be easiest would need to come first.

For this reason, I pulled Mother to the side shortly after the warming started.

"Mom, what plant produces the most food, or food for the longest?" I asked.

"Those are different plants, Elian, and you should know both anyway," she chided before answering fully. "Breadfruit produces the most, but tubers are the most consistent, why?" She looked at me suspiciously when she realized that I was planning something.

Breadfruit wasn't the name in the elven tongue, because bread wasn't really a thing, but it smelled like bread, tasted sort of like bread, and looked near enough to the species that I remembered from Earth that I was happy to reuse the name. Of the tubers, there were a multitude of types, but some were almost always in season in some variety.

"I was having some thoughts. Would you be willing to help me grow some more plants?" I asked.

My mother frowned. "Growing things too fast is bad for them, Elian, and bad for the land they're on. You know that, right?"

"I don't need them all the way grown, just made so they grow strong," I answered.

She pulled the corner of her lip in. "Maybe, show me when you're ready."

I sped off, having most of today free. Things were like that sometimes. Everyone had their own work to do—either things they needed to eat or things they wanted, but we had a lot of free time, and I mean a lot. Even when the women were out gathering food, it was only about half actual work, the other half chatting and relaxing. Food was plentiful during good times, so it wasn't laborious to get the plants which made up the majority of our diets. Hunting was done regularly, but also at a slower pace. The hunters went out in groups when they wanted to try and catch what they could, but often enough, they just ended up wandering in the woods for hours at a sedate pace. I'd never been out with them, but based on how some of the women talked, I suspected they did significantly less hunting and far more goofing around than was let on, at least when times were good.

We boys went out a lot, ostensibly to learn and practice, but today several of the members of our group were otherwise busy, so I wasn't. That had been planned for, though, and our traps taken in. Catching something you weren't going to eat was wasteful and just lowered the amount of already limited game. I wasn't the only one off on my own. I passed several other children and young adults who had little to do and were relaxing near the central fire pit. It was still cold, and that place was most often warmed magically or at least had a nicely sized fire.

I wasn't going far, but I wanted to scout out some places for a potential . . . not quite a farm, but close. Large scale monoculture was not really within my grasp yet—too involved, too large, and it needed too much infrastructure that we just didn't have yet. That said, I could still start us on the path by doing things like putting plants where I wanted them, and where it was convenient. The current plan was to try to grow several examples of our preferred ones all in one area where they'd be easiest to harvest. If there were other things, I'd cut them back, but for now I was just going to try to concentrate some.

We had a lot of woods around our home, but with the current cold season, much had died back, opening up a few holes in the otherwise dense forest. Places where trees were sparser, and I could perhaps find some workable land. I found three spots within a few minutes, and each had their ups and downs. The underbrush in all of these areas was dead, but there were factors like water and how the land looked.

I gave the first spot a quick once-over and immediately tossed it off the list. Half of it was on a hill. I hadn't gotten a good look under the vines that had crept over it. It only took a few minutes for me to clear out the rest of those to realize that this whole area was angled up and down in a way I didn't really want to mess around with too much.

The second and third areas were similar in makeup, but I eventually decided on the second. The third was closer to one of the many little creeks that covered the land, and not only would that flood every now and then, but it also meant that the few trees that were in that area were old monsters, hundreds of feet tall, and likely with root systems that would either be a pain or ruin my planting attempts.

All of them had some trees; that was just the way things were in large sections of the forest that was our home. Clearings existed, but most were already established gathering spots, and I doubted messing around with them would be welcome, so I had to clear a bit. At least the second had fewer trees than the others, and most were smaller. It looked like one of the older trees had fallen some years ago, carving out a path and taking several of its fellows down with it. There was also evidence of a fire in the bark of the few standing trees, but which had come first was unclear.

Over the next couple of weeks, I spent my off time at my little clearing, first cutting down some of the remaining trees, then doing what I could to turn over the dirt. The cold both helped and hindered me, as while most of the vegetation had been pushed back, what remained was very hard ground. Physically, this would have been impossible, as I was still the size of a schoolboy, but with magic, I could slowly make progress.

More than once, people came by to check on me, or to see what I was doing. Mother thought that I was weird for opening up the land, an opinion that soon formed consensus; but I wasn't causing trouble, so she didn't see the need to do anything about it.

"How are things, Elian?" Dad asked as he and a group of hunters stopped on their way back to the village, taking up seats in my opened-up area. The whole section was maybe a hundred feet wide and three times that long at this point.

"Good, how was the hunting?" I asked.

"Nothing at all," Larus answered with a frown. That was odd. Normally when he went out, they would at least bring something back with them.

"Shame," I said. It meant there'd be no meat at dinner tonight.

"How big are you planning to make this, Son?" Dad asked as he looked around. There weren't really property laws for land, so it wasn't like anyone would stop me from going as large as I liked.

"I think I'm done," I answered. "Big enough to test."

"Test?" one of the men asked.

"I'm going to put a bunch of trees and stuff here, see if I can get them to grow where I want," I answered.

"Why?" came the response from several in the group.

"Because it will be easier to gather the fruit from them if I can."

I got a lot of blank stares. They all knew that gathering fruits and the like was easy if you knew where to go, so it didn't make sense. If that opinion prevailed, it didn't matter if my test was a success; nobody would care. That was something I hadn't really thought about—the perceived usefulness of an invention.

"For times when the women want to stay near the village but we still want some fruit, like if it's raining bad or something. I want to see if I can," I answered. That actually got me some nods.

"That's a nice thing to do, lad," Larus said. "Hate to come home after being rained on to find that the girls called it an early day, too, and we're out of the freshest things. By the way, what are you doing with all the wood?"

He seemed satisfied enough that it was a mix of curiosity and trying to be nice, before getting to the real reason they'd stopped by.

"Nothing at the moment. I might build something with it, but I haven't decided. Do you want some?" I asked, looking at the small pile of trees laying along one side of the field. Once things got warmer, I'd have to do something quick or it would all rot, but for the moment it wasn't an issue.

"Actually, yes. It won't be great firewood, but we can use more, and if we cut it up and let it dry for a few more days, it'll do well enough," the older man answered.

"I mean, I can try to dry it . . ." I said before reaching out. I tried to visualize and find the water in the wood of one of the nearest logs. I focused on its structure, on how it held to the wood, and pulled. The action was much more difficult than I'd anticipated, but with some effort, fluid began to flow out of the lumber. The wood cracked and broke in a few places from the rapid shrinking before I was done, but it mostly survived, and would be much lighter too.

Larus smiled and broke off pieces for everyone to carry home. He was strong enough that he could just snap the foot-thick tree if he felt like it, and picking lengths for everyone was an easy job. Most people got smaller bits for the short walk to the village, while he took a much larger log.

"Hey," one of the men I spent little time with said idly. "You know, this feels like it would be really good to carve with." That comment got several pairs of eyes far more interested in the lumber, as large sections of dry wood were something that were harder to come by.

It looked like my first attempt at farming would be primarily ignored, but maybe I could jump-start some larger woodworking instead?

CHAPTER 32

JOINERY

It was a real disappointment that my attempt at agriculture had been brushed off, but I wasn't going to let that keep me down. I hoped that people came to see the benefit in time, and until they did, well plants grew, so there was no big issue letting my garden slowly expand. It was something I could do on the side, cleaning things up every now and then until they realized that I'd slowly made a bounty of food for harvest.

Now, though, I was going to try my hand at woodworking. This would be a real challenge because it was something I'd never really done in my previous life. I'd be working off of half attempts to make basic things in my memories, and a few videos I'd seen on TV shows. I might not have much, but I could at least work on that.

Wood was an odd material in this world, heavily used for some purposes, but very ignored for others.

For smaller objects, like tool handles and a few smaller tools and utensils, it was the go-to; but for construction, at least in our village, it was largely ignored by the adults. When you could have someone grow you a house in an afternoon, you didn't really need to do complex woodworking. Anything more than the little makeshift huts we boys had built was pretty much nonexistent.

For that reason some skills were far more advanced than others among my tribe. Carving was a pastime that a lot of men got involved in, and some of them were absolutely amazing at the small details that they could transfer over to things like their tool handles and toys they made. As far as joints went, though, there was almost nothing other than simple pins in holes. Everything that needed to stay in place was either tied in place or made some other way.

So I got some of my dried logs and began what seemed to me to be a simple project to start with. I had, in the past, aimed too high with my attempts at new things, and there was no reason for me to do so here. Aim small, win small, lose small.

"What are you making, Son?" my father asked as I began to set my wood out.

"A basket of wood," I answered. The description was close enough.

First things first, making boards. These I hewed, because it was the easiest way. Splitting the logs magically with something like a chisel-shaped blade of force and slicing until I got the sizes and pieces I needed. Blades were far, far easier than making a saw out of force, something I'd tried once. The teeth were the hard part, and keeping them in the right shape, which I had to figure out through trial and error, while it was moving was a real pain.

After carefully shaving the planks down to the sizes that I wanted, using little more than the power of my mind, I began to make a template. I remembered this from one of the trips my school on Earth had taken to one of the colonial towns. The carpenter there had shown us how we could make dovetails, and the simple shape was easy to transfer to a piece of wood. I was pretty sure I could do them with just a chisel too, which was a bonus.

My father came over to watch me work, but kept quiet. He liked to watch how things were made, and he looked over some of my boards. He even gently ran his hands over the surface of one of them and smiled, seemingly happy with the shape it'd taken before returning it to the others.

With immense care, I sliced away material, cutting here and there to leave the dovetail on the first pair of boards. By the time I finished up, I discovered that I'd been too careful and restrictive in my cutting, and the joint was so tight that it wouldn't go together properly. That wasn't too big a deal, as removing material was always easier than adding it, so I just reworked it until it fit with comfortable snugness.

Once I'd finished with all four of my boards, I began to put them together, at which point I discovered that I'd crafted my joints backwards on at least one of the four. With a small amount of irritation, I remade the board—no big deal—and got all of the boards into a mostly rectangular shape.

I picked it up, looking at all the sides. They fit together, but I'd have to somehow glue them together for long-term usage, along with some cleanup here and there. Then I looked through the center . . . through the center.

"Looks good, how are you putting the bottom in?" Dad asked innocently.

As far as I knew, the elven language lacked the sort of breadth and depth of obscenities available in English. There were some naughty words, sure, but not the kind of massive cursing that I could've achieved in my first native tongue. That was something I needed to work on.

I felt my right eye begin to twitch as I took it apart again. There was no need to get too complicated here, so I just made a small magic chisel and carved out a groove that a small board could fit into, then another piece of wood to size to fit.

"Need something to hold it all in place, like you do with your tools," I said to Dad, looking up.

My father made a lot of tools, and even managed to summon a sort of glue-like substance from nothing. The texture was more like sap, and it was something I personally couldn't replicate no matter how hard I tried. Trying to figure out why he could do that kind of thing was on the back-burner for now, but it still grated sometimes.

"I can make you some," he offered.

"Mind helping me finish it?" I asked instead.

My joints were . . . rough—in places a bit too loose, in others a bit too tight. The boards themselves were in dire need of sanding and, if possible, some kind of finish.

Dad smiled, like all dads tended to smile when asked to help with a project like this. I wondered briefly if I'd gotten myself into more trouble than I'd wanted, but with the look on his face, I just couldn't back out now. He was happy as he began to look it over again.

"Of course, Elian. First, let's get some reeds and smooth it out, and then we can do the wood like a tool handle to make it last longer. I think I have everything we'll need already."

I was launched into his explanations as it was sanded, the fit checked and altered ever so slightly, and then something that made me clench, even if I'd seen him do it a hundred times.

Dad's favorite way to finish off any wood project, of which he mostly made tools, was to burn the outside ever so slightly over a hot fire. He had me hold it while he watched until the outside of the wood began to get hot and burn, just slightly, darkening the grain. Water was then applied, and another round of sanding.

I'd have said that the glue came last, but after letting it sit overnight, I was asked to sand the thing once more in the morning, right after I woke up. That was unexpected, but he was right—some of the glue had dried on the outside and was crusty on the edges.

At the end, I had a box; not a large box. It was barely bigger than a cigar box, and without a lid, but it was a box. Dad eventually put it down in front of me, smiling.

"I like it, and there's more you could do with it if you wanted. Where did you see that shape before?" he asked.

"Hmm? It's just something I thought would fit, and I wanted to try it out. I think there might be better ways to do it, but I'm not sure."

He thought on that for a while. "There might be, but that works. If you could make more big pieces of dry wood, then we could do some really good things with it, but getting dry wood slats like that isn't easy." He'd effectively found one of the reasons that this hadn't been put forward yet. "Also need a really sharp chisel . . . hmm, that might be a problem for those without a light like you . . ."

"I'm sure you could make one," I said, trying to encourage him, but he was right. Metal might be the best way to go for those.

"Do you mind if I borrow this to show to some of the others? I think they'll want to try something out too," Dad finally asked.

"Of course not," I said, smiling. This was exactly the kind of thing I wanted to encourage.

CHAPTER 33

TRADER

Weeks had passed since my introduction of the dovetail, and I had to admit that things were going mostly well. A lot of men had been interested in the technique, and many more had stepped forward when I'd pointed out that, with a few changes, we could probably make things like basic beds, chairs, and storage chests. It had launched a large push for wooden items, until Mother had gotten involved.

Many of the trees around the village had been cut down, leaving large patches of barren land nearby, something my mother felt was both visually unappealing and harmful to the local wildlife. She gave a loud, impassioned speech at one of the village dinners about how it was wrong.

That, of course, didn't stop everyone, and the next day several had gone out to take down a few more trees. She didn't move directly against them; she didn't have to. What she did do was make arguments, promises, and a few outright threats of retribution to their female kin—wives, sisters, mothers, daughters, all—and let them bring the offenders to heel.

She wouldn't hurt them, of course; she would just refuse all aid to them. As would Father, because she would make it so. That meant no healing, no new houses, no extra crop growing if someone found a really good spot. It also meant that all of her products, and all of Father's, and all of mine would be denied as well.

I'd known she'd had strong feelings about protecting nature, but it seemed I had underestimated her druid-like drive. While I got a firm talking to about killing a lot of trees, I quite plainly told her that the reason I'd done it was to plant more vegetation. It was the truth, and I added that I hadn't meant for anyone to start trying to remove the forest. My age also got her to forgive me, at least after I promised to not dry wood for anyone unless it had fallen naturally. I was still a cute kid, and I wasn't the one doing the damage.

Since winter had finally passed, I had to deal with another growing change. Ninden was leaving us to join the hunters. It was sad, but he was over the moon while he prepared for the day.

Every culture like ours had some kind of coming-of-age ceremony. Some action proclaiming that someone was no longer a child, but an adult, and was due all the respect therein. For the men of our tribe it was a multi-day hunt where the new man would be taken out and ceremoniously go after game with his male relatives.

There was preparation of course. He needed new clothes, a new spear, plenty of body paint, and a big party. He would remain with his kin in the woods until he managed to take down some worthy game, the bigger the better, and then return to regale us with the story of how he bested it.

The women of the tribe had a ritual when a girl started puberty as well, but those were done in secret. All I really knew was that the girl in question would be taken away for a time and when she came back would be accepted as an adult. There were a few changes in her clothing, little as we wore. It was cut to emphasize the change, but that was about it.

It wasn't until two days after Ninden left that we got our biggest surprise. When the women of the village returned for the evening, we found them gathered around an unknown elven man, and they were rather irate looking.

The stranger's hair was a light brown, and he smiled when he saw us. He sat atop a massive wicker backpack and had clearly been rebuffing those around him for some time. Before him was a large skin of some kind, reptilian in appearance.

"Ah, there everyone is! And if my eyes do not deceive me, your elder is with them too. Please permit me to introduce myself, Elder Elaya. I am the merchant Orran, and I seek to trade in your village." He rose and gave her a deep bow of respect.

"Have you made an attempt to trade before greeting me?" Elaya asked, looking down at the man.

"Of course not, Elder." His tone made it clear that *Elder* was a title to him, and a formal one at that.

Elaya's eyes flicked up to one of the men who'd been standing near him, a younger man who lived in the same hut as her.

"He refused to even show his wares, or discuss what he'd brought in detail," the man confirmed.

Orran seemed to have suspected that something like this might happen, and I could see the smile creeping up his lips ever so slightly.

"Very well, let's see what you've brought," Elaya said to the merchant's obvious relief.

He began to lay things out on the skin, and I realized a few things quickly. Most of what he had was small and either decorative or something that was extremely rare in these parts. Elaya began by looking over his goods and trading him some of our fresh fruit for some salt. My guess was that this was simply a confirmation from her that things were truly open, and a gesture. After that, though, she fell back and let others take a look at his goods.

He was flooded with work. He had shells from species we'd never seen here, bones and tusks of various colors and grades, and many herbs that paired well with food and were irritatingly difficult to find in our area. The latter was cleaned out by Ninden's family since they planned to have a party for him anyway; those herbs would be a huge boon.

I hung back for a bit to see what he had, but I didn't do a lot of cooking or need anything decorative. It would be easy enough to see what people bought afterward, and listening let me learn more about what he had.

Auntie had run back to the hut to grab some of her better pieces of pottery, and when she returned, she joined Mother and me as we stepped forward to look over the goods. I could see Orran's eyes light up as we came closer, flicking both to my aunt's goods and Mother's, and then finally onto me—though at my head, not my face.

"Please come forward," he said as we stepped up. "Has something caught your eye?"

"Yes, those shells. Would you be willing to part for some cups?" Auntie Atie held forward one of her wares, and the man took it with care, looking over it with a keen eye.

"I've never seen one like this before. Something new?" he asked.

"Found it myself," Atie proudly proclaimed, the truth so far as she knew.

"Easy to make?"

"As if I'd part with how to make them," she scoffed at his question.

"Fair, but new is good, and . . . it can hold water, I assume. Looks like a stone bowl, but not quite the same. Mind if I try it?" he asked.

"You may," she agreed.

He poured some water into the little cup and felt the edges. Then he downed his drink and tapped it a few times, checking the sound it made with a smile.

"Those shells?" he asked, pointing.

"Mmm," she nodded.

"Agreed, but if I might ask another question of you two." Now it seemed he was looking to bring Mother into the equation. "You seem to have a lot of those," he said, indicating the purple beads, and I could see him doing calculations in his head. They're new too, aren't they?"

"They are new, and made by us, but only rarely. It takes a lot of effort and the use of light to make them," Mother said, not totally lying. It did take a day or two, and I had to use magic to get the flames right.

"I see, I see. Do you have anything you desire in my wares? I would like to get a few of those, if I could, at the right price."

"I want that," I finally said, pointing to a particular rock.

"A good eye! I just got that recently, came from up in the mountains—" he began.

"My husband works stone, and he was a merchant," Mother said from behind me, cutting him off. "If you take advantage of my son, I will be most displeased."

"Not too rare though, pretty, but not too rare." He changed his tune nearly mid-sentence; impressive. "Probably not worth one of the purple beads, but worth more than the wooden ones you've got separating them, I'm afraid. Perhaps you see something else you like?"

"How many of those would you add?" I asked, pointing to a small pile of what looked like cowrie shells.

"Those too are fairly common, young one. Why don't you look at these instead?" He pulled over a small bag of similar shells that had a slight opalescent coloration rather than the darker speckles of the ones I'd pointed to. "I could give you five of these, and the rock you like for one of your purple beads." I could see his eyes flicking up to my mother for confirmation as he offered, trying not to offend what was clearly one of the more influential women in the village, and one who had something he wanted.

"Ten," I countered. I didn't actually care about the shells, but going back and forth was a tradition I wanted to uphold, if only for appearances.

"Si— Seven?" he tried.

"Seven is fine, I'll trade for that." I undid the little tie I used to keep my money out of my face and pulled off one of the few purple beads I had left.

He breathed out as we made the trade, and I picked up the shells, along with what I actually wanted. My new little rock was a mixture of colors. It was bright green and worn down to expose the veins of native copper inside. Nobody had bothered to get the material out, or knew how to, but with magic, I had a good sense that I could finally get some metal. I was all smiles. I'd gotten a better trade than I could have hoped for, and I even learned where it came from.

CHAPTER 34

COPPER

I honestly don't know why you bought that, Son," Dad said, looking at me as he messed with the copper-laced rock. "It's not useful. The bits inside are weird, but they don't carve at all."

"How about we get them out and try some things on them?" I asked.

"You'd have to break it up, and you just bought it. Your mother will be mad if you paid that much just to make a mess, Elian."

"You said they were weird though," I replied. "I like weird things; weird things make new things."

"Fine, it's yours, but don't expect me to help you," he said.

"Can you at least help me get the weird bits out?" I asked.

My father frowned, but he helped. He showed me that he could carefully meld away the stone, leaving only the chunk of copper behind. That alone was more help than I thought I'd need, so I left him after that and began experimenting with part of it.

I did some things I didn't need to; I only did them for show. I didn't want anyone to suspect that I already knew how to do; that's why some of my failures didn't bother me. Making success after success perfectly would be very eye catching, but being the weird boy who beat on odd rocks until they did what he wanted just made me a bit odd.

The merchant had left well before I'd finished even the initial run of testing. I tasted the metal, tossed it, put it in water to see if it dissolved. I did every weird thing I could think of to the odd spikey blob of copper while also playing with my pretty green stone. Dad had saved the rock itself, which I might be able to make into something later, but for now I was just playing with it.

None of this was important at all, of course, nor all that surprising to me. Some of the other boys, mostly Rindal, began to tease me off and on about how I was way too interested in my weird rock, but I ignored them. We'd see who was making fun of whom when I made a copper . . . something.

It wasn't much copper all—less than a pound—so there were limits to what I could do with it. Mother would want beads if she knew what I could do, and at some point, she might get some, but not from this piece. I was leaning toward making a knife, a metal one that would make so many things so much easier; stone ones just weren't the same.

The first thing I tried was mixing some of the green copper-laden rock with some of my glaze. It went in with a number of other random types of rock I'd found. I didn't know what these might do, but I intended to find out.

"Auntie," I said one afternoon. "There's something I want to try, about maybe getting different colors on pots and stuff."

"What's that Elian?" she said, looking up.

"I want to try putting a bunch of different things into the mix in small amounts."

"Why?" she asked.

"To see if it does anything. Maybe it doesn't work, maybe it does nothing, maybe we get some new colors," I explained. "Or maybe something else I don't expect; who knows."

"Okay, I'll make up some pieces and we can try later. Let's do fancy ones in case they do well!"

"I was just thinking a couple of trials on a flat piece of pottery to see what it does . . ." I said, trying to back out.

"But that's boring."

"But it's repeatable and quick."

"No, that won't do. Making pieces is hard enough that we shouldn't waste the time," she argued.

"I can just do it myself . . ." I saw her twitch in anger. I'd come to her, so I should at least do something she wanted.

"Fine, whatever, we'll make something pretty, but simple okay? I've got some things I want to try. What about you?"

"I'll think of something," she said in a singsong voice.

After the daily work was done, the two of us made about a dozen small bowls. They weren't big enough for much, but it made her happy, and that was what mattered. I ground up my green rock, along with bits of other slightly colorful rocks, and added them into the basic glaze we had, making sure that each bowl had a distinct marking so I could tell which was which. Auntie was trying out a bunch of different sands, I honestly had no clue what that would do, but it wasn't like we needed these.

The results were . . . interesting actually. I'd been hoping to get a pretty green glaze, but it had come out light blue instead, probably some reaction with whatever was in the local clay or ashes; I didn't know. There were a couple of other colors in muted reds and blues. This took us away from the normal purple into something new, but nothing truly stellar. Small wins though. Small wins would add up into big ones eventually.

Months after getting my copper, and at a time when my patience was seriously being tested, I borrowed a hammer from my father, and I did what I'd wanted to for a long time. I began to hit it. It bent slowly on the rock I was using as an anvil as I struck it again and again.

"What are you doing?" he finally asked.

"Trying to get it to move into a different shape," I said.

"It won't, I've tried to knap it before and it just crumbles."

He was right, it wasn't a bar that could be shaped, and as cold as it was, the piece began to break very quickly. When it did, though, I wasn't bothered; everything had been planned out already.

"Hmm, could you make me some glue?" I asked.

He sighed and began to sing some into the world. I could tell by the unhappy look on his face that he was disappointed in me for "destroying" the thing I'd wanted, but I knew that in the end I would be right. The glue was just another distraction. After it dried, I broke the piece up again, separating out the dry bits of adhesive.

"Are you happy now that you've destroyed it?" he finally asked.

"No, maybe if I get it hot . . ." This was what I'd been waiting for.

With another sigh, he pointed me to the generally unused spot in the hut where we sometimes had small fires. Safety was important.

I floated the copper dust in my hands, magically gathering it all up and forming it into a ball. Then I held it there, between my two open palms, and began to generate heat. I went slow at first, but gradually the temperature increased.

"Careful, Elian," Dad said, looking up from his own work. "How hot do you need to make it?"

"Don't know," I said. "Until something happens, or it burns I guess." I knew it wouldn't be too hot. It was something that could be done even in ancient fire pits or covered mud foundries.

"Fine, Son, but be careful."

I moved around my hands and made a dome to hold the heat in. It wouldn't do to have him get worried and stop me here. Of note, there wasn't a need to use your hands when casting, at least for me, but doing this seemed to be a sort of focus aid, making things just a bit easier to visualize.

Hotter and hotter, the little ball of metal dust got. There were a few worrying moments when small pockets of missed glue or some other impurity ignited and I thought my dad would come to do something, but he was busy and trusted me not to hurt myself with my magic.

With time and effort, the ball began to glow, first a gentle red, then brighter into oranges, and finally yellow. It was hard to tell when exactly it all became liquid, as it seemed to happen gradually at first—a little droplet on the surface here, another there, until finally . . .

"Hey Dad, come look," I finally said, drawing his attention.

When he saw the glowing ball of molten metal he rushed over. "Elian, be careful! You don't know what will happen! Remove your light now!"

I did as he bade me and stopped heating it, letting it cool quickly through the reds until it settled back into the color of the reddish metal. I smiled and finally let it drop, watching it bounce on the stone of the fire pit for a second.

"It worked! Look how neat it is!" I enthused, internally thinking, "welcome to the copper age, Father."

"It is still smoking," he said angrily, unhappy that I'd let it get that hot.

"I told you I was going to get it hot . . ."

"Not that hot, and not *inside*."

My father had never been the one to punish me before, but he took that time now. He went for the ears, because of course they always went for the ears first. I wasn't sure how long he roared at me about the dangers of unleashing that much magic inside the hut, but eventually the other people who lived with us arrived. Mother and Auntie Atie both stood back, eyes wide as he lay into me about responsibility and utter foolishness, and how I was going to hurt myself.

When my ball of copper was fully cooled, which he checked, it was taken. If I was going to do stupid things with it, then I apparently wasn't allowed to have it any more. When I opened my mouth to complain, that only led to another lecture and another round of ear twisting.

CHAPTER 35

COMING TO TERMS

I had to flee to my mother for protection from her angry spouse. In my years on this world, that was a first, but one I could tell she rather liked. Apparently, it was hard to stay mad at me because after only a short while, I found myself pulled into her lap and my ears gently rubbed to make the pain go away. I was still the size of a child, so it was probably rather cute to her.

I seldom let her do things like this; it was still weird to me, but she didn't actually ask this time, and I was tired. Where to go from here wasn't clear. It might take a long time to get more copper, as I had no clue where the veins were, or the easy to find bits. I doubted my father would help me right now; perhaps later, but I was getting tired of later. I'd waited months for this just to lose it at the moment of success.

"It worked," I complained.

"Perhaps you should go and explain that to your father." I didn't respond. We both knew how that would go. "No? Well, then what did you learn?"

"Do things where nobody will see them," I responded.

That was clearly the wrong answer. I felt the hand that'd been so gentle only a few moments ago begin to press harder.

"Try again, and seriously this time."

"He wants me not to do things like that inside because it could be dangerous," I parroted what had been yelled at me. "Even if it works."

"Do you need another punishment?" she asked sweetly.

"No, I will do it outside, and away from burnables next time."

"Or you could just not make huge fires," my auntie suggested from nearby.

"Perhaps you should stop using fire. It would mean you have to give up pottery though," I suggested.

"Even when he should be sorry, he's still mouthy," Atie said, frowning.

"I'm mouthy when I'm right," I pointed out.

"You weren't right," my mother said with finality.

I could keep arguing, keep trying to convince them that I knew what I was doing, and that I knew it was safe. That wouldn't work though. I'd spent so much time trying to convince everyone that I was doing everything I could think of and everything I could try that it didn't track. It also seemed to fall on deaf ears that I knew the dangers of fire well—to keep it insulated, since I was still technically a child.

What I needed was a workshop, something private, where I could do as I pleased. That didn't seem likely, though, as we were very communal here. People were always around one another, always doing new things together. It was safer that way if something went wrong, which happened all the time.

"What will Dad do with the thing I made?" I asked.

"I don't know. That depends on if it's dangerous or not. If he thinks it is, he'll get rid of it. Otherwise you might get it back if you act good," Mom advised.

"I always act good," I complained. Upon seeing their eyebrows fly up, I tried again. "Most of the time . . . sometimes . . . when I feel like it. At least I'm generally safe." They kept looking at me after the last one. "Come on, when's the last time someone got hurt because of something I did."

"Safe and lucky aren't the same thing," Mom hissed.

"Fine, I'll try to come up with a better way to do things, in case something goes wrong," I answered before she could start the ear twisting again.

"Do more than that, Elian," Auntie Atie said. "Come up with what happens when it goes wrong, then what happens if what you made to protect you fails, then one after that too. Try to think of the worst that could happen and plan for it."

Her words reminded me of elevators and how they were made back on Earth. There were layers of fail-safes, and it was almost impossible for one to completely fall as long as physics was working and it was still in the elevator shaft. Frankly, if either of those two things were no longer true, there were much larger problems than a falling elevator. Though, I supposed physics remaining true seemed slightly less likely in this world, magic and all.

"How would you have done it?" I asked her.

"Depends on how hot you got it," she commented.

"Glowing brightly, and way hotter than your pots get."

Both of them fixed me with glares. "In the house?" I was asked.

"Yes, that was definitely the first problem," I answered cautiously. "What else though?"

"Ask your father," Mom finally said. "But not now; tomorrow or when he gets time. He's still mad at you."

So I sat back and waited. I didn't like it, but sometimes that's what had to be done. While I waited, I went back to pottery with my aunt and playing with the other boys. I even spent one afternoon with Isha, just relaxing as she made some baskets and I worked on tool handles. One could never have enough tools, in my opinion.

Soon enough, though, there was a good time, a day when both Dad and I were at the village rather than out and about. He sat there working on spearheads, replacements that were always needed as the stone ones broke often.

"I want to talk," I said, sitting across from him.

"About what?" he asked gruffly.

"I know you're still mad about me getting the weird rock stuff so hot."

"I'm not angry anymore. I was angry, but no, I'm not mad. I am disappointed. I am disappointed that you would do something so foolish, without properly talking to others and making sure there was nothing that could harm the hut, or, more importantly, yourself. Particularly after you've done so many good things." His words hurt a bit, and I frowned.

"All right, well what would be a better way to do it?" I asked honestly. "I plan on trying again, and maybe with different things, so how should I go about it? Not inside, I understand that was the first mistake, but what else?"

"I would prefer you not try again," he said with a slight frown.

"I know, but I was onto something; I can tell. I will try again, with or without your help. If I have to hide it from you, I will, but I don't want to." I was not giving up on metal. It was too big a thing, and I wasn't waiting for years when I'd already met success.

I could tell that my dad was angry. Being told by your young son that he was going to do what he was going to do regardless of how you felt about it would rankle any parent.

"You will fight me on this?" he asked with furrowed brows.

"It isn't this. When I . . . when I dream, I see a different world, a world where we are so much more than we are right now. We could be so much more, see so many wonders. I see towers of stone and crystal, roads connecting everywhere that are clean and without dirt. Crossings over water made of wood, or rock, or ropes. I see a world where monsters like the ones that destroyed our home and took so many, flee. Where the dangers of the forest are pushed back by the light. Where death almost never comes, and everyone lives to be like Elaya, or even Atal. That is what I want, that is what I will fight for, and not for me alone, for everyone."

He listened, and put aside his work, and then rose to come and hug me. "That is a beautiful dream, my son, but you must live to see it. You must do things right so that you can make your dream happen, even if only a little bit. Promise me that; promise that you will keep yourself safe."

"I promise," I said, and I meant it.

"Then let's go and build you somewhere you can try again, somewhere safer. Also, tell me so I can watch and help if you get hurt."

"Okay, Dad."

CHAPTER 36

KNIFE

Father and I looked over our handiwork, and I smiled. We'd come to some terms for safety after our disagreement, and this was part of it. I needed to work here, and under his supervision, if I was going to be using magic to make fires that hot.

The area in question was just outside the village, about ten feet around in a circle with some poles holding up a little thatched roof. Most of that had been my father's doing; my work had been focused on the ground instead. It was barren, charred to a crisp, then wiped clean, and compacted. There were also a number of stones and holes for making fires, and a small pile of both wood and charcoal sitting to the side; though the latter was of poor quality, if I had to guess.

I was surprised they even had charcoal. But in truth, it was so easy to make, a person could almost do it by accident just by leaving some burnt wood out during a rainstorm. It had been discovered long, before my birth, though it wasn't used frequently.

I'd also brought in some rocks under Father's watch. There were some that would serve as makeshift anvils, and a few more that I placed around the main fire pit. I had memories of the various different ways to build a construct like this. I wasn't an expert by any means, but it would still probably serve us well.

I'd been going through those rocks with a fine-toothed comb over the past several months, pulling useful bits out of them. There were some that were really good but many that also didn't help my current objectives, or were too obvious to explain without drawing lots of attention. I could do one or two things at a time, and needed to slowly grow, at least for now.

"Look ready to you?" I asked my father.

"Hmm, almost, but there is one more thing you'll need. Wait here." He left me there, coming back quickly with a small item in his hand, which he handed over. "Don't make me regret this," he said as he returned my copper.

It wasn't much, but it would be enough for what I wanted.

"Let's try to make a knife," I said.

"Can't chip away on that," Dad replied.

"No, but when I was playing with it before it melted, I noticed it bent when you hit it. Maybe we can hit it into shape."

We worked on forging it, but cold didn't work well, and even with heat is was suboptimal. My dad watched, but it was clear that he didn't think that this would work. I didn't know how to forge metal, and it was hard work to try. Soon enough, the misshapen lump was there, slightly elongated and very bent up.

"I don't think this is working, Son," Dad said, looking at the bit of copper that nearly resembled its native form. No matter how hard I tried, it just seemed to bend strangely.

"It isn't . . . Maybe if I melt it and put it into shape then?" I seemed to remember some shows and stuff casting copper, and that looked like it worked pretty well.

"Give it a try, and we'll see how it goes."

The first thing I needed was a mold, and I was sort of already an expert at making physical walls of force from my magic, so I just did that. It was the easiest method, and it let me do things quickly. With a few movements, I snapped together an outline of a simple knife, one that was a little straighter than most of the flint ones we used, and with a rather thin handle, but one that anyone could understand.

The point went down, and I put the copper into a sort of sphere over the end of what would be the tang, keeping a blockage between where it was melting and where it would flow through. Then I began the process of heating it.

No matter how much I learned, or how much I did it, magic never ceased to bring me a smile. It wasn't like anything else; it was like pure imagination had been given form. I was reaching out with little more than my mind and making the world bend to my desires. I couldn't do anything, but I could do so much, so much I'd never been able to do in either of my lives without it, so much that would just let me act in ways nature wouldn't.

Once the metal was liquified, I opened the separation between the two constructs of force and watched the liquid flow in. It was brightly glowing and beautiful, flowing almost like water as it filled the shape I'd given it, and then slowly it began cooling. I could try later to see if rapidly cooling it would be feasible, but for now I just watched with joy as the heat slowly bled away.

It took time for the object to cool, but that was fine with me. It just meant that I had plenty of time to watch. The layers dimmed and dimmed some more, showing a slightly mottled surface to the metal, with odd places where bubbles had been or still were under the outer layer. The casting, even in a nearly perfect shape, had been imperfect. The metal was probably full of other elements, and maybe not at the right temperature or properly handled, but none of that mattered. What mattered was that I'd succeeded, a major first step in advancing the world.

"That's different," Dad observed, looking at the blade. It was perhaps four inches long.

"Is it still hot?"

He put the back of his hand near it and frowned. "Yes, very. Water, you think?"

At my nod he summoned a ball of water around the little knife, and we got to watch as it sputtered and spat steam. This did not seem to reassure my father, who'd of course never seen anything quite like this before. He spent long moments rubbing his chin in thought as he hummed until the bubbles subsided.

"It was hot because I made it hot, but I think we'll need to remember that it's a rock and gets hot without looking that way," I said by way of reassurance.

"Yes, and make sure it doesn't get hot on its own," he said.

"Are there rocks that do that?" I asked.

"A few things that are like rocks, but this isn't really a rock. You should name it."

Names were hard, because a lot of them just didn't quite fit in our lexicon. The sound could be made, sure, and even put in the same place sometimes, but that didn't mean they sounded right in the language. Sometimes words just had feeling to them, and that was how it was.

"How about Cypri for this type?" I said, remembering that copper was derived from the name of Cyprus.

"Sipry huh?" Dad said, unintentionally changing the pronunciation almost instantly. I just went with it.

"And if there are others we can form like this, let's call them, Mae-atal." That was about as close as I could get to metal, so I was going with it.

Dad waved his water away with a smile. "I like that, and others will too." He cautiously took the small knife, looking it over before handing it to me.

"Needs a wrap for a handle," I mused. "And it's dull. Think we can sharpen it like an axe?"

"I'll get some stones of the right grit and we can try, but don't get your hopes up. Normally, to get a good edge you need to break things the right way. For a handle, I think I've got some older leather from the cold season we could wrap it in."

Together we continued working. There was just something about doing this with my father that brought a smile to my face. Perhaps it was the encouragement he sometimes gave me, or the light caution; I didn't know. Hopefully, one day I'd find out, though, so I could treat my own children the same way.

CHAPTER 37

NEGOTIATIONS

My new knife was rough. It was also the talk of the village. It took almost no time at all for people to begin looking over it and trying it out themselves. I only smiled and let them try; all according to plan.

"It cuts differently than stone; the motion is not the same," Larus said as he used it to slice up a piece of meat. "It's also very thin; gets in places easier."

He handed it back to me, and I took a few moments to sharpen it again. It didn't need to be super sharp, but displaying how to maintain something like this would make it easier for people in the future so they could do it and not complain to me.

"So, what do you think? Worthwhile to make?" I asked.

"Not sure on that one Elian. They're pretty hard to make, right? And your father said the stone to make them isn't common around here. Can you make anything else with the same material?" he asked.

"Need to test, it but I think so. I'm also pretty sure that when they wear out, we can just melt them and remake them again, not have to start from scratch. As for how hard it is, with my light it's pretty easy; without it you could, but it might be harder. The right stones being far away is a problem." I frowned at the last part.

He looked at my dad and shrugged. "If another trader comes we could ask him to get some, or we could make a run ourselves. These might be good for spear tips if they can be melted and remade. Break a flint one, and it's a tossup if you get anything out of it."

He and several other men had gathered to give their full impressions, and so far it was good. People could clearly understand the usefulness here, so it didn't take long for them to start parsing ideas.

"Is it far to go and get more?" I asked.

Everyone looked at my father, since he was the resident expert on rocks. "It's outside of the valley, ten days or more for both ways of the trip. We'd also need to take Elian to get the metal from the rocks. I'd need to go to find the right ones and keep an eye on him while we do, maybe Larus as well. Elaya won't like us taking so many of our strongest from the village at once, and someone will have to deal with that mess too."

There was grumbling on his observation. The elder couldn't outright forbid something like this, not if so many of our people thought it was worthwhile, but she could raise an awful stink and cause problems. She was the political power for a reason, and if we wanted to do this, we'd need her permission. This was assuming my mother didn't join her in raising a fit, something which might actually sink this mission.

"We still have the stone from where I made it. Perhaps we can get more of the copper out of it? Make them some beads or something?" I suggested.

"Your mother likes her trinkets, Elian, but she won't risk your life for them. Elaya is the same as well, and is far more concerned with the village than pretty things. Even if you could, which we should check if you want to risk it, that won't help. We need to show them the knife and convince them it is worth sending so many out," Dad said, furrowing his brow.

We took a couple of days to plan, during which time we managed to smelt down the rest of the ore into a few more ounces of the reddish metal. That in itself was helpful, as it was possible to do without nearly as much magic. Dad agreed that if we needed to, it would even be possible without it, though we'd need lots of charcoal.

We met with Mother and Elaya as they prepared dinner, asking both to come observe a deer being dressed that had been generously donated by our hunters. They looked skeptical, but some of my weirdness had panned out in the past, so they humored me.

"I want you to try this," I said, handing the little blade to Elaya.

With a shrug, she began the work of cleaning the animal. It was messy, but the first few movements told her most of what she needed to know. My mother had used the knife already, being that I'd made it and had been doing my best to get people's opinions. During this whole operation, I took the time to explain how it might be able to be reformed into other things when the knife wore out.

"It is odd, but good," the elder finally declared. "Can you make more?"

"Yes, but several of the men will need to go to gather the materials," I answered.

"Who? And how long?" I could already see the gears turning, trying to find why she was being consulted for this.

It was Dad who spoke. "I would need to go, as well as Larus, to make the trip worth it. We'd also need to process it there, so Elian would need to come. It would take at least ten days . . ."

"Absolutely not!" Mother cut in. "You are not taking my son off like that for so long. You wouldn't even be in one place, but taking him who knows where all over the countryside! He's not even an adult, just a boy . . ." A hand on her shoulder stopped the tirade before it could continue.

"She has a point. The two of you would be one thing, but he is still a child. We would also be weakening the village with you all gone. Is there no other way of getting what you need?" Elaya asked calmly. "If it came from that green rock he was playing with, we do see some like that in the river every now and then."

"Not enough," I answered. "It would take forever to make even a bit more metal using those." I had even checked; if there were more than a few flakes of something usable every now and then, I wasn't finding it.

I could see my mother fuming, only kept in check by the fact that Elaya was already leaning toward opposing our mission. Her eyes were mostly bearing down on Dad as she crossed her arms over her chest. I was getting a few of those glances, too, and knew that I'd be getting it when we got home.

"Let Adia and I speak for a while and consider this," the older woman said.

"There is nothing to consider," Mother retorted.

They had a complicated relationship, both wanting to be in charge of certain things, and clearly not wanting the other to butt in. If it had been anyone else wanting to venture out, I think Mom would have dropped it, but it wasn't. It was both Father and myself, and she could be very protective sometimes. Elaya, too, might have acted as the sole decision maker had it not been our family, and she already seemed tired by the argument they were sure to have.

"Let us talk," she said again, with more hardness in her voice this time.

Mom didn't talk to us again until we were all done with dinner. She spent the whole time deep in conversation with Elaya, who was using some kind of magic to keep others from overhearing. I wasn't fully sure what they were going back and forth on, but both looked very frustrated until the very end. Mother left with a wicked smile on her face, while Elaya just looked tired.

She looked at Father and I as if she'd won when we got home. "You should have come to me before you went to Elaya with this absurd request."

"I knew how you would react, my love. If I hadn't gone to her at the same time, you would have refused outright," Dad answered.

"Because taking our son out into the wilds is madness! It wouldn't even be in the normal hunting grounds, Eduan! The beasts out there . . ." she began.

"I know what the beasts are like, Adia, and I know my way better than most. Do not forget that I lived as a trader, that I know where to go and how to travel safely. Do you think that I would allow Elian to come to harm? That I would take him anywhere if I thought it was dangerous? He's young, but strong, and with both myself and Larus there, little could threaten us. Pah, even the boy has fought powerful beasts and won nearly on his own," Dad said, unhappy with her assumptions.

"May I say something?" I asked.

"No," they chorused; it was pretty funny.

"I'm going to anyway," I declared. "Mom, this could help us, all of us, a lot. Also, Dad's right. If he didn't think we could do it safely, we wouldn't go. I know you want me safe because you love me, but you also have to let me grow when it's safe to do so."

Her expression softened at that, but she still looked unhappy. "Son, it's very dangerous out there." Then she sighed, and with a slightly harder look sat back. "We did come to a conclusion. Elaya is interested in your claim that this metal can be melted and remade into different things. You can go,"—I perked up—"*if* you remake your knife into something else useful before you go. Are you willing to destroy your new favorite thing?" She looked triumphant, clearly thinking she'd won.

"Okay, we'll do it tomorrow," I said.

Her face fell. "What?"

I could see Dad trying not to smile as I continued, "I've got enough for a small hammer, and I wanted to try making one anyway. I'll do it tomorrow."

We gave her space for the rest of the evening until bedtime. She was the one to come and get us and pull us into the group, though positioning me between her and my father rather than the normal arrangement where she was between us. She was still mad, particularly at my father, but being mad and loving someone weren't mutually exclusive.

CHAPTER 38

FIELD TRIP

I checked my gear once again, while Mother gave Dad a few last rules. He let her, even if he didn't need to; it wasn't like he didn't know what to do. She was still quite mad that I'd remade my knife into a hammer, so I was getting few words.

"Elian, stay safe," she finally said to me. "I love you." She gave me a hug.

"Love you too, Mom." I hugged her back, fully intending to not take unnecessary risks.

The hammer was in the hut now; it was small and nice. Casting it into shape had been almost comically easy, and when it was done, Elaya almost instantly approved it and our trip. It was clearly useful, if small, and a good example of what could be done. The only real issue was that it was soft, as copper tended to be.

In total, there were only five of us going. Anyone else would just slow down the mission, and we only needed so much metal for now. Larus and Father were leading our group, and the rest were in charge of me. I was going to be doing the smelting when we got there, and the other two men were backup for carrying extra metal and helping with any creatures we might come across, though we were hoping for none.

When we were ready to head out, only a few came to see us off. Most people were out doing their daily work—gathering food or processing materials, all the things that needed doing. That suited me fine, as more would have just slowed things down further.

Just before we stopped for the night on the first day, Dad called out to me. "Come here, Elian. It's a good view."

I stepped up onto a large rock on the path and looked back at the village.

"Whoa," I said in near shock.

"I know. It's a beautiful valley, isn't it?"

I wasn't shocked at the beauty, though it was beautiful. No, far more shocking was what it was. It wasn't a valley at all. It was a crater, a massive, enormous crater. Something had blown up here with a power normally reserved for extinction level impacts.

Oddly, our village wasn't at the true middle. From here, I could see that much clearly. No, it was off to the side, a few hours walk at least from the true center. I tried to compare the angles, the shape of the land and the like, trying to figure out where it was.

Quickly, I concluded where it must be.

"The cave we stayed in is at the very center?" I asked.

"Hmm? Oh, the one for the winter, yes. It's the middle of the valley, Elian."

Well, that settled it. When I was able, I would definitely be going back there. It was too far to just pop off on my own, but I needed to know what it was that was making all of that magic. Was it some meteorite that had landed, blowing things to bits? Was it an ancient civilization that had destroyed itself? Or maybe some magical phenomenon. I just had to know; I was almost salivating.

"Come on down now, Elian. We need to get camp set up before it gets too late," Dad said, helping me down from the vantage point I'd taken.

"Okay, how are we doing the camp?" I asked.

"It's easy, I'll show you."

The sleeping area was little more than a lean-to with branches piled up over it. It wasn't much at all but would serve to keep the rain off of us should any fall. We didn't need much else, as the weather right now was roughly perfect for our bodies. We spent most of our time outside and with little clothing, so there was no real problem there.

The only other big addition was a fire.

"We could just use light from Father or me?" I suggested as we piled the wood nearby.

"Two reasons for using fire," Larus explained. "One, smoke keeps the bugs away. I don't want to be bothered by them, so it'll be better. Two, it repels most beasts; even the strong ones don't normally like fire. There are exceptions, but the majority of them, particularly the smaller ones, will stay away from fire. Putting up lights like you two have will attract some.”

After everything was set up, one of the other men asked a question.

“What is the watch going to be like?’

“Larus and I will each take one, as will you two,” Dad answered.

“What about me?” I asked.

“You don’t need to stay up, Elian. You need sleep, but if you really want to sit up late, you can with me. You okay with that Larus?” he asked the bigger man.

“Sure,” he answered lightly.

I didn’t stay up too late, but late enough to enjoy the stars. The stars on this world were so vibrant, so alive. I knew that on Earth they’d been prettier in far off and dark places, but I’d never been to one. Here, though, the clouds of gas stretched and arced across the sky in blazes of color. I stared at them until sleep took me.

The sun was barely starting to light up the sky when I awoke in the three-elf pile under the shelter. It still weirded me out sometimes that we always seemed to sleep on top of each other. Not just families either, but whole groups, all together and close as we snoozed. There was something comforting about it, though, and almost bond building.

“You’re up early,” Larus said as I rose, his eyes snapping to me for a moment before he went back to observing the forest.

“Yeah.”

“Good, we’ve lots of ground to cover today.”

He wasn’t lying either, and by the end of the day, I was using magic to help myself along. I couldn’t fly yet, and my first attempts had shown that it would be really difficult if I wanted to learn. It required a sort of control and quick reaction that I didn’t possess. It was very disorienting. However, I could sort of lift myself, giving myself short boosts. It was rather like walking on the moon, just a slight lightening to take the stress off my feet a bit.

We traveled three days in total, mostly keeping to rivers and streams, but every now and then cutting through thinner parts of the jungle to get to clear landmarks. As we got closer and closer to our destination, I started to see changes. There were bits of the copper ore we were after in the water, and there were a few trails that were decidedly not game trails, too wide and well worn.

“Are there other elves here?” I asked my dad.

“There’s a village about half a day from where we’re going. We might even see a few of their hunters when we get closer,” he answered calmly.

"Will they care what we're doing? We are taking their rocks."

"Elian, they have more than enough of them, and traders take them for trinkets all the time. Anyway, we're on good terms with all of our neighbors. Meeting them will be nice, and once they see your metal, they might trade us something for it. Don't let them know how to make it though."

"It will spread as it spreads," I said cryptically.

Before we got to our destination, we did indeed meet some other elves. There was a small group of mixed men and women, and they waved as we approached.

"Eduan, is that you?" one man asked. By his small shock of white hair, I assumed he was the elder.

"It is. It's been too long, old friend." Dad embraced him. "And this is my son, Elian. Come here, Son." He beckoned me over.

"Greetings, elder," I said politely as he smiled down at me.

"And to you, little man. What a light you have for one so young." Then he leaned in conspiratorially. "Any good stories to tell?"

"I think I can come up with one or two," I said, smiling.

Several of the women came to look me over. Children were valued by our people, mostly because we were pretty rare, and magical children even rarer. It gave me a chance to look them over too.

Physically, they were a lot like the women of my own village. They all looked young and in good health. There must be a healer of some kind in their village because they lacked the deformities or scars one associated with living as roughly as we did. Their style was quite different though.

Other than the standard braids and beads, they almost all used the same color body paint, but in varying patterns. The bright green lines covered arms and legs, and some were complex, some simple. That kind of thing was done sometimes in our village, too, but normally not in all the same color like this. It was perhaps a style here. One woman who was leaning against the elder had the most complex markings; not surprising.

"Well, when your business is finished, why don't you all come stay in the village for a night? I'm sure we can find a comfortable place for you," the elder offered.

"Thank you," Dad replied. "We will; though we'll be out here a day or two."

"See you then, Eduan. It is good to see you again."

"You know them?" I asked Dad after they'd left.

"When I was still a trader, a sickness came through their village. They didn't have a healer at the time, so I stayed and did what I could for an entire wet season. Before I got there it was pretty bad, but we got them all sorted by the end of it. I was even offered a place with them when I settled down, but your mother didn't want to move," he explained.

"He said they were friendly," Larus said, laughing. I was sure my face was showing surprise. Dad had never told me that story before.

The gathering location was just over the hill, and when we got there, I realized why the village wasn't territorial about the copper deposit. It was a canyon, hundreds of meters long and brilliant green along both sides. This deposit was absolutely massive.

CHAPTER 39

THE OTHER VILLAGE

We had a pretty good system going in short order. Larus was gathering and crushing ore like a machine and was getting help sorting of the best pieces by our other two. While they did that, Dad and I ran a pair of forges, trying to get what we could out of all of it.

He was still learning to put more power into the fire, and while we worked, we all sang some old song he knew, which seemed to make his magic better somehow. I wanted to know how that worked, but magic was weird and, well, magic.

I was making bars of metal, slightly more rectangular than one would normally associate with such things from movies and the like. Those would be easier to carry and would work out better for us in the end. We were also taking frequent breaks, as we were burning through quite a lot of magic in the process.

It was during one of our breaks that I looked over at my dad and said, "So, are we going to go and visit the other village when we're done?"

"We should, since their elder invited us and we're on their land," he replied, chewing his lip. "He'll be curious about what we're doing, though, and may try to do it himself if he learns."

"You know I don't care about that, right, Dad? I want these things to spread. Heck, we could even show him how to make pots and stuff if you want."

"Let's not do that right now, Son. It would cause problems. As for telling him, I think that, too, is unwise, as he may try to stop us from continuing. There are other sources of the copper, but we'd need to travel farther for it. Perhaps we could make him a gift though? Any ideas?"

I weighed that over for a while. There were in fact a lot of different things we could make, but many of them had issues. It was unwise to eat from copper bowls, depending on what you ate. It was likely the elder had several, and very good, tools, not something we could replace instantly. Though a knife might be a good one if worse came to worst. A decoration probably, maybe something he could show off would be good.

"I'll think about it, see if I can come up with something," I finally said, tapping my lips. "What does he like?"

"Games, any kind of game is something he'll like," Dad said. "He'll like it if it's a game he can play with others, too, so nothing too hard to learn," he added quickly.

I nodded, continuing to mull it over as we got back to work. The plan was to do as much as we could today and tomorrow and then go spend the night with our hosts. Most of the games I thought of were a little more complicated than I'd like though. I settled on one of two games and looked over at my father after several more hours of on-again, off-again smelting.

"For the elder, does he like games that are simple to learn but hard to be good at, or games that are simple to learn and easy to be good at?" I asked.

"The first I think is better," Dad replied. "What are you thinking?"

"Oh, nothing much, just trying to get the right idea."

We slept well that night, with our watch continuing to rotate, and the next morning I got to work.

We had plenty of skins to carry things in, and getting a few was no problem at all. The board was simple to draw, only needing straight lines, and while it could have been done on the ground, making one right was slightly nicer. A quick application of heat drew the grid, and I was done. Since copper was all the same color, I cast the pieces into circular and cubical ones, the easiest shapes to make, and tossed them in a few of our smaller bags.

"All done," I declared as we finished up breakfast.

"Really?" Dad asked.

"Yup."

Another day of work, and by evening, we had more than we would need for quite some time. All of us would be carrying a bit of copper back to the village, and everyone would be getting a copper knife as payment. With Larus getting a few other odds and ends from Dad, it was a good arrangement.

My father led us to their village as the afternoon waned, and we were greeted with a cheer. Lots of people knew my dad, and lots of them liked him, which made it easy for him to come here, and easy for us to join him. Of course, the first thing we did was go to greet their elder.

"Hello, old friend. Thank you for having us. My son has made a gift for you, if you'd like it," Father said.

The older elf was elated, smiling big. "Certainly, show me what you've brought, lad."

We found a place to sit, and I pulled out the pieces. A few members of his tribe came to see, and more joined when they saw him holding one of the game pieces. He looked it over intently, rolling the small cube in his hand.

"I've never seen something quite like this—heavy, pulled from the stones and shaped somehow?" he asked, curious.

"We call it copper, and we are still playing with it to learn more about it. I think it has potential," I said.

"Maybe, maybe, pretty too," The elder's wife said, leaning in and rolling the same game piece around in her hand. I could see the gears turning for both of them. "So what is this game?"

"I'll explain, and then would you like to play a game or two?" I asked, and he nodded along.

I briefly ran through the rules, as it would only take a few minutes, and he smiled. "Oh, easy to learn. We get traders and the like, and I think some of them will love this."

Playing a round didn't take long, and I won, but I'd played before.

"Do you like it?" I asked hopefully.

"I do, and you could make the pieces out of anything, even rocks. What do you call it?"

"It's called *Go*, and yes, white and black rocks would be excellent and look very pretty."

I was not a good *Go* player, not by any means, but the rules were easy, and I ventured that people would find it endlessly entertaining. It was also an easy way to show off the copper, which was working well. After our first few games, other members of this tribe took to playing against their elder, to varying levels of success.

Father was fielding a number of questions about the copper, since he was the most well-known of our group. While he answered questions, several of the children came to introduce themselves to me as well, asking about our village and the differences there. We talked about the recent cold season, and I told a few stories about some of our trapping and the hunt for the deer.

I left out the stories about the magical beasts I'd fought. Not because there was any shame in it, but because it was good to have people underestimate you. I just told a few short stories here and there and talked about the road and all we'd seen. That proved popular, since most kids here had never been that far.

The next morning, I woke up early and really had to pee. As I made my way outside and the sensation faded, I began to suspect that I'd been awoken by an outside force—the village elder was also awake, sitting in a relaxed posture in the grass.

"Good morning, did you sleep well?" he asked politely.

"I did, did you wake me?"

"Getting straight to the point, huh? Yes, I wanted to talk."

I joined him cautiously. Our elders tended to be powerful, and this was his village.

"What about?"

He rubbed his chin, thinking. "When your father came here years ago and helped us, I offered him a place here. He'd proven himself a friend, and a man such as him would be valuable to us. Not today, but when you come of age, I want you to consider the same offer. This thing you've brought me, I think you're right that there's something there."

"You wanted to offer this while we were alone?"

"Your father rebuffed my attempts to learn more about the process of making things with copper. I suspect you might tell me if you join our tribe, and you have a power to you, brighter than most," he said.

"Whether or not I join your tribe, I will tell you in time. If you ask again when I come of age, I think I will."

He blinked at that, seeming to roll it over in his mind. "Why?"

I shrugged. "I want the world to grow, and this growth requires spreading knowledge. If I do tell you, will you try to stop me from getting more materials?" I asked.

"I did not get as old as I am by not showing gratitude. Tell me when you are ready, and you'll still be welcome here so long as I am the elder of this village." With that he sat back, calm.

"I'm surprised you're letting this go so easily. I thought you might push for the information now."

He laughed. "I also did not get as old as I am without patience."

CHAPTER 40

PRODUCT REQUESTS

Everyone was tired when we got back to the village, myself included. We had all overestimated how much we could carry, because the metal was small, and we struggled the whole way back. This had made the whole trip take about a day longer than it should have, and many of us had blisters by the time we got home. Needless to say, proper backpacks were going on my soon-to-achieve list of inventions as well.

We brought our haul of material back to the hut, happy that few were around at this point in the day to see us, and dropped everything there. I made my way, unceremoniously, to the sleeping mat and promptly collapsed, letting the dreams take me.

The next time I opened my eyes, Mother was standing above me, looking cross. "Your father said the trip was easy enough, but the way you're laying says otherwise."

"Easy enough depends on what you mean by it. We didn't encounter any monsters, so that was good," I replied. "Things went mostly as expected, though I am sore."

"Hmm, well, good to know it wasn't something too fun for you. Maybe you'll wait before doing it again."

"It was fun, but I will wait. We have enough copper for quite a few projects now," I said calmly, not wanting any more trouble.

With a wave of her hand, the few aches and blisters I had disappeared. "Come, it's nearly time for dinner. You should help, and tell stories if you have any."

"Their elder said I should come live with them when I come of age," I said, not wanting to hide that from her.

She pressed her lips. "You could, if that is what you want."

"It's not what you want though, is it?" I asked.

"No mother wants to see her children go far away. We'll talk about it later if you want to, but now, dinner."

We ate and talked, and told the story of our trip to everyone. It wasn't a particularly exciting story, but it was news, and everyone liked news. We talked of the other nearby village, and I described how many of them used the green rocks to paint themselves, which got several of the ladies in our audience interested. Sadly, we'd not brought any of those back with us.

Father told of the game that I'd made and handed over to the other elder. This of course led to several people asking for the rules, and a number of impromptu games of *Go* played in the dirt with rocks and small sticks as pieces. I smiled. It was true that you could play basically anywhere with anything.

Isha looked over as we played through a game ourselves. "So you brought back a lot of that copper?" she asked with a glint in her eye.

"I did, why?"

"I was just interested in what you were planning to make with it," she said, a mischievous smile on her lips.

"If you want something, just say so and we can trade," I said, placing down one of my pieces and taking several of hers.

"Needles, I want needles," she said.

"Planning on stabbing someone?" I asked with an amusing tone.

"No, not currently, though that's not a bad idea. I know this one boy for example . . ."

As she trailed off and giggled a little, I said, "I'm not against the idea." As a point of fact, I was all for it. "But why needles?"

"Because I'm out of bone needles, and they're a pain to make. My father hates making them, as does everyone else. Do you know how long it takes to get new ones? Just getting the right bones is a pain, but I hear you can make things easily out of that copper, and it made a really pretty knife, so needles."

She wasn't wrong, making a needle was a pain. First you needed a large piece of thick leg bone, something sought after for a number of different purposes, and then you had to drill and grind it into shape. Father couldn't shape bone like he could stone either; it was annoying.

"Fine, and I'll tell you what I want for a few of them," I said.

"What?" she asked suspiciously.

"Two things. First, I want you to tell me how it goes, and then tell everyone else if it goes well. Second, I want you to think of some other things to make that would be useful—tools and stuff."

Isha narrowed her eyes at me. "You're up to something, Elian."

"Of course I am, Isha. I'm handing over the work of coming up with ideas to you, and you'll need to convince others that copper is worth the time," I said, laughing. "And only for the price of some needles."

Eduan

I watched my son work from a ways back. He was drawn in by what he was doing, heating and shaping the copper like it was nothing at all to him. As I looked on, I felt the presence of another move beside me. Elaya had come to watch too.

"His power is amazing, and at his age too," I observed. "I don't know what to make of it."

"It's not the power that surprises me," she said intently. At my raised eyebrow, she continued. "I've known your wife's side of the family for a long time. No, it's his control. He's still growing in power, but look at how he uses it. Here he's only putting forth a fraction of his light and working it into a project smaller than most of us would bother with. He's also using elements of the light that few make work for them in anything other than large attacks. When's the last time he accidentally made a fire?"

"One that he didn't immediately put out? He's lit things on fire when putting down his work but puts them out almost without effort."

"We knew he was using his light for years without knowing what he was doing. I'd bet it was things like this, things you'd only see if he let you," she said, tapping her lips, considering.

"Agreed, and he sees potential everywhere. Do you know how long he messed around with that copper? Like he knew there was something there but couldn't put it right. Never giving up until he got what he wanted," I added.

"I'm worried about what he wants, or will want though. You know how some people can get."

"He told me," I said. "He told me what he dreams of."

She blinked in surprise, staring at me. "What?"

"A better world," I answered. "A better world for all of us. Better in ways I don't even really understand, but the way he described it, you could tell he wanted everyone to be safe and happy."

As we kept watching, Elian finished, giving his creations a light polish and a few quick once-overs, each and every one of them, whatever he was making, they were very small and thin. Some time passed, and he came to me holding two small threads, each with five or so of the objects dangling from it.

"What do you have, Son?" I asked, interested in what he'd come up with this time.

"Needles. Isha asked me for needles. I made Mom some too. I hope she likes them." He seemed perfectly pleased, looking at his creation.

They were thin, far thinner than was really reasonably doable with bone unless you had a lot of time and were very careful. "I'm sure she'll love them."

"What did little Isha pay you for them?" Elaya asked from beside me, looking over the product he'd made.

"Words and ideas," he said, laughing. As he turned to make his deliveries, he was still chuckling under his breath and added, "The most valuable things of all."

After he'd left, Elaya turned to me. "And he says weird crap like that all the time too. Not wrong, just not what you'd expect from a boy that age."

"Um," I agreed half-heartedly.

"Also, I'd like some of those needles if they work well."

"You'll have to discuss that with him, and it's *when*, not *if.*"

"No, not if, *when.*" On that note she turned and left me, shaking her head and mumbling under her breath.

CHAPTER 41

TOOLING UP

The needles were in fact a huge hit. They served as both a good tool and a show of display that someone could afford the work, which wasn't unsubstantial. I thanked my lucky stars that Isha had the good sense not to tell people what she'd had to pay for them, or I would be having to fend off far more unhappy women than I did anyway. It wasn't that I minded making them; it's just that there was a finite amount of time I cared to work, and more things I wanted to make.

For example, I'd had to make knives to pay back our helpers on the copper run, as well as one for myself. Father similarly requested several small hammers to work stone, and I had one more thing I wanted to make.

I was currently working on an auger. The build was simple enough—a bar, twisted with a point on one end and a loop on the other. This would allow me to make replicable, simple holes, a nice addition if I wanted to make bigger and better things.

"My cousin wants you to make her some beads, if you're willing," Isha said from where she was seated nearby. "I told her I would tell you."

"I am not making beads out of copper right now, not for her, and not even for my mother, who I will point out is quite unhappy about that situation," I responded without even looking up from my work.

"I figured something like that would be the answer, but like I said, I told her I would tell you. What are you making now? That looks weird." She pointed to the tool as it finally started to take shape.

"It makes holes if it works right, but I'm not sure it will. Might be other things we could do with the same shape." I really was unsure, as I'd never made one of these before. "Father was messing around with those earlier for some pieces, and I think this will help."

"Okay, that's a good idea actually. Could you create something that makes crafting those boxes you came up with a little better?" she asked innocently. Excellent.

"Like what?" I responded, finally looking at her.

"Well, one of the men in my hut was trying to make some boxes, but getting the cuts clean enough is hard. Maybe something for that?" My, my, what a wonderful idea. Paying her had been well worth it if she could keep bringing me ideas that weren't my own.

"That's a great idea, Isha. I don't suppose you might know how to do that?" I prodded hopefully.

"Hmm, no. Maybe you should ask him," she suggested, tapping her chin as she mulled it over.

"Oh, don't worry. I'll be sure to."

As a point of fact, that evening several of the men of the village got together with me and Father, and we all began discussing ideas.

"I would like a spear," said the massive hunter, Larus. "Just one, to see how it works."

For only a moment, Father looked taken aback by his friend's request, but then he began to smile. "Not happy with stone anymore, huh?"

"The knives are good, Eduan. I want to see if a spear would work too. Though, with how they bend a bit, I'm not sure," his friend answered with a grin.

"Someone told me that working wood might have some uses? Something someone might need?" I asked, prodding them to look for more tool ideas.

"Ah, been talking to little Isha again?" one of the men said with a grin any boy would know. "Yes, the stone chisels are good, but I'm having a hard time getting cuts as good as that first one you did. How did you do it? The copper or your light?"

"I used my light, but with tools we could get a really good fit. Where are you having problems?" I asked.

"The cuts just aren't clean enough, the edges ragged," he clarified.

"All right, maybe a copper chisel will cut better; we can try that. Other tools we haven't tried yet?"

"Something to cook with perhaps? Like one of your auntie's pots or something, though I don't see much point to it," one of the other men answered.

Part of my problem was that a lot of people didn't see anything wrong with what we had. They'd been using it for a long, long time at this point and didn't see any reason to change. After all, if it had been working for centuries, why change now?

"I'm concerned about bits of it coming off, but we'll try if Mother agrees to watch for any signs of a problem while people are eating from the new pots." I could still remember that people had told me to be careful of copper cups, but never why, and it was driving me nuts. I also remembered that copper pots were definitely a thing, at least for jams.

"String," one of the younger men said. "You haven't made any string. It's a weird one, but it is a tool. Can you even make copper string?" I could have kissed him for inventing wire before I did.

"Huh, suppose we can try. If it doesn't work out, it doesn't work out. I'll send some over to you if it does so you can try using it."

After our meeting, there were some complaints, but none of them really mattered. Father was the one who did most of the stone knapping for the town, and like any good father, he supported me. Others, though, were not so sure, and I got a feeling that the Luddite feeling was alive and well within the elven population.

The biggest part of that dilemma, though, seemed to be that we got way older and stayed young looking and vibrant. One old man who was an expert with a tool could do wonders with it because he was still in his prime and knew it like the back of his hand. He would, of course, not want to change to something new, and newer workers learned from him, or *her* in the case of my biggest complainer.

"The new needles are too small, the holes too close together. I don't like them," the woman said, only having approached when the men had left.

"Then don't use them," I said.

"The girls in my hut are already making clothes with them, even if they might not last the same. The seams could rip, and then the leather would be wasted. I don't want to waste leather," she continued.

"Then don't use them," I repeated, already done with this argument.

"I'm just trying to look after them," she huffed.

"Then convince them, not me." I knew she had zero chance at convincing them; the needles were a hit.

"But—" she began, only to be cut off.

"Enough," Father said, both calmly, and with finality. "If you do not like them, don't use them. If you don't want others to, then talk to them, not us. My son is right—a tool is a tool, and if it doesn't work, nobody will use it, but if it does, they will."

It was nearly a week before I got some time to sit and chat with Isha again. Between making things and hunting and fishing with the other boys, I was pushed hard. It wasn't bad, and I really did enjoy it, but it took a lot of my time. She, too, was busy, of course, with much the same kind of thing.

As soon as she came over, I noticed the changes. She'd made a new dress, and it was long since she wasn't anywhere near fully grown, but the seams were so different.

"New clothes, and I see you changed how you did the sewing," I said with some humor.

"I like the small stitches, and with the little holes from the small needles, they look good," she answered with a grin.

"One or two of the women complained about that," I said, trying to gauge her reaction.

"They complain about everything, and how we *do* everything. The clothes, the hair, even what decorations we like. I guess you did a lot of those too, huh? Maybe you should have been a girl," she teased.

"No thanks. At any rate, the hair?"

"Oh yeah, the older a woman is, the more she likes the older hairstyles and braids. Have you noticed how Elaya, and everyone in her hut, do their hair differently? It's because that's what she likes, and it's really, really old," she explained.

"Okay . . . so you girls do your hair and stuff based on how old you are?" I asked while I tried to sort through the styles in town.

"Not really, no, but based on what we like. If we've liked one thing for a long time, we don't want to change it, right? A lot of girls pick one style and keep with it, and it will be a lot like their friends' or family's hair. Your mom and auntie have basically the same style, and if you think about it, most of the young girls now all have similar styles, or ones you taught us," she explained, seemingly finding humor in my lack of understanding.

"Huh, I never noticed that," I said.

"Never mind. It's good you were born a boy if you don't even see that kind of thing," she teased.

"Good, Mother would never have let me leave the village to get copper if I'd been a girl," I said, teasing her right back.

"Oh, good point. Yeah, things are best this way."

We both understood. It wasn't that girls were really kept down, but they were decidedly not encouraged to go out on adventures like we boys were. Evolution, I supposed. Lose a few boys, and maybe the ones you get are stronger each generation. Lose a few girls each generation, though, and it would be hard to replenish with our abysmal birth rate.

"Yup, I really like going out like that."

"You know, you're getting pretty strong, and I'm not bad myself," she said slyly. "Maybe one day we can go do something like that together."

"Is that what you really want?" I asked, and at her nod, I made her an offer. "All right, one day when I'm strong enough, I'll take you on an adventure. If that's what you want."

I could only chuckle as she made a little cheer.

CHAPTER 42

TEENS

I watched as the last of my childhood friends left the village, spear in hand. Unlike those that had come before, Olond was armed with copper weapons. He would be the last of those I considered friends, and I was sad to see him go.

By my reckoning, I was now fifteen. Of course, elves didn't age quite the same as humans, so I only looked to be thirteen or fourteen, and it would be a few more years before I was ready to join the boys—now men—whom I'd called friends. Even Isha wasn't so little anymore, having grown into quite the talk of the village.

Of those who'd been boys when I arrived, only Rindal remained with me, and we were not on the best of terms.

"I can't believe I'm still stuck here with the little ones," he said venomously.

"Larus said that you were just growing slower; it's not a bad thing," I replied, tired of him already today.

"Everyone treats you like an adult already, even if you're clearly not one." The jealousy was clear, and frankly, it was tiring. He'd been like this for the past couple of years now. "Just because your light is so strong."

"Because I do things that are good for the village, nothing more, and you know it. I've offered to bring you on our copper trips several times now, but you don't want to go; and frankly, I'm not offering again. Small suggestion though. Before you become an adult, maybe grow up a little," I snapped. Part of it was my friends leaving me, part of it was just not wanting to be around him anymore.

In some ways, our village was slightly different than when I'd arrived. We now had metal and pottery, and tools that nobody had made or thought of before. Wire-work was beginning to catch on as well, for art-work and decoration. It came with new problems—we had a nearly rolling line of traders these days.

It had taken a year for another to come after I'd first introduced metal, but he had been shocked. The man had traded for every scrap he could get, and the next time he came, he didn't come alone. Goods we'd never even seen were brought in. We had shells and art from all over, spices for food brought in from far away, even salted and dried fish from the ocean, wherever that was. The tools and weapons we made were now considered the best of the best, and Elaya had been forced to set up a small post where trading was done.

New people had tried to join our village, only to be rebuffed by our elder. There had even been a few people trespassing on our hunting grounds, looking for anything they could. We still had our trading part-nership with the neighbors whose land had the copper, of course. They were getting a large quantity of both the raw metal and finished goods from me, along with the promise to their elder that I would share my knowledge when I came of age, and this kept relations quite friendly.

Elayatol was now a booming hub of industry—well, as much industry as a society just entering the copper age had. According to Earth's time-line, there had been only a short period where copper had been king, before bronze took the throne. Sadly, I had no idea where to get the tin I would need for that metal, so we'd be skipping ahead a step or two. When I got to it, we would have iron tools. Waiting seemed prudent for now, though, so people could get used to the first type of metal before bringing in another.

"How are you, Elian?" Dad asked when we got back to my shop.

"All right. I guess. It's just, it's strange, not being able to play with my friends anymore. I enjoyed it, you know?" I said.

"They didn't leave, Elian; they just changed. Everyone does."

"Yeah, but we had good times."

Honestly, I was having trouble with the younger boys now. There hadn't been any more for some time, and when there finally were, it just wasn't the same. They were all of a similar age, and so there was a sort of distance between us. Sure, I tried to teach them things, but there were so few connections there.

It was weird, being able to look back on those memories like they were almost literally happening again, but it wasn't the same. They were like a recording, beautifully done, but ultimately false. They lacked the emotion and happiness that came from current action. That time had passed, and there was nothing I could do about it.

It almost felt like a waste. I'd been given another childhood, and I'd spent a lot of it working. When I thought of it like that, I wanted to punch myself. How many people would give up limbs for the chance I'd had, and here I'd wasted so much of it. And for what? A few extra years of advancement? We were ageless. I could have spent that time having fun. I looked down at my workshop in near disgust.

"Elian?" Dad asked from nearby, reading my expression.

"I think tomorrow I'm going to go and play," I declared. "I should do more of that while I can."

Dad laughed and laughed.

I went to find Isha, since going out and playing alone seemed foolish. Most of my other friends would be busy at this point, but like Rindal, she wasn't quite considered an adult yet. Many of us would be there by eighteen, but as we got older our aging slowed—it was an odd thing—so some of us spent much longer as children. If Mother was to be believed, almost everyone was considered an adult by twenty-five, as that was the way of the world, but it was based on how you grew, not how many years you had. Elves cared less about the years when we lived for so long; rather, the physical maturity mattered more.

Isha was easy to find, as she'd taken up helping my aunt with her pottery. Those, too, were taking off as an industry, and since we were far more willing to share how to make them, they were now spreading like wildfire through the region. A lot of traders still came here, though, since we were the only ones glazing the pottery.

"Hey, Isha," I said as both women turned toward me. "I'm thinking of going out to one of the old caves tomorrow to explore. Wanna come?"

"Yes, yes, yes!" Isha answered, smiling.

Auntie Atie gave me a hard glare. "Does your mother know about this?" she asked.

"It's still in the valley, Auntie, and I won't be alone. With the two of us, there won't be anything to worry about." My mother had accepted a couple years back that I could wander a bit, but she still didn't want me going too far, or alone.

"Not alone," my aunt declared, pointing at us. She looked like she thought I might be up to something.

"That's okay. Cala, can come. She's from my hut, so nothing will happen. Not like I'd let Elian do anything naughty," she said, smiling at my aunt.

"I didn't even think of that," I answered honestly. Isha was still young in my eyes. Having lived two lives made dating a strange prospect for me. All the girls near my physical age were so young, it made me feel gross even considering it, and all of the older women had watched me grow up.

Isha, on the other hand, took my response rather poorly and tossed a bowl of dirty water at me. "Go clean yourself up," she commanded, "at least before tomorrow morning."

CHAPTER 43

RETURN TO THE CAVE

The four of us gathered in the morning and prepared to go. Yes, four. Of course, Cala had to bring her boyfriend along. I really should have thought of this possibility, being that her current suitor was Rindal.

The dating pool in a village our size was pretty limited, to the point that many young men would travel to other villages to find a wife. Almost everyone was directly related, sometimes on both sides, and with the fact that many places restricted who'd they allow to join, such things were sometimes a real difficulty for young men.

There were exceptions, of course. Those with magic, particularly elves with very strong abilities, were allowed to join almost anywhere. If I left the village today and sought to join another, I would have no big issues, save my age. I was still clearly too young to be considered an adult, but that was the only hangup.

Cala and Rindal were currently making eyes at each other while packing up the last of their things. We weren't bringing along all that much for this excursion—a few snacks, a couple of leather bottles of water, and our day-to-day items, like spears and knives. Between me and Isha, even an extended trip would be easy.

"So, where exactly are we going? The girls were a bit unclear," Rindal said when they'd finished up.

"You know the old cave we stayed in when the twilight beasts attacked? It goes deeper, but nobody knows what's down there," I explained, already tired of having to deal with him. "I plan to find out."

"Why?" he asked.

"Because I want to know. If you don't want to come, then don't."

"If he doesn't come, I don't come, and if I don't come, Isha can't go," Cala said defensively. It was clear she planned to take his side on any argument we had.

I was tired of these two already. "Fine, I want to go because there's something strange about it, and I'm curious. Who knows what we'll find down there. Maybe something valuable, maybe something interesting. I doubt it's too dangerous, but I plan to go slow."

"Okay, it's silly, but with all of us, there's no real danger right? Nothing has ever come out of there that's hurt anyone, and mysteries are cool," Isha offered.

I might be an elf, but I still found my people odd sometimes. They didn't mind exploiting new things, and when they found them, would sometimes obsess over them and work toward perfection, but they seemed to have almost no interest in exploration. I understood that new villages were sometimes built in empty areas of land, but not because people wanted to see what was there, but because they wanted to be free from their previous homes.

We began to walk briskly through the forest. The cave was a good ways away, but unlike other times I'd gone there, we didn't have anyone small or weak with us, and we were in a very small group, so we could cover the distance in good time. It still took a couple of hours, but we'd make it by noon with ease.

"Don't look so glum," Isha said to me about an hour in.

"I wanted to do this for fun, not deal with him," I responded. We'd walked ahead of Rindal and Cala, as they too wanted some privacy.

"And I'm sure he feels the same, but you're the one who decides if you're going to have fun or not, not anyone else." She poked me as she spoke, teasing a bit.

"Maybe, but still, the guy has never liked me, and I'm just done with him."

"Do you know why? Sometimes if you know why, you can make things right."

"As far as I can tell, it's simply the fact that I'm good at things and have a powerful light," I said, shrugging. I really couldn't think of anything other than jealousy.

"Maybe you'll find out on this trip. At least try to get along, please."

"Fine, fine."

Isha's hand took mine and we walked, her humming as the birds and small animals flitted by. There wasn't much to it, just a nice afternoon stroll through the woods, but it was nice, peaceful, and I had one of my few friends by my side.

"Mind if I ask what's so special about this cave anyway?" Isha said as we rested briefly by a small creek, Cala and Rindal not far away.

"You didn't see last time we were there, did you? No, that was before you got your light. I'll let it be a surprise then," I said, chuckling. We weren't far, at any rate, this creek being the same one that eventually fed the pool near the opening in question.

They all looked my way with a mixture of expressions. Rindal seemed unhappy, as always, while Cala and Isha were both quite curious. I picked up on a few more of those looks as we approached the maw that we'd come here to explore.

Someone, my guess was Elaya, had blocked the entrance again. It didn't do much to hide it, as the location stuck out like a sore thumb; it wouldn't even slow us down much. With a wave of my hand, the offending piece of stone pulled away and rolled off to the side.

"Show off," Rindal muttered.

"He's kind of right you know, you could have at least looked like you thought it was hard." Isha poked me in the arm. We both knew she'd struggle to do what I'd just done.

As I'd grown, so had my magic, by leaps and bounds. The fact that I was constantly using it seemed to help, as did a certain quantity of my knowledge about the world. The more I considered things, the easier things were, and I was slowly training myself to think of what I was doing in terms of physics. For instance, I wouldn't simply light a fire, I would cause an oxidation reaction in the carbon in a given piece of wood. I wasn't moving things; I was adding forces to them in a certain direction. It was odd, but it really helped.

"Come on, that wasn't big and flashy or anything, and we needed it moved," I replied, rolling my eyes. "There's another one inside we'll have to get once we get there. If you three want to move it instead . . ."

"No, since you seem determined to do this, you can," Isha said, scoffing playfully.

She and I both sent up small lights as we padded softly into the darkness. It was cool, and damp, but also oddly quiet as we made our way forward.

By the time we reached the boulder inside the cave, the small glowing plants that littered the walls were bright enough to light our way. The cave wasn't that deep—a few hundred feet at best—and we'd all been there when we'd evacuated the village, so there were no surprises.

Isha got a surprise when I moved the boulder, though, which was perfectly timed with a little bubble floating gently forward and popping against a wall, sending a wave of energy outward.

"What, what is that?" she asked, eyes going wide.

"I don't know," I said. "Isn't it exciting?" I couldn't hide my grin. This was sure to be fun.

CHAPTER 44

✧

ACROSS THE DARK SEA

The cave we were traveling down was normal enough at first, other than the few bubbles of magic floating up and popping every now and then. There really wasn't much to it. Caves after all, were beautiful, but only if properly lit and displayed, and this one wasn't. It was pretty, but nothing of note yet.

"So, it's a cave, with light coming from it?" Isha's friend asked as we continued downward.

"Yes," Isha explained. "I know you can't see it, but it's really quite pretty—bubbles every now and then, almost like Elian's light."

She was right; the magic was floating upward in bubbles. It was unexpected, something different from what I'd seen. Normally each person had their own sort of aura around them when they had or made magic. Mine happened to look like bubbles floating around me. Most of the time I sort of tuned them out.

"It's odd though, right? I can see them, and they look like they're glowing, but they don't illuminate anything," I said.

"Huh, I didn't notice that," Isha said, tapping her chin. "Suppose not."

While she chewed that over, we came to a crevice. I stopped to take some careful looks at the rock and how stable it was. I knew little about cave delving, but I did know that people got stuck and died a lot back on Earth, and I didn't want to add to that statistic.

"What are you doing?" asked Rindal.

"Making sure it's stable and I won't get stuck."

He scoffed and began to work his way into it, turning sideways as he slipped in. It didn't take long until he was out of sight of us.

"This is wonderful! Guys, you need to see this place!" he yelled from inside, voice echoing weirdly off the stones.

With a shrug we began to follow. The girls went first, then I followed, bringing up the rear. It was a squeeze, but other than one moment where my chest rubbed against the side, it went smoothly. The opening twisted and turned, and my bobbing light was barely enough at times to see where I was going, but I managed it.

When I made it through to the other side, the rest of the group was standing in stunned silence.

"It's huge," Cala muttered, looking up at the massive room in awe.

"And beautiful," her boyfriend added.

It was both of those things. The chamber was massive, easily a hundred foot tall with dripping stalactites all hanging over a massive underground lake. There was a bit of light from both Isha and myself, but we could have dropped them, as the massive amount of luminous growths from the walls cast the room in an eerie twilight.

While they were all looking up, I was looking down. I couldn't place what it was, but I was trying to sort through my memories as I looked at the hidden body of water.

"Very pretty, but it's so cold," Isha complained, still staring upward.

"Because we're underground." With a flex of will, the air heated around us by a solid ten degrees.

"What's that?" Rindal said, pointing at the water.

"Where?"

"There, something moved, fast."

I flicked and sent a ball of light forward and down into the depths. If there was something down there, we needed to know what it was. Magical beasts were a danger not even someone like me could ignore. It took a few seconds for my heart to stop pounding.

"Fish?" Cala asked.

"They look sick," Isha added.

"They aren't fleeing the light at all," Rindal pointed out.

"Blind, look at the eyes," I said. "Pale white, and no color to them. Probably not enough light for them to see anything down here. Wonder if they eat the mushrooms or something else." I'd seen photos and documentaries on them before, but never seen such things in person.

"I'm more worried about what eats them," Isha said, looking spooked.

"Maybe something, maybe nothing, hard to tell," I replied. On Earth it would have been easy. There was nowhere near enough room down here for a large predator, but by this point I knew magic liked to point and laugh at logic, particularly when it came to animals.

"You think this is where the weirdness is coming from?" Rindal asked.

"No," Isha and I answered in stereo.

"There's definitely a flow coming from over that way," I said, pointing to the far side of the lake.

"Should we . . . what, go in and swim?" Cala asked.

"No, look, there's a ledge," Rindal said. He and I pointed, used to having to find ways around obstructions in the woods.

Slowly, we crept along the small cliff, staying back from the shore and eyes on the sightless fish, watching for whatever else might be creeping along in the deep, dark waters. Here and there were spots where the ledge was too short, or fell away completely, but magic solved such obstructions with ease. I constructed glowing planes of force to form bridges.

"That what you're looking for?" Rindal asked, one hand pointing toward a far-off point of light.

I followed his hand, and it had to be. There was another shore, not too far off now. Everyone could see it, as the many magically active flora shone around it. The hole poured out magic, waves of it. It shone in the magical perception those like myself seemed to have, like a geyser spurting its presence to all.

"Are you sure we should be doing this?" Isha asked, her concerned voice alerting the others to the sheer quantity of power coming from the next tunnel.

"No, but I'm going anyway. I need to know, Isha. I need to know what's down here." I left out the part I was thinking, that surely this had to have something to do with why I was here. This much power, and this close to my birthplace, it had to mean something. I couldn't just walk away now, not when I was right here.

There was a snort before Rindal spoke. "At least you're telling the truth about it, let's go."

It only took a few more moments to arrive at the tunnel, and we began to head down, down, the path sloping sharply toward whatever the source was, whatever deep secret lay beneath the stones.

CHAPTER 45

NIGHTMARE

I do not know how long we went down, but the cave was mostly smooth. There were turns here and there, to be true, but it was always headed down. Sometimes there were things that looked almost like steps, and other times there were flat, slippery surfaces on which we had to walk.

The glowing plant life was omnipresent and was the only thing guiding our path, and it was getting brighter. Every step we took deeper into the cave, the magic got denser and denser, and it had been some time since I dropped the ball of light I'd been using to see; it was certainly no longer needed.

Hours seemed to pass, and eventually, Isha made us all a small meal. We sat in silence, each looking at the world around, trying to figure out what this was. Our eyes roved over the mosses and fungi, looking for a clue as to what we'd found. If anyone saw something that shed real light upon it, they didn't speak.

After trekking long and hard, the walls fell away into a room of prodigious size. The others stared as I fell to my knees trembling, fear overtaking me.

"Elian, Elian!" I felt someone shaking me and looked up, seeing Isha's terrified face. "Elian, are you okay?"

I was forcefully pulled back from the doorway, even as I turned back to look. "You're here, you're still here, right Isha?" I asked.

"Yeah, yeah I'm here, but you're hurting me."

That statement pulled me from my fugue state, and I looked down. One of my hands had gripped her arm, and was now white-knuckled as I squeezed hard. When I pulled it away, there were spots on her skin, my fingers bruising her without my intent.

"Isha, I'm so sorry," I said, pained that I'd hurt someone I cared for.

"I'm fine, what happened?" she asked, still concerned as I picked myself up.

"It was . . . a dream. I saw myself all alone in a place just like this for so long, so long without anyone. I couldn't leave, couldn't get help. It hurt so bad, Isha, and when it all ended, my body burned, burned with me in it." I lied partially, trying to tell her what I'd experienced, but unable to articulate it properly.

"Just now?" Cala asked, looking afraid.

"No, no, years ago. I remember it though. I was so scared. Seeing this just brought it all back in a rush." It hurt that I couldn't tell them the truth, but that would just be too much. Isha seemed to understand that there was more, but she wasn't the only one here.

"Pfft, so you had a bad dream years ago and seeing this scared you so bad you went and hurt Isha? Good grief, at least try not to be a coward. Look, I'll go first." Rindal pushed past, heading for the exit into the chamber.

"Rindal, I don't know if we should!" Cala reached out as he slipped past.

"It's fine. I'm fine, see?" He'd walked out a ways, slipping between vines that I recognized all too well and across the floor covered in swirls and fractal patterns well beyond my understanding.

A few moments later, the young elven man came back to us and took his girlfriend's hand, leading her in. To him it was a wonderland of pretty plants and light, whereas to me it was the site of my worst nightmare.

"Elian?" Isha said from nearby, rubbing her own wrist. She hummed a tune to heal the minor injury I'd caused her.

"We can't leave them there, but promise me you will be careful what you touch, and don't eat anything," I implored.

"You're normally not like this . . . Okay Elian, I'll be careful."

I took her hand, far more gently this time, and we walked in after the other couple. Quickly, I realized that this place wasn't quite the same, if for no other reason than the patterns were slightly different. My memory was really good, and my past trauma stood out brightly in this place, but these swirls and fractal markings were different than those I'd seen before, if only slightly.

"Look at how big it is!" Cala called out, her voice echoing on the far-away walls and ceiling.

She was right. The World Cup could be held here with plenty of room left over. That was another change from the place I'd found myself trapped, another I noted carefully. This room was far bigger than that little grove.

"The vines are beautiful," Isha said. "And what are these markings on the floor?"

"I don't know how they were made, but they're math," I answered without thinking.

"Math? Like one and one is two?" The elves had little in the way of math. They could count, but even basic geometry was still unknown to them, as well as concepts like zero as a discrete number.

"More complex than that, but like that yes."

"How do you know that?" she asked, looking at me like I was strange.

"It's a long story, Isha, and one I don't really want to share," I answered with a sad smile.

She kissed my cheek, causing me to pull back in surprise. "That's okay, Elian, but one day I hope you'll feel comfortable talking to me about it."

Before I could think of anything good to say to that, there was a short, high-pitched scream. Our eyes locked, and I turned to run to Cala. I could feel Isha hot on my heels as I sped over the vines, feet finding the spots between them with ease.

"What happened? Are you okay?" I shouted as I made my way to her and Rindal.

"I'm okay," Cala shouted from somewhere I couldn't see. "I climbed up on this hill and fell into it. Give me a moment. There's some kind of tree or something."

It took her a few seconds, but I could see the little mound shifting, and the plants covering one of several little hillocks in the area began to shift. A few seconds later she appeared, and we carefully pulled her out.

"It's hollow," she said, looking at the hole she'd made. "Weird!"

I began to shift the leaves and stems around to get a look into the weird trellis-like structure. "No, it's not a hill," I informed her.

"Then what is it?" Rindal asked, checking over his girlfriend a bit too thoroughly for any injuries.

"A skeleton."

I spent a few moments slowly unwinding some of the runners from it when Rindal got frustrated.

"Come on, just rip them away." He stepped forward to do just that, only to pull back and jump like he'd been burned.

"What happened?" I asked, suspecting the answer already.

"It was like, like it felt bad to damage them. Sorry, guess you weren't too weird for doing it your way."

I didn't have to get all of it cleaned off to begin developing some new concerns. One, it was big, really big, with massive claws and teeth, and structures that could only be wings, and swept back horns flowing from its head. I had a word for it, but I'd never heard of a beast like this among the elves here.

"Rindal, you ever seen something like this?" I asked.

"Four legs, wings, and big enough to eat a village? No, but I'd hate to fight one."

At my questioning look, the girls shook their heads.

"At least it's no longer alive, and if any of its fellows were here, I think we'd be dead by now," I said, hoping none were.

"This place is weird. Should we continue?" he asked, seeming spooked by the idea of running into one of these things, but trying to look tough.

I looked to the pool of water that shone in the center of what must be a crater, the crater that made our valley. It still sent chills up my spine just thinking about it.

"I know you're still spooked," Isha said with a soft smile. "Mom always says if you're afraid, you have to face your fears. Why don't we go to the little pool there, Elian? We'll see where this all came from, and then we can go home." Her hand gently urged me forward.

I could run, but if I ran, would I ever stop? Would I be able to get over this fear that gripped me at the very thought of this place? Maybe, but I could just face it now, face it with the power I'd gained because of it, and if it came time to fight, I would be ready.

"Let's do that."

We were much more somber as we moved inward to the small lake in the middle of this cavern, passing more of the same plants and more of the odd symbols on the ground. There were ripples that became rises here and there, but it didn't take that long to make it to the water.

The magic coming off of it was something else. It was almost like the water here was boiling, massive quantities of it pouring out of what could only be described as massive eggs. Dragon eggs? Here? Why? I had so many questions.

Isha pulled me off to the side so we could talk. "That's it, eggs for those things. We have to inform Elaya. If one of those hatches, it would be bad."

"But we can't break them either. Just look at the amount of power coming off that liquid. What if something went wrong, or their mother showed up? How long have these even been here?"

She nodded, but as we turned back toward the others, another scream sounded. This one was much deeper, and it didn't stop; it just went on and on and on.

CHAPTER 46

RETREAT

Rindal lay on the ground writhing, constant screams pouring from his mouth. Beside him was a small wet spot on the rocks, one that was quickly turning into pure magical energy. Cala was over him, her hands on his shoulders as she tried to help but had no idea how.

"What happened?" I asked as Isha and I made it to her side.

"I don't know," the distraught girl said over Rindal's screams. "He just went to take a drink! It's just water!"

From where I stood, I could see several things happening to Rindal in quick succession. The first was that his body seemed to be taking the infusion of magic poorly, very poorly. Black and blue veins glowed across his skin, starting from around his mouth and spreading quickly. He wasn't burning like I had back on Earth, but he might well still die, and all this from just the water here.

He was also gaining an aura around him, and in a hurry. Little red and black bolts of energy began to manifest in my own magical sight. While most auras I'd seen looked natural, like part of the creature, this one looked anything but, it gave off the very feeling of being wrong. Something about the way it moved around him shouted to the world that it wasn't natural, wasn't right.

"We need to get him to Mother, fast!" I yelled at the girls. "Isha, can you heal him?"

My hands were already moving, helping me shape the magic to lift him up from the ground and keep him in place. Isha began to sing, little bits of her magic flowing over the writhing young man. I didn't like Rindal, not at all, but I also didn't want him to suffer like this, or die. I'd been through that, and I wouldn't wish it upon anyone.

Our group sped back the way we came. The trip down had taken hours, but we'd gone at a sedate pace. Now we all but ran. All of us were in good shape—part of living like we did—and we could jog for hours if need be.

I didn't know how long it took, but Isha looked like she was flagging when we made it back to the underground sea. Her constant use of magic here was more than she could handle. I was still holding, as I used my light nearly constantly, but it wouldn't last forever. Even Cala looked like she was having problems keeping up, panting from the run.

We could have taken the same route back, but it would take time, time I didn't think we had with how fast the veins were spreading all over our companion's body. This was unexpected, and I didn't know how to deal with it. We needed aid.

Instead, I froze some of the water. Ice magic wasn't my forte, but I knew enough about how it worked for me to sort of force my way through it. The boat was crude, and the girls looked scared as I led us all in, but it would shorten the trip drastically. A bit of forward force was all we would need.

We were about halfway across when something slammed into the bottom of our boat, rocking it for a few moments before showing itself. One of the largest eels I'd ever seen popped out of the water. The beast was easily large enough to swallow one of the fish in this little lake it inhabited.

The poor monster had drastically misread the situation. Without hesitation Isha turned and screamed, disorienting it enough that my blade of force smacked into its throat cleanly. It sprayed blood as it fell back into the inky water. Within seconds there was a churning in the depths as something, or many somethings, descended upon the dying creature. I didn't know if it was the fish, which were now swarming around the area, or others like it, but I had no desire to learn. Instead, we sped to our escape, heading the way we'd come.

"What was that?" Cala asked, looking back at the water, the splashes and movements unceasing.

"Monsters," I answered dryly.

The crevice awaited us, and while most of us made it through with ease, one particular member of our party got stuck. He couldn't move himself in any meaningful way, though he wasn't screaming and shaking nearly as much as he had been.

"Well I hate to say I told you so," I grumbled as I carefully tried to slice away some of the floor to get him through; messing with the ceiling was a non-starter. It took time, time I didn't want to use, and magic I could hardly spare, but we needed to move him fast if we wanted to save him.

By the time we were halfway through the last corridor, Isha stopped singing.

"I can't," she said, rubbing her temples and looking pale.

"It's fine," Cala and I said in stereo, and I turned to pick up Rindal, dropping the makeshift magical stretcher I'd been using.

I was by no means the strongest of our people, but I had to start saving some of my own magic, or I'd run completely out too. Using my physical strength for this would have to do, so I wrapped him up in my arms and began to climb.

He was still groaning, and still trembling, and I saw his eyes flicker open briefly. They were glowing just like his aura, and now in the visible spectrum, small red lights were flickering within the black irises. I knew Cala had seen it, too, but she'd said nothing, just staring at him.

Finally, we reached the cave mouth, and I raised my hand, sending out the distress signal our tribe used. The bright light hovered over our location while we breathed for a moment, watching it fade before we continued on into the woods.

While Isha and I were flagging, Rindal's aura grew and grew, spreading out from him. His body was still looking horrid, the poison-like effects turning his blood vessels colors, bit by bit. Something was clearly happening to him.

I got two more emergency flares sent up before one of our hunting parties finally found us. They came running out of the woods at speed, looking panicked. Ninden's father, Niyen, was leading this particular group, his son not far behind, and both men's eyes went wide when they saw our injured companion.

"What happened?" Niyen asked as they began to make a proper stretcher, something I should have thought of.

"He drank something. Looked like water; lots of power in it," I wheezed, now quite tired. Adrenaline had kept me going, but now that help was here, I could feel my energy fading, leaving me spent.

Three men in the hunting group ran off with him, heading for the village, while the others stayed with us, leading us back. We were all drenched in sweat and tired, and it was late in the afternoon when we finally stumbled back into our village.

Cala wanted to go to Rindal's side. We all wanted to know how he was doing, but before we could do so, we were intercepted. A furious looking Elaya met us before we could make it far, hands snapping out. One latched onto my ear, while Isha's was snatched with the other. She turned to Cala and I could see the magic move as she, too, was grabbed by the ear, and we were all pulled behind her to her hut.

The others who lived with her scattered as we entered, seeming to sense that she wanted to talk to us alone.

"What have you children *done*? That cave was sealed for a *reason*!" she began.

"You knew?" I asked, surprised, standing back up as I was released.

"Of course I knew, you stupid boy. That's why I closed it off! We've lived there for decades. How could I not know?"

"Why didn't you tell us it was dangerous then? Why didn't anyone tell us?" I questioned, angry that such things had been hidden.

"I do not have to explain myself to you!" the older elf shouted back, her magic flaring as she reached up to my ear once more.

"Yes, you do," I replied with cold fury, slapping her hand away and letting my own power flow from me. I was tired, but I wasn't going to take this. "If we'd known what was there we might not be where we are now."

Elaya seemed taken aback that I would both push back and stand up to her like this. In the past, I'd let her do as she pleased, mostly because she tended to be right, but she wasn't this time. We both knew she was stronger, older, more experienced, and we both also knew that if we fought it would still be an ugly fight.

She hesitated, staring me down as she gauged my conviction, and that of little Isha, who seemed to also be frowning at her from my side. "Because, I don't want anyone going in there and dying; we'd lost enough. Young, curious boys tended to think they might make it, that they might get stronger by drinking that water. Other than us, maybe two others in the village know about it—older folks who saw some of what happened."

"Is Rindal going to be okay?" Cala finally asked weakly.

Elaya looked saddened by that question. "No, he's going to die. Perhaps not today, or even this year, but soon enough."

After everything that had happened, hearing this was too much for her. Cala fell down to her knees and wept.

CHAPTER 47

NEW MAN

Cala had been taken to rest and to sit with Rindal while Mother tried to do what she could for him. Once she was clear, though, the real fight began. Isha kindly stayed, waiting to see what would happen.

"Tell me what you know," I demanded, furious that I'd been to that cave several times and Elaya had still hidden this from me.

"I will, but you'll watch your tone with me, boy," Elaya responded. "You'll need to know, if only so you don't try and figure it out yourself. One death is enough." She seemed to consider her words carefully for a few moments before continuing. "Your mother had a brother, Jolin. Did you know that?" she finally asked.

"Sort of? She never speaks of him." The name was familiar. Mother had used it against Elaya once, a cudgel for some wrong she thought our elder had done.

"You're a lot like him," Elaya said. "Both of you liked to explore and learn as much as you could, both with such potential. He was the last one who drank from the pool, curious about it when he found it, much like you did. I found him not long after, already gone. Your mother was too young to hear the details, but she remembered—remembered that I'd returned with his body from the training I'd taken him on."

I knew Mother had been furious, and very unwilling to send me away with Elaya as a child, and now that piece fell into place. I didn't know the details and probably never would, but if someone's brother had been taken away only to come back dead, anyone would hesitate to allow another of their kin to go away with the same person.

"The water though," Isha said. "What is it?"

"Light, but too strong, and not in a way that people can use. I'm not sure why, but there are things like that in this world. They force the power into you, but . . . it's not natural growth; it destroys the body rather than strengthen it, like a disease," she explained.

"So Rindal will gain power?" I asked.

"Yes, of the same kind you and I have, but it will destroy him. The more he uses it, and the stronger it is, the more it will destroy him."

"You know a lot about this," Isha said quietly.

"I've been around a long time, and I've seen it here before, and other places too." At our questioning looks she shook her head. "You're both so young. Ancients sometimes fight, and when they do, they drag along everyone else. Atal has gone to war before, our elder of elders leading a host against others. I was very young then, but I saw the same kind of thing happen. Forbidden arts to concentrate light from beasts and plants into mixes for desperate soldiers to drink."

"What happens to them?" I asked. I wanted to know. If this was a danger on our world, then I wanted to be prepared.

"Everyone's light grows with time, little Elian. If Rindal had lived long enough, he would have gained power like any other, but those mixes, and that water forced it in." Elaya shook her head. "Those soldiers knew they would die, but they wanted to save others, so they accepted it—a sacrifice to protect their loved ones. They got strong—very strong—but within five years, all perished. That is what will happen to Rindal—getting stronger, but dying as a result."

"If it's a poison, we can draw it out; I know Mother can do that much. Maybe some way to drain away the power before it corrupts him . . ." I began to think of ways to maybe do something.

"The damage is already done, Elian. If he consents, you can try other ways, but many have tried. The best thing for him would be to never use it, but you and I both know what he will do with that strength."

"Rindal has always wanted to have a light. If you tell him not to use it now, he'll rebel and probably use it more," Isha said.

"Yes, and he'll need to be made safe, which he'll hate. It may be even more dangerous to train him, dying as he is," Elaya answered. "Dying men are unpredictable."

I sat beside Isha, wrapping an arm around her. It was clear that she felt as horrible about this as I did.

"I'll help you seal the cave. If and when the time comes," I told our elder.

* * *

Later that day we went to see Rindal, my mother having returned and told us that he was awake.

"How are you?" I asked my fellow villager, motioning him to stay on the small mat where he lay.

"Feel like I fell off a cliff. That water packs a nasty punch. Suppose I might have made a mistake on that one," he admitted. "But look at you two. Is this the light you were talking about? It's beautiful."

He poked at my aura, his own angry energy pushing it away as he did so. In a moment of thought, he turned his hand and a small ball of light appeared there.

"Hey Rindal, maybe hold off on using it until Elaya gets a chance to talk to you," I said, trying to smile. "There's a lot going on, and it might not be good for you at the moment."

"Pfft, it feels . . . good, like it wants to be used. I get it now, get why you use it all the time. It's amazing, like your body is warm and strong." I wanted to sigh, but it was clear that soon Rindal would be using magic as much as he could. A part of me felt terrible about it, but another just didn't care; it wasn't like I liked him.

"Still, I'm sure Mom will come by and help when she can, but you should listen to Elaya; she knows more than she lets on," I pressed.

"Maybe, but honestly, people just obey her because she's so strong. Well, others can be strong too. We can tell the others about the water, and maybe to drink a bit less. Think that's how she got so powerful?" He tried to rise now, a smirk on his face.

"Rindal, that water makes you sick," Isha said, reaching out, only to have him pull away.

"Isha, I've never felt better." He rose, and I could see where he was supporting himself with his magic. It was sloppy and inefficient, and he was using a ton of it.

I held Isha and let him go. We needed Elaya to tell him the truth of the matter. Even if I wanted to help, he didn't trust me, and pushing now would only cause more damage. If we were lucky, we might be able to extend his life for a few more years, but if we weren't . . . I supposed he'd burn hot and fast, and leave nothing behind.

Over the next few days, several of the older members of the village tried to rein Rindal in, but to little avail. Larus had the best luck, as pretty much everyone respected him, but even that was limited. Rindal either didn't believe that using his magic was killing him, or didn't care.

I was worried because he worked his magic more and more. He was sloppy, but he was throwing around massive amounts of power, more than I had. The few lessons he attended with Elaya didn't seem to help much, and he outright refused to leave the village with her for training. That was unusual, as was the fact that she let it happen; normally she was quite set in her ways.

I sat back outside my shop one afternoon, watching him juggle rocks in the air before a cheering Cala.

"It won't be long," Elaya said, coming to my side. "And I told him as much. This isn't your fault."

"Doesn't he feel it?" I asked.

"Some poisons feel good before they kill you," she answered.

"Will he know when it is coming?" I questioned, turning to her.

"I don't know." Her answer was hardly comforting.

✧

CHAPTER 48

CRACKS ON THE SURFACE

I was with some of the younger boys, showing them the basics of trapping. We didn't do this every day, but as their senior, it was part of my duties to lead them as best I could. Sadly, they were all too young for me to speak to properly, all too fresh to the world and all of its wonders. As they ran off again, my mother came to my side.

"They're so small, she said. "I remember when you were that small."

"I don't know," I said. "I think I've gotten bigger. And I'll get bigger yet." It was the truth; I was in my growth phase, but based on the pains in my bones I was nowhere near done. I still stood almost as tall as my mother, even now.

"You're nearly ready to become a man though," she said, sounding sad.

"Don't worry," I said, hugging her close. "You'll always be my mother, no matter how big I get. I'd wager you came here for something else though."

"Hmm, Elaya told me about what happened with you kids."

"Yes." I didn't try to hide the fact that I was unhappy about not being told about the cave ahead of time, and I knew Mother had been withdrawn recently.

"As soon as either your father or I are old enough, we're leaving," she said with hard finality. "I don't know if you'll join us or not, or if you want little Isha to come, but we should have those conversations soon. We also need to be prepared."

"Prepared for what?" I asked.

"If you come with us, our whole family will be leaving. Larus is so close to your father, he's likely to come with us, and if little Isha does too, that will leave Elaya as the only one in the village with any light. She might try to stop us."

"Do you think Isha would come?" I asked, concerned.

My mother blinked at me for several seconds. "My, my, how could I have ever raised such a dense boy?"

I had to take a few moments to go over all of the more recent months. She wasn't like Cala with Rindal, or like the girls Ninden or some of the others were always with. She didn't hang off my arm, or come and lay against me at night, but I had to admit, she did always seem to want to spend her extra time around me. Perhaps I was being slow on the pick-up. It was something I would need to consider.

Then again, there was also the real concern of a fight between our side and Elaya's. Realistically, she couldn't do much about my parents, particularly once one of them started to grow white hair. At that point, it would be expected for them to go off and form their own little village, and as a couple they weren't supposed to split. I, of course, as their child would be going with them; that too was expected.

She could, however, raise a stink over Larus and Isha coming with us. That would leave the village without any healing, and with only her as a heavy hitter in case of monster attack. That could be a death sentence to a village like ours; monsters weren't common, but it only took one.

"Do you think it'll get violent?" I asked my mother. "With Elaya, I mean."

"Hard to say, and hard to say where people's loyalties will fall if it does. Larus will at least stay out of it, to protect the villagers that survive. Elaya is stronger than either your father or I individually, but together we'd win. And you with us, it wouldn't be much of a contest unless she gets support from another."

"Like Rindal," I said.

"Yes. You've seen him around more than I have. What do you think?"

"He's strong, stronger than me in raw power, but he lacks control. If a fight breaks out, he'll side against us, no question about it," I answered with a frown, unhappy that it was true.

The young man in question was nearby, entertaining some of the younger boys with small light displays. As always, Cala was nearby, clapping and cheering. Frankly, I had no idea how she was getting her own work done.

"Talk to Isha, see what she thinks," Mother finally said before patting me on the back and leaving.

It wasn't until later in the day that I had a chance to speak with Isha. On our way back from gathering I moved to her side, letting a lot of the others in the group pull back. I turned my hand up and let a bit of magic flow out into a globe around us, focusing on trying to mute sounds. It wasn't something I'd practiced much, so I wasn't great at it, but I was good enough.

"Mind if we have a chat?" I asked nervously.

She gave me a playful smile. "About what?"

"Mother thinks we'll be leaving the village soon, as soon as she reasonably can. Both her and Dad are kind of close to becoming elders, so in the next few years . . . That doesn't matter though. When we do, do you want to come with us?" I sputtered, unsure of how to address this. "She wanted me to talk to you about it."

Isha studied me, her eyes clicking across my face several times. "That depends. Are you proposing something more serious between us?"

I knew she was still too young. Even if elves stayed young forever, she was still many years my junior when it came to age, including my Earth years. Some gap, even a large gap, wasn't that odd among our people, but it didn't feel right to even consider her like that. She was, for the time being, still only my friend, and that must have shown on my face.

"Isha, you're one of my few friends, but . . ."

There was palpable disappointment. The air between us spoke of the test she'd put forward, and how she felt I'd failed. I couldn't explain things to her, to anyone really, and if I could, I felt she'd understand, but for now it was as it was.

"You are still such a child sometimes, Elian," was all she said before turning away, singing a note and dispelling the bubble of silence around me.

The rest of my day was not great. As a matter of fact, most of the next week was quite bad. I did a little work around my shop, but I just felt so separated, so apart from the people around me. A secret was a horrible thing sometimes, and trying to keep this one may well have cost me greatly. The younger boys were now radiating around Rindal, who was showing them more and more magic that others of the village were far more restrained about using.

I ended up working with my aunt at the end of the week. Auntie Atie was a good advisor for some things, not too close to feel weird about consulting with her. She had a few new glazes she was working on, and my aid at getting things hot enough was a big help to her. One day we were going to have to build her a better kiln; her current kiln was still a bit primitive.

"Any advice?" I asked.

"Time, Elian," she said. "Figure out where things are, and where they will go, and take your time. Now, can you do this one?" She handed me a new piece, a rather strangely shaped bowl that someone had requested, though I didn't know why.

She wasn't wrong, and though she was still obsessed with making the best pieces of pottery she could, spending time around someone else did seem to help. The fact that my aunt actually liked me was relaxing, even if she could read my face like a book.

CHAPTER 49

THINGS FALL APART

I crawled out of my workshop late in the morning, all the gatherers having left for the day. I'd been asked to come along today but had been in the middle of a casting when asked. Being a little late was okay, and it wasn't like they were going to be far from the village.

It was a short jog to the spot today, one of the better areas for berries that bloomed just before the rainy season began. The clouds gathered, but it wasn't raining yet. The clouds were shading the whole valley in a deep coolness, a welcome respite from the usual tropical climate.

"You're late," Isha said, acknowledging my presence as I loped into the clearing.

"I was busy. Where are the boys?" I asked, my own quick glance at the field showing that none were around.

"Hunting," she said without looking up.

Something felt off, but I couldn't place it. It was like the air was just wrong, like an item in the house was out of place, but you couldn't figure out which one. I looked at each group of gatherers closely, examining for the issue. It took me several tries, my eyes circling the field before I stumbled upon it.

"Where's Cala?" I asked.

"What? Gathering. Where else would she be?" one of the women replied, her eyes rising to look at the groups of girls. It was clear that one was missing.

"Where's Cala?" both Isha and I asked some of the other girls.

"Um? She's been around Rindal a lot recently, going off into the woods and . . ." one of the older girls said, not finishing her sentence. Teenagers were teenagers, but with so many gone, it raised the hairs on the back of my neck.

"What about Elaya?" I inquired, since she too seemed to be missing from the clearing today.

"Back at the village, working," the same girl said.

"Isha, can you call the hunters?" I asked. "And send them to the cave."

She was already forming the flare spell she would need, and said nothing more until I turned to leave.

"Where are you going? They're hours ahead," she said as I made my way to the tree line.

"I'm faster on my own."

Of all the magic I did best, walls and movements of force were my best. It and fire had been some of my earliest experiments, and putting a push into something was hilariously easy for me. It was weird trying to do it to my own body, and decidedly dangerous. I wasn't supernaturally touched, nor did I have insane reflexes, but I could push myself, so I did.

Every time there was a straightaway in the dense jungle, every time I could get a clean shot, I rocketed forward, magic pulsing to throw myself ahead as fast as I dared. Flight was still a far leap for me, but I could do this much, steering and catapulting between the trees.

As a child, this trip had taken many hours. Even not so long ago with only a few others it had still taken the better part of the morning. I was fresh now, and alone. There was no need for me to worry about pacing myself to anyone else. It felt magnificent as the wind blew in my hair, and my magic flowed around me, and in under an hour, I was approaching the cave once more.

I found them there, Rindal standing before the sealed rock with swirling power around him, Cala and the young boys standing well back. Elaya had called in both myself and Mother days ago to block off the potential danger in the cave, and it was now nearly seamless—molten rock and thick growths blocking what used to be the entrance to the underground world.

"What are you doing?" I yelled, moving into the little clearing near the pond.

"Ah, Elian, you're here," Rindal said, turning. "So, you gonna help? Or are you trying to stop me?"

The other boys looked concerned as the two of us stared each other down. "You haven't answered my question," I said, locking eyes with the young rebel.

"Isn't it obvious? I'm making sure our little brothers grow up strong. This power—it's theirs, ours, all of ours. With it, our village can finally be safe from the beasts, and we can become great. Nobody will oppose us once we all have the power." His eyes sparkled as he spoke, but there was a hard undertone to it.

"That power is death, Rindal," I said, moving forward slowly. "You know this."

"Lies," he yelled. "Elaya just wants to keep us from opposing her. You know how she is, Elian, how she does what she wants and makes us all bend to her will. We don't have to, none of us do, and if we were all strong, we could."

"You almost died, or don't you remember?" I asked, trying to push some reason into his head.

"You're right, and that's why we'll be more careful this time. Just a sip at first, just a bit. Now, are you going to help, or not?"

"No, the hunters are already on their way, Rindal," I explained, angling so that if and when magic started flying, the younger kids would be out of the crossfire. "It's time to stop."

"You just want it all for yourself," Cala interjected, angrily shutting my attempt at peace down. "You're just jealous that he's gotten so strong, that we could all be so strong." The kids were all listening to her words, too, unsure of what to do.

"That's how it is, huh?" Rindal said. "Well then, I'll just have to beat you, and then get them their power before the men arrive."

His angry aura flared up, and we both started to move. Rindal let loose a blast, like the one he'd been using to rip away the rocks, only for me to pull myself out of the way, the wind roaring as it flew by, lashing and shattering the ground behind me.

I had other concerns—the kids. Children were a blessing to elves, and protecting them was always a priority. They were so rare, so vital to keeping our village going that they mattered too much to keep near a fight.

I formed a box of force around my opponent and hurled him, trying to get him as far as possible from this place, from the innocents he might hurt. It snapped into reality with little more than a flex of will and flew back, crashing through trees into the forest beyond, me in hot pursuit.

Once we had some room, I stopped the cage in the air. "Rindal, just stop, it doesn't have to be this way," I pleaded.

"No, no, it does. Goodbye, Elian." He threw back his hands, and my cage exploded, a quick shield being the only thing that stopped the wave of power from pulping me then and there.

Rindal stood there, in the air, and the amount of energy he was emanating whipped and tore at the trees, peeling bark and snatching leaves from branches, rendering them into little more than bits of confetti.

The last thing I could do before we began battling was send up the emergency flare. Who knew if any of the hunters who saw it would be able to help, but I had to try. As I looked at him and he at me, I could feel it—this would be a battle that would decide the fate of our home. Either it would continue to grow and prosper, or it would fall to tyrannical power and the desire for more and more.

CHAPTER 50

WOODS BATTLE

I pulled myself to the far right as a wave of energy slammed into the ground destroying the vegetation and leaving an indent where the plants were once rooted. The power seethed and buckled, spreading like water over the dirt as it flowed, missing me by inches.

I didn't have time to worry about the others, for now I had to fight. I shot forth twin lances with fire so hot that it turned the very air into plasma—brilliant streaks pulsing across the sky. If they landed, they would be fatal, sure as anything, but Rindal intercepted them with another wave of power.

We circled like two predators, each looking for an opening in the other's defenses. He had height on me, and raw strength, but he was sloppy, a like a giant swinging a club at a wasp. Either could kill the other, if only we could connect.

I also had the double-edged sword of time on my side. Backup was coming to aid me, but it remained to be seen if they would be fodder or something to turn the tide. If I could wait him out long enough, I might win by default. Perhaps one of the hunters could even make him see reason.

Rindal, on the other hand, had his own plan. He wanted me dead. I had to admit that as far as simple, achievable plans, this one was pretty damn good. Who knew how it would go for him if he managed it, but he really might.

Another dodge and a bolt from Rindal shattered a tree as wide as I was tall, the ancient giant beginning to tumble down. It took little effort from me to alter its path, sending it careening toward the young man who'd felled it, hoping to slow him.

Rindal barely even blinked at the tree, turning it into splinters that he sent in my direction like a wind of needles. The tree creaked and screamed as it was ripped and imparted with direction, an angry gale of death.

"Stand still, coward!" he screamed as I took cover behind another tree, adding a weak shield to keep any excess debris from tearing me apart.

"No, I don't think I will," I replied before launching myself upward, a mix of magic and quick hands pulling me from the ground.

It wasn't a moment too soon, either, as his next attack obliterated the trunk of the tree I'd been hiding behind. I moved as fast as I could, seeming to flow up the wooden growth like water. He was strong, but he wasn't thinking clearly, and I could use that to my advantage.

"Ha! Got him!" he declared a moment before I sprang out onto a still-moving branch, more bolts of burning heat shooting out from my hands.

I fired a half-dozen in the span of a second, several dissolving against his protections, two missing, as he finally had to dodge or take the shot. One grazed the side of his face, leaving a scalding line deep in his cheek.

He dropped his offense entirely for a moment, and a plan began to form in my mind. I threw out more and more of the bolts, most of lesser power. I let some bounce off his shielding, while others began to land in the vegetation all around us. As I did, I ran, trying to pull myself far from the limb I was standing on. After all, soon it, too, would meet the ground.

He began to get lower to the ground, too much of his power being focused on protection, while I rose. Maybe I couldn't fly, but I could leap from tree to tree, minimizing my use of power while setting everything around us ablaze.

Fire was my strongest ally. Day in and out, I practiced with it, I knew it, and I could wield it with the lightest touch or the fiercest edge. Perhaps I could not match his might, but I would use my weapon to its highest potential, pulling it and encouraging it as it flowed around me.

With practiced ease, I drew away the moisture, fanning the heat higher and higher. The fire responded like an old friend, leaping upward as my enemy fell. He began to cough and sputter as he got lower and lower, and then I heard a roar.

Rindal released a wave of wind, managing to call it not through knowledge but through will alone. It was a mistake, as it just fanned the flames higher.

"I'm going to kill you," he screamed. "I'm going to kill you and that little bitch of yours!" The sound resonated through me, and for the first time since this fight began, I felt something.

"Burn," I declared, letting my fire resonate.

The heat leapt forward, surrounding him in the inferno. A ball of burning fire pulled itself around him, the wind keeping the flames from touching him, but it kept them growing. Bit by bit, the sphere of flame grew.

"No more!" I yelled. With a wave, my orb shattered, showering the forest in embers and heat.

Rindal stood there in the middle of the forest, a small circle of ice around him. My own shields had barely held, and the forest surrounding us was now aflame. I was breathing hard, trying to think of where to go now.

My opponent looked horrible, stumbling from magic use, with black veins now covering his skin. While he'd managed to push my spell back, he looked like he would fall any second. His eyes turned toward me, flashing like his aura, which was sputtering now.

"You, what did . . ."

I didn't let him finish. He'd threatened those I cared about and had nothing to say that I cared to hear. With a swipe, I sent a blade of pure force forward, right at his throat. There was a short gasp, and a spray of red, and then he fell, the useless lump from atop his shoulders falling to the side as his body spurted more blood, staining the little ice circle crimson.

The branch I was on began to waver underneath me, and my legs gave way, my body spent. I tried to slow myself as I fell, only to feel warm hands snatch me from the air, catching me before the darkness could take me.

The last thing I could see were the gathering hunters. Larus had caught me, while Father looked around in shock at the destruction. Knowing that they could take charge now, I let myself fall asleep.

When I returned to the waking world, I was not alone. There were many, many people gathered around, all of them looked afraid and alarmed, and it was clear to see why. Though darkness had fallen in the distance, there was red light. There was billowing smoke from what had to be a forest fire. Elaya was gone, as was my father.

Nearby, Isha had a group around her, sweat pouring down her face as she sang, creating water which she sprayed all around the village. I tried to rise to go to her side but found that I was still weak, tired from the battle.

I could see Cala off to the side and noticed that she wasn't alone. All around her were unhappy looking men and women, keeping her from moving. The children were also separated, getting a mighty talking to by one of their fathers.

When it was noticed that I'd stirred, I was joined by several of the hunters, notably those not associated with either my family or Larus.

"Stay where you are, and do nothing. Elaya has questions, but for now you are to remain in place," one of them said, visibly nervous.

He knew I was strong; they all did. They also knew that without another potent person here to stop me, there really wasn't much they could do if I decided to just go crazy. I settled back to lie down and nodded. I, too, had questions, ones that needed answered.

CHAPTER 51

JUDGEMENT

The forest is on fire." Those were Elaya's first words to me when she returned. "A full quarter of the hunting and gathering areas are burning. Larus and your father are desperately trying to do what they can to slow or stop the spread, but there is little to do, because the forest, is, on, fire."

"Do you wish me to help?" I asked, not sure what else to offer.

"I wish you to explain why in the world you two were so determined to kill each other that you released such wanton destruction on our home!" she screamed.

"He was trying to take the boys and Cala to the pool, to get them to drink," I said as calmly as I could.

"And you didn't wait for help? You didn't think that I, or one of the others, would have done something?"

"You weren't there, and I did call for help. I didn't think there would be enough time, and there nearly wasn't."

She sat down. "I like you, boy, more than I like most, but this . . . We will gather in the morning, and we will decide what is to be done."

I spent the night alone, save a few guards she'd assigned. Under the stars and moon I meditated, waiting, hoping that all would be well, but fearing it might not. Ideas and theories ran through my mind, things I could've done, but didn't. I'd been in the right, and I knew it. There was no other answer.

As the sun rose, many of the adults in our little tribe moved to the center of the village. I looked around at them, counting the faces of friends and family one by one; it was hard to read some of their faces. My mother looked ready to slaughter everyone present at the drop of a pin; whereas Father held her tight, trying to rein in her fury. Larus looked sad and worried. My old friend Ninden locked eyes with me, along with some of the other boys, and nodded in support. Auntie Atie looked worried, as did Isha, who was standing beside her. Elaya just looked old, and tired.

There would be a trial here, and Elaya would decide our fate, weighing the odds against the needs and desires of the rest of the group. Too extreme a judgment would lead to riot and combat; too light of one would lead to our group splitting, something it was already in the process of doing.

"I have spoken to both of you already, but now you will tell all what happened," the elder declared. "Cala, you will begin."

"He came from nowhere. Rindal was just trying to lead us over to the old cave on a trip, and Elian ran from the woods screaming and slinging spells. We all know how they've hated each other forever, and he killed Rindal, murdered him in cold blood. Rindal tried to protect me and the boys, but Elian wouldn't have it, and they ran off into the woods to fight. That's where he killed him," the girl spat out angrily, pointing and gesticulating the whole time.

"Elian, what do you say to this?" Elaya asked.

"When it became clear that Rindal had left with the boys and Cala, I suspected where they might go. I got Isha to send up an emergency flare to alert everyone to try and make him stop, but didn't have time and chased myself. I tried to talk him down, tried to convince him to stop, but he wouldn't. We fought, he died." My story was short and to the point, easy to tell, because it was true.

"Isha, did he do so?" the elder inquired, responding with a nod when the girl answered in the affirmative.

The other boys were called forth, each one in turn interviewed. Most of them supported my version of events, stating that I'd tried to talk, tried to get Rindal to stand down. A few, though, clearly fell on the side of the now dead boy, saying how he had been trying to help them before his death, how it was clearly me who was in the wrong.

Elaya said almost nothing, letting each of us have our turn. She sat back, watching, listening to the proceedings. Once or twice she asked for clarification, but little more than that. When all had spoken, only then did she raise her voice again.

"Elian, I would have the truth of this. Who released the fire?"

I could lie. Rindal was dead and nobody else was around to confirm or deny my story. That said, nobody would believe it. I used fire, and I used it well, everyone knew this. Was this a test? I wasn't sure, but regardless, I made my decision.

"I did," I answered to a chorus of gasps and intakes of breath.

"Such destruction and danger cannot be ignored. I appreciate that you did what you thought right, and that you meant no evil, but a punishment must be given." From the corner of my eye I saw my father physically holding my mother in place. She looked like she was ready to foam at the mouth.

"You are banished," Elaya declared. I heard Cala make a noise of victory under her breath. "You shall not again return to this valley so long as I am elder here. Neither of you."

"Neither of you?" Cala asked, seemingly confused, but I understood.

"Did you think you would not be punished? You were told the danger of that place. You were told that it would kill, and you still took so many of the children there to die by their own hands. You too, Cala, are banished, not to return." Her eyes fell back between the two of us. "Due to the fact that Elian has his light, and his abilities, he will leave with the sunrise. Though I shall show some mercy to young Cala. She will have a full phase of the moon to make arrangements. Do any object?"

"You'd better believe I object," Mother shouted, teeth bared.

"Stop," I said to her, since it looked like she might well leap at Elaya, and I'd seen how deadly her magic could be. "We will talk."

That mollified her somewhat, but she saw my face and acquiesced. I did not envy Elaya, for once I was gone, she'd have one very angry opposing force to deal with. None others spoke, though, keeping to themselves. Even if they weren't pleased with how things had gone, they'd said nothing. I could tell that Cala's family was furious that their child was being forced away.

When the trial was over, a few guards each followed Cala and myself. I headed to my workshop, as I had so much to do and so little time to do it in. My family followed me.

"That whore, I'll rip her face off, I'll—"

"Enough, Mother," I said. "I know you're angry, but fighting her like this doesn't help us." I turned and addressed the two guards. "You two, give us some privacy."

"We were told to—" one of them began.

"I have already been banished. I assure you that Elaya can do no worse to me if I break your legs and throw you across the village. Also, consider the chances of someone healing you if I do." I really wasn't in the mood to hear it.

The guards shared a concerned look, and then they backed off. There was the choice they wanted to make, but there was also the smart choice. I was rather happy they'd made the smart choice.

"Elian, we can break off to form a new village now," Father offered.

"No, nobody will respect a village without an elder, and with all the turmoil, you won't know who will side with whom. I know you will, and when you do, I want you to send for me, but for now I'll go. I've kind of wanted to see Atal anyway. It will be better for all of us, I think." I gave my mother a hug, and she just watched me with big eyes.

"We can . . ." she tried again, only for me to shake my head.

"I love you Mom, but this is for the best. One day I'll return here, but not now. Right now I need to get some of my tools and things put together. I've got a long trip."

"I'll get your things from the hut, and food. You'll need food." There were tears in her eyes as she turned to leave, and I knew she'd pick the right things.

My father and I began going through my many, many tools. I'd not gotten around to reinventing proper wheels yet, so most of what I was taking would be in a litter on my back. Weight and size were a concern, as were things that I would absolutely need, versus those that I just wanted. It saddened me to leave so much behind, but I knew that others could use them for themselves.

In the afternoon, Isha showed up, looking rather conflicted.

"You're actually leaving?' she asked.

"I think it's for the best. Isha, there's a lot of things I couldn't tell you, and still can't, but I want you to know that I care about you." I gave her a kiss on the cheek, the closest thing I'd ever done with her.

"Where to?"

"Atal. I told my parents to send for me when one of them becomes an elder and makes their own village, and I'd be happy if you joined us then," I told her honestly.

"Will you tell me the things you can't now if I do?" she asked, eyes questioning.

"Everything," I answered without thinking.

"Everything?" she asked again, unbelieving.

"Yes, everything," I said, this time with more conviction. I wasn't sure how she'd respond, but if I met her again, I owed her at least the truth.

"I brought you this," she said after we both contemplated in silence. She held out a small sack, the end tied off tightly. "Honey, for your trip."

"Thank you," I answered awkwardly. "Anything out of the shop you want?" I was leaving, and Dad was getting most of my tools, but it seemed right to ask.

Now was her turn to be off kilter. She looked about for a moment before finally pointing to one of the many copper knives that I'd considered taking with me. It was not quite the right size for me but seemed just perfect for her—a simple blade with an intricately carved handle. I passed it over, along with a small leather sheath.

"Be careful," Isha urged, giving me a light hug. "Are you sure you're okay?"

"Don't worry, when you meet me next, I'll be even cooler than I am now," I answered, patting her back.

I ate dinner with my family, and we talked and enjoyed our night. A few more visitors came to see us, but not many. There was a plan in motion already, and I was now ready for it.

CHAPTER 52

TRIAL

I awoke well before dawn, and I was not alone. My whole family was there, all of us ready for the coming day. Things were checked and rechecked; everything needed to be right, needed to be ready for my travels.

Mother and Auntie Atie sat behind me, each braiding my hair, putting bead after bead into it. It wasn't lost on me that the ones they were using were the best we had. Normally, we held back on what wealth we'd share, but it seemed if I was going to leave the village, I was going to go with a fortune on my head. Copper cast trinkets joined colored ones of every variety that my aunt knew how to make, most hidden in the layers between so that nobody would know just what I had, a few cheaper ones on the outside.

As the sky began to lighten, my father picked up the rolled bag, and we all rose. The goodbyes were long and tearful, but there was a limit on time, one that approached by the minute. Eventually, I was released from hugs and was told to be safe, as we walked out of the home we shared.

Elaya met us at the exit to the village, and she was not alone.

"I do not hate you, Elian, but this must be," she said.

"I don't particularly like you, Elaya, and I know," I responded.

"If you return, it will be to a fight, one that will only end when one of us falls," she warned.

"Don't worry, Elaya. I don't intend such a thing."

"Good luck."

"And you." And with that, I left.

Father was coming along, too, and had even produced a nice spear for me, one from his shop. He'd added a few decorations to his workshop while I'd not been looking. It occurred to me that he might have been up all night working on it, and I could only smile in thanks.

As we passed through the valley, I saw the destruction the battle between Rindal and me had wrought. Soon the rains would come again and the land would heal, but for now there were still small plumes of smoke. Entire sections of forest were gone, hunting grounds destroyed. Now it was clear why Elaya decided I had to go, and I couldn't truly blame her for it.

I stood at the lip of the valley, prepared to keep going, as I looked out over what had happened. It saddened me, but one day I might make it better; one day I might get to sit with my family once more in our home.

As I contemplated, several shapes flitted out of the woods. Larus was there, as was Ninden. So were a few men I didn't know too well but soon realized were the fathers of the boys who'd supported me. All wore half-cocked grins.

"Something happening?" I asked.

"Well, we can't let a boy leave our village alone. Certainly you must be a man before that can happen," Larus said with a booming guffaw.

"The elder will be pissed," I said, laughing.

"Pah on her," Ninden said.

"Pah on her," I agreed.

Paints were smeared on me in the traditional way and our hunt began. We left the valley, and though normally I wouldn't be carrying so much on my back, it slowed us down only a little. As we ran through the hills and across the animal paths, bits of advice were whispered to me.

"Always keep your word," one man said in a low tone.

"Defend your people," Larus advised as we knelt by a stream. "Though you already know that."

"Do not forget your family, or your wife," Father told me, as we lay under the stars on the first night. "They will need you."

The second day, we found tracks, massive ones. Each of us employed our skills, but I was to lead, and lead I did, following after the large paw prints in the mud. Here and there it seemed we might lose it, but the trail always picked back up.

As the day wore on, the trail got clearer and clearer, and by high noon we'd finally found it.

I suspected what it was from the first few prints, but there really was no way to confirm until we were upon it. The bear was just like the one that had attacked the gathering group when I was little—huge, spiked, and angry as it dug into a deer carcass.

Our group split and surrounded the bear. I led with bolts of potent force, slamming against the defenses of the monster as my fellows looked for an opening. Kinetic force slammed into the bear, taking moments more than it needed to bring up its magical defenses.

It roared and turned, charging only to be met with thrown spears from the sides. Blades of copper on wooden staves slammed into the beast's flanks, and it soon realized that it had been cornered. It fought, as all things at risk of death do, but bit by bit we weakened it, running it around like any other beast.

Once it was protecting itself from magic, I moved to boulders and hunks of dirt ripped up from below, hurling them with heavy force one by one at the magical beast. The fight was long, and it was hard, but strikes to the legs, to the back, to all the weakest places on its body bled it, and soon it fell, wheezing.

All the men looked at me, all of us covered in sweat, and I approached, taking the spear my father had landed and carefully angled it before thrusting it into the animal's chest, aiming for the heart, lungs—all the vital organs it would need to live. With a twist I pulled it away, spraying myself with crimson.

There was a cheer and congratulations all around. Soon the beast was slaughtered and cooked over a small fire, the choicest bits handed over to me. As the sun set, we all danced, moving around the small fire, and then we rested, the ritual finally done.

When I awoke the next morning, all but my father were gone, along with the beast. If not for the ashes in the fire and trampled earth, there would be no sign it ever happened. That was all fine and good.

Slowly that morning we walked to the path that would lead me to the next village over, the one where we got our copper. There was no talking, no words, just the peaceful sound of our feet on the floor of the jungle.

When I got to the path—now a proper road—my father stopped, looking at me. "Son, I'm proud of you."

I gave him one final hug, answering in my own way. "I love you too. Until we meet again."

He heading home, and I began my trek. Time was not my friend, and sleeping outside and alone was not something I desired to do, so I ran. I ran along the twisting road that had grown ever wider over the years, ran from the place I'd been born. I ran not away, but toward whatever would come next, for this world was still so young, and with a gentle push, we could make it so much better for everyone.

CHAPTER 53

ONWARD

The sun set as I pulled close to the village, our neighbor, or formerly my neighbor, since I didn't really live in Elayatol anymore. I'd spent the better part of the day in a solid jog, and even if I was in way better shape in this world than I was in my last, it was still a tiring run.

I was spotted by one of their lookouts.

"Who goes?" the man there inquired, trying to get a look at my face.

"Elian, son of Eduan," I answered.

Soon I was showed to the elder, and the proper introductions were made. I'd caught him right at the beginning of his dinner, and he looked up at me curiously after I'd gone through the ritual.

"You're alone, lad? Has something happened?" I was glad to see that he seemed concerned, like an uncle or family friend, which in many ways he was. Then he saw the markings on my skin, the smallest flecks of paint from my own adulthood ritual. "No, not lad, not anymore. Come, we'll talk."

He took me into what I supposed was his own hut, and I told him most of what happened. I explained that I'd had a fight with another of the boys from my village, that things had gotten far out of hand, and that I'd been exiled. There was no need to lie, as he'd know the truth soon enough.

"I'm hoping you'll give me shelter for the night, Elder," I said, head bowed.

"Just the night? I offered to let you join us once," he said.

"That would be a bad idea. This close to Elaya's territory and there would likely be problems. I came to you because we've had good relations in the past, and I still haven't shared the secret of smelting copper with you yet. I think my first act as an adult should be to keep that promise."

His eyes twinkled. I knew that was something he wanted, a secret that would catapult his own village's wealth. Sadly, there was a bit of hesitation. "You didn't tell me why this fight broke out between you."

"Rindal was doing something that would have endangered many of the boys' lives, even though he'd been told as much. I tried to stop him, and talk to him, but he wouldn't listen."

"Then the fire?" the elder asked.

"Partially my doing, yes. I can't say I blame Elaya too much. I'm not happy about it, but that is a lot of destruction."

"I don't know that I'd have exiled you, but I'm satisfied with your explanations. Similarly, you're right, staying here would be asking for trouble, though it pains me to admit it. Tonight you may stay, and tomorrow you'll teach us how to make copper, but the dawn after you should leave," he decreed.

"I thank you for your generosity," I replied. He easily could have told me to beat feet.

"Now, my friend, put down your burdens and join us for a meal. You look hungry, and surely you've at least one good story to tell, or game to teach us!" he enthused.

We talked well into the night, sharing stories of hunts and other fun anecdotes. I even dredged up a couple of variants of checkers to play with them from my memories. That night I slept in the hut with the elder and his family, separated from them a bit, but clearly still welcome. It was nice.

The next day, we made a run up to the copper mine and had a lengthy explanation of how to smelt copper. They'd seen some of what we were doing, and may have eventually worked it out, but with my help, the small group of men that came along understood what to do by the end of the day. We even made a small chunk of the stuff, which caused my host to smile a wickedly bright grin.

I didn't need payment, but the village refilled my supplies and sent a few of their hunters to the edge of their territory with me by way of payment, showing me the path I needed to take to head toward Atal. For that I was grateful.

Over the next week, I bounced from village to village, heading east toward the coast. Traveling merchants weren't uncommon, and while many of them wouldn't go alone, it wasn't impossible. So long as I kept to the prescribed behaviors in each village, properly greeting the elders and offering a token for my night's keep, I was unbothered.

Food was no issue at all. It was impossible to spend as much time as I had around the gathering parties and not pick up at least the basics on where to find edible plants. Though for the most part it meant that I was eating a vegetarian diet if I wasn't in a village. Yanking things from vines or trees with magic as I jogged along made for an easy enough trip.

I noticed a few changes as I moved east. One was that the paths were far clearer, with even a few other travelers passing me on the way. The other big change was that the villages got bigger and bigger, and tended to be near larger and larger rivers and creeks.

After nearly a month of travel, I knew that I was getting close. There'd been a few delays here and there—villages that I'd had to go around and days when I'd gone slower than I'd like—but all in all, I wasn't doing too bad.

I strolled down to the entrance of the next habitation, and what a place it was—easily three times the size of Elayatol, maybe more. There was a hustle and bustle here that most of the outlying villages lacked, with people constantly working. There was also a daytime lookout, a luxury many smaller places couldn't afford.

"Another merchant?" the elder of this village asked, sitting back on a comfortable looking log. It didn't escape me that her hair was nearly a quarter white, indicating a far higher age than most of the older elves around.

"A traveler, Elder, toward Atal," I answered.

"Where from?" she inquired curiously, leaning forward.

"Elayatol."

"Oh, oh, I see. I've heard many interesting things about that place. Your home has been sending out lots of pretty trinkets of late, and new tools too. I don't suppose you have any you could part with?"

I gave her a good deal on one of the colored beads my aunt was making. She probably wanted copper, but I was doing my best to hide that for now. I'd even taken to keeping my spear in a thin leather cover while in towns—the shining red metal attracting attention I didn't want.

This particular village even had a hut for merchants and guests to stay in—a big expense—but when I saw how full it was, I wasn't surprised. I even saw a face I knew.

"Orran," I said, approaching the first traveling trader I'd ever met.

"Elian? What in the world are you doing here?" he asked, clearly surprised at my appearance so far from home.

"A long story, and one I don't care to share. How goes the trading?"

Orran and I had done a fair amount of business over the years. He would appear with many of the odds and ends we wanted, and I would give him quite a bit of our product in exchange. There were a few others that had been going to Elayatol, but he was the first I'd met.

"Good, good. My friends and I got here just a bit ago. Which way are you headed?" he inquired.

"Toward Atal. Come find me the next time you roll through town there, and I think we might manage some good trade."

"You're staying? Ah, I'll not pry. My companions and I are headed that way as well, if you want you can join us for the last leg of the trip."

"I'd be honored. Thank you, Orran."

Orran explained his business to me while we ate that evening. He, and many of the other merchants that he knew, would travel out, getting rare goods from the most outlying areas when they could. They would then head back to Atal. Before they got there, though, they would lose some of their load, replacing it with bulk foodstuffs. Normally, those were near worthless, but with the size of the larger city there was always someone buying food.

Atal was like a tree, the villages around it, its roots. It would suck up all the best goods, and excess food, and then they would be swapped for what others wanted before going out again. The traders marched in and out in waves, getting things they knew the villages on their route would want, and bringing so much back.

Many of the travelers also had a base somewhere, either in one of the larger hub villages like this one, or in Atal itself. They would grow their wealth, handing it off to their families, and then go off again. This served as an outlet for wanderlust but was not a popular way for young men to find wives. Parents or siblings in the city would keep a merchant's wealth while they ventured, looking for a woman to bring home.

We set out early the next morning, everyone in Orran's group carrying a sledge, save myself. Each and every one of them had loaded up on dried fruits and nuts, and by mid-day we saw it.

As we turned around a patch of trees, the city of Atal came into view, and what a city it was. Atal couldn't possibly be called a village, and I couldn't even form a guess at the population. It stretched along the coast and well inland, a low stone and mud wall covering the outskirts. They'd also taken the time to clear out the area for visibility. No monster would sneak into this place easily.

"Pretty, isn't it?" Orran asked me.

"Wow" was my only response.

CHAPTER 54

CITY TOUR

It took us time to get to the wall, and it was perhaps twenty feet tall, and almost as wide, with an opening that was clearly a gate. No metal though; the blockage was made of wood. A man with a spear and a sash of red leather across his chest was watching people go in and out, examining all of them.

"Guard?' I asked Orran.

"Mmm, yeah, though they won't mess with you unless you try to bring in something dangerous." He was right, of course, and they hardly even looked at us, as normal as our group was.

"Mind if I ask for some advice?" I asked Orran.

"Not at all."

"If I were looking for a place to live . . ."

"Depends on what you want," he said. "Now, I've got a small place near the seashore, and it's good, but for you, I think another spot would be good."

"Why?"

"You're young, and there are cheaper places. A lot of the fishermen work near the shore, but with the power you have, you won't need to do that. I'm assuming that you'll be making copper like you were in your village, right?" he asked, leaning in.

"If I can get the stones, but I've another option if I can't, which might work better anyway."

"Right, right, so a place near the market would be better. If it were me, I'd want something on the upper side—better view and more food vendors up there."

"What's on the lower side?" I asked, curiously.

"That's where they sell beast materials and . . ." He said a word I didn't recognize and continued. "Stinks like you wouldn't believe."

"Beast materials and what?" I asked.

"Oh, people who were sold? Like for debts or war." Slaves, he meant slaves.

It shouldn't have surprised me, though it sort of did. There were no slaves in my village, and no need for them. That alone was probably why we didn't have any. I'd hoped that elves were more civilized than ancient man, but it seemed that wasn't the case.

"So you can just own someone, do whatever you want with them?" I asked.

"Not whatever you want," he said. "There are rules, and contracts, and a time limit. You don't need to worry about that though. Nobody would try to take someone like you, with your fire—good way to die."

He gave me some brief explanations, and it assuaged some of my worries. While people were enslaved, they never tried to keep anyone with magic. The danger of such an individual turning on their master was real, and any slave that developed it was quickly given another way to pay off their debt. There was also the fact that certain types of work had to be voluntary, and abuse was very frowned upon. These people would one day be free, of course.

"I need lunch, then to find a place," I finally said as we split.

The houses were also a cut above what I was used to. The bottoms were cut stone bricks, nominally forming a base structure, with cut-outs for doors and windows. Above the stone structure was something I was more familiar with, grown roofs and second, sometimes even third or higher floors. While they were still working with very low-tech materials here, it seemed the city of Atal was pushing them to their very limits.

I stopped only for a few seconds to find a man selling roasted fish and headed toward the sea. There weren't docks as such, since all the boats were rafts and canoes, but there was an area with an opening in the wall where you could see the people working the coast, fishing and paddling small rafts or canoes along the nearby tides.

A trash heap took the remains of my meal, which had been, at the very least, tasty as I continued my circuit around the city. The wall continued up through some workshops and areas that looked like they were poorer, with people going in and out of gates like the one I'd entered earlier.

As I moved into the market, I watched, looking for information I wanted. There were some major differences between this place and my home, and one was the money. They still used beads—that seemed to be universal—but there was at least some amount of standardization. Small shell beads were the go-to for transactions, rather than the mixes I'd seen up until now. Some of these were even put on strands, forming the base for larger exchanges. Others were still traded and exchanged, but these must have been rare enough to maintain value and cheap enough to be a standard, useful.

I found someone who seemed to be acting as a money changer and watched for a while. He had a few bags and a small mat on the ground where he did his business. I didn't have any of the currency that was most common here, something I'd have to change, but I also didn't want to get taken to the cleaners for not knowing the value of things. Once I was sure, I approached him.

"Finally stopped looking, eh? See something you like?" he asked with a smirk.

"You noticed? How much for one of these?" I asked, pointing to a small crystal bauble he had.

"Oh, a good eye, my friend. Fifty-five shells, or trade of similar. I've got two for a full strand through . . ." A strand of the shells was a hundred then, and I'd learned from Orran that that was quite the sum.

"Hmm, what about these?" I undid one of my hidden braids, dropping two of the colored ceramic beads from my village into my hand. They shone brightly in the light and clinked as I set them on the table.

The eyes of the money-changer sparkled. Ah, I've seen their like before, but only once. Out from the west, huh? And good colors, better than most. I'll give you the same as I'd have asked for the crystal ones." It was plain he was low-balling me.

"A strand and fifty for them," I countered.

We went back and forth, eventually settling on a strand and twenty-five. That was good enough for me and would let me trade in something that wasn't of obscene value. I didn't even bother taking out any of my copper; it needed to last and would only make me a target.

Cash in hand, I moved around the section of the market where the slaves were being peddled up around the north. With a sigh, I began to head back south, hoping to find the right area that Orran had described to me, but I struggled because nothing was labeled with signs. My perfect memory was the only thing that really kept me from getting lost, since I could always identify somewhere I'd been before.

The kid and I spotted each other at the same time, and I instantly knew that I was what he'd been looking for. He stood out, a small aura pulsing around him as we locked eyes, and he smiled, running off. I'd just turned onto this street, and I considered turning off now, rather than deal with whatever mischief the child might bring—scams or the like—but I'd have to learn what was coming eventually, so I readied myself for a fight and followed after him.

He zigzagged down the road, not even trying to hide, and stopped in front of a number of the businesses there. Whatever he said into the doors caused a stir, as I slowly followed behind, trying to work out what exactly the deal was. The only hint was that the plants forming the upper parts of the businesses all had vibrant flowers, something I'd not seen elsewhere in the city.

As I passed the first of the buildings, several women appeared in the windows and door, smiling and waving at me. It was weird, but I just continued on. Each one ended with more of the same, the girls clearly having been told I was there. There were beauties and girls who were less so, tall and short, and they had various hair colors. I frowned as I noticed some with the markings Orran had told me indicated slaves.

Realization hit me as I passed closer to one of the buildings. One of the slaves leaned over a small balcony, parting her dress to give a full view to those on the streets. "Come, newcomer," she cooed. "Sina will help you rest."

The world's oldest profession was alive and well, and I'd wandered into the city's red-light district. Magic was power, and everyone knew it. If I had power, I had money, and since I was new, clearly I didn't already have a favorite girl. My face began to burn as I realized that all of them probably thought I was shopping and were keen to advertise.

I was flashed several more times before I'd reached the end of the road, and was given quite a few offers that my hormones urged me to accept. That was not what I needed, though, and the day didn't have infinite time. Some of them looked after me as I passed with slightly sour faces, though many kept calling.

When I got to the end of the street, the boy I'd seen was there, and he seemed most displeased that I'd passed all the way through.

"Hey buddy," he said, marching up to me. "Look, the girls hire me to find them good guys. You not find something you like? I know all the girls. Tell me what you're looking for, and I'll find her for you? Then I get paid for finding you, and you get just what you're after."

"Never been down this street before, kid," I explained.

"Clearly," he retorted.

"Didn't mean to head down it."

"Ah, well shit." He sulked. My guess was he worked on commission or something, getting a cut when customers were found. "Guess I ran all up and down for nothing then. Don't suppose I could convince you to change your mind?"

"Not today," I said, shaking my head.

"Bugging people again, Chien?" a man said, moving beside us. He had the same red leather sash as the gate guard. "Thought I told you not to harass people?" He looked rather stern.

"He's not bugging me, just helping me find my way," I answered.

"Oh? What you looking for?" the man asked. "Nothing here, clearly, if the faces I see behind you are any indication."

"A house," I answered. "Friend of mine sent me up this way but didn't give me great directions."

The man laughed as the child slinked away. Chien would be seeing me again, as a kid well acquainted with the city and willing to work for cash would be an asset, but for now I'd deal with the guard.

"Ah, well, how about I take you over to our guard house. Someone'll know where the house you're looking for is," he offered.

"I'd appreciate that. The name's Justin by the way," I said, offering a hand in greeting.

"Weird name, Justin. I'm Ian," he said, taking my hand and shaking it.

CHAPTER 55

✦

HOUSE

It took me some time to explain to Ian—name pronounced the same as it is in English—that it wasn't a specific house I was looking for, but rather a place to live. By that time we'd reached the local guard station, and they all had a good laugh at my mistake.

"Ah, first time in the city then?" Ian asked, sitting on a small stone bench, which looked like a massive rock.

"Yeah, needed a new place to live, and Atal seemed the best around," I explained, still feeling embarrassed.

"He was in the right area at least, maybe not that street, but around there are some good spots," one of the other guards said.

"Aye, what are you looking for?" Ian asked, his interest piqued like he might have something.

"Don't need much room for myself, but something close enough to the market and an area for a workshop," I explained.

"What sort of work you do?" one of the others asked. I supposed if I was wanting to move into their city, that was a fair question.

"Sort of hard to explain," I said, looking for the right words. "I work with pottery and metal mostly."

"I've seen some of that. Weird stuff. You actually know how to work it?" Ian asked, one eyebrow going up.

"Yeah, if I can get the materials. Some of them might not be available around here though." I had no doubt about my next plan, since it could be anywhere, but making more pots and the like might prove difficult.

"My cousin had a house over that way, sold it off to our grandfather when he left. If you've got something to pay for it . . ."

"Maybe I should talk to your grandfather then," I said.

The guard's relatives all lived in the area he patrolled, a rather sensible policy, if one that would undoubtedly lead to a bit of favoritism. Perhaps I should have worried about that, but since it would benefit me, I was more than happy to be the one to benefit from it.

He even took me by the house that he thought might work, and I had to admit, it would. It wasn't tall, only two floors, but it was sturdy, and with some repairs it would serve as an excellent workshop. There were even a few extra rooms here and there for storage and any guests I might have.

Upon agreeing that it was a good place, I was shown to a large house, one with many people milling about. There were several floors and more than a few workers attending to small tasks nearby when we approached. It still had the standard architecture and build but also had murals painted on the low stone walls, a way to display that the owner had wealth.

Ian disappeared while I was taken to a room with a well-cleaned floor and a small clay oven to heat the room. There were even woven grass mats for sitting and a small raised area to serve as a table, set with wooden cups. As the guard left, a woman appeared and filled my cup with some kind of juice mixture—pleasant, if a bit sour.

When Ian and his grandfather returned, I almost stood, only to be stopped by a raised hand from the older man.

"Elder," I said, nodding.

"No elders here in Atal, my boy, but I would be considered such in the countryside. You may call me Shorin. My grandson here tells me you work with copper?" The man had long hair with a white stripe off to one side in the otherwise brown locks. His clothing was also longer and covered more than most people's, and it was made of a thinner, finer leather.

"Yes, I do."

The older elf pulled out a small skinning knife, one of mine. I'd made quite a few of these over the years and had gotten pretty good at it. As he turned it over, the reddish metal gleamed.

"I bought this last year, and found it to be rather magnificent, but as time went on, I find that the edge has dulled. If you truly work with such materials, can you make it sharper again?"

He passed over the implement and the problems became immediately clear. Nobody had given instruction on proper care and maintenance. We'd made sure to instruct people on how to sharpen them with stones, but somewhere along the line, the method had been lost. It pained me to see that someone had even tried to knap the edge of it, leaving rather ugly marks.

"May I?" I inquired, gesturing to the blade.

"Of course," he said, nodding.

As I pulled some tools from my pack, I used magic to reheat the metal. Taking it to nearly molten and using planes of force to clean up the blade quickly. That done, I cooled it back down and with care began to hammer the edge. That seemed foolish to most people, but copper needed to be hardened, and a few moments would make all the difference in the end. Finally, I took it through a series of stones to clean it down and bring it back to proper alignment. The whole process took nearly an hour, with both Ian and the older elf watching intently. When I was done, the knife could have sliced paper, and I handed it back to its owner.

Shorin tested the blade on a finger, and when it sliced deep and drew a line of blood he began to laugh uproariously.

"I take it you're satisfied," I asked.

"Oh, more than, more than. Can you make more like this knife?" he asked, a smile on his face.

"There is a certain stone needed to make copper. Without it, I may be unable to make more just like that, but I have some ideas on how to make similar things," I said, not willing to commit at this moment. "I do have a merchant friend who's supposed to be bringing me more of the materials, but it may take time."

"Good. Ian here will take you to the house, and if you like it, I want one more knife like this for it. If you can't make one . . ." he seemed to think for a few seconds.

"Done," I said, pulling out a skinning knife of my own and setting it down before him. Mine was nicer, but I could make more.

Shorin began to laugh again as he scooped it up. It was of slightly nicer quality than the one he'd bought because it was one of my personal tools, but it was something I could easily replace.

"You had another this whole time?" he said, smiling. "What other things might you have?"

"I may have other things, but if I'm bothered and lose them now, you'll not get more in the future," I said, which got me a more genuine smile.

"Smart as can be, aren't you? Good, if you need help moving some of your products, I'll do it; give you a fair deal too."

"Perhaps I'll take you up on that, Shorin, but not today. The evening is coming and I need to get set up still."

"Then go, my boy, and enjoy your new house."

Ian shook his head in good spirits as we left. I knew the older man was overcharging me, but that was fine. He had one of the city guards vouching for the place I was trying to buy and was ready to deal. If I played my cards right, I could make Ian a friend and have a good place to start my work here, which was worth far more to me than a skinning knife.

When I got to my new home, I still used my magic to pry up one of the stones in the floor and hide my valuables beneath it. There was no point making myself easy to rob. Then I went about deciding where exactly I wanted to sleep, going up and down through the rooms until I found the old bed. It was a group of vines, all soft and grown together to form a sort of net, and was as comfortable as I could really hope for on short notice—something to work on later.

As I drifted off to sleep, I wondered briefly how my family was doing.

CHAPTER 56

SLEDS AND SLAVES

As I rose, finding the sun just cresting the edge of the sky, I looked around in brief confusion. Moments passed as my mind righted itself, reminding me where I was and what I was doing before I rose. There was much to do today, and in the coming days. I had only a limited amount of savings, and there was no easy way to put it, but I needed to get working or I would find myself in a rather hard place sooner rather than later.

First came the general cleaning and organization. There wasn't much to it, as there just wasn't much here, but it was the right place to start. Once I was sure that everything was in order, I began the process of getting set up to start my labors.

I needed a forge of at least some form and had none of the materials required for it. Luckily these were fairly simple to attain, primarily consisting of mud, hay, and other building materials. A small offshoot of the house, which lacked a proper covering, would be the location, and after making some measurements, I began to go about gathering.

The city would not serve for most of what I needed today, so I made my way to one of the gates before heading out into the countryside. This was not at all unusual, and in fact a huge number of people were doing just the same, mostly headed toward the nearby sea, but some were off to achieve similar goals as me, and I fell in with them on some of the paths leading from the city.

Most of what I needed for now was either plant material or clay, and once I'd arrived at a small creek cutting through the local brush, I began gathering supplies. A small sled was easy enough to throw together with magic—cuts to shape it and shims to hold everything in place made the construction speedy and clean; the wood would serve me well, as it served many purposes.

I got looks from some of the other elves, but nobody bothered me as I heaped a mixture of clay from the creek bed and dried grasses atop my small vehicle. I knew what I wanted and roughly where it would all be. Most of those around me were far more interested in the edible plants than I was, since I only needed to pick up a few for my meals today.

Before long I realized that the people here were in smaller groups, all very spread out. Within each group there seemed to be a magic user, who was making the plants grow to be harvested, but they were all so far from one another.

Except for one girl, who had moved over to my sled while I was meticulously choosing some clay, and she was hovering over it. The rest of her group wasn't far off, getting baskets of nuts and the like, but she'd come over.

"Can I help you?" I asked, appearing behind her with an armload of my own choices.

"Eep!" she said, turning quickly. Now I could see the markings on her shoulder, a large number of hashes under something that looked like a shell, with a few characters beneath it that I didn't know.

I looked her over. Other than the marks on her skin, she seemed fairly normal. The basket in her hands held a variety of small plants but none that I'd been after, so it was immediately clear she hadn't taken anything. That said, I still didn't like it that a stranger was getting too close to my things.

"Well?" I asked.

"Ah, please, I meant no offense. I was just looking at the thing you made," she stammered, clearly nervous.

"A sled," I said. "It makes carrying things easier." That, at least, wasn't an odd concept for this world. People would sometimes build things like this to drag loads on the ground, though normally it took a lot more work from them than I'd put into this one.

"Oh, yes, it's just that some of the connections are different, and you made it very fast . . ."

I looked at it briefly. Without really thinking, I'd put several of the joints used back home into it. There were a few quick dovetails and many mortise and tenon connectors. I'd nearly forgotten that things like that weren't very common around here.

While I went over those things, another from her group walked up to us. This time it was the caster, who immediately took the girl by the ear and twisted harshly, far more harshly than I'd ever seen anyone twist before.

"I hope my girl Sala isn't bothering you, sir? Sala, apologize to the nice man," she said with a slight smile.

"Aah, I'm sorry, please forgive me!" Sala quickly said, her head bending and dropping as the other woman brought her hand down to force her to bow. Somehow, by either luck or long practice, the girl didn't drop the basket she was carrying.

"That's enough," I said, anger at this casual cruelty slipping into my voice. My aura flared, the magic responding to the fury I felt.

With a slightly shocked expression, the woman released the curious girl. Sala didn't rise. She was shaking like a leaf as her eyes stayed low, focused on the ground. Putting two and two together wasn't hard. Clearly this girl was property, owned by the other woman.

"If you say so, sir. I'll make sure she doesn't bother you again. Come along, Sala," the owner said, turning on her heel and leaving.

As the two retreated, I wove a small spell, one that would amplify the sounds from their direction, letting me listen in.

"Well, how did he put it together?" the magic user asked.

"I-I saw some of the things he used, and we could copy them easy, but some I didn't get a good look at . . ." Sala explained, clearly still afraid.

It seemed that my demonstration had attracted attention, and rather than just coming to ask me, someone had decided to spy. That was stupid beyond reason. If they'd just requested it, I could have made another, but this place was different. There was also no doubt in my mind that the girl had been sent; she'd not come on her own. It was an insight into the way things worked in this area, and one I didn't much like.

"Tch, useless, why do I even keep you around." A small whimper followed, but I didn't look, pretending instead to be absorbed in my work.

"He didn't seem unkind. Maybe he would trade you one?" Sala suggested in a small voice.

"Oh? And what would I trade him? You?" she asked with dripping sarcasm.

I let my eyes wander over to their group and saw that, save for the mage, all the other members of the group were marked. With a brief look over the area, I could clearly see that many of the groups, though certainly not all of them, were of a similar makeup. Perhaps that was one of the ways people with magic made money around here, using their power to control groups of slaves.

As for those I was spying on, I could see that other than Sala and her owner, all the rest were studiously keeping quiet and out of the way. I had some thoughts on this as well.

In both worlds I'd noticed that men were more prone to acts of extreme violence. Men killed, for the most part, and often were the ones killed. However, when it came to casual cruelty, women reigned. Even in my village, the boys might fight, but after that, it tended to be over. Some of the women, on the other hand, had kept small grudges that could last for years, sniping and being mean for as long as I had paid attention. It was one of the reasons I had no doubts Elaya would deeply regret sending me away.

Briefly, very briefly, I considered going and finding some way to buy the girl. It was clear that she was the whipping boy for her owner's bad moods. Affording her would be no issue with the wealth I had. However, what about the next slave I met, or the one after that? I couldn't afford all of them, and even if I could, there'd just be a new crop taken.

No, this girl wasn't one I could help now, but there was a solution. It was simple enough, and that was to get enough power—be it magical, political, or otherwise—to end this institution once and for all. That seemed a good goal for me, and bringing society into a more modern world would help on all fronts.

With nothing left to do here for the moment, I took the hauling ropes of my craft and pulled. After all, I had so very much work to do.

CHAPTER 57

SETUP

It took me nearly a week to get my house set up. Now it was . . . well, it was still subpar, but I at least had things in working order. There was a good set of stone tools, and the proper benches, and a slightly more comfortable setup, with a better bed and some food packed away.

Each morning I'd been going out, gathering the materials that I needed and doing a few projects, but after that is where the real fun began. I just watched people. I wandered the city streets, committing the layout to memory and observed all there was to see. I tried to understand people's living arrangements and distinguish them from different sections of the city; whether they were poor, or rich, or perhaps tradesmen. I even attended an auction of new slaves once, to understand it better, even if I had no intention of participating.

What I learned was significant, and in some ways rather surprising. Food, one of the main imports of the city, was cheap as dirt, and plentiful. Large quantities were brought into the city by traders, but this was, from what I could tell, actually not the main source.

Today, I wandered down to the shore to watch gathering that I wasn't as familiar with. While the woods were worked by those like my mother, many of the magic users down here were far more like me. There were, of course, shore-based groups doing things like digging clams or catching the many small crabs and the like roaming around, but there were also some elves out in the water.

With great interest, I looked on as two men hauled in several woven traps, dumping the struggling contents out to pick through them. Other than those traps, there were larger ones near the tidal pools, with platforms that, if I had to guess, were always, or almost always, manned. Outside of the walls, private property wasn't really a thing, so a guard was posted to dissuade people.

Several of the magic users here were the physically enhanced types, diving deeper and throwing spears with superhuman power at the nearby fish. Others were more like me, and were using their magic to pull their surprised quarry from the waves. This was all new to me, since fish back home were mostly just speared, and much, much smaller.

Back in town I knew there were also people performing to make food. They were like Isha and could quite literally sing for their supper. Unlike the larger scale gatherers, though, they focused on specialty foods—spices in ground form or sweet things like nectar and honey. It made sense since those would sell for more.

While watching on I began to consider what I called my various types of magic. In Atal there were many, many different opinions, but I wanted one of my own. Video games and the few experiences I'd had with tabletop games helped with this, as obviously the magical energy should be called "mana.'" The kind of magic that Isha and Father used was also easy, as I'd seen magical performers called "bards" many times over.

What I should call my type of magic was up in the air though. From a tabletop perspective, I was clearly a mage, but what kind? Maybe a wizard or a sorcerer. Frankly, I liked the latter for thematic reasons, but since I also used knowledge, and I wasn't generally a problem, the former almost seemed to fit better. Then again, a lot of the tropes didn't apply, since a staff or wand would just be useless to me. I could only shrug, putting it off for later.

I also wavered on the kind of magic my mother used. My prime instinct was to call her a "druid," though I wasn't sure if that fit well either. Sure, she cared about nature, but some of the others like her that I'd met in Atal didn't seem to. Instead, they grew plants because they wanted them to grow, not in any service to the world. Druid would work for now, though, at least in my mind.

"Hey buddy," a man called from nearby, getting my attention.

"Yes?" I asked, looking past him to the group of men he was with. Several were looking at me doubtfully. Many of those men were covered in odd looking tattoos, not something I'd seen before.

"You looking for work? My team here brings in a good catch, and I can see you're no slouch. We'd be happy to give you a trial run, if you're interested." I looked at him and saw the small aura leaking from his skin.

That was probably why he'd come over to talk to me, since he could see mine too.

"Thanks for the offer, but I'm just here to enjoy the sea for a bit," I explained with a smile.

"Ah, it's beautiful, eh? Old mother ocean gives us our food, and so much of it." He gazed out at the waves, sort of wistfully. "Well, if you change your mind, come and find me. Like I said, we'd give you a chance."

He and his buddies left, carrying small canoes. They were simple things, but, as with most items elves made, very well built. My new people were many things, but above all, some were absolute perfectionists. Those boats might not be complex, and they might not do much good on longer trips, but they were exceptionally well made. It was an odd tendency, but one I rather liked.

There was one more thing I wanted for now, though, and that was to have a chat with a certain kid. It didn't take me long to work my way back to the city and begin striding through the streets. I circled the red-light district several times, looking here and there for the kid without drawing too much attention to myself. I'd rather avoid the same issue I had last time.

Sadly, my search was fruitless, and with a bit of nervousness, I walked to the street where I'd first seen him. Predictably, I soon began getting attention, though much less than last time. Word had gotten around, it seemed, and the girls who'd seen me before remembered my face, and that I'd not taken any of them up on their services. Chien was standing on the opposite side of the street, being a lookout, eyes scanning.

"Hey kid," I said as I approached him.

"Oh, it's you. Decide to take me up on my offer to introduce you to some of the ladies?" he said with a smile, leaning forward.

"Actually no, I'm here looking for you."

"Woah there," he said, waving his hands around. "First, I'm way too young; and second, I'm not into guys, so I'm afraid I'm not on offer here. Though if you are more into men, I might know someone."

"Not for that, you little pervert. I need someone to do some work for me, and I get the feeling you know people and places," I explained before he attracted attention I really didn't want.

"I have, in fact, done a little bit of messenger and pick up work for the girls at times. Why, I know them so well that I can get you the best deals . . ."

"Could you stop trying to be a half-sized pimp?"

"What's a pimp?"

"Not the point," I said, and began to explain as simply as I could. "The point is, I need someone who knows the city better than I do, and I can pay."

"Well, if you're paying, I'm sure I can work you into my busy schedule. Why don't we discuss some terms over food?" I smiled. Sure, the kid was going to try and milk me for whatever he could, but a street rat would be able to get me places I'd otherwise be turned away from, and paying was not something I would have any issues with for a long, long time.

CHAPTER 58

FIRST EMPLOYEE

Chien and I found a nice spot where we could sit and eat the basket of clams I'd bought. It wasn't anything fancy, but the seller had managed to roast them inside the container with plenty of water and fragrant herbs. Oddly, the meal was probably better tasting than most of what I'd had on Earth—less fat, but the way it was cooked and prepared was just right.

"All right, so what is it that you want?" the boy asked while leaning against a wall.

"Mostly, I need someone to help me figure out where I can send my inventions, and how to spread the word on how others can make them well themselves," I answered.

"You're just going to tell people secrets? What are we talking about anyway?"

"Lots of things. Back in my village we did pottery and copper, along with a few other things, which are a little less known," I replied, turning to watch his reaction.

"I've heard of pottery. Neat, if not particularly useful. I mean, what's the point of pretty cups and stuff?" He seemed doubtful.

"They can hold water and are easier to make than you'd think. You can also make larger ones for cooking and the like, or just storing things that don't keep in baskets easily," I explained.

"Okay, but if they're so good, why don't you make them?"

"Chien . . . there are a lot of things that I want, but I don't want to be the one making them all the time. You enjoy food like this, but do you want to cook it all the time?" I asked, pointing to the meal we were sharing.

"Not really," the boy answered after some consideration. "Looks like a lot of work. I can also do things that make me more money easier."

"Exactly. I don't really want to mess around with a lot of things, but that doesn't mean that I don't want them to be made. The problem is getting them into the hands of people who might *want* to make them. I also need someone who generally knows the area and can help me find the materials and people I need."

"That all sounds like things you could do yourself, and without much effort," he answered with a frown.

"Ah, but there's a problem—I don't want everyone knowing where it all came from."

"Why?" he said, looking at me like I was slightly mad.

"Because if too many people follow too many paths to the same place, others will come looking."

Chien took a few moments to consider this, eating several more of the shellfish as he thought it through. "People will eventually figure it out though."

"Yeah, but that's fine. If you're worried about how long I'll need your help, I can help you with your magic, depending on what kind it is. Just because things change, doesn't mean I won't need more help anyway."

"Why me?" he asked.

"Because, you'll be helpful, and I like your attitude. You went out and found a place for yourself at your age; not everyone does that." I then brought up the one issue that might arise. "Your parents won't care though, will they?"

"Never knew Dad, and Mom doesn't care about much of anything," he replied flippantly.

That was kind of depressing, and while I couldn't be sure, with the company he kept, it wouldn't surprise me if his mother was a working girl. Not that it mattered. I may want to use the kid for my benefit, but he'd surely gain too.

"Look, I understand if you're doubtful, but I'd like you to give it a chance. I already know what some of the gathering teams want, and if you come by in the next day or two, I'll show you. It's nothing hard, so you'll be able to put the info out there pretty quick. I'll even pay you to do it, a bit when you first go out and more when I see others using it."

"I'm still not completely following the *why* here. Why do you want stuff spread around? I mean, if you were getting something from it, I could understand, but you won't be. Your whole explanation about wanting it around doesn't really follow either; you could just make it for you." He sounded like he thought I was a complete moron.

"Maybe I could explain, but honestly does it matter? The goal is to make people happy, and I'm willing to pay you for it. Do you need to know much more than that?"

The kid shrugged. "No, I guess not. Where are you showing me this stuff?"

"Come by my place for now," I rattled off some basic directions. He already knew the city better than me, and with the way elves' memories worked, finding it shouldn't be an issue.

I'd just finished my breakfast and was still putting some of the basics for the day together when I heard a call from outside. "Oi, weirdo, you there?"

"You know you can just call me Justin, right?" I asked the boy, looking down at him.

"Got you out, didn't it?"

"Fair enough," I said with a slight laugh. "Hold on and I'll grab the pieces we need."

The first thing I was showing him was my sled design. Those women had been interested in it, and it was so simple to make that all someone really needed was to see one working. The magic was all in the joints, the little bits that fit together to make it, so I didn't need to tie everything three ways from Sunday with vines and ropes.

I had to give it to the kid, his eyes flashed over it with heavy scrutiny, looking at each part in turn. He wasn't just judging the item either, but my work, and seemed pleased with what he saw, a small smile creeping up to his lips.

"How'd you get such clean holes and cuts in it?" he asked. "I don't see any marks from tools or places where the wood was worked down."

My explanations here were brief, but I soon found that Chien was the same kind of caster I was. With some effort, I made the same planes I used for cutting and drilling, letting him take a good look at each before showing him how they were used. I even handed over some of the wood I'd be using for fires later so he could get a bit of practice in. After all, he needed to be able to show people how to make things.

"I like it," he finally declared as we finished, just before lunch. "And I can see why others will too."

"Payment, as promised," I said, handing over some shells. My research had paid off, and I knew that this was about a week's worth of wages for someone doing basic magic. "And more will come if I see others using it."

"What's your part of what I get for selling the idea?" he asked, broaching a subject I knew he'd be most interested in.

"Nothing," I said. "You sell it, you keep the money. Now head out kid; you might catch some of the gatherers coming back from their work, and I have things I need to do today." I laughed as I sent him off to put the sled into the world, knowing that small changes would create ripples.

As he scampered off, I turned back to my own work for the day—two simple clay pots hidden inside crude looking baskets. I didn't really want to advertise that I had those yet, but I needed a container for small particles. I picked them up and headed for the beach. It was time to take things to the next level.

CHAPTER 59

BLACK SAND

The beach awaited, and magic awaited, and oh, was this something I was itching to try. There was something about the many ideas I had, a dreadful thing. In Elayatol they were either not very useful or something I didn't want to have to explain to anyone. I wasn't in my village anymore, though, and I didn't have to explain shit.

I reached my hands over the sand once I'd set my carrier down and began to focus. Inwardly, I'd prepped for years for this, visualizing the lines, the spin, the equations, even the outward appearance, everything I knew about magnets. Just over the sand, I pumped mana into the spell, making the strongest magnet I could.

There was a slight movement, a small shifting as the construct gained power and pulled. Bits of black sand, barely large enough to be grains themselves, were pulled from the beach, zipping inwards to the construct and hovering there. As they began to form a small ball, a small smile began to creep along my lips. This would do quite nicely.

Iron may have been one of the more common elements on Earth, and I suspected here as well, but that didn't mean there was a ton of it in a usable form just sitting around. There was some, surely, but not a giant deposit here or anything, just a few grains here and there that were sticking to my improvised magnet.

Even if there wasn't much of what I was looking for, I still had a whole beach and all day to work. Over time, I began to shift the sands around, hauling up parts before dropping them down around it and letting my magnetic field grab the little specks of black. After a few moments, I found the process almost meditative, repetitive and calming.

Even with the small amounts I was getting, it still only took me an hour or two to get all the iron dust I needed. My small pots now sat in their baskets with a black billing, the tiny grains shifting ever so slightly as I picked them up. They were also heavier than I'd anticipated. I used my magic to help lighten my load.

I was getting strange looks from some of the gatherers, clearly curious as to what in the world I was doing. Nobody had yet approached me, though, and I had to wonder why. Perhaps they saw that I was quite busy moving a large and potentially dangerous spell around, or maybe . . .

A man approached me, sporting some of the odd tattoos that many who gathered at the beach had. "Me and the boys were wondering what in the world you're gathering."

His approach was straightforward, one I liked far better than sending a slave to come and poke around my stuff.

"Black sand," I explained. "I'm a craftsman and am often after new materials."

The man bent down and looked at the small pots of sand, tapping the outside of one. "What you making?"

"Oh, all kinds of things. I'm not exactly sure what to do with the sand yet, but I've got some ideas."

"Interesting, did you make these? They're harder than I'd expect." Now he was clearly interested in the pots.

"I did make those. They're called pots, and I'll be making more in the future," I said with a smile. Pottery might be a good way to make money while I kept spreading designs. Knowing the basics of ceramics already meant that I could spread the word easily, and it was something I wanted encouraged.

"Expensive?"

"Not as bad as you'd think. They're neat, since they can hold things like sand and water." That got his mind turning, and I could see him thinking about the possibilities already.

That was one thing that always made me smile. Time and time again on Earth, cave men and those who lived in societies like mine were depicted as stupid, but these people weren't. They lacked a lot of knowledge, sure, but that didn't mean they were dumb. If shown something they'd never seen, they investigated, and if they found some use for it, they immediately took it up without issue. They weren't dumb, or particularly backwards; they just lacked information.

"That's interesting, very interesting," he said, tapping his chin in thought.

"Mind if I ask a question of my own?"

"Not at all."

"Those marks all over your body, the tattoos, what are they for?" I said, dying to sate my curiosity.

"Oh, they're ink made from a certain plant. If you put them in your skin, they can refill your lungs if you run out of air. Most people can only use them once or twice a day, but it's still enough to save your life if you start to drown."

A magical tattoo. That really was something. "How are they made? By who?"

"I'm not sure exactly, but some of the more powerful gatherers make them, and some village elders up and down the coast. I don't know that it's secret, but I think it's supposed to be hard to do." He didn't know the answers to some of my questions, perhaps many of them, but that information alone was something quite valuable.

"Are there other kinds?" I asked, excited now.

"Oh a few, but like I said, they're hard to use, and using more than one is really difficult from what I hear. I know a guy who does them if you want one."

At my vigorous agreement, he rattled off some directions. One day I'd have to go and pay the tattoo artist a visit, but not today. Today I had lots of fresh ore to work with, and a furnace to put to work.

Soon enough the stranger and I parted ways. He'd not gotten everything he wanted, but he did manage some of it and probably thought that the black sand was for pottery. I wouldn't be disabusing him of that notion for now, as getting iron or steel out into the environment wasn't quite on the docket yet.

When I got home, I had just enough time to start cooking the ore I'd gathered. While I might not know all of the details about how iron ore was turned into metal, I knew a few things, and one of them was that it had to get extraordinarily hot. Letting even a bit of water into that kind of heat seemed foolish, something I'd learned long ago; therefore, I needed all of it dry, very dry, before I began.

Chien showed up the next day about halfway into my first attempt at smelting. He looked between the two burning stacks—one full of pottery I'd thrown together quickly and another, which was being charged with equal parts iron ore and charcoal. For this first run, I was only using magic to increase airflow and using a variant of the same furnace I used for copper making, since I knew it worked.

"Morning kid, how goes it?" I asked, sipping from a small ceramic cup.

"Good, lots of people want sleds like the one you made, and more info on them."

"Glad to hear it, sounds like you've got your work cut out for you," I said, still sipping the small herbal blend I'd concocted from local plants.

"So about getting more of them?" he asked, hesitantly.

"You know how to make them, and I assume you're selling them?" I asked.

He nodded, and it was clear that he'd managed that much. "Yeah, but soon everyone will know what to do. What then?"

"Then I teach you something else, don't I?"

"Like what you're working on now?" He looked interested at the two flaming towers.

"Those will come in time, one much earlier than the other. I still have plenty of ideas, kid, and plenty of things that work well. For now, though, I need you spreading that sled design. It forms a baseline of skills needed for working with complex wooden joints." I didn't mind explaining, particularly since I hoped one day this kid would become my assistant in these endeavors.

"Who are you? Really?" Chien asked, eyeing me.

"Didn't I already tell you? I'm Justin," I answered, nearly losing my hard expression when I noticed his confused look.

CHAPTER 60

VISITOR

Iron was hard. Not in the sense that it was physically difficult to move. Well, it was that, but in other ways too. It was not as easy to shape as copper, leading to a whole plethora of problems.

I looked down at the chunk I was holding in place with magic with a small bit of rage. It was a chunk of the bloom, since the whole thing was rather unwieldy. There was metal there; I could even see some of it. Irritatingly, it was not doing what I wanted it to—it was not coming together.

Copper was mostly cast into shape and then worked lightly afterwards, but that wouldn't work with iron. Iron needed to be folded and worked. I knew this; I didn't know exactly why, but I knew that it helped with impurities somehow. There was a problem though.

Delamination was my newest enemy. No matter what I tried, my little hunk of metal was just not staying together. There was probably a really simple explanation, and a really simple fix, but for the life of me, I didn't know what it was.

I tried getting the metal hotter, and while that seemed to help, only once it got to a state where it was just beginning to melt, even then I was having issues—less issues, but issues. Perhaps heat was part of the problem? I was sure that was a factor, but it didn't seem to be the only one here.

I quenched the metal and then, using magic, sliced it in half. I needed to take a closer look to see what was going on. First I used only my eyes and that gave me a good bit of information. There was clearly something in the broken welds, some kind of undesirable inclusion, but that didn't tell me what it was. It could be impurities in the metal, and that was almost certainly part of it, but it could be . . . oxidation? Carbonization? Hmm, hard to know without a tool to test it, something I had little chance at getting any time soon.

So I needed something to keep whatever it was out of the join, a flux. Sifting through my memories was easy enough, and I found a few potentials after a couple hours of meditation. A video of Japanese sword-makers told me that they put burnt straw ash in their joins, so that probably would help. There were several references to borax, but that was less useful. Perhaps sand or lime would work, or even some of the black sand I was using as ore. Those should melt at the temperatures I was using, but I wasn't sure what they'd introduce.

There was only one proper solution—science. Taking the time now to work this out would save me unbelievable amounts of effort in the future, so I began to chunk out my bloom into roughly equal sizes. It wouldn't be perfect, as I lacked some of the tools, but I could at least get a good idea of what would work best.

Some of this was going to be subjective. Figuring out which flux or technique worked best for me was not something that would carry over to everyone, but I also aimed to learn more about the metal itself. To that end I was now leaning over one of my pieces, focusing my magic with intent.

I was trying to bend the light, to create a lens I could use to watch the structure of the material as I worked. Slowly, very slowly, it began to focus. The first version wasn't that much better than just my normal eyes, but as I refined it, I started getting clearer and clearer pictures. In time I hoped I could get close enough to see the crystal structures, but for now getting a better look at inclusions would be enough.

The next day as I was working, someone called from the doorway.

"Come in," I answered, after popping my head out to see who it was, not wanting to leave my forge alone. I'd already ruined one of my test pieces doing exactly that.

"Came to see how you were settling in, and you certainly have," Ian said, looking around the part of the house I was using for work. His eyes settled on the stack of pottery I'd finished, quickly making his way over to it.

"Think those will sell?" I asked with a smirk, already knowing the answer.

"Yeah, I do. These colors . . ."

"Honestly, not quite what I expected. The materials around here are different. Not unhappy with them though."

Even unglazed, the vessels were vibrant shades of orange and yellow, much more so than the clays back in Elayatol had ever been. I was sure it would mess with the glaze recipes too, but how I wouldn't know until I tried some out.

"And are you working copper?" he asked amazed, watching as I pulled one of the pieces of iron out of the forge.

"Not quite. This is a different material, and one I'm having issues with. If I can find a way to fix my problems, I'll let it out into the wild, but until then, it's kind of useless. Stand back; this can be messy." After adding flux, I brought it over to my small anvil and pounded it, sending out a shower of sparks.

"Thunderous death!" he cursed, jumping back. "Are you mad?"

"Ha, Chien seems to think I'm odd too, but no, it's quite safe." Ian was still giving me a concerned look. "If I was worried about it, I'd be doing something about it."

"You're working with the kid?" When I nodded to him, he shook his head. "All he wants is money. You know that, right?"

"People who want money are easy to predict, Ian. I'd rather work with someone who is telling me exactly what they want rather than with someone who is hiding their intentions."

"He's right, you are weird," the guard said. "I suppose wanting money does explain your actions though."

"Oh, I don't want money," I explained with a smirk. "I want the world to be a better place."

"That is something I can get behind. One of the reasons I took the job I did. Question is, though, how does all this make the world a better place?" he asked, motioning to the room.

"Small steps, little things that can make people's lives better. There are times for big changes, big things, but mostly it's the small ones. Bit by bit we can add, improve. It's like walking through a forest. You don't have to jump high or far if you can just put one foot before the other. Do that over and over again and soon you'll make your way through." I looked him in the eye as I spoke, because I knew the steps I could take, and that they would lead me forward; perhaps the road would be rocky, but it was clearly set out before me.

Ian just nodded, seeming to process all that.

"By the way, Ian, if you don't mind, could you take this to your grandfather, get his opinion? He said he might be interested in selling the things I make, and I think that might work well for us both." I passed him one of the bowls with a smile. "And I can see you want one."

I knew that soon enough pottery would be spreading. Even now it should be, and I would be seeing that it did. For the moment, that bowl was a rare product, something worth selling, but in the future? Probably not. That, and I rather liked Ian, he seemed a decent guy.

"Thanks, I mean it," he said. We both knew that piece of pottery would fetch a good price in the market right now, even if I didn't overly value it. We said our goodbyes and he left, letting me get back to the task at hand.

CHAPTER 61

SHORIN

I walked down the avenue and into the largest structure in the city by a large margin. All around me, staff and servants moved in waves here and there, each on their assigned tasks. Of course, I too was here on an assigned task, one that would take me deep into the center of the building.

Most of the places in the city of Atal were some mix of grown and stone architecture, but this one was not. This building alone was all stone, each of the huge blocks moved into place with care over the course of centuries. They were massive, and I knew for a fact that it had been done by hand. I'd even been around for the most recent expansion, overseen by the owner of this place himself.

The innermost hall was massive, a room dedicated to business—the business of ruling the city. For all of that, though, there were few people here, only singular visitors, a few guards, a handful of advisors, and at the center of it all, Atal himself. He sat in a stone chair covered in furs at the very center of the room, pits filled with fire lined the approach all the way up to the ramp leading to him.

I stopped at the bottom of the dais, upon which his throne sat, and I bowed low. "Greetings ancestor. I bring news, and a gift." I held out the little bowl my grandson had brought me, the first of what I hoped to be many useful items.

The servant on duty took it from me and brought it to the ruler, who regarded it calmly, with eyes that had seen ages. After some time, he leaned forward, pure white hair spilling over his shoulders as he looked at me more closely.

"A worthy gift, from the newcomer you spoke of?" he inquired.

"Yes, ancestor. He sent it to me for evaluation. My grandson tells me he has made many more, and is experimenting with metal."

"He has found a new source of it? I was informed it was made from stones not of this area," the ancient elf said with a hint of confusion.

"Some other source, and a different metal. Details are still scant," I answered, not yet having a full picture.

One of the advisors took this time to speak, adding his thoughts. "Ancient, we could still bring this youngling here, have him work at your order." His form of address indicated that he was not a direct descendant of Atal, not an unusual situation, but one that would keep him from rising too high in rank.

"Hmm, no, a tree raised in captivity bears less sweet fruit. For the time, have him watched, and gain what we can from him. Shorin, you said your descendant was in contact already. Have him continue. I wish to see what this child can do. If he can make a weapon capable of withstanding my strength . . ." I looked at the small knife my ancestor had put to the side. It was bent and destroyed, but not reduced to the bits most things he held were.

"I still believe . . ." the advisor didn't get a chance to finish, as our elder moved. There was no blur, no indication he'd stood. He simply disappeared from his place upon his throne and appeared before the advisor, one hand upon the man's shoulder. An instant later, there was a gust of wind and a sound like thunder, the mark of his movement.

"I have spoken," he said, firmly. "Argue no further."

"Yes, ancient," the advisor said, bowing.

Atal was not known to rage, or scream, or show any form of anger. Never had I so much as heard him raise his voice against another in all my years. No, those who displeased him were simply ripped apart, be they youth or elder, and on more than one occasion, another ancient like himself. Other than another ancient or some beast of unspeakable power, none could stand against him.

I knew, though, that some things about that potency grated upon him. Every warrior loved to have a weapon in his hand, but with that much power, nothing could withstand him for more than a single use, if that. Wood splintered into bits, and stone broke into sand in his grip.

My eyes fell on the little copper knife he had. It was nothing special, but it had survived. True, it was bent into uselessness and twisted, but it was still mostly in once piece, and this was the work of a youngling. If he could make such things already, what would be possible as he grew in skill? A few years to my ancestor was nothing if it gained him such a useful piece, and the advantage it would give over others like him couldn't possibly be overstated.

"Shorin, your work has been done well, now continue it." With the dismissal, I quickly turned and left.

I hurried back to my home, mind racing the entire way. How did I want to handle this—what method to take, who to use? Ian had already proven himself capable, and I knew he got along with this Justin, so he, of course, would continue to be sent out. A friend like that could help my grandson, in more ways than one.

As I arrived home I found Ian waiting for me, an odd look on his face.

"Is there something wrong?" I asked him.

"Something odd," he replied.

"Many things in recent days have been odd," I said. "What is it now?"

"I told you the newcomer had hired a waif to help him. I've discovered what he has the boy doing."

"Well, out with it!" I urged.

"Justin's got the kid spreading designs for things. The boy's going around selling information on how to make wooden connectors of various types."

"Why?" I asked.

He could only shrug at me helplessly. "I don't know."

"Then . . . oh, it doesn't matter. Keep an eye out for new metal, and anything that could be a new weapon. We'll send someone to look after the boy, try to find out what he's spreading exactly and why. If it becomes something that needs to be stopped, it will be, but I don't see a reason to right now. There's no damage he can do like that, is there? It's only wood, and only ways to put it together, not a threat."

"Should I speak to the child? See if he knows anymore?" Ian asked.

"Do so, but be polite, and see if you can learn these techniques, and anything else he may start to spread. Now go."

"Yes, Grandfather, as you wish." Ian turned and marched off into the city. He was a good lad, if a bit naive sometimes.

CHAPTER 62

IRONS IN THE FIRE

I washed my face, tired, exhausted, but satisfied. It had taken months of work, but my testing was finally done, for now. The final bar of steel was tested and placed on the small rack in a hidden compartment in my floor.

There had been a number of problems, all of which overlapped in the first few batches, but slowly I'd worked them out to the degree that I was currently happy with. My steel wasn't near as good as some of the modern alloys, but for where I was and the materials and knowledge I had, I felt it held up well.

A big part of the problem had been gas, particularly oxygen and carbon-dioxide. It had taken an embarrassingly long time for that to occur to me as well. The presence of those gases in the right amounts and at the right times could cause success or disaster, and getting them where I needed them was no easy feat, but I'd managed.

I moved a block of stone over the secret compartment, which would soon need to be expanded. Perhaps an underground lab, or a private workshop would soon be in the mix. Building something like that would be a pain, but it would be well worth the time invested if it worked well.

For the moment, though, I'd other projects to work on, and so I turned to my current headache. Laid out across part of my workshop were various plants, all of which had been washed and beaten, washed again, boiled, in both lye and soap, and were now laying out. Some were clear failures, some were still potential successes, the most likely of those a form of coconut which lived on some of the nearby seashores.

Leather was the current choice for clothing, and one I doubted would be replaced any time soon, but there were places where cloth was just needed. I knew about as much about it as I had smithing, and would be handing it off far, far sooner, but I needed a proof of concept first.

"Hey boss, you here?" came a call from my door.

"Yes Chien, come in," I replied.

"More secret projects?" he asked as he looked over the drying fibers.

"Trying to recreate something I saw once. Never done it before, so it's not working as well as I'd like. This one I'll teach someone else just as soon as I get it working," I replied.

"Don't like it?"

"Not in the least, and it's very time intensive. That's for later though. How did soap fare?" I asked.

He chuckled. "Better than I thought it would, boss. I showed it to some of the girls down on the flower street, and they're losing their minds over it. If you showed up with a few blocks of that nice-smelling one you made, you'd have your pick for a night."

"I could do that anyway," I replied. "Though introducing hygiene to the world is worth the effort."

"Don't know what that is boss," Chien admitted.

"Being clean, like, very clean. Not the 'I soaked in the ocean for a moment three days ago' clean."

"Whatever you say, boss," he said with a shrug.

"On another note, I saw some pottery in the market the other day. Your payment." I pulled a small bag off of a nearby shelf and tossed it to him—what I owed for his work.

"Nice!" he said weighing it. "Got to admit, though, their work looks garbage next to yours." He looked over at a few of my newer pieces as they dried in the corner.

"Perhaps, but that isn't the point."

"The point is to spread it," he said with a sigh, repeating what I'd told him a horrid number of times.

"Glad to see you're finally getting it," I said with a sarcastic smirk.

"No, no I don't get it at all, but you pay well, and I'm learning things that will make me rich one day." He thought for a moment. "What'll happen when people make things better than you?" he asked.

"First, I'll celebrate, since that means not only have they learned what I'm teaching, but they've also improved on what I know. Then I'll move on to something else."

"Some of your ideas are weird, though, like that lime stuff. Works good as white paint, which is cool and all, but not really anything else," he complained.

"Ah, that is setting the stage," I remarked.

"Huh?" the boy replied, clearly confused.

"Getting ready for bigger things to come."

"Oh, you mean readying for the hunt?" he asked.

"Yeah, that too. Lime is used in a number of things. So is lye, for that matter, but those will come later."

"So what does this mess become?" he inquired, poking a few of the drying fibers.

"Something like leather, but not," I replied. "Thing is that they're all kind of rough and shorter than I'd like. I need something like long and soft hairs, but no animals around here really have those."

"Mom told me about something called a catch beast from back where she came from," he admitted. "If what she said was right, those might work."

I could have hugged the kid. his was the kind of thing I kept him around for, things about the area I didn't know . . . wait. "Are they from around here?" I asked.

"Two days north is where her village was. So I guess they're close."

"Tell me about them then."

"Sure, she said the hunters would practice on them. They've got fire, like you and me. They're fast and hard to catch, and nobody really hunts them for food since they don't have much meat and taste bad. They've got this really long hair, though, and if you can get close and grab some, it'll pull right out. The beast runs off and you can try again later. Kind of a challenge for young men and those who want to show how good they are."

"Explains why I've never seen their hides in the market. Two days north you said?"

"Wait, are you actually planning on going for those things?" he asked.

"Of course. I need a good source of fibers, and in order to figure out if they'll work, I'll have to at least take a look at one of these beasts. Maybe I'll even catch one myself and get a little bit of the hair to experiment with."

"Listen Justin, I know you're smart and all, but are you any good at being a hunter? They're supposed to be really hard to catch."

"I'll manage," I answered. If all else failed, I could just use magic. I was pretty good at magic. "Have to clean up the house a little bit first . . ."

Finishing up the current batch of pottery and the fiber attempts would have to happen first, but after that . . . Even if it failed, maybe I could make something from some of the things I'd already found, felt was a cloth, right? That seemed reasonably possible. I rubbed my hands together and began to get to work.

"You've got that look in your eye again," Chien said as I turned and began going over things again. I barely registered it when he grumbled, "Guess I'll head off then. See you later, boss."

CHAPTER 63

VILLAGE DISPUTE

As the city began to fade behind me, I let out a sigh. It had taken almost two weeks to get everything in order, and it was frustrating. That said, I couldn't just leave my house alone and full of things others might want, so divesting myself of some of my goods was needed. The proceeds had been hidden well enough that nobody should be able to find them.

It had been years since I'd come to this world, and still things surprised me. Most people never really understood what the stone age was like, and even now I was only starting to get it. The fact that there was not only a city, but a massive metropolis, was surprising to no end. Perhaps it was only possible due to magic, but still, it was impressive. Of course outside of it, the small villages that dotted the countryside were much more like what one would expect.

It was to one of those villages that I was headed now, with my hair tied behind my long ears. I wanted textiles, and this seemed to be one of the few places I might be able to find the fibers needed for them. There were doubts about how much I might be able to get at the moment, but in time things might come together better.

The path northward was only marginally a road, but it was at least visible well outside the city. Chien had gotten me all the information he could on this particular direction, even if he thought I was mad, so I knew roughly where I was going.

The path I was following wove in and out through the dense forests, mostly following creeks and small rivers. These were the standard, since cutting a path through the woods would be both laborious and a waste of time. We were solidly in the tropics, and anything cut would quickly grow if it wasn't studiously maintained. Creeping vines and trees edged even on the path I was using, eager for a chance to get more sunlight.

By noon of the second day I should have been pretty close, but I was spotted before I found the village. As I rounded a corner, there was a man looking quite displeased at my presence.

"Greetings, stranger," he said in a manner that communicated that I was roughly as welcome as a hemorrhoid.

"Good day," I answered, the feeling of being watched tingling up my spine. "I'm seeking a village that's supposed to be nearby. Do you happen to know of it?"

"Perhaps, what is your business?"

"Oddly enough, I'm after some hair from a local animal," I told him with a shrug.

The way he squinted his eyes told me that he didn't believe a word of it, but he wasn't attacking yet. Something was going on, probably something I wanted no part of, but I could only wait and see. Well, in theory I could also leave, but I'd come an awful long way to get here, and I wasn't about to give up that easily.

"You will come with us," the man commanded, and slowly several forms shifted out of the local brush. I got the feeling there were more to be found that hadn't revealed themselves, but there was only one way to test that. "We will speak with the Elder."

For now I decided to play along, letting them lead me. Nobody had yet attempted any actual violence, and if they did, I could always just start laying down the hurt on them. Perhaps I wasn't the strongest magic user in the world, but if I really wanted to I could certainly bring the pain. None of them had auras, so none of them were likely to be able to defeat me alone.

Everyone was on edge as we made our way back to their village, slowly picking up our pace along the trail. Behind me were a pair of hunters with spears, with two more on each side of me. Their leader was alone ahead of me, and he didn't seem worried that he had his back to me. Either he had a plan, or he had absolute confidence in his men.

They didn't try to take my spear or pack, which was wise, as I wouldn't be parting with either without good reason. I didn't really need them that badly, but it was the act that was important. When dealing with others, it was good to be polite, but showing weakness to these men would be foolish beyond belief.

Before long the village came into view, and I could see the women and children coming back from the day's gathering. Many things struck me about them. The gatherers were not alone. Another group of hunters escorted them. More importantly, they looked thinner than I would expect—not gaunt, but they'd clearly missed a couple of meals.

Before long I was shown to the local leader. She was older than Elaya had been and had a hard look in her eyes. I went through the task of greeting her and giving her a small bowl as a gift. That kind of thing generally kept everyone happy.

"Why are you here?" she asked as soon as I'd finished.

"I was told of something called a catch beast and of its hair. I wish to acquire some." Honesty seemed the best policy for now.

The woman looked at me like I was a fool, which perhaps I was. I awaited her words with patience though. Hurrying her along would serve no good.

"No other reason?" she questioned.

"No."

"I would like you to lay out the items in your pack, leave none hidden."

That was an odd request, but one I could at least abide. It was clear that she didn't trust me, and that she was looking for something. She'd also made it a request, not a command, something that wasn't lost on me. From where I stood, she certainly could have her men try to force the issue, but I got the feeling they wouldn't.

Once I'd set out everything I had with me, which wasn't all that much, I looked back to her. "What are you looking for?" I asked.

"Poison," she responded flatly. She didn't touch any of my things, but I could see her looking over the few copper tools I'd brought with great interest.

"I do not have any poison. Why would I need such a thing?"

The older elf's fingers tapped on the ground for a few moments. "What do you know of our village?"

"Not much, if I'm being honest. I was only led here for the hair. An acquaintance of mine knew of it in passing and thought it might work for one of my current projects." Things were getting odder and odder.

"We recently split," she explained. "Not on good terms."

I briefly felt my memory flash back to Elayatol and my former home. They were on the road to a similar situation, though there were still questions that needed answering here.

"And they're poisoning people?" I asked.

"Not people, water sources. They want our territory and are trying to drive us out." At my look of confusion she asked another question. "You're not from this area, are you, young man?"

"No, much farther west," I explained.

"There is little territory here, and little game in comparison with the more outlying regions. While it may seem foolish for them not to move, there are few places the split-off group could go, and as they grow, they will need more space, as will we."

"So they're trying to get you to leave or die? You are near Atal. Perhaps you could receive help there?" I asked.

She actually laughed at me at that one. "And prove I am unable to hold my own lands? They would not help me, but we have plenty of that hair you want. Perhaps . . ."

Internally I sighed. I was going to get dragged into their conflict.

CHAPTER 64

✧

FARMING TAKE TWO
AND A BIG HOLE

Over several hours of trying to negotiate, I learned that this elder's name was Ina, and the village was, of course, Inatol, Ina's home. We weren't really getting anywhere, but that seemed to bother her little. One thing I began to seriously hate about older elves was how patient and hard-headed they could be. Ina wanted my help killing her foes before they managed to poison the water supply, and I wanted nothing to do with her little war.

"You frustrate me, boy," she said after a long time. It was a clear attempt at disrespect, as it was clear I should be an adult.

"And you frustrate me, Elder. I want to trade, but I am not a warrior for sale." We'd gone back and forth on this quite a bit, and were getting nowhere.

"I can see your power, and I have what you want. Certainly you can see my point, can't you? My people are hungry, it is simple enough. They're poisoning the watering holes, driving off game, and even trying to kill the best gathering spots. They are few, we are many. We will starve before they will."

"Do you not have a singer who can summon food? We used one all through the winter recently where I came from; it made things much easier," I retorted. "It might even turn the odds in your favor."

"Yes, and they have one as well. Neither can produce enough for either group, So we need plants, and it's not like we have them beside our village," she snarked.

Something pinged at that. It took me far longer than it should have to come up with that answer.

"Why not?" I asked.

"What?"

"Why can't you have plants right beside your village. If you have some-one who can make them grow, you can get them to grow there. Your ene-mies won't want to come so close, will they? And then you won't need to go out and gather them."

"Because . . . that's . . ." I could tell she was looking for a retort.

"Ina, it can be done. As a matter of fact, I've done it. I made a little plot like that back where I'm from. Nobody really cared though." That admis-sion kind of stung; farming had been one of my biggest failures to date.

"Tell me more," she said after a few more moments of thought.

I ran her through the very basics of gardening. There was no real way to test soil pH and nitrogen levels here, but there were some general things she could do. Some plants grew better in sun or shade, and the best way to guess would be to look where they grew in the wild. You could bury fish into the ground to make it better, though not many. I even told her that if they were quick growing plants she'd need to rotate them, or the soil would go bad, but a proper bit of magic might be able to help with that.

For her part, Ina listened intently, tapping her chin the whole time. A crease formed between her eyes—either she didn't like it, was unhappy, or had to poop. I was having a hard time telling which. She asked a few questions here and there and even brought in one of the local spellcasters to listen and ask me other questions.

"I believe you have done this," she finally declared, something of a relief.

"Good, because I have."

"But it solves only half of our problem," she retorted. "We cannot make enough water for everyone either, and with the local sources being set upon, we still will run into conflict."

I wanted to scream! We were living in the tropics. That didn't mean good sources of water were everywhere though. Other than rivers and streams, which were being poisoned, there were few places. This was par-ticularly bad in the dry season, but there were solutions to even this.

"Fine, fine, you want a source of water? Very well, but if I give you this, you give me the hair I came for. No more arguments, no more trying to send me against your foes. Agreed?"

The elder laughed at me. "If you can, I shall give you all you can carry, young man."

"I need stones, and I'm not cleaning up the mess," I said, and then I rose, turning to leave her hut.

In a huff, I marched straight to the center of her little village and plopped down, settling as well as I could on my bag, then I began to cast. This was a spell I'd cast many times, but never like this. In my mind, I formed the drill, the same one I used for wood, but longer, and wider—far, far wider. It made it to a few feet across before I decided that was enough, and then I sent it down.

The progress was slow, but the first few feet weren't too bad. This was the kind of magic I did all the time, and while I'd never actually dug a well before, it wasn't all that complicated. Only the size was a bit of a strain; the rest of it was easy enough.

At ten feet I was feeling the strain, and the mounds of dirt I was dumping were really starting to get attention. Elder Ina came out of her home to look at me strangely but said nothing. Personally, I thought she was hoping I'd fail, but that wasn't going to happen.

Around fifteen feet I was tired, but the dirt coming up was significantly wetter, and those that had been watching me like I was a madman were now coming closer, touching it and looking at me like I might not be mad after all. I began to smile at that.

By the time it reached twenty-five feet, I was done. My magic was beginning to sputter like an engine out of fuel, and I had to stop. As I did so, I collapsed back on my pack, using it as a pillow.

"That's a very deep hole," the elder said as she approached and looked down it. "What's it for?"

"How many stones did people get?" I asked. She pointed to a small pile nearby of varying sizes, mostly river rocks.

"Right, so those are for covering the sides. They don't need to be perfect, but they need to keep the dirt out and hold the sides basically in place. You need a layer on the bottom too, but kinda loose, I think? I don't know, I'm tired. I'll look at it after a nap." My piece said, I fell asleep.

Using too much magic at once was exhausting, in an almost physical sense. I wasn't sure how long I'd been out when I woke up, but it must have been hours. I was at least glad to see that people were working, and at a frantic pace.

"You're awake," the elder said from nearby.

"Ugh, kind of wish I wasn't," I responded. I felt like I'd been hit by the proverbial truck—fitting, since I found myself in some kind of fantasy world. "But I am glad people are getting that done."

"At first, everyone thought you were a fool," she answered. "Even I thought you were a fool, and then I realized the hole was quite wet."

I began to snicker, which got me a raised eyebrow, and more pain in my head. After I waved her to continue, I began rubbing my temples.

"Yes, there's water down there. You should line it with stones and put something over it so nobody falls in, but it should be drinkable. Maybe boil it first, but nothing else should be wrong."

"I was dubious about it, but I think I'll put a good bit of effort into this 'farming' of yours too."

"If it works, you should share it with your opponents. If both of you have food and water, there's no reason to fight," I said.

"That is . . . worth consideration, but they've made us quite mad. Perhaps once we are resupplied, we will deal with them in other ways," she answered.

"Fine, just leave me out of it." I was still feeling under the weather, but I could see her nod.

"Oh, and your reward. Our hunters don't really need this, since it's just gathered during practice. We've mostly been sewing it up in skins to sit on or use in beds. I hope this is enough," she said, pointing to a bulging pack full of what appeared to be fluff.

"Yes, that should do quite nicely," I said with a smile.

CHAPTER 65

HOMEWARD

As I made my way home, I began to contemplate how my life had gone so far. This new life was something I could never have expected, and the world of magic it had brought me was—while sometimes tiring— still . . . full of potential. There had been struggles sure, but so too was there hope.

One day this world would see magical wonders and beauties the likes of which its people couldn't yet understand, and if I had my way, I would be at the forefront of it. We could have magical computers, magical cars, magical buildings stretching to the sky where people might well live in peace. Perhaps it would outpace me, and that was fine, good even. Being part of something bigger and more wonderful was always a boon.

At the same time, there were problems, problems that one day would need to be solved. Magical beasts would haunt us for a long time yet and may never fully be beaten back. In my first world, the worst of the predators had been brought to heel, driven to the wilds, but even there, things happened sometimes. They might even be needed for the ecology here. That was good to know before going after them.

There were also the follies of people to deal with. Elves weren't human, but they also weren't much different. My new people tended to stick with what they knew, and push it to what it could do, rather than exploring new options, both a boon and a folly. Unfortunately, they still had some of the cruelty that inflicted mankind—the desire to control, which allowed men to see other men as things, or even livestock. The latter was something I wanted to eradicate in time, if I ever grew powerful enough. As it stood, there was little I could do.

There were no roads as of yet, but as I got nearer to my new home, the paths changed. Small game trails, barely able to be picked out from where they meandered near the shores of streams, turned into wider dirt concourses, pounded flat by the ages of people passing along them. The solitude of the forest gave way to occasional meetings, passersby waving in greeting as we moved.

People here were still just people, living their lives, trying to make it through the day. The gathering parties and the occasional group of guards near them carried their pickings for the day on their heads or at their sides. I smiled as a few were even pulling along larger sleds, all packed full of fruits and roots on their way to market.

I approached the city as the sun began to sink toward the horizon, perhaps an hour or two before it truly fell, but it still hung low in the sky, the light just starting to change as it set. I stood briefly upon a hill, looking out at the place. To the east, I could see the barest strip of shore, with fishermen the size of ants bringing in the last of the day's catch. To the west, I could see meadows and forest through squinted eyes, the paths into my home filling slowly with people headed back to their homes.

South of me was Atal proper, and it looked like a painting. The city had dark stone walls, full of buildings of much the same, over which sprouted the trees that made up so many of the second and third floors of the buildings. The greenish tones made it look less like a city and more like a patch of rocky forest, in which lived the elven nation that ruled this land. Ancient elders and younglings like myself dwelt here, among stone and living wood, learning crafts and magic as we gained knowledge and power in each.

I made it to the gates before sunset, if a gate was really the proper word. Here I slipped in, just one of many headed back home for the night, or to see what the night brought to the city. While it got dark, there were still stirrings here and there, places where people put up small torches, or in a few cases, even shone magical lights, just now coming on to let everyone find their way home. I passed by streets one by one, going down some, letting others fall behind me. The street of flowers was one I passed by, some of the girls still out, looking for patrons in the night, even winking and calling to passersby.

Step by step, I drew nearer to home and thought back to my first home here, to my village, Elayatol. They'd banished me, sent me away for the destruction I'd caused while trying to defend them. I couldn't say they were totally wrong, even if it stung that I'd been ostracized for protecting my home.

My parents were still there, as far as I knew. They, along with a few friends, would be there for a time yet. Would they split and fight like the village I'd left not so long ago, trying to drive Elaya and whatever supporters she had away? I didn't know, but if it came to pass that they split, I would happily join them again. A good family was a treasure.

Then there was Isha, one of my closest friends, and one I'd made a promise to; that sometimes made me worry. She knew I had secrets, and after her questioning, I'd promised to share them with her when we next met. Was that a promise I could or would break? Would I even need to? I didn't know yet, and only time would tell.

Before I could reach my door, I ran into my two closest confidantes in this city. Chien and Ian stood there, glaring at one another before my house. The guard was, at least officially speaking, probably the one with the greater right to be here, but the waif was my employee and sometimes student, so he was quite welcome as well.

"My, my, I wasn't expecting a reception," I said with a smirk.

"You walk slow, Justin. Asked some folks to let me know if they saw you coming back," the boy responded.

"Good to know you care," I replied.

"Eh, wanted to know if you died out in the wilderness," he answered, shaking his head.

"Bit of the same," Ian said when I raised my eyebrow in his direction. "Also wondered what you're working on that took you away for days."

I chuckled. "Well my friend, that's no secret, even if it's not working yet. Why don't you two come and join me for dinner. I managed to pick up some fresh fruit on the walk home, and there should still be some dried meat in my pack." They both looked at me like I was weird. "It's been too long since I got to sit around and chat with friends, or whatever. It'll be refreshing."

"You're actually going to share your projects?" Ian asked with a doubting look as he followed me in.

"Don't question it. Justin's just weird," Chien said, laughing.

ABOUT THE AUTHOR

Wandering Agent is the North Carolina–based author of the Melody of Mana and Elevation of Mana series, as well as other fantasy and isekai stories.

9 781039 466517